For TRACY —

Hope you enjoy the book

Dian Iessy

THE DOG WHO SPOKE WITH GODS

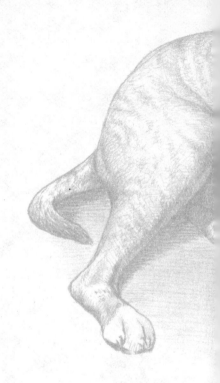

DIANE JESSUP

ST. MARTIN'S PRESS
NEW YORK

The DOG WHO SPOKE with GODS

www.stmartins.com

Book design by Michelle McMillian

Title page illustration by Dee Dee Murry

Library of Congress Cataloging-in-Publication Data

Jessup, Diane.
    The dog who spoke with gods / Diane Jessup.—1st ed.
        p.   cm.
    Includes bibliographical references (p.).
    ISBN 0-312-26662-6
    1. Human-animal relationships—Fiction. 2. Dogs as laboratory animals—Fiction. 3. Women medical students—Fiction. 4. Pit bull terriers—Fiction. 5. Women dog owners—Fiction. 6. Dogs—Fiction. I. Title.

PS3610.E77 D6 2001
813'.6—dc21   2001021957

First Edition: June 2001

10 9 8 7 6 5 4 3 2 1

This book is dedicated to those dogs from which Damien was first drawn. To have known them was the honor of a lifetime, and the void felt now that they are gone proves false the saying "Time heals all things."

In memory of The Three:

ARROW
A yellow Labrador
Who taught me many things, but mostly that Damien exists, and that the friendship between a human and a dog truly can be among the closest bonds of this earth.

OTTO
A Doberman
Who taught me all I ever needed to know about the heart.
And heart doctors.

SAXON
A Doberman
A trust betrayed; she understands why I had to write this book.

And for The One:

DREAD
A Pit Bulldog
With whom I shared a soul.

ACKNOWLEDGMENTS

I am a solitary person, and the writing of this book was a solitary event for years. It was just something I did for fun and for catharsis. Not being the scholarly type, my efforts were undisciplined and inexpert, and the thought of anyone actually seeing my story filled me with horror. I was finally coaxed into sharing a few pages with one friend, Dee Dee Murry, a world-class wildlife artist whom I felt, because of the rigors of her own lonely craft, could understand the emotion that accompanied the creation of art. Poor thing, once she showed the slightest interest, her fate was sealed. I then spent endless hours on the phone agonizing over every detail, to which she always listened with the utmost patience and kindness. A true friend!

Dee Dee and I laughed at the very idea of the book ever being submitted for publication, let alone published. How we laughed at our shared joke that one day she would paint the cover for it—when it was "discovered"! And then, like magic, it was being published. We laughed in amazement. Then, like more magic, she was doing the cover, and we laughed all the harder. Everything associated with this book has had a kind of magic to it—a word I dislike. But how else to explain the amazing chain of events associated with *The Dog Who Spoke with Gods*? In my heart there is a secret belief that, as the character Barbara says in this book, the only real "magic" is the power of true love. Looking back over the chain of events associated with the publication of this book, I can't help but feel that somehow, somewhere, my soul mate Dread still feels the depth of my commitment, and that the love that made our lives together so special continues on.

But if Dread—or the power of my love for him—is somehow behind all this on some supernatural level, there is a human who is behind it all on a very real, concrete level. Her name is Jane Berkey, and the story of her association with this tale is, really, stranger than fiction. She entered, dramatically, on the afternoon of my fortieth birthday.

Coming to terms with the loss of Dread, my best friend and working partner for a decade, and recovering from a grueling ten-year stint as a canine behavior consultant, which took Dread and I to several countries and many, many engagements, I made a solemn vow to myself, on the morning of my fortieth birthday, to "never do anything again." That was the exact term I used, expressing my desire to end all travel, stop all deadlines, and take serious time out to work with my dozen dogs and my beloved garden. It was a solemn vow, and I meant it.

That was in the morning.

I returned from lunch to a phone call from a person identifying herself as a "serious New York literary agent." I had a vague idea what a literary agent was, and so that piqued my interest (as Jane knew it would). However, I wondered what a "serious New York agent" would want with a small-time dog book author such as myself. I remember being terribly impressed with the layers of people I had to go through to get to her, and being in a perfect panic. Turns out this woman from New York was interested in pit bulls (of all things!). More astonishing, she was interested in rescue!

Only the most die-hard, true-hearted people are interested in rescue dogs. She was not just another breeder or dog-show person, but someone who loved the dogs enough to simply want to help even the least of them.

Jane wanted to fly me back East to check out her small rescue kennel. I politely refused. I was firm—I was never going to "do anything again." I meant it. Then she spoke those fateful words. "Well," she sighed, "I wish someone would write a novel about a pit bull. That would really help the breed."

There was, as she remembers, a very long silence on my end of the phone, which ended in a strange sort of gurgling sound. I mentioned (oh, so casually) that I had a little manuscript, nothing really, just something I worked on when I wanted to relax, and nothing I had ever seriously intended to submit to anyone (that was true). I could hear (I swear it) the pain in her voice as she politely suggested I send it to her. I felt sorry for her. I knew she had gambled that I wouldn't be one of those "take-a-look-at-my-manuscript" people, but she had stepped in it now. She was stuck.

It took me two weeks to get around to sending the thing off. I hadn't read any books on submitting manuscripts, so it was single-spaced, not very well spell-checked, and pretty rough. It wasn't even really finished and was just plain horrible in the middle, but I sent it anyway. I can honestly say I wasn't even nervous; I just felt sorry for Jane. She seemed a nice sort. I sent her a video of my place, outlining a few ideas for the care of rescued pit bulls, and left it at that. I figured if the manuscript didn't put her off, the video of my madhouse would.

The call came at work, and my coworkers, stacked four deep outside my office window, watched in glee as my face drained and I sat, head resting on table, as I got the news.

A miracle—she loved it.

But there was more magic. Much more. Her dear friend Michael Denneny, one of the "last great editors left in New York," was visiting her farm the weekend the manuscript arrived. Jane left the manuscript lying on the table when she went to care for her horses. Michael, firmly not a morning person, staggered about looking for the *New York Times.* The paper hadn't come, so, as he put it, "what is a vacationing editor to do?" He picked up the single-spaced monstrosity on the kitchen table and found himself eighty pages in when Jane came back. He liked it, and took it back to New York City with him.

A real live New York editor—a good 'un—liked it, she said.

I don't smoke, but I staggered outside at the conclusion of the conversation and was handed a cigarette by the compassionate kennel staff. I smoked it. Then another.

It just went like that, on and on. Jane and Michael gently but firmly gave me a crash course on writing, advising on how to fix the story's many problems. Not only was my manuscript being looked at, but now I had two mega-professionals giving me personal assistance! I had to pinch myself. Repeatedly. Dee Dee howled, unable and unwilling to believe that a New York agent had called me asking about a manuscript. We laughed. Jane kindly officially submits the new and improved manuscript to Michael Denneny at St. Martin's Press and they buy it. Dee Dee and I stop laughing and go into shock. My coworkers, trying to understand, want me to explain who is who and what is going on. I patiently explain that these two people are deities, and if they call, I am to be considered in conference with God, and not to be disturbed for any reason.

I am left alone for six months to fix the manuscript's problems. I have never had to write with a deadline before. I get up at four in the morning, write, play with thirteen dogs, go to work, come home, play with thirteen dogs, write, fall asleep on the computer, and start all over again. I do most of my editing while driving to and from work. Or sitting beside the dogs' treadmills and springpole. Sometimes I remember my vow to "never do anything again," to stop and smell the roses. I don't have time to smell a rose pinned to my shirt front.

Now it is time for Diane's Big Adventure. I am to make that trip to Jane's pit bull rescue kennel (where I meet and fall in love with the wonderful Tori Rose, and bring her home) and meet my editor and all the people who have helped me get to this point. I go to St. Martin's and then to my first, real live author lunch with the head of sales, Jeff Capshew (he has a bull terrier, so we know he is OK), Jane, Michael, and Michael's assistant, Christina Prestia. Nicer people never lived. I sit at the table and remember my vow. But now, surrounded by these wonderful people working so hard to make this all come true, it seems worth it. And so, Jane Berkey, Peggy Gordijn, Michael Denneny, Christina Prestia, David Rotstein, Jeff Capshew, and all the folks both at St. Martin's and at the Jane Rotrosen Agency, I want to thank you from the very depths of my heart. This book has become something so much better than it ever could have been without your help. I am very, very grateful.

And many people on the home front have lent their wonderful support and encouragement, and I hope you can all appreciate how much your help and support has meant to me. St. Martin's Press says they have never seen such a long acknowledgment, so while the remainder is short on words, please know it is long on love!

My human family: my parents, for being the truest, most honest, most loving people I know. I measure the world by the standard they set. My brother-in-law Robert and my sister Danene, who taught me to love the right kind of books.

My canine family, past and present: with whom I have shared my life and fortunes. Who have always been there for me, and who continue to teach me so much. Thanks for the ride, guys.

And the following people who have meant so much to me: Virginia Knouse, cofounder of the Progressive Animal Welfare Society. I met her once when I was fourteen years old and she has remained my hero all these years. She is the single most sensible person in animal welfare I have ever met. My local friends who mean so much to me and continue, through their selfless and wonderful support and assistance, to allow me to have these crazy adventures. Unbelievably good friends: Joyce Marks, Heather Ringwood, and Dee Dee Murry. Thanks also, Dee Dee, for painting a cover that catches so masterfully the essence of "Damien."

Kerrie Haynes-Lovell of Australia, seal and bear trainer extraordinaire and my mentor, who opened up new worlds for me and taught me (so patiently) to really listen to my dogs.

Sincere thank-you's to friends and professionals who have lent me important technical support, moral support, and life lessons. Each made the book much better than it was. Each contributed significantly: Theresa Meadows, Carla Restivo, Tony Houston, Amy Morris, Shannon Johnson, Jan Dowling, Kate Lamont, Dr. Patti Schaeffer, Dr. Jeff Miller and Sheila (Ludahla) Miller, Jen Martin, Lynn Smythe, Deanna and Jill Johnson, Wayne Johnson of the Northwest Animal Rights Network, Brent Max Jones, Ph.D., Susan Hilliard and Debra Bacianga, Cydney Cross, Kerrie Taylor, Anne Gordon, and Lesli and Dean Taylor. Thanks also to my boss and coworkers at the animal shelter who have always been very kind with their support and encouragement.

And to dear friends who have gone on before and are sadly missed: John Marks, Mary Marks, and Orla Marks-White. And Anne Beck, who was there at the beginning, so many years ago.

AUTHOR'S NOTE

This book considers, among other things, how we as humans interact with our unique associate species, the dog. To no other animal save the dog will a man, in his absence, entrust the guardianship of his home and loved ones. Nowhere in all of Nature is there duplicated the absolute trust of a woman leaving her children to roam the woods in the company and care of a large, carnivorous animal—the dog. It is a wondrous and truly unique aberration in the natural order of predator and prey.

Not all cultures appreciate the dog. For some, familiarity has bred contempt, and for some he is an abject slave, reduced even to a source of food. For others he is something to be pampered and spoiled and made useless, as unfair and unkind a fate as any. Without a doubt, the dog is exploited by many, often treated cruelly or with indifference, and yet the greatest threat to the dog today comes from those who would cause his extinction in the name of animal welfare or public safety. These people seek to sever the ancient bond of man and dog to satisfy their own narrow agendas—yet another form of exploitation. Surprisingly few people recognize the dog for what he is—a precious gift to our species, who asks nothing more than to be allowed to accompany us always, to help us, protect us, to share our joys and sorrows. He is a gift whose origins are unknown. From whom did this gift come? And when? We don't know, and every culture has a different mythology to answer that question. Whether he came from wolves or gods, it appears the faithful dog has always been with us, functioning as companion, guardian and helper. He is our species' soul mate.

The dog inhabits a no-man's-land between human and animal. Unlike the cat, the pig, the sheep or the horse, he cannot, if given the opportunity, take up where he left off with Nature. In one sense, he is no longer truly an animal. Nor is his canine brain the equal of our primate one, and for this he is forever doomed to be misjudged. We struggle to quantify his intelligence in terms of our own particular endowments, which cannot be done. The dog cannot read or write. He speaks with his body and his eyes. He does not use tools. He possesses loyalty, perception and patience in quantities we cannot comprehend. He shares with us our full range of emotions; he can sob with terror or sorrow and grin with good humor. He is more similar than different from ourselves. And the similarities in the ways we think and feel are such that a dog and a human can have perfect understanding, acting together as one while performing complex tasks. A single glance between dog and human companion can communicate subtle and complex emotion and meaning, proving without question that we have more in common than not. Friendships between humans and dogs have proven to be as strong as, or stronger than, those found between many humans.

Listen to your dog.

The medical and psychological research protocols and procedures mentioned in this book are real.

The use of the electric shocking collar is based on its actual and increasing use in all fields of dog training.

THE DOG WHO SPOKE WITH GODS

PROLOGUE

Viktor Hoffman came through the doorway first, holding it open as Seville passed through followed by his research assistant, who was carrying in his arms an emaciated dog's body.

"Right here please, Tom." Hoffman moved to a stainless-steel exam table and hovered while the tall young man deposited the limp body onto it. The animal's legs made weak, disjointed paddling motions, as if it were trying to run, and its head raised a few inches off the table. The brown eyes were glazed and focused on the middle distance.

"Tom," Seville said softly as he approached, pointing with his chin at the animal. His aide promptly pressed the dog's head to the table, holding it so as to avoid touching the neck, most of which was ulcerated and bleeding. Dr. Joseph Seville stood looking critically at the brindle body of the pit bulldog while he gloved himself. The dog's ears had been trimmed very short, and were inch-tall triangular spikes on either side of his broad head. His base color was rich gold, but he resembled a very small tiger, with thin black stripes all through his sleek coat. There were traces of blaze orange spray paint on his side.

"So what is this?" Seville asked as he lifted the dog's lip and checked color and capillary refill time.

"Joe, I appreciate your meeting me here on such short notice," Hoffman said. "This is the dog my undergrads have been observing through radio collar tracking, for our feral dog project. We've been out there a while but we came in during that windstorm last week and lost track of him for a while. It appears that while we were gone the collar got wedged in some rocks and hung him up. By the looks of him he was stuck up there pretty much the whole time we were away. He was dropping weight fast, but he had quite a bit more flesh when I last saw him."

All three men stared at the feebly moving animal. His emaciation was complete.

"He doesn't weigh twenty-five, thirty pounds now," commented Tom quietly, remembering the feel of the cold, bony body in his arms.

"I assume that if you called me down here to look at this, you want to try and save it. I guess, Viktor, my question is—why?"

Hoffman shrugged, then grinned in good-natured embarrassment. "Well, I suppose it's silly, really." He looked up to meet Seville's dubious glance. "I'm embarrassed to sound so dramatic but, here it is: I can't help feeling I owe this dog a favor. He helped me out one night, up on the mountain before my students arrived, and saved me really, from a rather uncomfortable situation. In point of fact, his actions kept me from quite a nasty experience with hypothermia. It's possible he . . . well, in any event I'm going to return the favor now." Growing serious he nodded at the pit bull. "Can you pull him through? Will there be permanent damage?"

Seville looked up from under his dark hair, leveling stark gray eyes across the dog's body at his friend and associate. "What *I think* is that you're a new classification for DSM IV." He shook his head in a dismissive gesture and continued to examine the dog. "I give you less than a twenty percent chance of pulling him through," he announced at last, straightening up. "If you wanted to do it, we'd have to get an IV going, get him stabilized." Seville shook his head slowly with disapproving amusement. "Where do you want to set it up?"

Hoffman glanced at his watch. "Katharine should be here any minute. I haven't the facilities to keep him while he's critical. For now, I'm going to see if she has an open isolation kennel I can use."

The door opened and Katharine Novak stepped into the room. All three men glanced up at her but the petite blonde marked only how Seville's eyes swept her as he noticed what she was wearing. He always did that, looked her up and down when he first saw her, and it always produced in her the same, sharp, pleasurable chill that swept through like a shudder. She paused to put on the glasses which hung from her neck before looking at the object on the table. That, despite her considerable beauty, gave her a distinctly administrative appearance. "Good Lord, Viktor, what is that?"

"Katharine." He nodded. "I was just explaining to Joe that this is a subject my group's been observing as part of a project, and his tracking collar got stuck in some rocks. He's in a pretty bad way, but," he said with cheerful evasiveness, "I'd like to try and save him if possible. Joe has agreed to work on him, so I was wondering if we could set him up in receiving? In an iso kennel perhaps?"

As the director of the Laboratory Animal Resources Department came around the table, Tom nodded politely. He knew her well; Dr. Katharine Novak was his boss' lover.

"Certainly Viktor, I'll take care of the paperwork. This is a random source animal?"

"I brought him in from a field study, yes, not from a dealer."

"That'll be tricky. We have to be *very* careful about bringing in randoms, very careful, but I'll see what I can do. I'll find something for you. Joe," she said, turning to Seville, "what do you need?"

"If we're really going to do this, I need a place to work *right now*. I'm going to want to get the fluids started. Send me a naso-gastric tube, something to feed it, and an IV setup. I need the solution warmed."

Novak nodded. "All right. I'm sure there's a spare ICU rollaway; that would be better, I think, for now. Why don't we have Tom come with me, and he can bring it back. I've got a four o'clock," she said looking at her watch. "Oh, and I'll send someone from nutrition up to get whatever you need." Tom glanced at Seville, who nodded slightly, and then his research assistant followed Novak out of the room. Seville stepped back, leaned against the counter and drew a cigarette out of a pack from the inside pocket of his lab coat. The dog on the table was now motionless, and the pathetic, huddled body looked dead. Professor Hoffman stepped up to the table and laid his hand on the dog's skeletal head.

"Don't you worry, Damien my boy, you'll get the best care in the world here. Your troubles are over."

CHAPTER ONE

You ask of my companions. Hills, sir, and the sun-down, and a dog as large as myself...

—EMILY DICKINSON

TWO MONTHS EARLIER

Viktor Hoffman set aside his binoculars with a grimace and a sigh. After hours holding still in a blind, his back was killing him. He wanted more than anything to reach over his head and have a giant stretch, but that would be seen by the dog.

The object of his attention was a brindle pit bulldog across the ravine. The young adult dog looked very much out of place in the thick woods; his short cropped ears and fine coat of fur marked him as a domestic, not wild, animal. The dog was resting easily, however, as if very much at home in the evergreen forest. The very fact that the dog *was* a domestic animal in this wild setting was what made it of interest to the scientist.

Hoffman sighed again. Dark, very dark, clouds were gathering to the south.

Carefully, so as not to let the dog see his movement, he backed down from his tree blind and struck off on a fairly well-marked game trail. Reaching an opening in the timber, Hoffman paused to watch the towering black thunderclouds drop their loads of moisture on the peaks across the valley. Moments and sights like this kept the professor coming out to do fieldwork far better left to his undergraduates. At sixty-two, even though he was trim and fit, living in a tent for weeks at a time each summer and fall involved larger and larger doses of ibuprofen.

By the time he reached his camp, his mind had one plan of action.

Coffee.

He stepped into his tarp-covered "kitchen" and took up the water container. Eyeing the darkening sky he figured he had just enough time to make it to the river and back before all hell broke loose. As he walked, he noticed how quiet it had become. The entire forest was holding its breath in anticipation of the coming deluge. Rain was nothing unusual in the western half of Washington state, but here in the coastal mountains it often came in epic proportions.

In defiance of the growing darkness the sun broke through one last time, shooting low rays through the firs, cedars and hemlocks lining the river. The golden light looked almost solid as it hung before him in bars between the tree trunks. He reached his "beach," a bar of sand barely two feet wide tucked into the slick black rocks along the river's edge. A dozen feet away on the opposite shore there were several yards of sand and gravel between the water and the tree line, but on this side the bank dropped away quickly, and the water ran swift and deep. This served his purpose well though, enabling him to drop the can straight down, filling it rapidly without getting any bottom sand in it. As the container filled, Hoffman glanced downstream at the opposite shore.

The dog was standing hock-deep in the water a hundred yards away, staring back at him. The sun was slanting in from behind, backlighting the animal, forming a bright halo around its fur. Hoffman drew in a quick breath—he had not wanted the dog to see him. Having left it sleeping beside the fallen and rotting tree trunk it appeared to call home, he had not expected to see it by the river. The water container, now full, began to sink, pulling Hoffman's hand into the icy water. He straightened up quickly and watched with a grimace as the dog moved hastily out of the river and into the heavy woods.

Viktor Hoffman was a research biologist with a particular interest in the impact of domestic animals on the natural environment. His current area of study focused on the life span of "feral" dogs; domestic dogs living without dependence on humans for food, shelter or social bonds. Unlike cats, which return with relative ease to an independent life in the wild, very few dogs survive without direct or indirect human intervention. While it was an intense struggle to find subject dogs living with no trace of human assistance, it was Viktor Hoffman's forte, and his unique papers, while often criticized by peers for their weak numerical basis, had found sufficient audience to make him an authority in the field.

His current research focused on solitary dogs living in remote locations and thereby unable to participate in group hunting or scavenging techniques. A decade spent carefully cultivating relationships with loggers and park rangers across the western United States had paid off; repeated inquiries had produced two very lucky finds so far this year.

Hoffman had arrived two days earlier to take the first critical step in the project; determining the animal's status. Far too often, dogs reported as "feral" turned out to be either free-ranging owned animals, or abandoned pets. Obviously, with cropped ears, this young dog had not been born in the wild, but had been lost or abandoned at some point in its youth. Over the next few days Hoffman would carefully determine the animal's true status. Should this dog prove out to be living independent of human care, the biologist's study would pose the question: could a domestic dog survive in the wilderness with neither direct nor indirect human intervention and care? If it could, *how* could it? If it could not, what would be the nature of its failure? Radio collar tracking telemetry and visual observations would reveal this particular animal's fate. This year's previous subject dog had succumbed to starvation relatively quickly.

The ranger who had brought this particular dog to Hoffman's attention assured him the animal was feral. The pit bull resisted all efforts to be lured into camps and somewhere along the way it had learned, like all wild animals, to fear humans, but for Hoffman that suited his needs perfectly. If the dog hung around their base camp and begged for food then it was not really feral, and it could not be included in the study.

The next morning, as he brewed his coffee, Hoffman noticed the pit bull standing fifty feet away, observing him from amongst the huckleberry and salal bushes. Only the end of its nose moved, as it tested the air for clues about the intruder. The scientist frowned, carefully watching to see what the dog's reaction to his presence would be. He needn't have worried, for when the dog noticed him looking back, it jumped quickly into the brush and disappeared.

Hoffman arranged the base camp to suit himself and then sat back to drink his coffee and enjoy the solitude. In a week or so, if the animal checked out, his students would arrive, and then the real work would begin. The dog would have to be trapped, measured, weighed, examined and collared. Then the monitoring would begin, ten readings a day, plus once every seven days the dog would be monitored every fifteen minutes for twenty-four hours. The animal's home range would need to be mathematically determined, his fecal material analyzed, his activity and temporal patterns charted.

Draining his third cup Hoffman leaned back, a thoughtful expression on his narrow, rather austere face, as he looked straight up into the firs and cedars which towered over him. He drew the chill air deep into his lungs, and the scent of the evergreen trees brought a flash of memory, followed unmercifully by another: Christmas Eve, holding hands with Helen as they leaned up against the couch in front of the fire, listening to carols and watching the tree's little lights twinkle—and Christmas Eve alone, his wife buried two months, sitting on the couch looking at the dead fireplace, just him and the tree there, both of them trying to be brave.

If the truth be told, his insistence that he be the one to go ahead and establish the dog's status was a thinly veiled excuse for getting some time alone in the wilderness. As much as he enjoyed the company of his students, this beautiful solitude was something the biologist needed. Alone, he could remember Helen as she had been when they were newly married. Without the distraction of the students, he could remember the early field trips, look out upon his present campsite and see her bending over the campfire, laughing as she blew on a fire which struggled with the persistent rain, and recollect how they had finally retreated to the tent. Several times that trip, if he remembered correctly. How many years ago was that? Thirty-eight? With her image fresh in his mind, it seemed no more than five or six.

With a huge sigh and a small smile to himself, Hoffman rose and started his workday. Setting out to collect hard data on the dog, he was unable to locate the animal all day. He returned to camp in the late afternoon when his coffee thermos ran dry. That evening the dog was back, the bright, disembodied glowing of its eyes the only sign of its presence. Sitting at his campfire, Hoffman mused that it really caused no harm—this approach behavior—so long as he was careful never to leave any food uncovered when he left camp. That the dog should be drawn to his campfire and his presence did not surprise him. It was a dog, after all, not a true wild animal. Even a feral dog would be curious about this stranger in its territory. The parameters of the project were strict, however: they must not impact the dog any more than possible.

As the evening wore on Hoffman sat on a tiny camp stool, his coffee beside him and his after-dinner pipe in readiness on his lap. Propping his feet up near the flames, he watched the eyes creep ever closer, slowly, until they stopped forty feet away. After a time the eyes dropped low to the ground, and Hoffman could imagine the dog's broad head resting on its outstretched front paws, as it watched him at the fire.

The wind switched to the north in the night, and the next day dawned clear and cold. Every object outside the tent was coated with a fine dusting of ice, and frozen water in the dirt below his feet caused the ground to crackle when he stepped on it. Hoffman emerged from his tent shivering and resolved once again to stick to summer fieldwork. One look at the day, though, and his resolve wilted.

Today he would continue collecting evidence of the dog's status, look for additional blind sites, and try to locate a high spot from which his phone would work. After breakfast and coffee he packed a lunch and set off.

What little hair he had left might be gray, Hoffman thought as he broke through the heavy brush, but he was still in damn fine shape for a man his age. After three hours of tramping steadily around the study area, he was pleased to note his breathing still came evenly. Hoffman knew that without the radio collar they would have no chance of tracking the dog's movements, and he continued searching for elevated locations where visual and radio transmissions would be unobstructed. He moved up the side of the hill he was on, breaking out of the trees and onto a steep slide of boulders which rose above him.

He started up the rock slide, and when he neared the top he stopped to rest on a large, flat rock. He unpacked his lunch and thermos of coffee. Overhead, the sky was the peculiar shade of dark blue found at mountain elevations. The ancient rock slide he had just scaled stretched below him seventy-five yards until it ended at the tree line.

A movement caught his eye and his composure shied like a young horse. A glance of tawny gold moving below and to his left reminded him that cougars were common here. He smiled in chagrin, glad there was no one to notice him startle, because it was only the dog, which had evidently been following him at a distance. The young animal, distracted from the trail he had been following, was sniffing furiously at a crack between two rocks. In another moment, when he heard the sharp alarm whistle of a marmot, Hoffman knew why. For the next hour he watched with amusement the antics of the young predator and the wise prey. There were several of the large ground squirrels, and they all took turns standing upright, watching the intruder, then diving under the rocks only at the very last moment before the dog reached them. Hoffman could almost imagine their sharp whistles were taunts directed at the pit bull. Then again, the scientist had to admit that the dog, despite not obtaining any food, seemed to be having the time of his life. Tail thrashing madly, he seemed to enjoy each new chase as much as the last. He never appeared to grow frustrated—only more and more excited. He only stopped when he was utterly exhausted, his tongue lolling and his face covered in specks of white saliva. He lay down then, stretching his hind legs out behind him, staring straight ahead, his eyes squinted shut in happy exhaustion. After a while the dog rose and moved back into the trees, while the marmots jeered his retreating form.

Hoffman spent the rest of the afternoon marking trails to likely blind and radio-tracking sites. Pleasantly fatigued and ready for fresh, hot coffee, he turned for camp, some three miles distant. The late-afternoon air was growing chilly and he rolled down his shirtsleeves. At a picture-perfect creek running steeply down a boulder- and fern-strewn course, he stopped and used his thermos cap to fetch up a drink of water. He drank, as always amazed at the sharp chill of mountain streams, and the glory of their flavor. His long-suffering mouth, much abused by a lifetime of scalding coffee and tobacco pipes, savored the clear taste. Stowing the thermos away he moved on, stepping lightly from stone to stone as he crossed the creek. As he reached the far side he slipped suddenly, regained his balance for a moment and then slipped again, his boots unable to get a purchase on the slick, smooth, mossy rocks. His left foot slid down between two boulders and as he fell he twisted, grimacing at the sudden sharp pain. He tried to land on the bank, but didn't. He landed on his back, in the water. It couldn't have been worse; his pack and clothes were soaked.

From where he lay on the ground, Hoffman tried to raise his left leg clear of the rocks but pain prevented him. With cold foreboding, he reached down and lifted the leg free with his hands. The pain was appalling. He moved himself up out of the water and huddled on the ground for several moments, nursing the badly sprained ankle and cursing himself silently and viciously for having been so clumsy. A sprain like this would take time to heal, and make walking in this rough terrain difficult, if not impossible, for the next week. Grimly he recounted in his mind how rare a find this dog was, and he resolved on the spot that this injury would not affect the study. Once he got back to camp, he could deal with a sprain, no matter how severe. He would simply call Tag, his grad student and research assistant, and have him come up early to finish the determination on the dog's status.

Oh no.

It occurred to him to look at the contents of his day pack. He pulled it around to his front without much hope. Everything inside, packed simply for a hike on a day with no rain expected, was soaked. He looked forlornly at the phone, thinking about the cost of its replacement. He set the pack aside and looked himself up and down. Camp was a long way away, and the autumn sun was very near the top of the surrounding peaks. He was not dressed for a night out in the mountains, and now he was wet. He *must* get back. And he must hurry for he would never be able to find his way in the dark.

With great difficulty and much wincing, he hoisted his pack on and struggled to his feet. He stood on one leg, looking at the stretch of rocky path ahead of him. If the ground were more level, he might be able to use a stick like a crutch, but here on the rocks, and in the thick underbrush, a crutch would be useless. He started forward, hopping on one leg, resting, and hopping again. In fifteen minutes he was, despite his cold dunking, covered in sweat. He stopped and looked at his ankle. It was purple and already swollen grotesquely.

He swung his backpack off and rummaged inside for the phone. Pulling it out, he *had* to try. You never knew, miracles could happen. He knew in his heart it would never work. He tried anyway, and wasn't surprised at his failure. *This is not good,* he thought grimly.

He stopped after another fifteen minutes of crawling and hopping and estimated he had covered about one hundred yards from the creek where the accident had occurred.

The sun settled below the peaks across from him, and dusk began in earnest. Hoffman was no stranger to survival techniques, and knew he must keep at it until he reached the camp. At this elevation, and wet, he ran the risk of hypothermia or even freezing to death if he stopped walking.

Hopping and hobbling, he moved toward his distant camp through the growing darkness. In time the underbrush became a dark gray mass all around him and he realized he could no longer see his markers or his way. It was decision time. He could try to build some kind of a shelter here and huddle wet and miserable through the night, but it just seemed too risky. He eased himself to the ground, grimacing in frustration as much as pain. He began to shiver as his body cooled rapidly. He knew then that he would have to walk it out. No matter how uncomfortable it was, it would be better to keep moving, even if he simply floundered through the woods all night. Hoffman was a scientist, and he was not afraid of the dark woods as many others might be in similar circumstances. However, he did find his thoughts turning to a journal article he had recently read concerning bear and cougar population surveys for this area. Quite simply, the woods were full of the big predators. He decided to think about something else.

Squinting down what portion of the trail he could still see, straining to catch sight of one of his trail markers, a movement caught his eye. The dog was a dozen yards away, watching him.

Nuts, Hoffman sighed to himself, *everything is going wrong.* The subject animal he was trying to keep from seeing him was standing there staring at him. He held still, hoping the animal would shy away as it had the previous times they had met.

It didn't. It was watching him with interest.

"Well, thank you at least for not laughing," Hoffman called to the animal. The dog's head was lowered, his neck outstretched as he watched the man. The professor chuckled. He felt a twinge of gratefulness for the dog's company as he sat all alone in the darkening mountains. "You don't look much like Lassie," he commented. With his pointed hornlike ears and flat skull the dog looked more like a demon than a guardian angel. "You look like a medieval gargoyle," the scientist joked. "A daemon." The dog sat down, his front feet close together, his head still lowered, furthering his resemblance to a sitting gargoyle. "Daemon. Yes, Damien would be a good name for you," Hoffman decided.

It became too dark to see the trail and he was still miles from camp. There was nothing to do but go on and hope for the best.

Now I know what they mean by the expression "you're not out of the woods yet," he thought grimly. High, thin clouds hid the stars. Sighing in frustration he leaned against a tree, angry with himself. An experienced woodsman, this situation made him feel like he had been caught with his pants down. He put his head back and shut his eyes, trying to decide on the best course of action. Stumbling through the woods injured and cold for the next several hours seemed to be his only option. He would never locate his camp in the dark; he only hoped he didn't get himself royally lost during the night, ending up miles from where he needed to be come morning light. When he looked down again, he was astonished to find the dog standing just a few yards away, still watching him.

For a sharp moment he felt concern; he had no weapon and the dog was, after all, a *pit bull*. They were alone together in the dark woods, and he was unsure of the dog's intentions.

You're injured Viktor, and obviously an easy target.

Then he stopped his mental fright tactics and chided himself. The animal was simply curious about him, and probably aware that he afforded no threat. *You could sell this story to the trash magazines and retire on the proceeds,* he thought with wry amusement. He pictured the front page of a tabloid, him pointing with a crutch to the spot where the "killer dog" had stalked him. An inset would show some dog's head (any dog's head would do) snarling with teeth dripping blood and saliva. *What would the headline be? "Terrifying Ordeal: Injured Professor Stalked Through Mountains by Bloodthirsty Pit Bull!"* He could probably make the TV talkshow circuit. Disgusted at the vein his humor was taking, Hoffman shook his head.

The dog crept closer and lay down, as if it were his pet, waiting patiently for him. A warning buzzer went off in Hoffman's mind. The scientist in him demanded he use this opportunity to do what he had come to these mountains to do: determine the dog's status as an independent, wild-living dog. It was not acting like a feral dog and he had to ask himself: had he gone through all this to find that the dog was simply someone's lost pet?

"Come here, boy." Hoffman held out his hand as if there was food in it and made chirping sounds. "Come on." He made his voice reassuring and gentle but the dog sat back up, obviously startled and suspicious, and for a moment Hoffman thought he would flee.

"You're afraid of that, huh? Well I won't hurt you. Come on now." The man continued speaking for several moments, but the dog stayed sitting, his posture one of wary uncertainty, watching the man without a dip of his ears or a wag of his tail to show he appreciated or understood the kind words. When at last Hoffman leaned back he had made up his mind—this was no one's pet. It was a domestic dog living without dependence on humans for food, shelter or social bonds. The dog was curious about him, that was all. Damien was a perfect subject for this study.

Complete, utter darkness had arrived and Hoffman's thoughts turned again to his own increasingly serious situation. Standing up, he determined to keep moving to combat the chill now entering his body. He heard a soft sound and glanced down to find the dog's form—the rich gold color muted to gray in the darkness—almost within reach. Hoffman drew back, startled.

What the hell?

The dog disappeared. Then it reappeared. Then it disappeared again, away from him, down the trail in the direction he had been taking. For a moment the professor hesitated, then, for lack of anything better to do, he shrugged and followed the shadowy form of the retreating dog. The dog reappeared, again and again out of the darkness, always staying just out of reach. In the absolute darkness of the forest under the cloudy night sky, the going was very tough for Hoffman. After just a few moments he stopped to get his breath, settling back against a tree trunk.

I'm in a jam.

The dark form of the pit bull hovered about. After a moment it lay down somewhere out past his feet. In his line of work, Hoffman had of course heard stories of dogs sensing when people were in trouble and helping them. As a behaviorist he looked at those stories differently from the other two "camps," those who either dismissed them as maudlin exaggerations of canine reasoning or those who embraced them as proof that dogs were furry little people. That a dog's behaviors would appear to be helpful to a human he did not question, but he *would* inquire into the actual, fundamental basis for the behavior.

By the end of his little rest, the scientist had to admit he was puzzled. He could come up with absolutely no reason why the animal was displaying these particular behaviors. If the dog had been merely curious, it was much more likely the wary animal would have stayed further out, hidden by darkness. If Damien was a lost pet, it would have showed *some* response to his friendly overtures. Whatever the reason, as he struggled to his cold, wet feet again, he couldn't help but feel gratitude to the creature which accompanied him so faithfully through the utter darkness. Though the dog was not large, Hoffman was reassured that Damien's sturdy presence would keep any curious cougar or bears away. They moved on again, the man and the dog, for nearly an hour before Hoffman stopped to rest. He was covered in sweat and hadn't the slightest idea where he was. He was following the fleeting glimpses of the dog as it appeared before him. He had a compass, but no source of light to see it with. He had failed to bring matches with him on what was to have been a day trip.

"I'd give five—no *seven*—years off the end of my life for a cup of coffee right now," he said into the dark, to the dog who was waiting for him. Damien came and curled up in a ball, so close that he could see its outline. The dog heaved a heavy sigh and settled its head into its turned-back front paws.

"Don't get too comfortable, friend, I'm going to have to keep moving." His cooling sweat was a chill sheen on his body. In the distance, he heard the river. That was encouraging. If he stayed near the river he could work his way back up or down it in the morning and find his camp.

After a few more minutes rest he rose again, and the dog again moved in and out of his sight, showing him the path. For another hour they moved on through the dark, the scientist covered in sweat but gamely struggling on, the silent dog patiently waiting, then moving slowly ahead, again and again.

Sometime well after midnight, the underbrush he had been fighting his way through suddenly ended, and the professor moved forward with relative ease. Sliding his sprained foot forward, he felt a strange brushing on his thigh, almost like a branch, but firmer. He felt with his hands and found a tightly stretched piece of rope. He laughed out loud.

"Son of a bitch!" he said in delight.

He had run into one of his tent's support ropes. He was in his camp. He was at his tent. His tent with his lantern, his pipe, his coffee, his aspirin and his sleeping bag. It was unbelievable good fortune. He glanced about for Damien. He listened but could not hear any sound of retreating steps. The dog was gone.

"Damien?" he called into the dark. "Hey buddy, I owe you one," he said, then crawled into his tent.

Hoffman did not see the dog again until after sunset the next evening. Having decided to rest his ankle for three or four days before he tried to hike out, Hoffman propped his foot up before his campfire and sat back to enjoy the beautiful solitude of his temporary prison. Other than short, painful forays out to drag more dead wood back to the campfire, there was nothing to do but sit back, drink coffee and enjoy his pipe. There were worse things, Hoffman mused, than forced relaxation. But the day did go slowly. By the time the dog came sniffing and urinating around the edge of the fire's circle of light, Hoffman was grateful for the company. Damien came within twenty feet of the fire and lay down, sphynxlike, blinking across the fire's orange flames at the man. Watching the dog, Hoffman was struck by the similarity of the scene to that portrayed by theorists who claimed the modern canine was simply a derivative of wolves tamed by men dozens of millennia ago. Wolves who were theorized to have hung about campfires like this one. It was a question Hoffman had considered before. Wolves *did not* hang about campfires, so it had always seemed just a little too easy of an answer. *Something* had happened, thirty, forty, maybe even fifty thousand years ago, between a man beside a fire, like himself, and a canine that came out of the dark woods, like Damien. Whatever had happened, it had resulted in the world's most unique interspecies relationship, and its most enduring. Damien, he reflected, with his short cropped ears and his smooth, short coat, was a rather unlikely character to portray the Primordial Dog, while he, sipping his coffee and smoking his pipe, an aging, balding biologist, was equally unlikely as Primordial Man. But the scene did set one thinking about the origin of the man/dog partnership. *Had* wolves come out of the night, like this dog, growing more and more comfortable with the noise, odor and behaviors of the primates behind the fire? Or had it been some other canid? Had man perhaps played a more active role, capturing wild canids and forcing them into domestication? Or had the mysterious joining together of two different species come about by some strange act of nature, as yet unthought of by man?

Viktor Hoffman knew as much of the available evidence of canine domestication as anyone, and he had to admit he did not know the answer to these questions. So he pondered the feral dog's strange, enigmatic loyalty.

The next night the dog came again, and again lay across the fire from the scientist. This time it watched him for only a few minutes, then curled up, businesslike in the light drizzle, to get some sleep. Hoffman decided to stay up, all night if necessary, to determine if the dog stayed till dawn or left sometime before that.

It was pleasant, sitting by the cheerful fire and smoking; the misty drizzle did not bother such an experienced Pacific Northwest outdoorsman. The fire sent sparks sailing up into the void above him, encircled by the great, gray tree trunks that ringed the small clearing. By midnight the drizzle ceased and the air became so still Hoffman's pipe smoke hung in the air like a miniature gray aurora borealis. Damien lay curled in a tight ball, his nose tucked in to his paws.

As he reached for the coffeepot once again, Hoffman became aware of the dog's head slowly rising, of the animal staring out into the black forest intently. For several long seconds they hung like that, the man with his outstretched hand stopped halfway to the coffeepot, the dog still curled in a ball but neck stretched up, staring with eerie intensity into the night. Then the sound of the dog's growl reached him, and it was so low Hoffman seemed to feel it rather than hear it. He listened to see if he could hear what it was that alarmed the dog, and then he heard it too, over the sound of his damp wood burning; the unmistakable shuffling and coughing sounds of a bear.

Damien exploded. The dog bayed, his hair erect all along his back, his tail stiff and straight as a class-bred pointer's. Hoffman smiled to himself hearing the anxiety in the young dog's voice. Had Damien been an older dog, or a dog with a well-defined territory to defend, the pit bull might have launched himself headlong at the far larger, far stronger adversary, in the fashion of his bullbaiting ancestors. As it was, he barked his warning from where he stood.

Hoffman could glimpse the bear at the very outskirts of the light. It was a juvenile, this year's cub. For an anxious moment he scanned the dark forest for signs of the cub's mother—that could be trouble—but only the one bear was in sight. His concern was tempered by his knowledge that it was highly unlikely the black bear would try to harm him. However, in his absence it could easily destroy his entire camp searching for food.

"That's right, Damien, give 'em hell," he encouraged the dog quietly. "Scare 'em away."

Damien glanced at the man, then jerked his head back to continue baying and barking. The bear moved off into the woods, away from the strange acrid smell of wood smoke and pipe tobacco, the man smell and the noisy, frightening dog. At last the pit bull stopped barking, standing stiffly and listening with obvious intensity, only occasionally "harumphing" as if muttering threats he had forgotten to use. After a few more moments he sat down, still carefully looking after the bear, then he lay down at last, but his ears swiveled continually, back and around, while he guarded the camp. It wasn't until the cold, damp early morning, when the only hint that sunlight was coming was a faint gray tinge to the sky, that Hoffman watched, chilled and tired, as the dog stood up, shook himself, and trotted off into the morning gloom. The scientist then retreated to his tent, where he slept till noon.

Four days after his sprain, Hoffman determined he was fit to hike out. Other than hanging his remaining food high above the ground from a tree limb, he left the camp as it was, for he would be coming back with his undergraduates. Picking up a large fir bough he had fashioned into a walking stick, he set out. Damien had been, as usual, absent when he awoke, but ten minutes from camp Hoffman noticed the dog tagging along behind him, thirty or forty feet to the rear. Less than a mile from camp Damien stopped and sat in the trail, watching Hoffman leaving. The research biologist made a mental note to compare the dog's location with the boundary of his known home-range when that data became available. Then, with a lift of his hand, he bid the strange dog farewell and went back to collect his students.

In three days Hoffman returned, his four students strung out behind him on the trail, their large packs and themselves draped with plastic ponchos. It was typical Olympic Peninsula weather, a perfectly diffuse gray, with a fine, soft rain that barely penetrated the heavy overgrowth. It was late in the season for fieldwork.

The first order of business after Tag, Seth, Susan and Devon had set up their own tents and stowed the sensitive research equipment away from the weather, was to assemble and set the wire dog trap. The animal would have to be captured, tranquilized, weighed, measured and outfitted with a radio collar and blaze orange markers to facilitate tracking its movements in the dense brush. Hoffman proposed setting the trap up near camp, as it was clear the dog would not hesitate to approach, and it would be easier to tend. It was quite usual for the traps to be tripped by nontarget animals such as raccoons and skunks, and a location close to camp would discourage these animals.

The camp established, firewood collected, the trap assembled and set, now began for Viktor Hoffman one of the greatest pleasures of fieldwork. Sitting with his still-tender ankle propped up before him at the campfire, he smoked his pipe and listened to the enthusiastic and earnest discussions of his students and aide. Around the shifting light of the campfire, debates raged about contour delineating options on home-range software, who was going to be the one stuck with determining habitat type distribution within the study area, and the statistical significance of crepuscular activity in relation to lunar cycles. The professor rarely interjected; his enjoyment came from being the catalyst for their expanding abilities and simply being party to their enthusiasm—that was something that was harder to maintain as one got older. Hoffman's happy marriage had, sadly for them both, produced no children, so now he found it strangely reassuring to know that these kids were building valuable, productive and rewarding careers as a result, in part, of his gentle guidance. These serious, polite, good-natured kids *were* his children. He thought Helen would have liked them.

The dog appeared late, about ten o'clock. The flashing of his reflective eyes was first noticed by Tag, Hoffman's teaching assistant and most promising student. He was an intense, dominant young man disliked by the other students for his monopolizing and overprotective attitude toward the professor. As always, he was seated close beside the older man, and he reached out now, touching his arm. He nodded in the direction of the animal.

"Oh yes," Hoffman said quietly. "There he is."

Having more sense than to speak out loud in the presence of the wary animal, Susan couldn't help but remark, low, "Wow, it *is* a pit bull," and Hoffman nodded. It was not a breed any of them would have expected to survive in the forest.

Tag and Devon had set the trap thirty-five feet from the camp, baited with a handful of raw hamburger. The trap was a long and narrow wire cage with one end propped open. When the dog entered, its front feet would step on a metal trip plate approximately three quarters of the way to the back. Once triggered, the door would slam down behind the dog, trapping it.

Damien neared the strange object with curiosity and none of the usual fearfulness of a wild animal. He approached from behind, coming up to the back of the trap. He sniffed the hamburger and then hungrily pawed at the wire. With a sharp metallic snap the sensitive hook holding the door in place was jarred loose, and the door slammed shut. Obviously hungry, Damien returned to the trap and dug at it vigorously until he succeeded in moving the trap several inches and exposing the hamburger, which had fallen through the bottom wire. Having licked up every piece, the bulldog looked questioningly toward the camp before trotting off.

For a moment no one spoke, then Devon said, "At least he's not afraid of the thing."

"No, he's not," Hoffman laughed. "Go tie a plastic sack over the back, so he won't be able to see the bait from behind. Let's try again."

Devon secured a black plastic sack to the back of the cage, then reloaded and reset the trap. The plastic worked, and the dog circled the trap looking for the food he could smell. Finding the opening, he entered cautiously. They could see him stretching his short, powerful neck, trying to reach the food without stepping in any farther than necessary. One step, two steps. They saw him glance down, most likely looking at the metal trip plate which stuck up at an angle across the cage bottom. He inched forward, then, by craning his neck, was able to reach over and lick up the meat without stepping forward any farther. When the food was gone he backed out carefully and sat looking at the researchers, as if waiting for further developments.

"Hey Devon, he's not going to leave you a tip if you keep him waiting," Susan joked.

The young man snorted. "He's good, you have to admit, he *is* good."

Devon wore a peculiar leather hat that lacked only a long pheasant feather stuck in the band to be a ringer for Robin Hood's. He pushed that hat back so far in a resolute gesture now, that the others around the campfire wondered how it stayed put. He went out again, this time with Tag's beef jerky, and he secured it tightly to the back of the trap with twist ties.

"We know what the animal is subsisting on tonight, don't we?" Hoffman joked with his students when Devon returned to camp. It was only minutes until Damien reentered the circle of light and approached the trap. Stepping carefully over the metal trip plate, he thoughtfully chewed the jerky loose and then backed cautiously out again.

"Too bad this study doesn't require the establishment of feeding stations, because we've done a pretty fair job of setting one up." Everyone laughed. Devon was sent out again with more beef jerky and instructions to lay fern fronds and fir boughs over the trip plate. While the young man was on his hands and knees inside the trap he saw the flash of the dog's eyes again, thirty feet away, and knew that the animal was watching him.

"Room service," he said. "I'll be out of your way in a moment, sir."

Devon backed out and reset the trap, making sure the release mechanism was hair-trigger.

They watched—Devon holding his breath—as the dog sauntered up to the trap and stuck his head inside. He scented the meat and stepped in, jerking back when his foot touched a fir bough. His shoulder hit the side of the trap and the door slammed down, hitting on his head and neck as he scrambled backward. In succession Damien looked at the trap, at the researchers, back at the trap, then walked around to the back of the trap and tore at the plastic until he was able to pull out the jerky from behind. The scientists in the camp watched in silence, feeling without a word being spoken that the dog had earned the jerky.

Without a word, Devon stood up, resettled his hat (this time pushing it so far forward he had to tip his head backward to see), took the last of the beef jerky from Tag's hand and walked out toward the trap.

"Why don't you just hand it to him?" Tag called. "Save yourself some trouble."

As the young man approached the trap the dog stood up, then backed away a few yards.

"We *are* smarter than you—I want you to know that. It just doesn't look that way right now."

The dog suddenly whirled and disappeared into the dark, and he did not return again that night. The professor concluded that the animal had gone off to digest his considerable meal.

Though the dog kept away from the trap the following day, the students and their professor had plenty of opportunity to observe his behaviors. The drizzle was replaced by brassy autumn sunlight that had no effect on the air's chill, and the day was glorious but sharp. From their makeshift blind overlooking a fallen log the dog appeared to call home, they watched Damien enjoy the day. Or, as Tag put it, they "recorded his behaviors." Damien had been resting curled up against the log's side when a wind gust blew a dried maple leaf across his line of vision. His head jerked up, then he sat up. The leaf paused, twirled in place, then moved on rapidly. The dog pounced, grabbing at the leaf and missing by several inches, overshooting it, turning back and pouncing again. He appeared to be intentionally missing it, allowing it to continue on, but striking at it with his paws and jaws.

"He acts like a kitten," commented Susan, to no one in particular. "Playing with a ball of string."

Without apparent cause, the game ended with the dog breaking into a spectacular running fit. With one last grab at the leaf, the dog erupted into an irregular figure-eight pattern at full gallop. The leaf was forgotten in the wild rush. Lips pulled back in a crazy grin, hind end tucked low in his intensity, the pit bull appeared to be avoiding an unseen companion as it zigzagged about the field. The wild rush stopped as suddenly as it had started, when the dog sat down to scratch behind its ear.

For the humans who followed the dog's activities while trying to remain hidden from his view, the day passed slowly, but for the young dog it was a long, glorious day spent playing, hunting, sleeping stretched out in the thin sunlight against his log, and hunting again. He spent an ecstatic hour digging up four voles, his primary diet, then ate copious amounts of deer droppings, had a glorious roll on the remains of a dead hawk and late in the afternoon patrolled the river bank for anything edible.

That evening Damien wandered far from the research team, just following his nose. He found the carcass of a deer left by hunters, gorged himself, then slowly made his way back toward his home base. It was in this way he had survived, a young dog alone in the wilderness, against all odds. The fate of dogs lost or dropped in the forest is almost always death by starvation, but the young pit bull, having stumbled upon the lucky remains of poached deer, had held off starvation long enough to learn to find and eat voles. Late in the night, he returned to the area of the humans' camp, and once again he approached the trap. He wasn't hungry but he entered the trap anyway, because food was to be taken whenever it could be found.

The trap door slammed down behind him, and he jumped, startled by the noise. He didn't panic—it was not in his pit bull nature—but when he found he was trapped he had a moment of consternation. He turned about and nosed at the trap for several minutes, then, unsure what to do, lay down with a sigh of resignation to await developments.

After a long, cold dawn, the first rays of sun angled through the trees, spilling across the campsite. Damien sat up at the sound of stirrings from within the tents. In time people emerged. When they looked his way they pointed, and called to each other, and he knew their tone to be excited. The human Damien identified as the group's alpha came out of his tent and, after a while, they all started through the underbrush toward him.

Damien felt very strange. Strong, conflicting emotions swept over him as the humans approached. The Voice, The Ancient Voice of his genetic make-up and bulldog heritage, reassured him that these approaching creatures were good; that in some strange way he *belonged* with them. Something really deep within him had been aching, aching like a hurt, to go to them and feel their hands upon his body, to hear their voices commanding him, praising him. The Voice told him he belonged *with* them, not apart from them. In their service, It whispered, he would find contentment.

But the voice of experience spoke differently, louder, and with a shrill insistence. It reminded him of what he had learned from hard experience; humans were to be avoided because they caused fear, and sometimes pain. The researchers were coming and he could not escape, so he circled anxiously inside the trap, remembering other encounters, all with people who had been intimidated by his wide jaw and powerful appearance. People who had shied rocks at him, shouted at him, shot at him. His every approach had been rebuffed. So he watched the approaching humans, bombarded by the conflicting emotions of learned fear and instinctual longing.

The humans surrounded the trap and he stood, facing them. His bulldog heart would not allow him to snarl or growl in fearful aggression. He was frightened, but he would not harm a human to save himself, for he was bred from an ancient line which had always served man. He pressed into a corner of the trap and awaited their will.

In a few moments, the girl assembled a syringe pole and began to try to inject him in the thigh with tranquilizer. Each time she tried, Damien would twist about, and the needle on the end of the pole would bend. The sharp pricks hurt, and the dog became very confused and frightened by their actions. Stamped indelibly now in that part of his mind where future decisions would be made, was the understanding that human hands *would* hurt him. He threw himself against the end of the trap in an attempt to force his way out. All he wanted now was to get away, and to take care in the future to stay out of the reach of human hands.

Frustrated with her efforts, Susan handed the syringe pole to Hoffman. The professor's calm voice did nothing to allay Damien's fears as he watched the man thread the hurtful stick through the bars at him. It came as a surprise to the dog that *this* man would hurt him, but in Damien's mind was now recorded the fact that Viktor Hoffman could not be trusted. With one swift movement Hoffman drove the syringe into the dog's thigh, injecting the sedative. Damien whirled about and bit at the pole, but the needle had found its mark.

Once the tranquilizer took effect, the young men gingerly drew the powerful dog out of the trap. His limp body was placed on a tarp and hoisted up on a small fishing scale attached to a branch held on the shoulders of Seth and Devon.

"Sixty-two pounds," Susan recorded.

Back on the ground Damien was measured and examined exhaustively. Seth walked back to the camp and returned with the electronic tracking collar that would make it possible to monitor the dog's every movement. The brindle pit bull's short, powerful neck was barely long enough to accommodate the width of the collar and large long-term battery pack. While Seth secured the collar, Tag sprayed the dog's sides with fluorescent orange paint to facilitate sighting him in the dense brush.

"OK, pack up the snack bar," ordered Hoffman, "and we'll let this dog get on with his life."

Later that evening, as the sun dropped below the dark shapes of the surrounding mountains, Damien sat hunched at the river's edge, thinking. The humans observing him from their blind would argue that it was not possible for him to reflect on past events in a way which could rightly be called "thinking," but he was, nonetheless, thoughtful. The scientists did not know dogs nearly so well as they imagined.

Damien was staying away from the humans' camp. He was a pit bulldog, born of a proud race of dogs exalted for courage, but today's events had shaken him to the core. When the drugs had rendered him conscious but unable to move, he had experienced profound panic during the moments the humans had laughed and talked over him as they handled his body. The drug-induced disorientation had only heightened his terror. So now, awake again and away from the humans' hands, he reflected pensively on what he had learned today.

He would stay away from humans.

The decision left him feeling empty. He bent his head to lap at the river's edge, and found that he could not reach it. The awful, chafing collar they had put around his neck precluded it. He had to stand up, and then lower his shoulders to reach his muzzle to the water. Earlier he had spent hours trying to rub the collar off, but had succeeded only in wearing sores in the fine fur under it. He was resigned to it now, though not yet used to the restrictions it put on his movements.

When he finished drinking he stood a while longer in the growing dusk, gazing across the blue-green water rushing past. He really couldn't remember it clearly anymore, but there lingered a distant memory from his puppyhood, of a pleasant feeling experienced while following at a human's heels. But with that memory came another; the sharp, cold, unbelievable moment of horror when he had realized he could not find his humans. Now, standing by the cold river sliding by, Damien's stomach jerked imperceptibly as he voiced his aching loneliness in a series of silent whimpers. He could not understand why the thing he longed for was the thing he now had to avoid.

Sleeping was bothersome and hunting became nearly impossible. He could still dig up the voles and mice which made up a large portion of his diet, but now for the most part the rodents could avoid his jaws. Lunges which had been lightning fast were now awkward. He survived the first week by returning to the deer carcass and becoming one of many creatures subsisting on the decaying flesh. In time, nothing remained but scattered bones and he began to go hungry, really hungry, for the first time since the day he had found himself alone in the forest. After each weary day of nonproductive hunting, he would attempt to curl up in a ball and sleep, but the collar forced his neck out at an awkward angle and he lay blinking in annoyance.

When his hunger grew, Damien's resolve to stay away from the humans weakened. As frightening and unpredictable as they were, they *had* been a source of food. He was starving. Fifteen days after the placement of the tracking collar, he had lost eight pounds. His gaunt, silent form became a fixture as he sat a dozen yards from the kitchen area, salivating at the scent when food was cooked, his eyes burning with his need.

Then desperation made him bolder. On a night of torrential rain, when the noise of the downpour hitting the tents and tarps drowned out all other sounds, he came into camp while the professor and students slept. He went straight to the kitchen area and gnawed through Seth's carelessly stored food stash, gulping down bars of butter and several eggs. He chewed open plastic containers, licking up the granola and dried foods which spilled out. He left when he could find nothing more to eat, and slept that night under his fallen log, licking his lips contentedly.

As the team of behaviorists watched Damien's decline with interest, they were unaware that their tracking collar was the source of the dog's distress. Tag, at least, should have known; before coming to work with Professor

Hoffman he had spent a year studying a population of wild geese on the Great Lakes. He and his fellow researchers had tagged a dozen geese with neck tubes made of PVC pipe marked with large numbers. When a harsh winter storm had spread the first ice across the marshes, ten of the geese had died, the plastic pipes frozen tightly to the ice. When the researchers returned they found the dead geese surrounded by faithful mates and comrades, unwilling to desert their fallen companions. There had been a stink about it in the local paper, and it was an unpleasant memory for Tag. But as Hoffman and his students carefully noted the dog's declining physical condition, they all assumed what they were witnessing was the normal termination of a feral dog's life cycle. They spoke in appropriately regretful tones when discussing the upcoming end of the subject and their project. They were not immune to the emotion of the dog's suffering, but they were scientists, they all understood the importance of observation, and the consequence of their interference or any emotionalism over the "natural" course of things. So they carefully locked their food away inside their tents and continued with their observations.

Days passed; chill, cold rain, often mixed with snow, began to fall in earnest, and Damien subsisted primarily on deer droppings and grass. He was fifty pounds now, his skin sliding over prominent back and hip bones, his head narrow and skull-like. He tired easily and spent most of the day sitting on the perimeter of the camp, watching the humans. When the hunger pangs became too much to endure, he would wander off in desperate search of deer droppings.

The time came when Damien, as some domestic, and even the occasional undomestic, animals do, sensed that he must go to humans. Damien did not understand the concept of a word like "intervention," but he understood that he was miserable, and that he felt somehow the humans could make it better. The Voice spoke clearly, though with no explanation. He *knew* the people in the camp *could*, if they wanted, provide food and warmth. And, The Voice prompted, they could provide something more. Something intangible that Damien did not as of yet understand.

The Voice said: *Your place is with the people.*

So he went. Wary, uncertain of his reception and yet with a dignity found only in some few dogs of character, he stepped carefully out of the dark forest into the light of the dying fire. Hoffman was up, attended as always by Tag, everyone else having gone to their tents. Both men saw the dog and watched its strange behavior unfolding. By the light of the fire Damien could see their features, the older man gaunt almost, with a high forehead and a thin, straight nose, the younger man chunky, with a round face and flaxen hair. It was the older man the dog watched. The dog came, step by wary step, closer to the men. Though his manner of moving was furtive, his eyes were not. His gaze was direct—holding Hoffman's eyes.

He was telling Hoffman that he was hurting, starving, dying. It was up to the man now, what would become of him—and somehow, to Damien, that seemed right.

The dog came within five feet of the professor, then sat, his steady brown eyes upraised to the man's. Hoffman gazed back, seeing again the Primordial Dog, and seeing also Damien's form coming in and out of the darkness, the night of his injury.

Tag watched them both, his eyes moving between the dog and the man. He decided, in his usual overprotective manner, that it was up to him to protect Hoffman from any misgivings the professor might be experiencing about the termination of this project. He watched the growing hint of a frown on Hoffman's face as the man studied the dog before him. The three of them sat like that, a frozen tableau, while the fire gently hissed and cracked, and the soft misty rain whispered as it fell upon the great, gray trees that ringed them. Then Tag acted. He stood up suddenly, making a harsh "Haaah!" sound meant to frighten the dog away. His hands waved at the dog, and he stepped toward the animal in a threatening manner. Damien turned and fled, disappearing quickly into the wet, cold dark.

Tag felt the need to say something rather quickly. "We're going to have to really keep an eye on our food supplies."

The older man's frown had deepened when Tag acted, but now his face composed itself and Hoffman sighed very quietly. "You're right," was all he said. They sat, in silence, another fifteen minutes, and then Hoffman, knowing Tag would not leave him alone by the fire tonight, went to his tent.

Damien awoke to a clear, sharp, late-autumn morning. Something odd; some strange sensation had awakened him. There was nothing unusual to be seen, heard or scented, but his skin tingled with an anxious feeling, and he got to his feet. As was usual now, his thoughts turned immediately to food. The crisp air brought him the scent of the humans' campfire, coffee and cooking mush. He shuffled off wearily in that direction.

A surprise awaited him as he sat in his accustomed place dully watching the movements of the researchers. The people were taking the camp down. In an hour they were done and, with almost all of the equipment stowed beneath tarps tucked protectively under some fallen trees, they simply left. Damien, too weak to follow, watched them go. He had seen hikers break camp before, and he knew what to do. As soon as the last student disappeared into the brush, he went forward and inspected every inch of the camp. He was looking for food, but found nothing except a pile of coffee grounds which he sniffed critically but licked up nonetheless. He sat down in the middle of the empty camp and heaved a large sigh.

He sat still for quite a while, until he became aware again of the strange sensation. There was a certain heaviness of the air, as if the sky was pushing down on him. The feeling made him uneasy, and he stood up, uncertain what to do. It was a beautiful clear day, but he felt the need to seek shelter. The warning was vague, however, and not nearly so loud as the insistent demand of his hunger. He *must* find food today.

Radio reports of the impending severe weather that Damien was sensing had sent Hoffman and his group scurrying for cover. Extreme winds were predicted—rare for this part of the state—and the forest would be far too dangerous a place for the researchers to stay. Tents were simply not safe among the trees in high winds. The professor made the decision to withdraw until the danger was over. They would restock their stolen supplies and pick up where they had left off when it was safe to return.

By late afternoon Damien reached the rock slide where Hoffman had watched his playful hunting of the marmots. The wind was blowing hard now, straight and cold down the side of the mountain. The marmots whistled and jeered but the dog stood staring dully at them for several moments. Then, with an obvious effort, he roused himself and went forward.

Cramming his head down between the rocks where one marmot had just disappeared, he inhaled the intoxicating scent of the big rodent. If he could just reach down a little farther between the rocks, he might reach one. His breathing quickened at the thought of the warm blood spilling over his tongue and the soft, broken body being crushed between his jaws. He *must* catch one. He drove his head inward, twisting his shoulders, the collar's box making sharp grating sounds on the granite rock. Perhaps in here he would find the animal cowering, helpless. Its scent was everywhere, taunting him, driving him to madness in his desire for food. He felt himself slip forward a couple inches, and his body corkscrewed wildly in an effort to get his muzzle just a few more inches into the space between the rocks. But it was no use, his shoulders blocked the way and he wearily began to back out, hunching up his spine, his hind paws scrabbling on the slick rock for a purchase. He went nowhere; he was stuck. He had forced the bulky collar through an opening in the rocks while his head and neck had been sideways; now, upright, the collar was wedged effectively behind the small opening.

Damien felt no panic but continued to struggle, sure that at any moment he would be free. For several minutes, the dog struggled but the collar was firmly stuck behind the crevice. Exhausted, the dog collapsed upon the rock, panting hard. He lay patiently, waiting for his strength to return so he could begin again to try and loose himself.

Six days later Hoffman and his students were regrouped and back on the trail headed toward their abandoned base camp. The storm had been severe, with gusts in excess of 100 mph on the nearby coast, and the hikers' progress was seriously impeded by the destruction dealt to the forest by the storm. Tag and Devon labored in the point position, hacking and pushing a way through the windfalls while the professor, still a little sore from his sprain, brought up the rear. It took them the entire day to get from their vehicles to the camp, and they arrived shortly before nightfall. They set up their tents again, cooked a quick dinner and fell into their sleeping bags too exhausted to even think about locating the dog.

The next morning Seth woke first and crawled from his tent, his equipment under his arm. After a quick trip to the "beach" to dunk his close-cropped, dark hair in the river and splash ice-cold water on his face, he fired up the equipment and located a faint signal north-northwest of camp. As the others joined him around the rock-ringed campfire where the coffee and tea pots boiled, they discussed the feasibility of following the signal through the downed brush.

"It's possible he's died," said Devon. "That would explain the stationary reading."

Hoffman nodded. "I think we have to consider it a possibility. Depending on how far out he is, we may or may not reach him today. We can get a good start though. Let's get to it."

After three hours of throwing limbs aside and climbing over tree trunks, the group retreated to camp. The faint signal had remained stationary all day, and there was no longer any doubt in the researcher's minds that their subject had perished. There was no rush now.

By noon the next day, they broke out of the woods onto the rock-covered hillside Hoffman recognized.

"The signal is strong here. He's close," Seth said.

Hoffman was silent, scanning the rocky hillside. The dull gray sky above blended with the dull gray of the rocks, and there was no movement anywhere. Even the marmots were absent. Then he saw the body.

"There," he said, pointing. "There he is."

The students looked where he was pointing and saw the gold and black striped shape, the head out of sight among the rocks. Even from this distance it was obvious the dog had died of starvation.

"He pegged out a while ago by the look of it," Tag said. They all began climbing up toward where the body lay.

"We'll be home for Thanksgiving," Devon said flatly.

"What a collar!" Seth said as they climbed. "Look how his head is stuck in those rocks, but we still got the signal, clear back at camp. That's intense."

"Wow," Susan exclaimed as they got close, "look at that—his head *is* stuck in those rocks. That's insane; the collar must have jammed."

They ganged around the dog's body, staring. "That's what happened," Susan continued, pulling her blond ponytail back and resetting the rubber band. "He got it stuck and didn't have the strength to pull free. God, I've never seen anything that thin."

"He tried. Look at the blood around his shoulders. He really tore at it— but when *I* put a collar on, it *stays* on."

"Yeah, your mother must be proud, Seth—why don't you see if you can get its head out, otherwise we're going to have to cut the collar off," Tag said.

Seth knelt beside the body and craned his neck to see into the rock crevice. Reaching in, he grasped the scrawny neck, determined to twist it around and ease the collar back through the hole. At his touch the body jerked convulsively, and a hind leg drew slowly up toward the belly.

"Oh my God!" Susan breathed, her face jutting forward in disbelief. "He's alive!"

Seth jerked back with an oath and stood up. His olive skin was pale. "No way, man. *No way.*"

Hoffman knelt down, grasping the dog's chest at the narrow point between its elbows. "There's a pulse," he said, his eyebrows raising, "but I shouldn't expect him to live much longer." There was silence. It was an awkward moment and they all avoided each others' eyes. The professor stood up and they stared down at the cold, starved body at their feet.

"Well," Devon said, "what do we do?"

"Should I take the collar off, anyway?" Seth trailed off.

"Well at least pull his head out of there," Devon said. "It can't make much difference to the study at *this* point."

Seth looked at Hoffman and the professor slowly nodded.

Seth returned to his knees beside the dog and reached into the crevice again, much more gently this time, and eased the head around until he forced the collar back through the opening. He grimaced and wiped his hands on his pants after he laid the dog's head down on the rock slab.

"Yuck, look at that."

The dog's vain struggles had worn the skin away under the collar, and blood and pus coated the collar strap. Lying on the rock in the cold mountain air, the dog's body was too weak even to shiver. It merely twitched spasmodically from time to time. It was a mere skeleton, its head a ghastly skull in which two brown eyes rolled weakly upward to the faces of the scientists. The pathetic form before them searched their faces, and then, the effort being too much, its eyes closed once again.

"Huh," said Susan uncomfortably.

"I wish we could put it out of its misery," Devon said quietly, picking up his hat and running his hand through his hair before he resettled it.

Hoffman sighed deeply. "No, let's just let nature take her course. We're simply here to observe—it's not for us to interfere. We'll come back tomorrow and record the end of the study. Let's go back to camp."

They filed away, silently, not a word spoken until they arrived back at camp. They ate dinner and sat around the campfire glumly. They had all experienced project terminations with their resulting loss of subject animals before—it was quite common for this type of work and not normally a cause for emotion. But somehow, sitting around the warm fire in their down jackets, thinking of the emaciated dog lying alone upon its rock on the open hillside stilled them all.

"He's probably dead by now," Devon, slumped under his hat, said into the silence.

"Oh, I would think so," Hoffman answered. "He won't make it through the night."

At first light Hoffman, Seth and Tag set off to retrieve the collar and record the end of the dog and the project. Susan and Devon stayed behind to pack up camp so they could leave when the men returned. Having packed up, and finding themselves with nothing else to do, Devon dug out the last of his stash and rolled a small joint which he and Susan shared, sitting, by force of habit, on the stumps around the dead campfire. Hearing the faint sounds of the returning men they looked up to see Hoffman and Tag, followed by Seth, breaking out of the woods. The professor had a sheepish grin on his face and Seth carried the brindled dog over his shoulders.

CHAPTER TWO

Passing through the animal receiving area, Elizabeth Fletcher noticed the door to one of the isolation rooms was open, though it was clearly marked with instructions to keep it closed at all times. Thinking to pull it shut, she leaned in to see if perhaps someone had simply stepped in for a moment.

She saw two men standing in the room. She recognized one of them as Dr. Joseph Seville, a veterinarian who had obtained his Ph.D. in behavioral research, pointed out to her by the animal technician who had shown her the ropes her first day, and she shyly ducked back into the hallway. It was too late. He had seen her.

"You, there. Come in here."

You there? she thought with a frown.

The technician, indicating the researcher to her with a quick and furtive nod of her head three days earlier, had called him a "stone-cold bastard" and said that the only things he had less regard for than the animals were the students and techs. The technician had suggested steering clear of the investigator at all costs.

Great.

She stuck her head back in the door. "Me?" She mouthed the word, pointing to herself.

The man glanced her way again. His eyes were a light, startling gray beneath his short-cropped black hair. Beside him stood a younger dark blond man with the strong, erect look of a high diver. "Yes, you. Come in here."

She stepped into the room but didn't come in any farther.

"I need this cage cleaned out. Stat."

Elizabeth was taken aback. She was in fact a premed student, soon to be the third generation of cardiac surgeons in her family to work right here at this University. Glancing down though, at the worn jeans and oversized T-shirt she wore when working here, she had to admit she probably did look the part of a kennel technician. Under the scrutiny of the man, she suddenly felt self-conscious. The doctor was wearing a dark blue shirt and black tie beneath his lab coat, and neatly pleated gray slacks. The younger man wore a spotless white collarless shirt tucked into immaculate jeans. Compared to these two, Elizabeth felt like a slob.

Something in the man's manner forestalled argument, and she didn't want any trouble after only three days at this job. Working here was all very clandestine anyway—of her friends, only Hannah, who had talked her into being a socialization handler, knew about it. She wanted to keep a low profile. If her father found out she was wasting valuable study time to "play with animals" as he would call it, she would never hear the end of it. Though she had no training in how to clean out cages, and it was not part of the duties of a handler, an instinctive respect for the older authoritative figure prompted her to walk into the room.

The younger man had knelt down and opened the door to the metal and Plexiglas intensive care unit, gently pulling an animal out of it onto the floor. The dark-haired doctor was watching him, a stomach feeding tube and three 60cc syringes of brown fluid in his hand. He glanced up at her again as she approached

"What are you going to clean it with?" His voice was soft, but his tone left no doubt he considered her an idiot.

"Oh, sorry," she mumbled and left the room. Elizabeth hadn't a clue what to do. As a handler, her job was to pet and handle the animals utilized in the research labs in an effort to keep them docile. This had the secondary effect of helping the University to meet voluntary animal care guidelines established by national humane groups. The job of handler, which paid so little it was basically a volunteer position, had simple rules; having sat through the orientation, she could now enter any nonrestricted area on the University grounds and handle any animal there, as long as she did not see the special no-contact sticker attached to a lab's door or to an animal's cage. She must wear her handler's card conspicuously at all times and she could not give food, water or any other substances or objects to the animals. She must obey any additional instructions given by the investigator and his/her staff, and she must wash her hands with a special disinfectant gel carried in her pocket between each cage or kennel.

However, cleaning cages wasn't something handlers were supposed to do. The only thing Elizabeth could think to do was find someone who might know how she should go about it. She sure wasn't going to ask that jerk of a vet anything. Seeing a senior animal technician she had exchanged greetings with the day before, she hurried to catch up with her.

"Hey—I'm sorry—I've got to clean a cage for this guy in there, and I'm not sure what I should use."

The girl was plump and had her blond hair done up in a bun. "*Clean* a cage?" she asked in a friendly manner. "Who is this guy?"

"A tech told me his name is Seville, I think that was it."

The girl's face set. "That figures. I suppose he's smoking in there too?"

"Not that I saw."

"Well, he does as he pleases, breaks every rule, and expects everyone to come running when he wants something. Nobody is supposed to ask you to clean cages—you're just a handler, right?"

"Well, yeah, I am. It's OK."

"Would you like me to do it instead?"

Elizabeth looked at the girl's friendly face and felt awful. There was no way she would ask someone else to clean a cage for her. She wasn't a prima donna.

"No, thanks, it's not a big deal, really. It's OK."

"All right, but don't feel you have to. Those guys know better. It's the little ICU in there, right?"

Elizabeth nodded.

"If you're going to do it, just get one of the buckets with the disinfectant—the pink stuff—in it, right inside that door there; the rag is already in it, and here's a baggy in case there's any big chunks. You put your hand in it, like this, grab it, and pull your hand out, got it?"

"Oh. OK, thanks. Thanks a lot."

She got the bucket and returned to the room. The two men were kneeling over the body of a dog that was lying on the floor. She could only see its back and she gasped at the sight of it.

"What *happened* to it?" she breathed. It was a skeleton with fur. She had never seen anything like it. How could it be alive? Her face was pulled back in a grimace of disgust, but she couldn't take her eyes off the grotesque spectre of the dog. The men ignored her. While the young man held the feebly protesting dog to the floor, the doctor threaded a tube down its throat and into its stomach. In rapid succession he attached each large syringe to the tube and expertly depressed the syringe plunger by pushing it against his thigh while holding the tube in place in the dog's mouth. Seville looked up once while he was working, looking right at her. He cocked his eyes toward the cage and then looked back at the struggling dog, and she got the point.

The cage the dog had been in was a portable intensive care unit, small and made of stainless steel. The front panels were Plexiglas, and the dog had been lying on a plastic-coated wire grill. The grill was soiled with urine, diarrhea and vomit. She felt her stomach lift, and then settle.

She wondered what was wrong with the animal. Was it a research dog? What kind of research would produce something like that? It was a repugnant sight, and her mind rebelled at the unpleasantness; instead of pity she felt disgust. She bent to her work and listened to the men talking behind her, curious to find how the dog had come to be in such a condition.

The researcher leaned back. "Go find me some Normosol R, Tom, and some injectible B."

"All right, anything else?"

"Yeah, get me a 35, or better yet, 60cc syringe and an eighteen needle."

Elizabeth watched from the corner of her eye as the young man left the room. The doctor stayed. Taking a smaller syringe from his pocket, he pulled off the cap with his teeth and injected the animal in the thigh. He replaced the cap and returned the syringe to his pocket. The dog was struggling harder to get up now, and the man placed his knee on the animal's bandaged neck to hold it down.

"Are you finished?" he asked Elizabeth.

"I, I think so." She shrugged. "I don't do this normally, so I . . ." She trailed off, feeling stupid.

"Come over here."

She moved up tentatively, as hesitant to do something wrong and earn the man's scorn as she was to get close to the hideous form of the writhing dog.

35

"Come on, come on," he reproached her, grabbing up skin behind the dog's head with one hand, and grasping its muzzle with the other. "Take a hold, here, like this. Hold the head up."

Grimacing, she imitated his hold, keeping the dog's head stiffly away from where she knelt.

"God," she breathed, "it's disgusting."

The man produced a small pair of scissors and swiftly cut away the soiled bandages from the dog's neck. The skin underneath was raw and oozing.

Elizabeth stared at the dog. It began to shiver in a violent, twitchy manner. Either the floor was cold to it, or perhaps, Elizabeth thought, it was frightened of her and the doctor. She wondered who had done this to the dog—maybe this very man? He seemed nasty enough, she reflected. Then again, even though he was kneeling on the dog's side to hold it down, he was now rewrapping the dog's wounded neck with obvious care.

The dog's head had been turned away from her since she entered the room. Elizabeth leaned forward so she could see the head she held in her hands without disturbing the angle of the neck the doctor was working on. As her head came into its view, the dog, helplessly pinned to the floor by the man's knee, raised its eyes to her face, and they stared at each other.

"*Wow.*" She mouthed the word so softly the man did not hear. The dog's eyes were small, rimmed in black and they were a rich, golden brown with a soft, diffused dark center. The eyes stared at her, and though they did not resemble human eyes, she saw a *somethingness* there, that bespoke a personality far stronger than she would have believed possible in an animal.

The dog held her stare, and she wondered what he thought about her. What did *he* see in her eyes? She looked away first.

Having never been allowed to keep pets, Elizabeth lacked personal experience with animals. She had suffered the deprivation keenly, keeping up a steady barrage of requests for puppies or kittens for years. Her father had steadfastly denied every one, refusing to even discuss the issue. His adamant refusal to even consider allowing her to keep a dog remained a mystery to her, for generally he denied her nothing. She decided to wait it out, looking forward to the day she could have as many dogs as she wanted. Some of her friends had dogs, but these were mostly yappy little housedogs that dived under the couch at her approach, threatening her from there. She found dogs like that unpleasant at best. She liked big dogs, malamutes and Dobermans, dogs like that. When she was feeling particularly rebellious, she imagined keeping an entire team of huskies, and taking her father on a wild sled ride someday.

Ironically, the place where Elizabeth saw dogs most often was in her father's cardiac research lab. From childhood on however, he had discouraged her from showing any interest in them *as dogs*. As receptacles of his handiwork it was another thing; he was always willing to show her some new device being tested, or to point out some particularly interesting new technique. As a result, she most often saw the dogs as anesthetized and draped lumps, consisting primarily of a gaping, pulsing hole surrounded by bloody drapes upon which instruments dangled, and under which only the remotest form of a dog was discernible. Here and there, a paw tied down to the V-shaped table poked out. She saw other dogs there, as she passed through the rooms to get to where he was working. These dogs were lying about in steel cages, charts carefully noting the number of days each animal survived the procedure done to it, the animals staring out at her, their eyes dulled to indifference by suffering.

That was why she had taken this handler's job; this was an opportunity to be around dogs—to pet them and stroke their heads—without her father's sharp glance of disapproval finding her from across the room.

"Does he have a name?" she asked the man when he had finished his bandage and motioned for her to release the dog's head. It was a ridiculous question to ask a researcher—she knew that—and she was shocked to hear herself asking it.

"A name?" The doctor seemed amused at her question. "Uhm. You'd have to ask Viktor Hoffman about that, it's his *pet.*" His tone was wry.

Tom reentered the room, a bag of solution in one hand and a large syringe in the other. Elizabeth backed away, unwilling to leave yet. She wasn't sure why, but she wanted to know what they were going to do to the dog with those strange, compelling eyes. She watched as Tom pulled fluid from the bag into the large syringe. He handed it to the doctor and then held the dog steady as the fluid was injected under the loose skin of its gaunt back. They repeated the operation several more times until the dark-haired man seemed satisfied.

The two men placed the dog back into the ICU, gathered up their equipment and left the room without a word to her.

In the silence following their departure, she stared at the dog as it lay inside the metal cage. Lying on his side where the men had left him, the

37

starved dog stared back at her, its gaze unwavering. At first she thought his expression cruel, then realized it was only an absence of affection which she saw. The other dogs at the Animal Resources Center were all mad for attention, greeting her with wild displays of cheap love. Tails lashing and eyes gleaming with adoration, they wanted her to give them the human contact they had reason to miss. It was obvious this dog felt nothing for her. She wondered if he felt affection for *anyone.* He looked so grim and savage with his short pointed ears and wide jaws. His emaciated condition made his appearance more frightening. And yet it struck her also that for all his fierce appearance, the dog seemed so alone, so defenseless against the actions of her fellow humans.

She kept looking at the eyes, the quiet brown eyes that held hers—searched hers—and she couldn't help but question what manner of mind lay behind them. Having never really *known* a dog she wasn't sure if what she was seeing was normal. There just seemed to be *something* behind those eyes—something she couldn't reconcile with what she had been taught.

The essential things she knew about dogs she had picked up from her father, and she had had no reason to question his basic assumptions about dogs. She had grown up in awe of all her father knew—he was a brilliant man—and she had never questioned his qualification to judge the intelligence or essence of the species he so often used in his work. Yet she knew *most* people treated dogs as pets, a thing her father did *not* do. It wasn't that he disliked dogs—she knew that was not true—and for the first time, standing there staring down at the brindle pit bull, she wondered vaguely if her father's attitude was a defensive mechanism that allowed him to exploit dogs the way he did.

The dog raised its head to stare back at her. She could see plainly that it cost the dog just to make that simple movement, and she saw its head wavering weakly as it continued to watch her warily. The dog, she realized, was concerned she might do something to it, like the men who had just left.

"Oh, don't worry about *me,* I won't hurt you," she said very quietly, almost to herself. The dog dropped its head, and its eyes half closed. She wondered if the dog understood her tone or if he was simply too exhausted to keep his head up.

Elizabeth realized now she really didn't know much about dogs, other than what she had read in a few books. Dogs, she knew, did not feel emotions or pain like humans, could not reason, simply reacted to stimulus and lived only in the present. They did not think about nor experience the world the way humans did. Her father said so, and the books—supposedly written by experts—she had read, had said the same thing. She puzzled at the enigmatic form, as remote and unknowable to her as an alien found lying in a wheat field. She wondered again what had happened to bring the animal to this condition, and if its owner—Viktor Hoffman the researcher had said—would come for it soon. With one last glance at the dog's starved form, she turned and left the room.

Her handler's shift wasn't over for another twenty minutes, but she went to her locker anyway, changed and left the building, which was laughingly called "the ARC." She felt subdued, and unwilling to handle any more dogs. Stepping out into the brisk autumn air she called herself a silly goose for getting so upset over one dog, yet the animal's image stayed with her. Wanting to clear her mind she walked for a while, concentrating instead on her upcoming twentieth birthday. It seemed an important and significant turning point. In another two years she should—no *would*—have achieved admittance to the medical program *here,* at the same University she was currently attending. Her father had graduated here, and now worked at the same University medical center where *his* father had also practiced in the years before his retirement.

Elizabeth repressed a tiny nag way back in the furthest reaches of her mind. It came around whenever she contemplated her admission to the medical school. For the past ten plus years she had prepared herself for nothing else, yet the thought of her future being so completely consummated at the moment of her admittance always caused her to pause, to mentally hesitate a beat before continuing on with her thoughts. She *did* feel the pressure of being the third generation of Fletchers to become an M.D., but it was nice to know that she could do something which was so meaningful to her father and grandfather.

Elizabeth sat down on a low wall outside the student union building and decided the nagging doubts were not about her chosen profession, but rather the natural result of her fear of failure.

To fail in this was unthinkable; it would break their hearts.

So the immense responsibility rested squarely on her shoulders alone. She must stick to her well-thought-out schedule, which would propel her toward an M.D. degree. Because she was a Fletcher, and it was her turn.

Because the fear of failure was so unthinkable, of course she thought about it. Her fears were unfounded. She knew that on a logical level; school was easy for her and her grades were exceptional. There was no reason she should not sail through without a hitch. As a consequence of her father's single-parent status, her childhood had been spent hanging around his workplace, witnessing thousands of practice surgeries and watching experimental routines being performed on lab animals. She was far better prepared than most people.

Still.

She couldn't help but worry, because it *was* so important. All her life, since she was old enough to understand the concept of a career, she had known what she would do, what she would be. The Fletchers were heart men; her grandfather a thoracic surgeon, her father deeply involved in cardiac transplant research. She might not be a son, but she could still follow in the paternal footsteps, and she intended to.

Drumming her heels against the low brick wall she was sitting on, she watched the other students pass. Elizabeth knew her friends envied the unwavering vision she held of her future, but was it true, she wondered, that *most* people her age had no idea what they wanted to do with their lives? She had known for so long what was expected that it was hard for her to imagine sitting on that wall *not* knowing exactly where her future plans would take her. She tried it, shutting her eyes and thinking:

What if dad had been a delivery man, and grandpa a car salesman? What if you had no family to consider—what if you were an orphan? What would you do?

She didn't like the feeling. She felt it in the pit of her stomach, a lost feeling. It would be strange and disheartening not to know exactly what steps to take, where you would be in your career in X number of years. She tried again. What would she do with a life free from predestiny? She frowned slightly and thought that *maybe*, perhaps, she could be a chef, for she loved to cook. She thought it would be pleasant to be surrounded by the warm smells of a kitchen, preparing food so good that others would speak well of it. But she opened her eyes. She was going to be a cardiac surgeon.

David, her father, and Bill, her grandfather, both wanted her to follow in their footsteps. It was a life she knew and was accustomed to, having grown up in an environment where discussions of surgical procedures more often than not dominated the dinner table conversation. Up until her grandfather's recent retirement, there had been times when it had seemed to the young woman that the two men could not speak, read or *live* any other subject.

But Elizabeth was proud to be a part of that tradition. How many people on the planet knew how it felt to hold another human's beating heart in their hands? In a few years time she would be trained to do such complicated and delicate work. She imagined herself in scrubs, standing before a helpless, unconscious human with a scalpel in her hand. *She* would cut through the bleeding skin, split the rib cage open, reach into the chest and hold the beating heart in her hands. How must it feel, at that moment, to know that a person's life was as surely in your hands as if you were a god?

No wonder cardiac surgeons are paid so well.

Thinking of it in those terms made her feel a little queasy. She put her arms behind her and leaned back, exposing her face instinctively to the late autumn sun. There was hardly any warmth to it, but it felt good to close her eyes and relax. For a little while longer she could afford to set aside thoughts of the future, and today was a good day to do just that. She enjoyed autumn, with its comfortable back-to-school feel, and she looked forward to the Christmas season. She was the driving force behind the holiday atmosphere in her home. Recently she had caught her grandfather up in her enthusiasm, so that now, right after Thanksgiving and much to his son's chagrin, he began to disgrace the house and yard with monumental quantities of outdoor lights.

"Hey!"

Elizabeth opened her eyes and saw her friend Hannah's round, dark-complexioned face before her.

"Whatchya doin'?"

Hannah was a girl she had sat next to in biology class her first year. It was she who had helped Elizabeth talk herself into sneaking into the handler's job, pointing out it was a good way to enjoy petting and playing with dogs without having to own one. Now their schedules had diverged and they found it difficult to work or study together this year. As friends, they were already drifting apart.

"Just got done at the ARC. What are you doing?"

"I'm headed home, actually," Hannah said. She set on the ground before her a book bag which could easily have passed for a Sherpa's bundle on an Everest expedition. "I just wondered what you were doing—you looked like one of those things on the front of a ship—you know, the statues of women?—the way you were sitting there with your face up." She jutted her chin out and tipped her head back, imitating Elizabeth's posture of a moment before.

"Oh my God, did I really look stupid?" Elizabeth glanced about, scanning for men who might have noticed her.

"No," Hannah laughed, "no, you didn't. I'm kidding. Hey, catch you later." Hoisting her bag back to her shoulder, she moved off in the stream of between-class students and disappeared from sight.

Elizabeth watched her go. She liked Hannah, but they had never gotten really close. Like the other members of her family, she was a bit aloof. For Elizabeth it was not out of any feeling of superiority, but rather because her affection was simply not given cheaply. Elizabeth's best friend, Colleen, with whom she had gone through elementary, middle and high school, had moved away to Florida ten months ago and she felt that loss keenly.

She gathered up her books and headed home. When she had turned eighteen, one of the concessions her father made for her, as an adult living in his home, was never to ask her about her whereabouts. Because of this she had been able to work the handler's job into her daily routine, undetected, the only hitch being the minor guilt associated with intentionally keeping anything from Dave or Bill.

The fall afternoon was beautiful. As she walked between the rows of cars in the tree-lined parking lot, she glimpsed some boys throwing a Frisbee back and forth. A blue- and black-spotted cattle dog ran, silent and intent, just beneath the disk every time it was thrown. His strong herding instincts fired up by the Frisbee's motion, he waited bug-eyed with intensity for each new throw. Elizabeth's thoughts turned, unbidden, toward dogs again. She wondered vaguely if her father would ever use any of the dogs she handled in his research over at the cardiac wing of The Med. He went through a tremendous number of dogs. Then her mind edged closer to where she did not want it to go. She considered the sheer numbers of animals housed in the ARC, and used annually by the University. The University's use of animal "models" was colossal. The vast majority of the dogs used were "random source" dogs, meaning former pets which had, by fair means or foul, become the property of USDA "bunchers," who then sold them to their fate. The cost of "colony dogs," those bred and raised specifically for research purposes, was prohibitive, and their use relatively rare. Arriving at her truck she got in and turned on the radio, loud, and tried to sing thoughts of dogs—any dogs—out of her mind.

That evening, sitting at the dinner table with her father while they waited for Bill to bring the lasagna from the kitchen, Elizabeth said, "I was wondering about something I saw today. I went over to the ARC building with a friend," she hated herself for this small lie, "and I saw something there that I . . . I was wondering about." Taking a breadstick from the middle of the table, she fiddled with it.

Her father was pouring himself a glass of red wine. He was a large man, tall, and while not really overweight, not svelte, either. "What?"

Bill came from the kitchen, carrying an oblong pan with oven mitts, a hotpad dangling from under his right elbow. "Here—take this El." He tipped his arm in her direction. She placed the pad on the table and he deposited the dish and seated himself.

"It was a dog. And it was really, I mean *really*, messed up. Just a skeleton. This guy was trying to save it, I guess; he was giving it fluids. But I was just wondering, do you think something that has been *that* starved can survive?"

"I'd have to know exactly what percentage of body tissue—fat and muscle—was affected," her father said, "and what *form* of starvation it had sustained, in order to know about possible damage—what caused the weight loss, do you know?"

"No. The guy didn't say."

Her father took a drink and set his glass down, then asked, "Where were you when you saw it?"

"In receiving. In an isolation area, actually."

"I wonder why it would be in receiving?" He resumed eating. Guiltily, Elizabeth was certain he was wondering what *she* had been doing in animal receiving as well.

"What's this?" Bill asked, having missed the beginning of the conversation.

"A dog I saw. I just can't believe it was still alive. I just wondered if it was going to make it, is all."

"What were you doing at the ARC?" her father asked.

She felt terrible. "A friend is signing up to be a handler. I just went with her."

"Uhm." His expression was noncommittal, so she decided to go for broke, and get herself out, if possible, of her present predicament.

"It doesn't look like a bad job."

Her father shot her a glance, but remained silent. He didn't *need* to say anything.

"How's the chemistry class coming?" Bill said. Chemistry was her Waterloo; they all knew that.

She made a face. "OK. It's tough."

Her father nodded. "Yes, it is. But you'll do fine."

Elizabeth sighed. Bill and Dave (she called them by those names at her father's request) were so supportive, and here she sat, having just lied to them. She felt miserable. She was fiercely devoted to them both and they were the only family she had. As the only woman of the house, she considered them *her* responsibility.

She decided to change the subject, which was SOP whenever the subject of chemistry class came up.

"Did Tony call?" she asked her grandfather.

"Yup. He wants you to call him this evening."

Tony was a third-year med student whom she had been seeing casually for six months. Elizabeth harbored a strong suspicion that the young man came over more to talk shop with Bill and Dave than because of any romantic interest in her. She knew they would simply be friends until they drifted apart, sometime soon.

They ate in silence for some time, then she said, "OK, so, do you think there is *any* chance of that dog surviving?"

"I would think so," her father said, "or else they would have just euthanized it, don't you think?"

"Yeah, I guess you're right." She hadn't thought of that.

"What made you so interested in this?" Bill asked.

"Oh, I don't know. I've just never seen anything that starved." She didn't mention how the dog had looked at her.

Her grandfather nodded. "You could probably check on its status at the receiving office if you're interested in knowing if it does survive."

Elizabeth had been raised by the two medical men since the awful time when her mother had simply left, abandoning her child and her husband without a word ever having been heard from her since. This had occurred shortly after Elizabeth's sixth birthday, and Bill had moved in to help provide additional care for her. The two men had raised her as best they could, juggling their professional careers with the needs of the child. Elizabeth had been a bright, loving child, almost too eager to please, and in perfect sympathy with the intellectual atmosphere of the home. For this reason it never occurred to either of the men to warn her against becoming attached to a research animal; it was not an idea they could even entertain.

Damien was young and of rugged breeding so his recovery, considering the severity of his condition, was quick. By the evening of the second day Seville pulled his IV line when the dog persisted in trying to chew it off. By the evening of the third day he was lapping weakly at the gruel placed before him and struggling repeatedly to stand. By the end of the week he got to his feet, swaying with weakness, when he heard the approach of the doctor in the white coat. Feeling more like his old self, he stared at the dark-haired man with a steady, level gaze that had in it neither submission nor threat. The man was alone, and he hesitated with his hand on the cage door while they scrutinized each other. Then, to the dog's relief, the researcher shrugged and retreated, having thought better of treating the formidable-looking dog without assistance.

Sometime later, other people came and Damien's cage was rolled a short way down the hall to another room. Damien was released into one of a line of twenty isolation kennels, each three feet wide by six feet long. The kennel walls were stainless-steel panels, the gate and roof stainless-steel bars. The floor was a stainless-steel grille, six inches off the stainless-steel bottom of the cage. When the animal technicians left he stood in the middle of his new world, wavering with weakness and eyeing the shiny, incomprehensible walls of his cell. Damien couldn't clearly remember a time when he had not lived outdoors in the cool, dappled forest, surrounded by the moist smell of moss and humus, the sharp, delicious, ever-changing odor of a swiftly flowing mountain river, and the intoxicating scent of small rodents in the ground beneath his paws. This abrupt and absolute disruption of his universe dismayed him. With a sigh he curled up at the back of the cage, and gave up quickly any attempt to get comfortable on the hellish metal grill.

He lay, his dog's eyebrows rising and falling as he glanced about, his consciousness filled with confusion. Lying on his stainless-steel grill, the dog felt desolate, empty, and the sight of a human outside his cage only persisted in making him wary. The memories from his puppyhood, when he had known human affection, now lingered more in his genetic makeup than in his mind. From that moment long ago when he had become separated from his owners, he had never known a kind pat, a word of praise, or the aching pleasure that came from pleasing his gods. Instead, humans had flung stones and sticks at him, shot at him, harmed him at every turn. Had he been a lesser dog, the sight of a human would have sent him cowering in terror, or snarling and snapping in defensive fear. But The Voice of his steady, resolute bulldog blood was strong—he would not turn against man simply to save himself.

Outside the University building where Damien lay, each day the thin early winter morning light came, strengthened, and passed into afternoons of cold, bright sun or heavy gray clouds which smelled of moisture. Each afternoon the sun descended into a sunset which blazed or smoldered, and then cold darkness came. Each night the moon shone down from an icy, clear sky, or through openings in great dark clouds which passed overhead on their silent, deliberate way across the sky. But inside the isolation ward, inside his metal world, the dog passed through his quarantine period living in a perpetual fluorescent noon which had no morning, no evening, no night, no shadows.

The sound of approaching footsteps, which he could just make out over the crescendo of barking that occurred whenever a person entered the room, was a source of both fascination and concern for Damien. The arrival of a human certainly broke the brutal monotony, but having learned to distrust humans, it was stressful for Damien. The lessons learned in the forest, coupled with what he had experienced since his capture, led him to believe that when humans came to stand before his cage, it was almost certainly to do alarming or painful things to him. The powerful force of his domestication was a persistent subtle whisper to his soul; that he was no longer a wild animal, that he *belonged* with these people, that he needed them, and that he must *serve* them somehow. Yet the more strident voice of recent experience continued to warn him to avoid their hands at all costs.

The two men no longer came to force the feeding tube down his throat. A woman who hardly glanced at him came instead, and twice a day she placed a food bowl in the holder in his gate. Hoffman came by now and then, kneeling down, smiling and snapping his fingers at him, but the dog remained curled up at the back of the cage. Damien no longer trusted him.

One other person came, almost every day, approaching his cage in a tentative, hesitant fashion, which Damien noted was quite different from the other, businesslike humans. It was a young woman and she stood back from the gate at a respectful distance making no moves to either befriend or harm him. At first her presence alarmed him, for he expected she was there to do *something* to him. So he had stared at the metal wall inches in front of his nose, his body rigid with stress, and hoped she would go away. After a time, when she did not try to harm him, he began to glance at her, then to raise his head at her approach, curious against his will. She just stood and watched him, with a somber, puzzled look on her face. She'd watch him for a while and then leave, at which point he would drop his head again and continue his desolate waiting.

When his thirty days in quarantine were up he was moved to the main ward to a kennel with a sign that read:

ADMIN HOLD FOR V. HOFFMAN,
AD/M/K-9 6DR514129V5S
AUTHORIZED FOR NON-LETHAL USE WHILE HOLDING
CAUTION!

He was in an entirely new area, in a new cage, and the barking was monumental. He stared around, baffled. His cage walls had changed. The sides were still stainless steel, but the top and gate were chain link now. The regime was very much the same. All night he lay in the unceasing dull fluorescent light, listening to the sounds made by two hundred bored dogs. At 5 A.M. the kennel staff arrived and the next three hours were filled with shouts, steam, the hiss of high-powered hose nozzles, the sharp scent of disinfectants, the blare of a radio and the raucous barking of his fellow inmates.

After the cleaners left there was more waiting. People came and went, pausing sometimes to glance at the kennel cards; dogs were put in, or taken out of kennels. Every dog there was happy to see a human come to their cage door, but Damien had no reason to be.

In the evening the cleaners came again, and the same noise and steam held forth for another three hours. Finally, the techs put scoops of pelleted dog food down the chute on the front of each cage. Then they left, leaving the lights on, and it was night again.

While "instinct" is not a word her father would have ever used in connection with human states of mind, it was the word Elizabeth found herself coming up with whenever she contemplated her reluctance to mentioning the strange, starved dog to Bill or Dave. She had been truly amazed to see that the dog survived, and she had followed his recovery with interest. There could be no real harm, she decided, in simply looking in on the animal from time to time. For his part, the dog seemed to recognize her now, but that was all—he remained as enigmatic as before. He had put on enough weight that it was now evident he would completely recover from the ordeal, and she made vague plans to stop her visits.

A week passed. Then another, then another. No one bothered the brindle pit bull. His steady, unwavering, somewhat grim expression caused the researchers and their assistants to pass by his kennel in search of more docile-looking dogs. He grew used to the routine and the people, and to the young woman who came every day to stand in front of his cage and speak softly to him. She didn't presume; she never commanded him or called to him, she simply spoke to him in quiet, sympathetic tones. He accepted her overtures without emotion, for she meant nothing to him, and he simply watched her face curiously until she left. The only thing that marked her as different from the rest of the humans was that he no longer felt anxious at her approach. After several more visits had passed, he even began to feel a strange, dull sensation in his gut when she walked away. Very occasionally, as he watched her retreating back, a tiny whimper of sound escaped him, but it was tiny, and quickly lost in the maelstrom of noise that surrounded him in the kennel.

One morning after the cleaners had left, a very tall, very thin man in a blue shirt and tan pants stopped in front of his cage. He had been coming down the line, peering at the kennel cards, and making marks in a notebook. He wasn't even glancing at the dogs. He jotted down Damien's kennel number and moved on, peering and blinking at the next dog's kennel card. That afternoon the dogs in Damien's row were taken away, one by one, by a man. This man was very businesslike, and didn't hesitate on opening the pit bull's cage door. He stepped in, looped a nylon kennel leash around the dog's neck and tugged on the line.

"Let's go, chum."

Damien had never been on a lead, and he instinctively jerked backward against the frightening choking sensation.

"Come on, come on, it's OK," the man said impatiently, pulling harder.

The dog reared back, panicked as the rope cut off his breathing. He didn't know what the man wanted, but he did know he was being choked, and his most primitive survival instincts were aroused. He bucked forward, coughing now, and the man pulled him out into the hallway, shutting the kennel door behind him.

"There, there, stop it, now! Why are you being such an idiot?" He tried to move down the hall, but the dog had lost all sense of place and reason, and was fighting, as far as he knew, a primordial struggle for survival. Damien's eyes bulged and he gagged as he reared back, trying to get the nylon rope in his jaws.

Working one row over, Elizabeth heard the sound of explosive barking from several excited dogs and came around the corner, curious as to what might be disturbing the animals. When she saw which dog it was, and that the man was struggling to drag the dog down the hall toward a kennel cart, she hurried up to him.

"Hey, please, could you stop that! Let him get his breath, he's choking."

The man looked her up and down while he held the taut leash in his hand. His sudden and unexpected fight with the dog had given him an adrenaline rush, and he was exasperated. "Stay back, I don't need you getting in the middle of this." He looked at her name tag, which identified her as a handler. "You people aren't supposed to interfere, you know."

"I know, I just want to help. Look, he's almost unconscious. Can't I try?"

"Try what? You're going to get bitten."

The dog was on his back, his jaws in a wide and ugly grimace, horrid gasping sounds coming from him. "Please give me the leash, I can help you get him in there—I *know* this dog."

That's a bit of a stretch, she thought.

The man shrugged. He liked dogs all right, and if she could get the dog loaded into the pushcart without a fight, that was fine with him. He handed her the end of the lead. "If you know him, knock yourself out, just don't get bit."

Elizabeth knelt as near to the gasping dog as she dared, trying to free the lead from around the dog's paws, and loosen the noose without reaching up near the wide jaws.

"It's OK, it's OK," she soothed. It was evident to Elizabeth that the dog was fighting the leash, not her. She got the lead loosened and in a few moments the dog righted himself and struggled to his feet. "There you go, Buddy, you're OK now," she said very softly.

The dog faced her, looking disoriented and panting, and she looked back, biting her bottom lip. The man was watching them. She had told the man she could help him get the dog in the cart. She'd just said that to get him to stop choking the dog. She had no idea how she was going to do *anything* with the dog. It looked savage. The dog had never shown her the least sign of affection in the weeks she had been coming to check on it. It was not a friendly dog, and now it was probably pissed off from being choked. What would it do if she reached out for it? She had to do something; the man behind her would not interrupt his work all day for her.

"OK," she said, as if to the dog but she knew it was for herself. "OK."

She reached out, slowly, her hand headed for the space between the dog's ears. She held her breath. The dog held steady, but his ears flattened tighter and tighter against his head the closer her hand came. Elizabeth visualized those massive jaws snapping upwards, lightning fast, and latching onto her arm. She wondered if the bite would break the bones in her arm. She wondered, if it did break the bones in her arm, would it permanently effect her ability to do surgery? What would her father say if he found out? Her father never handled his research dogs unless they were muzzled. His hands were too valuable to risk, he said.

"You know what you're doing, kid?" the man asked.

"Sure," Elizabeth replied very quietly. The dog's brown eyes held hers. Could she, she wondered, trust the being behind those eyes? Was it just an unthinking animal that would lash out at her in fear, or was it possible that this creature was capable of staying his teeth, even through his fear, because she was trying to help him? Her hand came down between the ears, and stayed there. The dog flinched, but remained where he was. She rubbed her fingers back and forth. "Good dog," she said. "Good boy."

"Come on, now." She pulled her hand back and slowly straightened up, patting her leg and backing away.

"You got more Won Ton than me, kid, that's for sure," the man said with grudging respect.

"He wasn't trying to bite you, he's just scared of the leash, that's all," Elizabeth said with more conviction than she felt. She was hoping like mad the dog wouldn't suddenly turn on her. "Where's he going?"

"Dr. Nelson's lab. He'll be back in a week or so."

"What are they using him for?"

"Toxicology study. He's just one of the control group."

"Oh." The dog had come to stand beside her. It gave her a strange feeling to have that powerful, dangerous-looking dog standing by her side looking, with her, at the man. She looked down at him and put her hand, very gently, on his head again. He glanced up at her face and again, strongly, Elizabeth saw what she had seen that first day.

There was someone in there, someone who gazed back at her, and considered her as she considered him. A powerful, fierce someone who did not attack the man who had been choking him, nor the girl he had found on the end of the same leash when he could breath again. She wondered why, but was grateful, whatever the reason.

She backed slowly toward the end of the row and the cart, coaxing the dog and patting her leg. The dog watched her but only moved forward when the man circled around behind him. To avoid the man he went toward the girl. Elizabeth never let the lead get tight, and soon she was at the cart. Each side of the cart had two doors on it, and three of the little cages already had dogs inside.

"Can you get him in there?" the man asked.

"Uh, yeah, I think so." She didn't think she could, but she didn't want to admit it. She was afraid of what the man would do to the dog to get him in if she couldn't. She opened the door and patted the cage floor.

"Come on, get in here." The dog stared at her. "Come on now, up here, get in." The dog stepped back; he had no intention of going into the frightening boxlike cart. For several moments she pleaded, but the dog refused to even step near the rolling cage. She noticed the dog was growing nervous. She was asking too much. It occurred to her she might push the dog too far and get bitten.

"How 'bout I walk him down there? You could push the cart, and I could just walk him along behind."

The man considered. "Why not? It's going to be a lot less trouble. Let me load one more, then we'll go."

Taking a dog from the kennel next to the pit bull's, he placed it in the cart. "OK," he said, and started down the hall, pushing the cart full of dogs.

Elizabeth looked at the brindle dog and shrugged at him. "If you don't want to go in the cart, you're going to have to walk. Come on, now." She started walking, patting her leg as she went. She was surprised when the dog followed her, stayed right with her in fact, almost crowding her legs as they walked down the hallways. His eyes darted left and right and he shied away from people and objects; he seemed overwhelmed by his surroundings.

"We'll take the skybridge over, rather than go outside with him," the man told Elizabeth. She dropped her hand to the dog's head one more time and, again, he looked up at her face at the touch. He did not wag his tail or fawn on her. Instead he searched her countenance with his brown eyes. Once more Elizabeth wondered what he saw.

The testing was being conducted in a small, poorly lit lab. It had the appearance of something makeshift. The light in the room was too yellow, and it annoyed Elizabeth. In a side room were several crates, half of them having red tags attached to the front, indicating those animals which would be receiving the test substance. Elizabeth made sure the dog was placed in a cage without a red tag. Pleased that he entered the crate here without a struggle, Elizabeth drew off his leash and spoke to him before she latched the crate door.

"You'll be OK. Just be good, and don't bite anybody or anything. Maybe I'll come by and see you tomorrow." The man was placing the other dogs in the crates randomly; just filling them up.

"Will the dogs in these red-tagged cages die?" she asked him.

"I don't know. Probably. That's why they call it *toxic*-ology. Nelson does a lot of LD 50 type stuff. Little tests, for this one contract he has." The man chuckled. "They keep trying to get a different result but they can't."

She looked at some of the dogs which had been placed in the red-marked crates. They stood at the crate doors wagging at her happily; their warm brown eyes full of their trust and their love for mankind.

"Well, that sucks," she said in reply to the man's answer.

"You better go now," the man said. "Thanks for your help."

Elizabeth nodded at him as she looked once more around the small room. The dog would be living here for a week or so, he had said. She glanced around and didn't see any no-contact stickers anywhere. As she walked away down a linoleum-lined corridor that smelled sharply of chemicals, she thought *I put him in there—he followed me, and I put him in there.* It was an uncomfortable feeling that nagged at her. She hoped he'd be OK.

The next afternoon Elizabeth changed into her handler's outfit and made her way straight to the toxicology lab. She cautiously entered the outer room. Looking around she saw with relief that it was deserted and quickly went into the room holding the dogs. The cages hadn't been cleaned recently and the small room was foul with the odors of urine and feces. Small food and water cups had been hung on the insides of the crate doors, and most had spilled. The dogs were standing in a slurry of water and wet dog food inside their crates. She found the pit bull and knelt down, poking her finger through the cage door.

"Hey," she said. The dog had recognized her and stood up in the crate. "Good boy," she said. "I wish I could take you out of there, but I can't." She spoke to him for several minutes while he watched her noncommittally from the rear of the crate, and then, feeling guilty, she stopped in front of every crate and spoke to the dogs inside. She noticed that the pit bull's eyes followed her as she comforted the other inmates.

The next day she returned again to the unattended lab and then it was the weekend, so she had to wait till Monday. But on Monday there were several men talking earnestly together in the outer room, and she didn't have the nerve to walk past them. She fled without going in.

Tuesday she made up her mind to go in no matter what or who was in the outer room. She needn't have worried, the lab was again deserted and she hurried to the room full of crates.

The first thing she noticed when she entered was a strange, sweet, sickly smell that overrode the urine-and-feces smell. She looked around. In the red-tagged crates three dogs were dead, and a fourth and fifth were barely conscious. The rest of the dogs in the tagged crates looked ill. The pit bull and the rest of the control dogs seemed OK. Standing in filth, he came to the front of the crate at the sight of her. His expression, she thought, could not rightly be called friendly, but it certainly seemed less grim than usual. *He's relieved to see me,* she sensed.

She was appalled at the condition of the crates. She considered cleaning out his while she was there, but didn't have the nerve. If she was caught messing around with the cages, or if she screwed around and could not get the dog back into the crate when she was done, she would be fired. She didn't need the money, but if she were fired she would never see the brindled dog again.

She looked closer at the dead dogs. They all lay on their sides, their eyes open and staring dully, their mouths open and lips wrinkled. She felt sorry for them, and she felt sorry for the pit bull, having to sit in the stinking room amongst the dead of his kind. There was nothing to do but leave. She hesitated at the door, raising her hand slightly in a gesture to the dog.

"See ya," she said sadly and left.

Wednesday she wasn't scheduled to work and on Thursday the dog was back in the main kennel. When she approached his gate he lifted his head and looked straight at her. His pointed ears dipped back slightly and his eyes narrowed. Elizabeth didn't know a thing about dog behavior, but she thought he was smiling a small smile at her. She grinned back at him.

"Back from your dream vacation, huh?" For a moment it appeared the dog would actually get up and come to the front of the cage; she thought she saw him start to rise, then sink back down. She knelt down and put her hand through the bars. "Oh, come on, you *want* to be friends, don't you? Come on, I'm not going to hurt you. You *know* that."

The pit bull lay for several more moments, just watching her with his deep, brown eyes. Then, without warning, he rose silently and approached the gate. Bravely, she held out her fingers for him and he sniffed them. Then he sat down in the corner between the gate and the left wall, his right side against the kennel gate, and stared at the opposite wall.

"There you go," she said softly, "you gotta trust someone, huh? Might as well be me." She tickled his neck and shoulders through the fence. The dog continued to stare away from her, as if he was not aware of her presence, but she noticed his eyes were half closing with the pleasure of her touch. "You sure got neat eyes," she told him confidentially.

She sat down on the floor and continued to pet him through the gate for several minutes. "OK," she finally said, "I really have to go pet some of the *other* dogs, you know." When she stood up to go, the dog stood up also. She refused to look back at him as she walked away.

Falling ill with influenza, to which she had always been susceptible, Elizabeth did not return for nearly a week. When she returned to her handler's job, and came looking for the dog, the pit bull was absent again. No one could tell her where he had gone—and it seemed too much bother to look it up for her—so she waited and wondered and was vaguely bothered by his absence. She tried to focus on all the other dogs which, unlike the brindled dog, clamored for her attention. She stroked the dogs, and patted their heads, but the image of the quiet, aloof dog who *wouldn't* beg for attention stayed in her mind's eye. She often wondered why she thought about the dog at all. It was just a dog, and not even a very friendly one at that. Whatever her bond with the strange bulldog, she didn't understand it.

In fourteen days he was back, lying in his cage with an ugly wound on his thigh. The whole leg had been shaved, and the wound sutured, but the broad, jagged scars still had a raw look.

"*Geez*, what happened to you?" She peered, frowning, at the wound. The dog stayed at the back of the kennel and stared at her enigmatically, his head resting patiently on his front paws. "Where have you been?" The question hung in the air between them.

"Wound lab," said a voice behind her, and she startled. A passing animal tech had volunteered the information. Elizabeth swung around to face her.

"What did they do to him?" she called to the retreating form.

"Oh, probably shot him. They've got a big government gunshot trauma study going right now." The woman disappeared around the corner of the kennel bank.

Elizabeth frowned. For the first time she felt doubt and even anger about what had been done to him. All the arguments for animal research seemed to pale when compared with the reality of the suffering before her. "They shot you, huh? Well that's just great."

The dog wouldn't come to her, so on a mad impulse she decided to try going to him. But she hesitated; he looked so forbidding. She decided it was one of those times when it was best not to think about it too much. She screwed up her courage and with one quick motion opened the kennel door. At the clang of the gate the dog's head came up quickly, and he watched her advance. When she neared him he turned his head away from her in avoidance. Elizabeth understood why he wouldn't look at her.

"Look," she said seriously, "you don't think *I'm* going to do something to you? I never have, have I? Come on now, it's me, your friend." She came closer and then stopped, considering as she did the powerful head and neck of the pit bull. They eyed each other and then the dog's tail thumped, just once, on the grating, and his ears went flat to his head. He was looking straight ahead, a part of him trying to shut out the troubling presence of the human, another part, the part that acknowledged the tentative friendship between them, glad of her company.

"Yeah." She grinned. "Yeah, you know who your friend is, don't you?" She reached out carefully and stroked him. "I won't hurt you. Good dog. Good boy." The dog's lips were pulled back in a lopsided grin, and he turned to her, leaning forward to sniff her pant leg and shirt. He sat up, with some effort, and gently sniffed at her hair and face. Elizabeth quickly pulled her face back and away—she wasn't willing to be that trusting yet. Some scent on her chest interested him intensely, and he stepped forward as she pulled back, his nose seemingly glued to her shirt. Once the dog was standing he moved around her, curious, and Elizabeth froze.

I'm locked in this kennel with this dog, and no one could hear me scream over the barking if he goes for me. Great.

The dog was behind her now, and she stood up quickly. She wanted him where she could see him. "Easy, boy." Then she noticed *both* of his rear legs were shaved and sutured. They had shot him in both legs.

"Geez," she said weakly. An unpleasant thought went through her mind. She had seen, often enough, shaved and sutured dogs lying in cages in her father's and grandfather's workplaces. Just like this dog. So how could she feel anger toward the people who had done this? She was thinking like some "animal rights" whacko. Of course they had to do the research—it *was* necessary. She chewed at her bottom lip. She would have to sort this out. She leaned forward, looking closely at the raw scars, not daring to touch them.

"Wow, I bet it hurt when you woke up, huh?" she murmured, incorrectly assuming the dog had been anesthetized while the shots were fired into his body. He had, in fact, been suspended in a sling, fully conscious, while the wounds were inflicted. Hoffman's instructions for the dog's use while in holding had been vague, indicating only that the animal was not to be terminated as part of any use.

Damien continued to sniff her, for he was as curious about her as she was about him. Her movements, body language and moods were as alien to him as his were to her. She fascinated him, and it felt Good when she came to his cage and spoke to him. In his bleak existence, she was now the one pleasant interlude. So when she pulled away from him, and then stood up, he could tell she was afraid—submissive even—and he flattened his ears and lowered his head, wanting to reassure her of his peaceful intentions.

Fourteen days later he was gone, in use, again. This time the first tech she asked knew where he had gone.

"Behavioral Psych took him—some study on mean dogs, aggression or something. Something to do with their chemical reaction to aggression, I'm not sure."

Elizabeth didn't like the sound of that. The dog was not mean. He was frightened sometimes, but how could he be considered mean? Were they basing it on his appearance? That didn't seem fair.

When she was done with her rounds she walked over to the psych complex to see if she could find him. It took her the better part of an hour just to find someone who knew vaguely what she was talking about. By that time people had gone home and doors were locked.

The next day she was back, but she got nowhere. Lab after lab was closed to handlers like herself. Her eyes squinted with suspicion. Why were psych labs so reluctant to let handlers in? Her only lead was a student who had heard of a study on cortisol release in dogs that were aggressively aroused. They were studying the difference in output among varying dog breeds. Aggressive, and nonaggressive types, he said.

After three days of questing after the dog she got a straight answer. The dogs were being tested for hormone levels, both while resting and after "arousal." However, when they were not being "aroused," they were locked in isolation chambers, to minimize unwanted stimulation. She could not see him. Elizabeth shrugged her shoulders and went home, wondering what they were doing to the quiet dog to arouse his anger.

The dog was gone a total of twenty-nine days. He came back gaunt and exhausted, and when his head lifted at the sound of Elizabeth's steps at his gate, the expression in his eyes was flat and ugly.

"Hey!" Elizabeth stepped back, startled. "Hey, it's me."

For a moment the pit bull remained still, staring, scenting, confirming she was not one of the researchers with whom he had spent the past month. Then his expression softened and his tail thumped his recognition and a small apology. Elizabeth grinned back at him.

"Geez, you scared me, man. What did they do to you?"

She opened the run and came in to sit beside what today, for the first time, she realized she thought of as *her* dog. That was silly of course; it wasn't her dog at all, it was just a laboratory dog. One of hundreds in this very room. Undeniably, though, they were friends.

"What's the matter, boy? Why are you so sad?" She stroked him gently. She knew that he couldn't tell her what he had just been through, and it made her stop to wonder at everything else he couldn't tell her. What *was* his history? Had he been someone's pet? Had he gone to the park and played Frisbee with kids? Why was he here? She didn't know, and information like that was impossible to find out. Most of the dogs came from bunchers, people who collected them from a variety of sources, and the dogs' histories were quickly, and very often deliberately, lost. She would probably never know anything about him besides what she could tell by looking at him.

As the two sat together in companionable silence, Elizabeth sighed deeply. Thinking about the dog's unknown past set her mind wandering in a familiar but unpleasant direction.

When people meet you they don't know about your past, either. No more than I know about this dog's past. People don't know what you have gone through. What makes you who you are . . . At an age where self-reflection seemed terribly important, Elizabeth had done plenty. Her mother had left her when she was six years old. Dropped her off at the daycare center and simply left, never to be seen or heard from again. The action left Elizabeth with a year-long phobia of being dropped off anywhere, and a quiet, lingering fear of further parental abandonment. There had not even been a divorce. A note from her mother—a note she had only heard about from Bill but never seen—had advised her husband to pick up the child at the daycare center and carry on without her. Of course, as every parent does, Dave had assured Elizabeth that the problem was between her mother and him, having nothing to do with her. And, like every child, Elizabeth had had her doubts about that. Elizabeth would never know. Her mother was obviously never going to tell her. That, or anything else.

She wondered if her mother had ever loved Dave, or if she had married because of his potential for income. When Elizabeth was a child, she had liked to think that her mother loved them both very much, but went away due to some desperate and tragic reason; perhaps so they would not have to see her die of some terminal disease. However, as she had grown older, Elizabeth had formulated more sophisticated and pragmatic scenarios, with one theme consistent throughout; her mother had felt forced to leave for (insert reason depending on mood) yet was counting on Elizabeth, with a mother's fond faith, to care for the men in the family in her absence.

Elizabeth sighed again, even harder. The dog moved his head so that it rested, very gently, on her outstretched leg. His eyes searched her face. She laid her hand on his strong neck and left it there. If her mother ever surfaced, ever came to take an accounting of how her daughter had turned out, Elizabeth hoped that her mother would be pleased with her. She had tried since the time of her abandonment, with a persistent concern not often found in young children, to take her mother's place. She had played at keeping house as a child, now she did it in actuality, enjoying domestic chores with a guilty enthusiasm. She would much rather pick up a homemakers' magazine than a medical journal, a failing she knew her father had noticed.

So, as she stroked the mysterious dog's head she realized that in this one way they were alike. No one, not even herself, coming upon him now, would ever know upon what foundation his actions were based, or where his fears came from. As for herself, when people met *her* on the street, they wouldn't know her motivations either. They wouldn't know that she was becoming a cardiac surgeon because it would please her father and her grandfather, and that pleasing them, and keeping them with her, were the most important things in her life.

Elizabeth considered the dog. Her father had always told her that dogs didn't think like people. That they lived only in the present, and were incapable of thinking about the past or future. But that didn't make sense. This dog remembered her after being away for weeks. If he could remember that, why couldn't he remember other things, like things he missed from his past life?

She felt the dog stiffen below her hand and when he raised his head, tense and hard, it frightened her. What was he doing? What had she done to alarm or displease him? Was he going to attack her? All around her the noise of barking dogs blocked out any other sound. But the brindle dog wasn't reacting to her, he was looking away, and his eyes were fierce. His lips twitched into an ugly snarl. Alarmed, Elizabeth slowly raised herself up, wondered if the dog was thinking he was about to be tormented as he had over the past few weeks in the psych study. She followed his gaze and saw a woman standing at the gate, looking in. It was the friendly tech who had helped her get equipment to clean the ICU when the dog had first been admitted.

"Hi!" The woman waved and then opened the gate to lean in and speak to her. The dog's reaction was swift. Scrambling to his feet he advanced toward the woman, his eyes hard and his tail up. Instinctively Elizabeth reached out and touched his shoulder in a restraining gesture.

"Easy," Elizabeth said, and the dog stopped.

"Hi!" the woman shouted again above the din, seemingly oblivious to the dog's reaction. "How are you doing?"

"Have you come for him?" Elizabeth asked with a frown.

"Oh, no." She smiled. "Professor Hoffman called and asked us to see if the dog was in. He wants to come see him."

Elizabeth's face fell. Viktor Hoffman was finally coming to get his dog. That meant she would probably never see him again. That would be fine if he was going to a nice place, but what kind of a man let his dog stay here? Doctor Seville had said the dog was Hoffman's "pet," but why would this man let his dog be *shot*?

"He's coming to get him, huh?"

"No, I don't think so; he just stops by every once in a while to see him. He doesn't take him out though, as far as I know."

"When is he coming?" she asked.

"I don't know. He just called and asked us to check his status. I would think sometime today or tomorrow."

"Viktor Hoffman—what kind of research does this guy do, do you know?"

"All I know is he's a behaviorist—studies, like, wild dogs—that sort of thing. He's really nice," she added. She shut the gate and walked away.

"*Wild* dogs, huh?" Elizabeth looked at the dog and the dog looked up at her face. She nodded to herself, reaffirmed in her recent line of thought concerning the mystery and motives of those you meet with unknown pasts. "So, is there something you haven't been telling me, jungle boy?" she asked him with a wry smile. She patted the dog good-bye and let herself out of the kennel. She paused at the gate, looking at the raw, sutured wounds on his rear legs, then into his brown eyes. Then she turned and walked away.

CHAPTER THREE

... but the fighting-dog, with his rarely given silent love, and deathless courage, claims both our love and respect.

—CAPTAIN LAWRENCE FITZ-BARNARD

That evening Elizabeth was disturbed by a persistent unsettled feeling which made it impossible for her to concentrate on her studies or enjoy TV. By nine o'clock, when she and the two men had settled into the masculine and darkly furnished family room where they generally did their evening reading, she was fighting down the urge to bake a pie. Baking a pie—generally apple—was what she had done for years to soothe herself.

So she sat watching the gas fire flickering feebly and listening to the rain sweeping in undulating waves across the picture window, and calculating how late she would have to stay up if she started a pie now. She wondered if it was the storm that made her edgy.

Dave was deep in a journal article and Bill was reading the evening paper. She set her book down quietly, staring at the blue tints in the gas flame. It really was too late to start a pie. Suddenly she was surprised to find that she was thinking about how the dog would look, lying there before the fire, its head on its paws and those strange brown eyes looking up at her. Then the vision was gone.

She stood up, picked up Dave's glass and walked into the kitchen. She rummaged in the refrigerator for herself, found nothing to her liking, glared at a bag of apples and returned her father's glass, refilled, to its place beside him. He grunted his thanks without looking up. Pulling her legs up under her she sat down and fiddled with the bottom of her shirt.

"Something the matter, El?" Her grandfather was looking up at her over his reading glasses, the newspaper lowered momentarily.

"Oh, no. Uh-uh. Just restless. What a storm, huh?"

Bill folded his paper and looked over at her. "Not a night to be outside, for sure." He continued to watch her.

"I'm going to go make a pie, want to keep me company?"

"Sure."

They rose and went into the kitchen, where Elizabeth started setting out flour and shortening for the crust. Bill sat at on a stool, watching her.

"I've known you a long time, Elizabeth—and I know when something is bothering you. If you want to talk, I'm here."

Elizabeth fussed with the flour, really wanting to speak about what troubled her, yet feeling instinctively that her family were the last people on earth to whom she should broach this subject.

Maybe I'm not being fair. Maybe Bill will have some good ideas, he usually does.

He was, and had always been, her best buddy. Always there, far more approachable than her father, it was really Bill who had raised her. "OK. Well, it's kind of awkward for me, I mean, I feel like you wouldn't approve." Her flour-covered hand swept the kitchen, as if entreating him to understand. "I mean that's kinda what's buggin' me. And I guess it seems trivial."

"Well it's obviously not trivial to you. That makes it important to me."

"Oh, thanks. It's, well it's about that starved dog I told you about a while ago at dinner. Remember?" Bill shook his head in the negative, unable to recall it for the moment but she continued anyway. "Well he *did* make it, and they have him in the main ward now—over at the ARC. I see him there." She hesitated, because to go on now meant either to lie about working as a handler, or to expose herself. She couldn't stand lying to her grandfather so she took a deep breath and went on. "I haven't mentioned it before—I knew Dave would disapprove—but I'm working part-time as a handler. I work with dogs for two hours a day, between classes. Handling them, you know . . ." Her grandfather hadn't changed expression, and he seemed willing to keep listening without comment, so she continued.

"Please don't mention it to dad, it would just freak him out. Promise?"

Her grandfather nodded, serious. "I won't tell him."

"So anyway, I see him *there*, at the main kennel, you know, when I'm working as a handler. I . . ." She started again carefully, picking her way through her concerns with an eye for anything that might offend. "I don't think what they've been doing to him is *right*. It's cruel really—I mean they *shot* him in his hind legs for Pete's sake. I just wish he . . . I don't know, I just wish he wasn't in there, that's all."

Bill nodded, thoughtful. "Out of all the rest, you've become attached to this particular dog, haven't you?"

Elizabeth shrugged. "I guess. He seems happy to see me."

Bill's lips pressed together. "El, you're going to be a medical student very soon. Specializing in cardiac surgery, like you will, you're going to be using a great number of dogs as you learn. It's necessary; I've done it and your father does it now. I think you need to come to terms with that very quickly, or you're headed for real trouble."

Elizabeth rolled out the crust, hearing his words and knowing they were true. "Are you going to throw a fit the first time they expect you to practice a procedure on a dog?" Bill's tone was harder than she had expected. "I would hardly expect this to be a problem, with someone of your background," he continued.

"Of course not, I know the work. I've been around it all my life. I just— that's what's bothering me. I can't explain. *This* dog is so proud, he's different in a lot of ways from the other dogs. I guess I feel sorry for him, and I guess I sh . . ." She stopped. She had been going to say that she shouldn't, but that didn't feel right either. She *did* feel sorry for him.

Bill let out his breath and continued. "Here's my advice, El. Stop going and looking at that dog—you're getting emotionally involved where you have no business to. It is going to cause you problems down the road."

Done with the crust, Elizabeth moved on to the filling, using frozen blackberries from a bag in the freezer; it would be quicker than apples. "The dog belongs to somebody. A professor. They said it's actually his pet. I just wonder why he keeps it there."

"It's none of your business, Elizabeth, why he keeps it there. It's his dog, not yours. No one is hurting it intentionally. If it undergoes some procedures, you can be assured that everything is done to keep the animal as comfortable as possible."

Elizabeth nodded. "I guess." But she didn't feel convinced at all. She felt more curious than ever to understand why Professor Hoffman left his dog at the ARC. And why he let it get shot in the legs.

She slipped the crust over the pie, crimped the edges, cut a wheat sheaf into the crust with the sharp tip of her knife and set the pie in the oven. "Dang," she said, "I forgot to preheat the oven." She took the pie back out and turned on the oven. "I'll be up all freakin' night."

By morning she had made up her mind to take a decisive step, seeing it as the only way to put an end to her turmoil and to get used to something that, as her grandfather had sensibly pointed out, would be an element in the rest of her life. She would look up Professor Hoffman and ask him, point-blank, why he let the dog stay at the ARC and be used in experiments. Her curiosity would not be satisfied until she knew why he left the dog there, and if indeed he knew how the dog was being used.

It was easy enough to look him up in the directory and locate his office, a tiny cubicle with a sliding glass door for the front wall. Taped to the glass door, along with several other notices, was his schedule, showing that he would be in his office in about twenty minutes. It would mean skipping a class, something she rarely did, but it seemed worthwhile to get this matter resolved once and for all.

Leaning against the corridor wall watching the infrequent between-class traffic, Elizabeth guessed it was him the moment he rounded the corner and started down the hallway toward her. The man just *looked* like a professor, with his balding head, brown tweed jacket and casual shoes. She thought his rather long, angular face looked kind enough, and he smiled at her as he came up to his door and fumbled with his keys.

"Are you waiting for me?" he asked her pleasantly.

"I think so. Are you Professor Hoffman?"

"Yes. How may I help you; would you like to come in?" There was hardly space enough in his office for them both. Boxes and files and books and computers were piled everywhere, the floor included. There was one plain wooden chair, obviously there for visitors, so she sat down in it. Hoffman removed a bulging pile of mail barely contained by several rubber bands from the seat of his chair and balanced it carefully on top of a similarly composed tower on his desk. He sat, looking politely expectant.

"Professor Hoffman, there's a dog in the ARC building—in the main kennels—a striped dog, medium-sized, little ears, and I've heard he is your dog."

Viktor Hoffman sensed the statement was a question and answered. "Yes, I know the dog you're talking about. And, yes, I guess you could *say* he was mine, so to speak. He actually belongs now to the Animal Resources Department. What about him? Why do you ask?"

"Well, what I mean is, do you have a special feeling for him? Like, was he a pet of yours?"

"No, he's not a pet, not at all. Why don't you tell me what this is all about?" His tone was still gentle, and he did not seem defensive. Elizabeth took that to be a good sign. She blew out her breath and started again.

"I saw your name on his kennel, and a man—a researcher up there that worked on him when he was starved—he said the dog was your 'pet.' Well, I wondered if you knew what was happening to him lately? Up there."

"What do you mean— I'm sorry, I didn't catch your name."

"Oh, sorry. I'm Elizabeth Fletcher. Sorry."

"Not a problem, Elizabeth, you just had me at a disadvantage. What kinds of things are you talking about happening? What's happened?"

Elizabeth felt immediate relief. He didn't know what was going on; maybe he would care.

"Well, they've been using him in different studies, over and over. And now they've shot him—in both hind legs."

"Shot him? Are you a tech?"

"No, I'm a handler. I know I'm not supposed to interfere like this, but I just feel sorry for that poor dog. I guess he seems special somehow—I know that sounds stupid, and I *do* know better, I want you to know that. My dad works over at The Med, you know, he does cardiac transplant work, so I know about this stuff, but this just seemed strange, you know, that they said he was, like your dog, and . . ."

She was babbling, and she knew it, so she shut up.

"Elizabeth, you're a student here, correct?"

"Yes."

"What program are you in?"

"Premed."

"I see. And your concern for the dog stems from, what? I'm simply curi-ous, I don't want you to think of this as an antagonistic line of questioning, you understand?"

She shrugged, unable to put into any meaningful statement what her interest or attraction to the pit bull was. "I guess I just like the dog, and he likes me."

"*Does* he?" Hoffman's eyebrows raised. "I hadn't realized his behavior had altered to that degree. Damien's a feral dog, you know."

"Damien?" Elizabeth said with a half smile. "I never knew his name. That's a good name for him."

"It's just what I call him," Hoffman said with a shrug, "he doesn't respond to anything anyway, and he's never shown any inclination to be handled."

"What is feral?"

"Certainly. Feral is a term which applies to any domestic animal which has returned to living in a state independent of human care. Feral cats are quite common, but with dogs it is much rarer, much more difficult. As a species, dogs need human support, either directly or indirectly, or they perish. One of the things I study is the ethology of feral dogs."

"You're saying Damien is a feral dog? Like a wild dog? That doesn't seem right. He's really a great dog; he's gentle. He seems like other dogs."

"You handle him? You pet him?"

"Sure, all the time."

"Really. Well, he's come a long way since I last saw him then. I'll go today and see him."

Sensing that a possible premature ending to the conversation was forthcoming, Elizabeth went for the gold. "Do you maybe have plans to move him out of there? Somewhere where he won't get used for research? Is that possible, do you think?"

Hoffman smiled a genuine, friendly smile. "You *do* like him, don't you. Well, Damien is a very interesting dog, though I would caution you always to handle him with extreme care." The professor then nodded thoughtfully, staring into the middle space and obviously considering his options. "I had planned on moving him to my dog enclosure in the spring, but maybe I'll do it sooner." He directed his focus back on Elizabeth. "Don't worry, Elizabeth, I'll go up today and see about having him moved."

Elizabeth sat, unsure what to say now. She was unsure where the dog was going, and equally unsure she should ask the man further questions when it truly was none of her business. It sounded as if he was concerned, and that the dog would be moved *somewhere*, and that had been her goal, after all. She stood up to go.

"Thank you, Professor Hoffman, I'm glad Damien has someone like you looking out for him. I'm not sure why I became so interested in his welfare, I just did. Is where you are moving him a nice place?"

"Oh yes, he'll enjoy it. He'll be outside with other feral dogs in a large enclosure. It's off campus, over attached to the forestry and agriculture satellite campus. He'll be fine, I don't want you to worry." He slid the door open.

"Thanks Professor Hoffman." She walked away down the hall, thinking what a nice man the professor seemed, and still wondering why he thought Damien was "feral."

The next day, when she arrived at the ARC building to make her rounds, the dog was gone. Viktor Hoffman had taken him. The kennel already had a new occupant, and Elizabeth absently chewed her bottom lip as she stared at the slender yellow Labrador that gazed up at her. The dog's tail swished gently back and forth and Elizabeth put her fingers through the wire, waggling them on the dog's nose. "Good girl," she said softly. She glanced at the paperwork and noticed without meaning to that she was available for any use, including those ending in termination. "Sorry, girl," she said to the Labrador, "good luck." But as she walked away she knew what a foolish thing that was to say. Research dogs left the University only one way. The dog had nothing ahead of it but unpleasantness, and ultimately death. Elizabeth frowned. She *was* starting to think like an animal rights person.

She went to her classes. She studied. She went out a couple of evenings that week with Tony. On the weekend she took breaks from her studying to go out into the inviting sunshine and watch Bill as he prepared his garden for planting. She couldn't just leave it like this; she had to know "her" dog was all right. She was sure he was, and when she saw that he was fine in his new situation, she could let it go.

Out of curiosity, she had looked up dog breeds on the computer. It had occurred to her that perhaps the brindle dog was some kind of undomesticated canine species. She didn't know dog breeds and she could think of no other reason Hoffman would consider him a "wild dog." After reading the history of the pit bull—the dog breed which closely resembled her friend—she was even more confused. The pit bull's roots stretched back as far as any breed's, and it was a well-defined type of dog that had assisted hunters by seizing and holding large game animals, and had been utilized by man for thousands of years, certainly as far from a wild animal as you could get. It appeared to Elizabeth that Damien was a normal domestic dog, so why was he of interest to Professor Hoffman? The question left her with an uneasy feeling and a resolve to not walk away from Damien until she knew the answer.

The pens and paddocks associated with the forestry and agriculture schools were located in a rural area fifteen minutes from her home. It wasn't until Saturday morning that she had an opportunity to go over and look for Damien. Parking her truck and ignoring a sign which clearly stated AUTHORIZED PERSONNEL ONLY, she walked between two enclosures holding native deer and started searching for the dog enclosure. She tried to walk purposefully—looking right and left only with her eyes, not her head, as if she knew where she was going. She passed another sign which warned her ALL UNAUTHORIZED PERSONNEL MUST SIGN IN AT OFFICE, and felt her heart rate increase another dozen beats per minute. She had never done anything like this, and she kept asking herself why *was* she doing it. The fact that she couldn't frame a reasonable answer to that question didn't slow her step.

Being Saturday, there were very few people about; she wondered if that would only make her more conspicuous.

You don't even have a good story ready if you do get stopped, she thought with exasperation. After ten minutes of walking she was on the outskirts of the campus. To her right was a screen of alders and cedars and behind them she caught a glimpse of chain-link fence. To get there she had to walk across ankle-high wet grass, her sneakers getting hopelessly soaked, but through the screen of trees she saw that the ground opened up again into a large field.

Pay dirt.

The fence was six feet tall and curved in at the top. It looked to enclose about two acres of level ground, with clumps of alders here and there and an occasional towering cedar tree. Scotch broom plants were trying to enter from the fields outside the enclosure, and in several places near the fence line, poisoned corpses of the primitive-looking vegetation showed where humans had succeeded in stopping the relentless invasion. Tracks from pacing dogs had cut trails through the lush green grass. Across the way she could see a brown wooden observation tower at the other edge of the field.

It reminded her of a guard tower in a prisoner of war camp. To her right, backed into the tall alder and fir trees that ringed the enclosure, were two chain-link kennels, side by side, covered by a substantial wooden roof with a large overhang. Inside the near kennel she saw a golden-colored dog lying curled up on the concrete floor. It was *him*, of that she was sure. She looked again at the "guard tower." The windows were tinted dark, most likely, she assumed, to keep the dogs from seeing the observers. If there was anyone in there, she would never know. On the enclosure fence she had noticed KEEP AWAY signs, and she wondered just how much trouble she would be in if she were caught hanging around. But she had come this far, and she intended to see "her dog" before she left.

She was thankful she was wearing her usual jeans and T-shirt, for she had to push her way through thick, wet brush to get to the back of the kennel. It was worth it, though, to see the brindle bulldog standing at the wire wagging his tail, his jaws cracked open in a happy grin. She hurried to push her fingers through the wire and he snuffled them joyfully.

"Wow, you really like being out here, don't you?" she asked him. "I guess this beats being in those crummy cages." She looked around, noticing now how nice out it really was. It was late April, and the sky was filled with towering white thunderclouds. The sun however, was bright if cool, and birdsong filled the air. She inhaled deeply, finding the air delicious. She was glad that the dog was glad. "But what *are* you doing here? You're *not* a wild dog." She glanced at the kennel gates and noticed they were securely padlocked. "I guess maybe he'll let you into the big yard soon. That'll be nice. I guess I won't have to worry about you anymore. You've been cooped up for a long time, but this," she looked out at the grassy enclosure, "this will be real nice for you." No other dogs were in sight.

She knelt down against the wire, stroking his fine, short fur with her fingers. Her happiness was edged with melancholy. She was happy for the dog, but she realized she should stop coming to see him now, before she got in real trouble. She was trespassing, and the signs made it clear trespassers were not welcome. She should tell him good-bye and get it over with. Damien was *not* her dog. She had just come to feel that way over the months of their friendship, and it was foolish. The dog was the property of the University, Hoffman had said, and that was that. He seemed fine here, and it was time for her to get on with her studies and get on with her life.

Damien suddenly dropped his chest to the ground, his rear still upright. He stared at her, his tail waving stiffly. Elizabeth was taken aback. What was he doing? Then the dog leaped onto a small pinecone that had blown into the kennel. Grabbing it up in his powerful jaws, he tipped his head back and juggled it in his teeth, teasing her.

"You think I want that thing, huh?" She was delighted with his joyful pleasure, and though the wire separated them, she feinted with her hands, as if to take it from him. Damien went wild. He raced about the kennel, still mouthing the pinecone, and each time he dropped it, he quickly pounced on it, again and again, hitting it with his paws, as if he could not quite get it. Each time he came near her, Elizabeth reached out, as if to grab him. When the pinecone was reduced to a pulpy fragment, Damien dropped it on his side of the fence, at Elizabeth's feet. He panted with his exertion, smiling up at her with wide jaws.

"Wow, that was fun, huh? You like to play keep-away?" She found it interesting that a dog would play a game with well-defined rules she could understand.

She sat for a half hour with the dog, noticing the little things he watched, amazed at the things he heard. Damien outside was a far different dog than Damien inside, she decided. Surrounded not by stainless-steel walls, but by Nature, he seemed competent and comfortable. He lay with one front paw tucked under his chest, his head upright as he calmly surveyed the surrounding area. Somewhere she had heard that dogs could not see as sharply as humans, but she found his sight and hearing as acute as her own. And he noticed things she would never have noticed, had not his steady gaze drawn her eyes to them. Together they watched small brown sparrows flitting in the leafing tree branches. Watching the branches steadily for some time, she noticed a nest among them she would never have seen otherwise. They looked up at a pair of geese overhead, honking in alarm at some danger the two earthbound companions could not perceive. They watched a young man walking hundreds of yards away, and they watched an ant, crawling across the kennel's cement floor. When she stood to go the dog stood also, and he looked at her expectantly.

"What? Don't look at me like that—you can't go with me." She raised her hand half-heartedly in a parting gesture. "You be good, I'll come back one more time, in a few days." For the first time Damien, a dog who was almost eerily silent at all times, barked as she walked away. It tore at Elizabeth's heart.

She came again, and then again. She told herself she would stop coming as soon as they released him into the large enclosure. The fourth time she came it was a humid, warm, late-April day, with lowering black clouds threatening, but no rain yet. She greeted the joyful dog, then she sat down on her book bag, intending to catch up on her reading. As she leaned back against the chain-link wire, on his side of the fence the dog leaned up against her back. Elizabeth reached her hand behind her, absently tickling the dog with her fingers through the fence. Abruptly the dog rose, his small, cropped ears tight over the top of his head, a low rumble in his chest.

She followed the dog's line of sight, looking back through the dog kennels in the direction of the "guard tower." Someone *was* coming. A man. *Oh, oh.*

"I'm in for it now," she whispered. She thought briefly about running for it, but that would be too undignified. She'd have to stand there and take whatever she had coming; she just hoped she hadn't broken any actual laws. She could just picture calling her father from jail; if she told him she'd been arrested for trespass and interfering with another researcher's animal he'd probably *leave* her in jail. The dog swung his head around at the sound of her voice, noting her reaction to the approaching man. His tail rose stiffly and he stood foursquare by her side, as if the chain-link fence were not between them.

Elizabeth got slowly to her feet. She could see now that the man was a lean, older man with a narrow face and high forehead framed by a ring of longish, graying hair. He was wearing a brown anorak windbreaker and khaki pants. Then she recognized him. It was Professor Hoffman. What would he think of finding her here like this? Would he consider her a busybody, or even worse? As he strode up to the kennel his expression was congenial; he smiled at both her and the dog.

"Hi," Elizabeth said softly.

"Hello, again. I see you found him."

"Uhm, well, yeah, I just like to sit here and read. I didn't see a 'keep out' sign here . . ." She gestured around the immediate area where they stood. "I'm sorry." That was a lie, and a lame one at that. The enclosure was ringed with KEEP OUT signs. It had come out before she knew she was saying it. It appeared the professor wasn't particularly buying her story either; he smiled slightly and she knew he knew that she had lied.

"The dog does seem to enjoy your company."

Elizabeth was grateful her nervous eyes had a place to alight. She stared at Damien, who was still standing stock-still beside her. "I like him and I think he likes me." She shrugged.

"You've established a rapport with him, but watch, now, how he reacts to me." Hoffman squatted down beside the cage, putting his hand up to the wire and snapping his fingers at the dog. Damien ignored him completely.

Without thinking Elizabeth put her fingers through the cage and the dog immediately came over and sat against the wire, pressing into her hand.

"I've been observing you from the blind," the professor said. "I'm curious about your relationship with him."

"I'm sorry," she said, flustered and self-conscious at the thought. "I didn't think it would hurt anything. I just wanted to make sure he was OK."

Viktor Hoffman straightened up slowly, with the muffled creaking of a man his age. "I made a commitment to this animal when I brought him out, and he'll live out his life with me here. You needn't worry."

"Where did Damien come from? You 'brought him out'?"

The man leaned sideways against the chain link, resting comfortably. "It's a long story, are you sure you want to hear it?"

Elizabeth was surprised and pleased that the man was so affable, and that he would share any information about the dog. "Yes, I'd really like that. I've often wondered about where he came from."

Hoffman nodded as if he understood her curiosity. "This particular dog's early life *is* a mystery. He somehow became lost or abandoned—most likely lost, no one would go that far back in the woods simply to dump an animal—anyway, he ended up far back in the Olympic mountain range, living on his own. Mind you, that is not something domestic dogs can readily do, especially this type of dog. It is usually just a matter of a very short interval of time before they starve to death. This particular dog," he pointed with his thumb at the pit bull, "survived rather well for a time, probably several months. When my students and I began to track him, he was already on the decline, and with winter coming on, it was probably only a matter of time before he would have died. However, after we radio collared him, his collar became stuck in some boulders, and he would have starved to death if we hadn't removed him—well, you saw him, evidently, when Joe Seville was working on him. He was a mess."

"Yes, I couldn't believe he was alive. He must have been stuck in the rock a long time."

"Well, he was pretty well on his way to starvation before he became stuck. The process takes time."

Elizabeth frowned, the implications becoming clear to her. "You were watching him starve to death? You weren't, were you?"

Hoffman tipped his head at her reprovingly. "Elizabeth, I think you understand the significance of research. You know that sometimes the work is not pretty, but it's how we learn."

Now Elizabeth nodded, slowly, more to be polite to this man who was taking the time to speak with her than because she agreed with him or understood his point. "So you saved him. You brought him from the mountains to here."

Elizabeth reseated herself on the floor at the man's feet. "Is he a pit bull?"

"Yes, I rather think so."

"You always hear about how mean they are. But he's not mean at all."

The professor glanced at the dog and nodded. "Mostly they get into trouble when irresponsible people get ahold of them, dog fighters, drunks, drug addicts, street punks, people like that. To be perfectly frank, I think these dogs are attractive to those kinds of people because the breed has qualities they lack. The truth is, if you give one of these guys half a chance I've always found they were rather charming animals. But," he added as a warning, "there is a lot we don't know about this dog's behavioral history, and you must not be careless. This is not your normal pet animal in any respect— he's been living just like a wild animal for some time."

Elizabeth took a deep breath. "Is it all right if I continue to come see him?"

Hoffman considered, rubbing his chin. "I don't think it will hurt for a few more days while he is in the acclimation pen, but when he is released into the full enclosure, I'm going to have to ask you to stop your visits. I don't want the rest of my dogs having human contact. You can understand that?"

Elizabeth wasn't sure she wanted to commit to something like that. And she didn't want to have to lie to this nice man. She hesitated.

Hoffman saw her struggling and admired her for not just blithely lying to him. "You could come to the observation blind any time, see how he's doing. You'd be welcome.

"You obviously have the makings of a fine ethologist. I don't know if your schedule would allow it, but consider taking some behavior classes; I teach a few myself, you know. You would always be welcome out here at the tower as a special friend of Damien's."

Elizabeth was crestfallen. Not only did she have no interest in studying the behavior of a bunch of dogs, she could tell the man was politely telling her that was the only way she would ever see "her" dog again. She could "observe his behavior" from a guard tower.

She had a sudden flash, ridiculous but exciting. "This will sound silly, but would you consider selling Damien to me?"

The man laughed and gave her shoulder a good-natured squeeze to show his appreciation for her effort. "No, no. Like I said, he's not suitable as a pet. He could be quite dangerous; he's really only suitable as a research dog. Consider one of my classes," he said again, "I think you'd find them interesting."

There was a long, awkward pause in which the professor's smile stiffened slightly but persisted. "I don't mind you coming out over the next few days, but in a week, when he is released into the enclosure, will you respect my wishes and not let any of the dogs see you?"

Elizabeth squirmed mentally. She sure didn't want to have to answer that question. Put so nicely though, it was very hard to refuse. She nodded, looking down.

Hoffman put his hand out, squeezed her shoulder again in a friendly, sympathetic way. "Thank you," he said and then he walked away.

She went every single day of that week of grace, spending as much time as she could. She caught only very rare glimpses of the other dogs but she saw enough to know they were nothing like the bulldog. The leader was a big white Maremma sheepdog, and he bayed in an unfriendly fashion every time he saw her. He was easily 140 pounds, and had a dense white coat of fur which Elizabeth thought hid any trace of expression on his face. The other three were females; one was a black-and-tan border collie crossbreed, while the other two bitches were nondescript yellow dogs, obviously related. True feral dogs, they were nervous and unfriendly, running at the first sight of Elizabeth.

For the most part Damien ignored the other dogs, his attitude disdainful of their cowardice and alarm. Elizabeth figured there would be trouble between him and the big leader. She fervently hoped the professor knew what he was doing.

Twice Hoffman saw her and came out to visit with her, sharing stories of the dog's behavior while it had lived wild. He told her about Damien's strange and inexplicable behavior when he sprained his ankle, and Elizabeth looked at the quietly resting dog with an even deeper sense of appreciation. But the day came when the kennel door was open and Damien was gone. Elizabeth stopped in her tracks. Viktor Hoffman had been very patient and kind to her when he could have been brusque and impatient with her interference. She would keep her word to him. She walked away.

She stayed away a week, thinking of nothing but how the dog was faring in his new world. She wondered if he enjoyed being outside, on grass, and she worried about how he was getting on with the other dogs. On the morning of the fifth day, after a night of concern over what had happened between Damien and the large white dog, she thought of something. The professor had said he didn't want the other dogs to see *her*. So she would go, and see if Damien was all right, and make sure they didn't see *her*. He hadn't said anything about her not seeing *them*. Even though he had invited her, it never occurred to her to simply go to the observation tower and ask Hoffman how Damien was doing. She had always done everything concerning the pit bull by herself, so that sneaking over to see him without asking Hoffman's help just seemed natural.

The problem with her plan was that Elizabeth didn't know anything about the canine sense of smell and wind currents. When she got within forty yards of the enclosure Damien knew it, and came trotting happily to the fence line, tail lashing, head lifted and nose working furiously in an effort to locate her. Elizabeth peeked out of the thick brush to find Damien waiting at the fence for her. As aggravated as she was with him for foiling her plan, she had to grin and wave to him just the same.

"Go *on*!" she whispered, gesturing at him, but she knew it was hopeless. But the dog simply wagged the harder. He was delighted at her appearance. Anyone in the "guard tower" could tell the dog staring through the fence wagging its tail was looking at someone it liked. She saw now, truly, that she must go away and not come back. The dog looked fine, the enclosure was nice and large, and the professor had said he could live there as part of the colony. She took a huge breath and let it out.

"OK, Damie, this is it. I *can't* come back anymore. I'm sorry, but I'm gonna really get in trouble. I told that Hoffman guy I wouldn't come see you, so, you know, that's it." She stared at him hard, trying to etch his chiseled face into her mind's eye so that five years from now, when she tried to remember the strange research dog she had grown so fond of, she would be able to recall his features.

Damien stared back at her. There was a joy in his expression, and fondness too, evident in the fierce brown eyes which were softened by hard-earned trust. Elizabeth's eyes stung, and she felt a part of her soul pull back, ashamed.

He's just a dog.

That's what everyone said. Just a dog, a research animal. Expendable. Her father sacrificed dozens just like him every month in his work. But it didn't feel like that. Not at all. They seemed like buddies, comrades who had somehow come through peril together. She put her finger through the wire one last time. Damien grew still and then leaned forward and touched it with his nose, very gently, as if he too, understood the finality of this parting.

"Bye, Damien. You're a *good* boy—take care of yourself." She stood up and turned away, walking quickly, her vision blurred by embarrassing tears. Damien made a choking noise and whined softly, which hurt her even more. Then there was a sudden sharp baying close behind her, and she jerked around, startled. The big white Maremma had spotted her—a sneaking intruder to his little world—and his ancient blood spoke to him. It mattered not that there were no sheep in the enclosure for him to guard. The Voice told him the sneaking, half-hidden human was an intruder to the area that was *his* responsibility to guard. Roaring his challenge, he charged the fence.

Damien had watched in desolation as The One snuck away, but the sound of the Maremma swung him around quickly. The big dog was charging—not at him—but at *the girl*.

Damien hit him when he was five feet from the fence, his powerful jaws closing on the side of the big dog's head, and there was a loud impact sound that made Elizabeth gasp as she swung around. The Maremma was more than twice Damien's weight, but the pit bull's intense and eager onslaught shattered the sheepdog's resolve in the first moments of the fight. It was breeding against breeding, purpose against purpose, whispered Voice against whispered Voice. The Voice the Maremma heard could only help him protect sheep against the sneaking wolf and human thief, creatures easily deterred by a strong voice and a large, impressive form. The silent Whisper the pit bulldog heard was different. For *his* bullbaiting ancestors, which had been sent in to hold the snouts of England and Ireland's great bulls, boars and stags for countless generations, noise and bulky size meant nothing. An agile, powerful body driven by a quiet, decisive mind and resolute fierceness was needed to survive the murderous hooves, horns or tusks. Only dogs with those qualities had survived to breed and pass on their genes. Only dogs that early hunters could trust with their lives, trust to die before they would release their hold and allow a beast to charge and kill their human companion—only those dogs were valued and bred. Because of this, Damien was not capable of wavering, not capable of indecision or tentativeness. And so the little bulldog struck, and clung to the giant bucking sheepdog with the grim determination of his kind. The Maremma roared and shook his head, but his growls quickly changed to yelps of terror as he realized this was no ordinary dog and no ordinary dogfight. The swiftness and suddenness of the counterattack had taken the white dog by complete surprise.

For several moments the larger dog made attempts to get a hold on its smaller foe. It managed to get one of Damien's hind legs in its mouth, and bit down repeatedly. The bulldog, however, knew he had a solid, well-chosen grip and he endured the pain knowing that, in the end, he had a hold he did not want to lose. Then, with a loud, hoarse yelping, the Maremma began to cry. He couldn't shake the bulldog from the side of his head, and he couldn't even reach him to fight him. *His* Voice could not help him—it had no advice against an adversary that worked so calmly and efficiently, who was not intimidated by noise or size. At that moment the big dog fell onto its back, his submission complete, just wanting the bulldog off of him. But Damien's blood and breeding would not allow him to release. *His* Voice told him one thing, over and over: *Hold 'em dog! Holdfast.*

Had Damien's ancestors been prone to releasing their holds when their opponents paused in battle, then a bear, a boar, a two-thousand-pound bull, would have crushed the little dogs to pieces. So Damien held, and it was a strangely pleasant feeling for the pit bull. The Voice reassured him that if he held proudly—even to his death—the girl, The One, would be proud of him. It would be Good.

Elizabeth had stared in horror at the fight, which she knew was a direct result of her illicit visit to the enclosure. Then, seeing that the white dog was twice the size of Damien she had run to the fence and hung clinging to it. Thinking the little dog was going to be killed *because* of her, she quickly realized that Damien was in fact overwhelming the big dog. Mistaking his clever hold on the Maremma's ear for a deadly grip, Elizabeth watched what she thought was surely the murder of the white dog.

Damien did not want to kill. He wanted only to feel the satisfaction of holding his opponent down, controlling him, holding him fast until *something* else happened. He wasn't sure what that *something* else was, for he had no experience working with man. Countless thousands of his generations had worked this way, but for Damien there was only the grim hanging on, and a strange feeling of incompleteness about what came next.

Elizabeth was frantic. That large white dog might be some important specimen for Professor Hoffman. What would happen to Damien if he killed it?

Damien showed no signs of stopping. He had attacked the dog in her defense, that was clear, and it was up to her somehow to stop the fight in order to save Damien as well as the white dog. Her decision came without conscious thought. She simply found herself climbing over the chain link. The fence was high but she was rolling over the angled top in a matter of seconds. She had no choice but to drop from where she hung, clinging to the angle wire until the last moment. She hit the grass beside the dogs with a tremendous plop, unharmed.

She heard a shout and looked up, alarmed. Two men were gesturing to her from the base of the "guard tower." A third came out of a door near them and he had a black object in his hand. That decided her on the spot—they were going to shoot Damien. She had no choice but to pull him off. Frightened and eyes wide, she watched the fighting dogs for several moments, trying to see how she could separate them. She hadn't a clue how one broke up a dogfight, let alone such a *big* dogfight. She glanced up at the men again, and saw that they had entered the enclosure. They were running across the two-acre area, gesturing frantically, angrily, their shouts carrying to her. One of them was Professor Hoffman. She knew she was in real trouble now, but she had no time to worry about what would happen to her, she *must* get Damien off the white dog. They wouldn't be able to shoot him if he was off the other dog and she was holding him by the collar.

Damien had on a narrow black nylon collar with his ID number tag on it. She took a deep breath and plunged her hand down into the dogfight, grabbing hold of the collar and pulling back for all she was worth. The white dog was squirming and squealing beneath Damien and Elizabeth had to dodge his wild snaps. The three female dogs circled about in agitation, darting in and out as if to join in but then thinking better of it. Elizabeth held her grip grimly, and shouted at the pit bull.

"Damien, *stop*! Stop it! Let *go*, let go!" She saw Damien's eyes roll back and he looked at her, noticing her for the first time since she had entered the enclosure. Her sudden appearance beside him and her sharp, disapproving commands startled the dog and his grip slipped enough that the Maremma was able, by leaving behind a sizable portion of his neck fur, to pull away and run, tail between his legs, to the farthest edge of the enclosure. The three female dogs followed at his heels.

For a moment Elizabeth struggled to hold the battle-eager dog, then he seemed to realize victory was his, and he turned and fawned upon her, his tail lashing and his mouth open in a wide, pit bull grin. He expected her praise for a job well done. At that moment, neither Elizabeth nor the dog realized the significance of his action in looking to her for praise.

"Good boy," she said grimly, patting his side, but her eyes were on the approaching men. The dog, hearing them coming, turned to watch them walk up. He stood solidly beside Elizabeth, and she held him to her with her hand through his collar.

Viktor Hoffman's face was red. She could tell he was angry even from a distance. Her actions had jeopardized his entire program, and there was no telling what the fallout would have been had she been injured breaking up the dogfight. His two assistants kept shooting quick looks at Hoffman's face; they had never seen the professor this agitated. One held the foot-and-a-half-long 150,000-volt stun baton out before him, pointed toward Damien.

"Get away from the dog," Hoffman said sharply, "come over here with us. Hurry."

Elizabeth made herself meet Hoffman's angry eyes. "I think it would be better—safer—for you guys if I hung onto him. I'm OK, really."

"You're in very real danger—I want you to do what I say. Come away from that dog, *now*."

She could feel Damien leaning into his collar, pressing forward. Hoffman's sharp command rang in her mind, but her stomach knotted at the thought of what might happen if she let go of the dog's collar.

"I'm really sorry I came here. I didn't know this would happen. If I let him go, you won't shoot him or anything will you?" She eyed the black object in the blond student's hand. "It's not his fault this happened. He was . . ."

Hoffman's undergrad stepped forward, holding the stun baton out in front of him like a sword. "You heard him, let go of the dog and get over here."

Having broken her word to him, Elizabeth could take Hoffman's wrath, but who was *this* guy to think he could order her around? She felt Damien lean forward even farther, responding to the man's aggressive tone and stance.

Hoffman stepped forward. "Elizabeth, you've done enough damage here for one day. Release the dog and we'll walk out together. Not only are you in very real danger, you're disrupting the natural order of things here. Can't you see that?"

"No," she said, surprising herself immensely, "there's nothing *natural* about shoving a bunch of dogs in a pen. They can't get away from each other. They could in the wild. There's going to be trouble between Damien and that white dog, and one of them is going to get killed or badly injured— just so you and your students," here she shot a quick, personal sneer at the student with the stun baton, "can watch. That's mean."

You certainly know how to smooth things over Elizabeth, she thought with a mental grimace. *Way to go.*

There was a moment of tense, ugly silence, while Hoffman regained his composure. "Tag, that's enough. Elizabeth, would you be so good as to walk the dog over to the holding pen for me? You're quite correct about one thing, the colony is no place for the pit bull now. Things were fine before you interfered, but he'll have to be removed now. I really thought we had an understanding—an agreement." His tone let her know that he intended to remain civil, but his disappointment in her was profound. Figuring she was in so deep she might as well keep wading, Elizabeth asked, "What are you going to do with him?"

"I don't know. I just know I want to get all of us out of this enclosure as quickly and as safely as possible. I don't think this is the time or place to discuss it."

She nodded, and suddenly she felt terrible. What *had* she done? She began to shake, hard, from the combined stress of the dogfight and this confrontation with the professor. She glanced about and located the holding kennel about forty yards away. How could it have all gone so wrong? She had only wanted to say good-bye, and now the dog was being removed to God only knew where. Because of her. She felt nauseated.

"Come on, Damien, this way." The dog limped along beside her, and she noticed he held his mangled rear leg up off the ground. "Sorry," she said so quietly only the dog could hear her. He glanced up at her, sideways, catching her eye. Whatever manner of soul resided in this animal, it now regarded her as a companion—a friend.

Elizabeth knew people who kept dogs as pets and seemed quite fond of them, but this friendship seemed different. She had been part of Damien's fate for so long, and now they were in trouble together. It was like they belonged together, as if their two souls were easy together. She knew the dog had attacked the much larger white dog on *her* behalf—watching her back for her—and she now felt obliged to do the same for him.

When she reached the kennel she opened the gate and gestured with her head. "Go on in."

The dog hesitated and looked up at her again. She knelt down on one knee beside him. Without thinking, she slipped her arm around his sturdy neck and pulled his head against her cheek. She hugged him silently, sorrowfully for a moment, and then kissed him on top of his flat skull. With a quick twist of his head the dog turned and licked her twice on the cheek and she smiled. Their friendship was sealed; they were in this together.

"Thanks for trying to save me Damien," she whispered. There was a shuffle behind her.

"Put him in, please."

She pointed to the kennel. "All right, Damie, go on in." Obediently the dog walked in, turning quickly to watch as the men came forward and shut the door. Tag took her arm as if to guide her away but she shook him off. "Let go of me—I'll go." Without anything more being said, the men walked with her toward the gate beside the observation tower. Elizabeth could see the white dog and the three females pacing nervously against the far fence. The white dog sat down and tried to lick himself on the neck.

On what seemed like an unnaturally long walk across the enclosure, Elizabeth had a vision of Damien sitting up beside her in the front of her truck—but stealing the dog would never work. She had thrown away any chance of that with this little stunt. If the dog came up missing now they would know who was responsible, and she was easy enough to trace. Not to mention the reception the animal would receive from her father and grandfather. Besides that, she thought miserably, they were going to take the dog away from here, and she would have no way of knowing to where.

When they had exited the pen Hoffman turned to face her. "I won't press charges *this* time, Elizabeth. I really think you didn't mean any harm in coming here—at least that's what I'm going to assume. However, you have caused a great deal of trouble and I can't trust you anymore. If you are *ever* seen *near* this enclosure again, I can and will press charges. Now, I suggest you go back to your studies."

Elizabeth was surprised she didn't feel more mortified, standing there, so clearly in the wrong, in front of those three disapproving men. She felt unrepentant and proud of the courageous little bulldog. She walked away from the men with her shoulders squared in defiance, but within her she felt cold fear for Damien's future.

Joe? Viktor here. You may be able to do me a favor. I remember you said something about starting a new project, the one you were mentioning to Sol? You're going to be using dogs, right? OK. And that's long term, isn't it? Well, here's the deal. I have a dog here, the bulldog you worked on sometime ago when he was admitted, and I need a place to put him, long term. So if you can use him, it would be doing me a favor if you could take him. I'd just as soon not see him sacrificed, and I believe your protocol doesn't call for that, does it? Great, when will you have someone there? OK, I'll send him over then."

CHAPTER FOUR

And they do well to hide their hell.
—OSCAR WILDE

Damien was in a new place, back Inside. The rooms, the men who came and went, the whole *feel* of the place was Bad, and he didn't like it at all. Through the open doorway, from his location in one of a row of eight stainless-steel cages, he watched two men talking as they moved about working. A third man he had never seen before had just left, but these two men he knew. They were the ones who had put the tubes down his throat when he had first come to this place. Many of the things these men had done to him at that time had been unpleasant and mildly painful, so he classified them as Bad, and their presence made him anxious.

Unlike a wild animal, the compelling force of Damien's domestic heritage had conquered his initial fear of the people who now surrounded him. The months lived outside the company of men could not erase his need for their leadership, a need which was a constant smolder in his dog's soul. Though he did not like these men, in their presence Damien felt a yearning fascination, a compelling need for their approval. It was a strange and puzzling magnetism for the dog, but it was not one which he could give consideration to. He could only experience it as strange waves of longing or dread that swept him alternately when the men were near. The men were as gods to the dog, and he submitted himself accordingly. The merest look or acknowledgment from them thrilled him with hope—he knew not what he hoped for—but if he pleased them, it felt Good.

Godlike, they expected from him—without the slightest question or complaint—complete obedience and submission to their will. Unlike many dogs of squalid breeding, it was not in his bulldog nature to resist the men who handled him with any treacherous acts of petty aggression.

He thought about the girl. His expectation that she would come here, to this place, to see him never wavered. She had always come, no matter where he had been moved to, and this would be no different.

He raised his head and tested the air. There wasn't the slightest trace of her scent. Putting his head on his paws he sighed and continued his vigil.

Elizabeth lay awake, staring into the darkness, her hands clasped behind her head. She and Tony had had, well it couldn't be called a fight, for that implied stronger emotions than either was willing to put into the relationship, but it had been close to a spat. He had an annoying habit of asking for specifics on her test results that put her over the edge. He was worse than her father. Elizabeth assumed most kids her age would accept "good" or "not so good" as a perfectly acceptable answer to "hey, how'd ya do on the exam?" But not Tony. He wanted a complete breakdown of the results and he wanted to know where, specifically, she had failed. Then, and this infuriated her more than she could understand, he acted like he wanted, on the spot, to review her weak areas. She was sure it was only his concern that she do well, but it irked her. On the rare cases where she didn't ace an exam she wanted sympathy, not analysis.

She craned her neck from side to side, trying to loosen tight muscles. She *was* tense. The incident at the dog enclosure, which was still on her mind, had been way too close a call. Any closer and her father could have been notified, or found out in some way that she had interfered with another man's research. He would be furious. Worse, her grandfather would be disappointed, confused and kindly in his attempts to get her to explain what had motivated her to such foolhardy action. Either way, disgrace before those two men was something she could not bear.

As a family, the Fletchers were undemonstrative in expressing their emotions. It seemed to be a family trait, the proud, almost stiff mannerisms that concealed very real respect and affection for each other. Elizabeth was aware that all through school her aloof and quiet manner had put off many children who might otherwise have been her friends. Particularly with her father, for whom she felt not only the deepest respect but also a profound gratefulness, she found it difficult to articulate those strong feelings, which resonated from deep within her soul and which were grounded in her earliest memories. It was upon his lap and clinging to his damp tie that she had, as a small child, fallen asleep many nights in a row, exhausted from an abysmal crying fit because her mother could not be produced at bedtime. Despite all the pressures of an escalating professional career, he had never set her aside, had never disregarded her fears of abandonment, but instead had held and comforted her until she cried herself to sleep. Old enough now to see how it was, Elizabeth was deeply touched by his devotion to her; he could so easily have sent her away to a school, or worse.

So Elizabeth tried every day to repay him. By her deeds she meant to win his approval, and she had lived by that creed, more for him than for herself, refraining from many of the dubious teen activities which might have won her acceptance from her classmates. She didn't go out drinking or partying, nor had she ever smoked pot, or even a cigarette. She had never put herself in a foolish position where sex was concerned. She had refrained from most of the petty crimes which mark adolescence.

And now, Elizabeth agonized, for the sake of a laboratory dog, to which her father would say she had become overly attached, she had nearly done just what she had always worked to avoid.

She attempted to reason with herself. *Now* was the time to walk away from the situation. Damien would be fine wherever they had put him. Professor Hoffman himself had said he would see that the dog lived out its life at the Center. But she couldn't help but wonder if "living out its life at the Center" was necessarily a good thing. Before she met Damien, she had never given the fate of research dogs any thought, but now she had an uncomfortable nagging question; what if Damien showed up at her father's office? If what her father would do to Damien in the course of his work made her uncomfortable, then how could she turn a blind eye to what he was doing just about every day to other dogs?

While she could agree with herself to admit that the life of a research dog was unpleasant at best, she could not yet focus direct, unwavering attention on the question of her father's involvement in animal research. For twenty years she had lived in a home supported by and supporting vivisection. Now, for the first time, that was difficult.

Viktor Hoffman had been very angry with her, and would probably warn whomever ended up with Damien to watch out for the foolish and interfering young woman named Elizabeth Fletcher. If she were caught hanging around the dog again, she had no idea what might happen. She wondered if they could even expel her.

She flipped from her back to her side, punching the pillow up under her head and neck. She was disgusted; no matter how hard she tried, she could not keep thoughts and concerns about the dog from her mind. She dropped off to sleep telling herself she could no longer be concerned about the animal—and wondering if he had been fed, if he was comfortable, and where he had been taken.

In the early morning hours, she dreamed about Damien for the first time. Like most of her dreams, it was clear and realistic; like watching a home video. She was walking on campus, the dog ranging out in front of her, looking back over his shoulder from time to time to grin at her. She wondered later, when she awoke, how it was she knew so clearly what Damien would look like running out in front of her—his expressions, his rocking gallop. She had never seen the dog running free, so she wondered at the detailed nature of her dream.

They walked along together, in that dream, and at one point a big gray squirrel undulated across their path, Damien chasing it up a large maple tree with utter delight. He leaped up against the tree trunk a couple of times and then ran back to her, urging her to follow him to the tree. Damien kept looking from her to the squirrel as if he wanted her to do something, but she had no idea what he wanted. He finally sat down and looked at her reproachfully.

They had walked on, and in her dream it was high spring. The leaves above them were so fresh and plush, it seemed as if they were walking through a bottle of green glass which filtered the sun into a strange verdant hue. The lawns of the campus were covered with little white daisies and bright gold buttercups. Rhododendrons caught the eye with brilliant red, purple or pink blossoms. They came upon some massive stone and brick buildings that loomed severely above the lawns. Suddenly the door to one of the buildings opened and a man in a white lab coat stepped out. It was the doctor who had been with Damien the first day she had seen him, the man who had told her to clean the cage, and he had a leash in his hand. Dreamlike, she was rooted in place, unable to move, and she watched in impotent horror as the man called to the dog and Damien, with the trust of his kind, trotted up to him. Slipping the leash over the dog's head, the man turned on his heel and walked back into the building, pulling the dog along behind. Damien suddenly resisted, and when he turned toward Elizabeth his imploring eyes were filled with such an expression of dread it cramped her stomach with cold terror. Their eyes locked, and then, as if in a close-up shot, she watched in dismay as the dog's mouth opened and he *called* to her.

"Help me."

Then she was running to the door, but it was locked. She pulled on the door's handle, seeing in her mind the terror in the dog's eyes, hearing the pleading in his strange, shocking voice. But Damien was gone, locked away inside a fortress of brick and impassable bureaucracy. She ran from door to door, window to window, frantic, but there was no way in. She awoke while she was still, in her dream-turned-nightmare, pulling futiley at the large, solid door. Lying in her bed with her eyes wide, she blinked up into the darkness of her room and tried to slow her ragged breathing.

Fight or flight, she thought to herself. That primitive part of her brain where her fear was born, could only choose between those two options.

Fight or flight?

In a human or dog, it made no difference, the hard wiring was the same. What else, she wondered, was the same?

What will it be? a voice inside of her asked in a mocking tone. *Fight or flight?*

For her sake, the dog had not fled— he had fought. He had attacked a much larger dog, against the odds, for her sake. Would she now, in a pitiful move, forsake him and simply walk away?

No.

Lying there, her resolve grew slowly, and spread, like butter melting in a frying pan. It oozed its way into her fear, her complacency, her desire to stay out of trouble. Her resolve seemed to push those things before it, until there was only the *knowing* that she could not walk away from the dog and his plight. For that she felt both grateful and chagrined; grateful to find that she was the kind of person that *couldn't* walk away, chagrined because she knew it meant a difficult time ahead, and possibly disappointing the people she cared about. That was a heavy consideration, and she determined to move ahead with great caution.

She lay in the chill, predawn gray and pulled the covers up around her. Through her open window she could make out the full moon, its bottom just touching the top of a summer fog bank nestled against the foothills. The unseen sun was lightening the air, and it occurred to her, for some reason, that the full moon would be setting just at the same time the sun rose on the opposite side of the sky. That seemed a strange coincidence. She watched the moon fall slowly and bravely into the dark gray fog bank, surrendering the sky to the more powerful sun, and wondered if Damien was conscious of the same dawning.

Her cautious steps to locate Damien got her nowhere. She spent fruitless weeks trying to trace him through stray information gleaned from techs and kennel assistants during breaks and after classes, to no avail. There was no official record of the transfer. Damien had fallen through the cracks and if she was ever to find him, she knew it would take persistence and resourcefulness on her part. But she was resolved on the issue; she had to know what had become of him—because of her actions.

The University was a very large complex, not even counting the satellite campuses. The dog could be anywhere, in any one of hundreds of labs. She had learned over the past several months that despite the positive but misleading information put out by the Animal Resources Department to animal welfare groups, handlers were, in fact, not allowed into the majority of laboratories. Any researcher could simply state that outside contact could alter test results, and their lab would be closed to handlers. Entire sections were marked NO-CONTACT permanently. If Damien were behind any of those doors, she would never find him.

Three worrisome weeks went by. With each passing day she continued to approach every new kennel or cage with a hopeful glance, only to step back, disappointed. She even visited her father's office and, as nonchalantly as she could, asked him about the dogs he had recently used in his work. She saw hundreds of dogs—nice dogs—but none that returned her look with a familiar grin, none that glanced up in recognition. Slowly she became discouraged at the sheer improbability of stumbling across Damien in a random fashion. She enlisted the help of Hannah, and a couple other handlers, describing the dog to them and waiting hopefully for news. Finally she had to admit that without hard information from someone who knew the dog, she would never succeed.

She covered a lot of ground, traveling back and forth across campus, and taking precious time away from her studies. For the first time in her life she got an eighty on a test (organic chemistry, of course), resisting the urge to chew up and swallow the paper lest Tony see it.

And then one June day while she contemplated her book cover and listened to an instructor's droning voice, Elizabeth had a thought. It came out of nowhere, she wasn't even thinking about Damien, and she sat up and squinted, trying to focus and strengthen the idea that swam before her mind. It was true she couldn't speak with the professor, but Hoffman seemed to have some kind of relationship with the man who had worked on Damien when he had first come to the Center. Perhaps that man might possibly know where the dog had been taken.

She slumped back down in her seat. But how to approach *him*? Seville didn't seem like the sort you could just casually walk up to and start chatting with. He had a reputation with the kennel techs as a bastard, and nothing she had seen of him so far altered that appraisal.

She sat up straighter. What about his aide, the young man who had been with him? He hadn't been any friendlier, but he hadn't been *unfriendly*. Then again, what if Hoffman had told Seville and his aide about her? About how she had caused problems. Hoffman had warned her he would call security, or prosecute or *something* her, if he caught her around the dog again. That made it tricky.

She exhaled so hard the girl sitting next to her in class looked over at her questioningly. She smiled back wanly by way of a reassuring apology, wondering what the girl would think if she knew what she was contemplating.

Elizabeth started what she thought of as "Operation: Shadow Seville" the very next day. She wasn't sure Seville was her key, but she *was* sure she had no better idea. She began by finding his building in the University directory. Then she set out to intercept his assistant.

She struggled with herself about leaving her 11:00 class ten minutes early in order to be sure to be in position by noon. The first day she did it and the instructor glanced up at her, she almost sat back down. But she went, cringing, up the aisle and to the door. Once she found Damien and saw that he was OK, *then* she could remove herself from his life. Wherever he is, whatever his fate, she told herself as she eased the heavy door shut behind her, it was because *she* had caused the dogfight and gotten him moved.

She had no illusions about how difficult and chancy the timing would be to catch the assistant alone. Seville's office/lab was located on the second floor of an immense building, which seemed to be made up entirely of old linoleum hallways and closed metal doors. Steps echoed there, and she could hear people approaching long before she could see them. She learned where the restrooms were and ducked into them on a regular basis to avoid being seen too often by the same people. There was security at the entrance, but her handler's ID tag got her in, no questions asked. Once she was inside, she just started walking around the second floor, trying to look busy and purposeful. Even during the lunch hour there were surprisingly few people moving about, and she was never challenged.

She was loitering before a wall display on the life cycle of the mollusk when she felt a sudden jolt of adrenaline. Seville was leaving his office, sports bag in hand. Breathing fast, she walked directly to the door Seville had just exited. As she approached on her first pass it suddenly opened. Her heart almost stopped because it was Seville's assistant and he was alone.

Ohmygawd. This is it.

She stood there staring, as he carefully pulled the door shut and nodded politely as he passed by her.

"Excuse me, excuse me." Elizabeth walked after him feeling like an idiot. The man turned around and regarded her through his small wire-rimmed glasses with an impassive expression. He was quite a bit taller than she, and a half dozen years older. His close-cropped dark blond hair and immaculate white shirt gave him a crisp, punctual look, and there was something about his erect, calm posture and trim mustache that fell an inch below either side of his thin lips, that made her feel especially young and ineffectual.

Come on! Ask him, you dork.

"I'm really sorry to bother you," she said with an apologetic smile, "but I'm trying very hard to locate a certain dog. I don't think it's in your lab, but I'm just wondering if maybe, you know, Professor Hoffman mentioned to you or Dr. Seville where it was sent." She felt a cold jab of fear as she realized he would have to wonder why she didn't just ask Hoffman—he would *have* to wonder about that. She bet a hundred dollars Hoffman had already told them about her.

But this was her only chance. "It really means a lot to me."

Tom's face remained expressionless, and he didn't answer her question.

She saw his eyes move, just a little, then come back to rest. Elizabeth was annoyed with herself for noticing he smelled pleasantly of aftershave.

"A striped dog," she said, deciding it was better to just press on than give him a chance to refuse. "Striped like a little tiger. Medium size, short ears, his name is Damien. Do you know where he's been taken?"

"The dog that was starved?" he finally said. "That one? *You* were there." She heard the recognition in his voice, which had a soft, polite, low quality to it that reminded her of family friend Jack Leroy, a heart specialist from LSU, born and bred on the Louisiana delta.

"*Yeah,* that one! Do you know where he is?" She leaned forward, her expression a combination of hope she would get some news of her missing friend, and fear that the news wouldn't be good.

Seville's aide hesitated. It was not his habit to discuss his boss' business with outsiders. But he wouldn't lie, and he couldn't think of a way to extract himself without answering. "Yes," he said. "He's here." He pointed to the lab door with his chin.

Elizabeth turned in a small circle, her fists balled tight and held before her chest. "Thank you, *thank you* so much for telling me, I *really* appreciate it."

Tom tried to leave, nodding politely.

"Wait! Please! Could I ask one more question?"

Tom stopped, and managed to show, even without the benefit of facial expression, a civil annoyance with her persistent intrusion into his employer's private affairs.

"What do you guys do in there? You know, what kind of research?"

The man's eyes changed then, just slightly, a lowering and focusing upon her that made her think he was seeing her now for the first time.

"Dr. Seville does basic research," he said carefully, politely, distantly.

Elizabeth screwed up her face. "I guess that doesn't really tell me anything," she said with mock confusion, hoping to draw a smile from him. His expression—or lack of it—didn't change.

He hesitated and she thought, for just a moment, he wanted to say more. Then he seemed to gain determination and he turned away again.

"I just really like the dog, that's all, I just wanted to make sure he's OK, you know?" Frustration foamed in her stomach. Tom sighed a very quiet sigh and turned back, polite to the end, to face her.

"I'm sorry," he said. Then, firmer, "I don't discuss the doctor's work."

Elizabeth's eyes widened. "Why? What's he doing to the dogs in there, Tom?"

She suddenly remembered his name from that first day she had seen him, and she could see he was surprised when she called him by name. She glanced at the door and he guessed her thoughts. "I don't think you should go in there," he said. "The doctor wouldn't like it—and *you* wouldn't like it."

Her eyes went wider still in apprehension. "My God," she breathed, "what *do* you do in there?"

"I don't discuss the doctor's work," he said again firmly. "The dog is receiving relevant care, that's all I can tell you." He turned and walked away and Elizabeth could only let him go.

From that moment on, she had one goal in life—to get into that lab. If she found that the dog was being treated cruelly she resigned herself to stealing him and, because she couldn't take him home, she would just turn him loose. To her mind, he would be better off as a stray again than in that lab. If she gave him to the animal shelter they might, if the University reported him missing, return him to Seville.

Tony was waiting for her outside her last class. He had been accepted into a summer intern course, was excited, and wanted to tell her about it. She went with him to the cafeteria, then sat, staring into the middle space, while he talked. He finally hesitated, frowning.

"What's the matter, Elizabeth?"

Her eyes jerked back toward his. "Oh, I'm sorry, nothing. I'm listening."

"No you're not."

"Yes I am, really. Don't be so uptight."

"What's that supposed to mean?"

"Come on, Tone, it's nothing. I'm just a little tired, and sorta thinking about something. I do want to hear about this, though."

"I'm done," he said, peevishly.

"No you're not, go ahead."

He leaned back in his seat, taking stock of her. "How'd you do on the chem test?"

This was tit for tat, but she was glad to change subjects, even to this perilous one. "I've done better," she said, not unhappy to know that that response would annoy him.

"Where did you fall down?"

"I didn't 'fall down'. I missed a few questions—honest mistakes—it's not a big deal."

Tony sighed, as if profoundly disappointed. "I think you need to put in extra time strengthening your weak areas."

"Maybe," she said, with a degree of coldness in her voice that made Tony blink. "I think I'm doing well enough. I'm passing; I'm in the top ten percent of my class. Why isn't that good enough for you?"

Tony had strange, pale eyes beneath his wavy red hair, and they opened wide now. "Why don't you want to try harder? You can do it, I know you can, and that's what I don't understand. You don't seem to really care."

"Well, you know I do," she snapped. Even as she waited for his predictable response, she had a strong and sudden vision that shook her. She was standing beside her father in his lab; she was gowned and assisting with the surgery. Dave was deep within the thoracic cavity of one of his dogs, pointing out an interesting development in the new suture material he was testing. Standing there, in her vision, Elizabeth realized with horror that she was not at *all* interested in what her father was showing her. Instead, she was trying to look under the drapes at the figure of the dog. She was trying to see if the dog was brindle.

Her plan of action was now even more difficult than catching Tom alone. Now she had to avoid Seville *and* his aide and the other occupants of the lab at all costs. Tom knew she wanted entry to their lab; if he saw her hanging around he would call security. If he called security . . . She had to be very, very careful.

At first it seemed an impossible situation. How to be sure all the men who worked there were gone?

She began by lurking outside Seville's office during her lunch hour again. At one o'clock every day she could count on Seville to leave, carrying his sports bag, obviously headed for some kind of physical activity. A workout, she wondered, or a game of handball? *If* Tom left the lab, it was some moments later. The other occupants of the lab she could do nothing about; their schedules were simply too erratic as they moved back and forth, she discovered, between Seville's personal office and the lab down the hall where his undergrads came and went. All she could do was hope for the best where they were concerned. She made up her mind to watch and wait until both Seville and his aide left, and then she was determined to try to enter the lab. If the door was locked, as she supposed it would be, she would go every day until it wasn't. She couldn't think of anything better.

The next day she took up her position, watched both men leave within minutes of each other, and then, grim-faced proceeded to the now-familiar door. She hung around in the hallway, gathering nerve. She exhaled sharply when the door swung open with a jerk and a young man stepped out. She found his appearance odd. With his shoulder-length blond ringlets and his sleeveless denim shirt open at the chest, she found him a most unlikely looking lab worker. She thought he had the look of a rock star or a surfer dude, and as he rolled down the hall with a careless swing, he winked at her as he passed. He went two doors down and disappeared into another doorway.

Elizabeth hurried to the door, holding her breath. She put her hand on the knob. She had her story straight. If there *was* anyone in the room, she was simply a handler who had come in to see the dogs. The no-contact notice on the door? Oh, that? She had simply failed to notice it—sorry! If the blond man came back she would say the same thing.

The doorknob wouldn't turn. It was locked, but the man had not swung the door hard enough to shut it. It was open a crack. He must mean to come right back. At that moment, when the door cracked open, she knew that if she entered that room against the wishes of the researcher, she was taking an irreversible step. If she found Damien and decided to steal him, with his status as a research animal, she would be committing a felony.

Good-bye medical school, she thought grimly. But at that moment she did not think of her father. She thought of the dog, who had no friend but her.

Her respiration was so rapid she had to stop and consciously fight to slow it before she went on. What was she *really* going to do if she found the dog? She hesitated.

Stealing him was just too big a step. Everything would come crashing down. She'd be fired for sure, not that that was any big deal. The real question was where in the world would she put the dog? She had no friends she could trust to take the dog—not if any pressure was put on them. There simply was no place for him to go. If the dog came up missing, Hoffman would know she had taken him.

She blew out her breath and opened the door about twelve inches. No one was in sight. In the middle of the lab was a free-standing counter, the top cluttered with equipment, most of which appeared to be electronic. It looked, thought Elizabeth, like a VCR repair shop. On the counters along the edges of the room were the more traditional microscopes and other medical apparatus. She paused long enough to glance at the jumble of unfamiliar-looking equipment in the middle of the room, curious, and with a mild feeling of anxiety as to what it might be. She looked at the name plates on several items: *Programmable Isolated Stimulator LX, Shock Floor Accessory ES-10, Startle Response Audio Source Module, High Amplitude Drive Aversive Audio Stimulator.* With a growing sense of dread she picked up a manual: *Startle Software V3.1.* A package with tiny screws in it caught her eye. BONE SCREWS, it said.

Feeling faint, she moved away from the table and toward a large desk crowded with papers and reference books. She noticed two doors with small glass windows running vertically near the door knobs. As she approached them she could see animal cages inside. The door was locked, and she stopped, hand on the doorknob, and leaned against the glass, craning her neck to see inside. Animal food bags were piled against one wall, and the rest of the room was filled with equipment. She moved to the next door and looked inside.

There were eight cages, and her heart nearly leapt from her chest when she saw Damien directly in front of her. The dog was pacing inside the cage, but due to the small size of the enclosure, it could more accurately be called weaving. His hindquarters moved only a little compared to his head and neck, which were rhythmically swaying back and forth from one end of the cage to the other, rubbing along the cage bars. On each pass his nose was pressed up into the corner of the cage, in the exact same place, with the exact same motion, over and over. His eyes were unfocused. His whole manner expressed a mindlessness Elizabeth found absolutely terrifying.

"Damien," she yelled, hitting the glass and then the wooden door hard, hoping to break his horrible trance. *"Damien!"*

If he heard her he gave no sign. "Damien!" She waved her hands in the window, hoping to catch his eye.

But Damien could not hear or see her. His elaborate "weaving" pattern was a stereotyped behavior, purposefully induced by the researchers, for the study of the affect of certain psychostimulant drugs on the catecholamine neurotransmitters dopamine and noradrenaline. When Damien weaved, the mindless, stereotypic movements induced the action of the analgesic opiate peptides in his brain, giving him a small but merciful measure of escape from the forces which had caused him to seek this relief.

Elizabeth was unaware that she was slowly shaking her head.

Had he gone mad or was he simply trying to escape the pen? He didn't look at all right. Once again she jiggled the doorknob in frustration. *"Damien!"* she called one more time, as loudly as she dared. Then she saw a strange thing. She heard, very faintly, a tone coming from inside the room. Suddenly two other dogs which she had not noticed in her attention to Damien, rose quickly from where they had crouched on their cage floors. She saw now that there were dogs in all the cages but one, and that they were all anxious and moving about in an aimless, hurried fashion within the confines of their stainless-steel cages. One dog suddenly froze in place and, turning its head to its flank, began to suck the fur there with a mindless, haunted expression. Frowning, she wondered what the sound could mean to them to cause such instant anxiety. Damien, she noticed, was performing the exact same weaving pattern but quicker now than before. Suddenly every dog, simultaneously, started upwards into the air with a grunt or yelp. Within seconds most resumed their mindless patterns of movement, as if the shock had not occurred. Elizabeth, as unfamiliar as she was with the thinking behind this type of lab, understood instantly that the wire-grid floors of the cages must be hooked up to an automatic electrical shocking machine, similar to the ones on the counter behind her.

Who could do such a thing?

The men who worked here. And many more like them, all over the University.

The bastards! Why?

To that she had no answer. She knew by heart, of course, all the arguments in favor of animal research; had, in fact, argued them herself on more than one occasion in the past. But here, in this lab, watching these dogs and looking about her at the reality of their existence, she knew that this was evil.

The minds behind all this were frightening. The *system* behind this was frightening. What *kind* of a company made Shock Floor Accessories? Even if something like this *was* capable of producing worthwhile results, the price was too high. Far too high. Who would *want* to do this sort of thing to an animal?

The tone sounded again and with a horror too strong to turn away, she watched, waiting without breathing like the inmates of the room, for the torturing shock to come again. She saw the same anxiety, the same quickening of stereotyped behavior but no shock came. She found the longer the delay, the more tense she became, waiting, waiting with the dogs for the pain. But it never came. Inside the room the dogs all continued their separate movements, each in its own nightmare world induced by unpredictable and disturbing events over which they had no control. The randomness of the shocks from grid floors was just one of the many erratic and distressing elements that had been carefully designed by the researchers to induce stereotyped behavior in them. The dogs had no physical escape and they knew it, but their remarkable minds worked desperately to ease the pain, by the repeated and predictable sensory input of the stereotyped movements which had a narcotizing effect. In a pathetic attempt to create for themselves a more predictable world, they shut out, as best they could, the real world. Damien could not see Elizabeth standing at the window. Nature had done what She could for him.

Why isn't this illegal?

Nothing, her father had said once, *is illegal in a medical research laboratory. Nothing. Anything can be gotten around, anything can be done.*

The law would not help Damien. Mankind, which cowered before the specter of disease, turned a blind eye in its selfish fear, and would not help him. Who then, her mind kept framing the question, who would help Damien escape from this pointless, unfair fate?

Elizabeth wanted more than anything to help him, but how could *she* get Damien out of this room? There were no easy, simple answers; the University, this doctor, his aide, security guards, her family, her future, they were all obstacles rising before her. Elizabeth had a sudden sense of being no match for the task. It was a cold, chilling feeling that wilted her as she stood watching the mad, mindless thing that had once been Damien.

On the fourth of July her father held his annual outdoor dinner party. As usual, it was catered, so there wasn't much for her to do. The guests were all work friends of her father and grandfather, most of whom she knew only slightly. Tony was there, pestering her to come meet this and that person who could "be instrumental" in her career until she had ditched him by pretending she needed to step into the house for ice. She carefully avoided him the rest of the evening, but she needn't have bothered; he forgot about her as he stood about, drink in hand, schmoozing with the surgeons in attendance. Elizabeth was thankful for that. She wasn't sure she could have taken both him and the heat.

Ever conscious of her role as lady of the house, she smiled, nodded and kept an eye on the caterers, while fantasizing about soaking her feet in ice water. It was nearly one hundred degrees, unusual for this part of the country, making the oppressive heat all the more dramatic. It was the talk of the party among the nonmedical spouses unable to join in the general shop talk. By seven o'clock it was still sweltering and Elizabeth gave up, slipping away to her grandfather's garden to run the hose over her feet in an effort to forestall their imminent spontaneous combustion. She kicked off her shoes and hiked her dress up, then sat on a bench Bill had strategically placed near the hose. He liked to sit here in the evenings and water his beloved tomato plants. Reaching over, she turned the hose on a trickle and held it over her feet.

Ouch!

The water in the hose was scalding hot. She jerked it away and let it run, waiting for fresh, cool water. She rubbed the top of her right foot ruefully.

In thirty seconds the water was cool and she gratefully played it over her feet. She set the hose between them and just let it run out, a small miracle of coolness in the unrelenting heat.

She looked at Bill's tomato plants. Already there were sizable clusters of cherry tomatoes on every branch, many nearly ripe. The bigger plants sported full-sized green tomatoes of enormous circumference. For some reason her mind was wandering in strange directions tonight, and she wasn't really surprised to find herself thinking about what kind of damage a dog like Damien would do to the rows of carefully caged and staked plants. Then she remembered where Damien was, and her mind fell silent.

At a soft sound, she turned to find her grandfather walking up. He smiled, loosened his tie and sat down beside her. He moved his feet slightly to avoid wetting his shoes.

"You've got the right idea, huh?"

"It's *so* freakin' hot tonight. I don't remember a Fourth being this hot, do you?"

"It's hot," he agreed. "Good for the tomatoes though; they thrive on it."

"Well, that's good, I'm glad someone enjoys it."

"Where's Tony?"

"I ditched him."

They sat in silence for several moments, and then Bill said, still looking out over his garden, "What's been bothering you these past few weeks, Elizabeth?"

His question startled her and she looked over at him. He turned his head to meet her eyes and she saw how kind they were. "You know you can tell me *anything*," he said gently, seeing her hesitation.

She smiled faintly to herself, then more brightly to him. "The thing that's on my mind," she began, choosing her words carefully, "you'd have a hard time relating to."

"Oh, now look," Bill joked, "it hasn't been *that* long . . ."

Elizabeth laughed a little. "No, it's nothing like that."

Bill leaned forward to pinch a yellowing leaf off of a nearby plant. "*All* problems," he said, "come back to either money, malpractice lawyers or the opposite sex."

Elizabeth laughed again. "Not *all* of them. I really don't know how to explain it to you, because it's something you'd have never encountered. Nothing personal—I just don't think you would understand. And . . . I think you would disapprove."

"Try me."

"OK. It's about one of the research dogs I worked with. I don't think he's being treated right." She saw the minute change in her grandfather's expression and exclaimed in both triumph and defeat, "*See*, I told you."

Bill composed himself but it was too late. "Well, let's hear it."

"Bill, with all due respect, what good would it do to tell you? You've used dogs all your life."

Bill leaned back with a sigh and crossed his arms. His shirtsleeves were rolled up to just below the elbow, and she looked at his sturdy forearms. For some reason they had always reminded her of a dusty Roman legionnaire, stocky and strong, standing in his sandals holding a spear. A Roman soldier's arms; not like the arms that belonged to someone who did the delicate work of repairing human hearts.

He was looking out over the garden, purposefully distancing himself from her in an attempt to be an impartial arbiter. "I'd like to think I was never cruel. I think I treated my practice animals as well as could be," he said. "If an animal is not being treated right, Elizabeth, there are steps that can be taken."

His granddaughter's head came up. "There are?"

"Of course. No one wants to see dogs treated badly. What's the nature of the problem concerning this animal's treatment?"

Elizabeth sighed and fiddled the hose about with her toes. Then she shook her head. "I don't even know where to begin—I don't think I can."

"Well, Elizabeth, I mean either it's being mistreated or it's not. You're certainly going to have to do better than that before you bring charges against anyone. However, sometimes experimental protocol calls for measures which may *seem* like mistreatment."

She turned then to face him, and her action drew his eyes to hers. Bill saw bewilderment, hurt and frustration in her brown eyes. She had seen something that was truly troubling her.

"What *is it*, Elizabeth?"

"I don't even know what it is they are trying to *do* to Damien. It doesn't make any sense. They have him in a cage, a small metal cage with a floor that *shocks* him. They've left him in the cage and shocked him so much that he looks like he's lost his mind. He's just weaving back and forth, wearing his fur off on the bars—they've made him crazy I think."

Her grandfather considered before he spoke. "Is this a psych lab?" He said the word "psych" with a dismissive tone.

"I guess; the guy's name is Seville. His aide said he does basic research."

"Well it's hard to say what they're examining; it could be something important, something beneficial. How do you know the dog's name?"

"I've known Damien for quite a while now. I've mentioned him before. Now he's in this place and I've *got* to help him."

Bill tipped his head to one side and gave her *that* look. "Listen to yourself. It was foolish to become attached to a lab animal—*you* should know that. And while I'm sure this man is doing everything he can to minimize the dog's possible discomfort, if you really have legitimate concerns, take them to the AUIC. That's what it's there for."

"What's that?"

"The Animal Use Investigation Committee? It's a board that reviews research and teaching protocols to assure proper procedures are followed."

"Oh." Elizabeth thought about that. It had never occurred to her that there might be standards of care for the animals. Who would suspect such a thing when one considered the very nature of their use? Who could say that it was cruel to apply shock to a caged dog's feet *this* way, but not *that* way? She shook her head. "Who's on this committee? What kind of people?"

Bill shrugged. "They're appointed by the Director of Animal Resources. I think they have scientists, and laymen, and even animal welfare people. I'm not sure."

"Did your work go before this board?"

"In a general way. It was never called up formally for review. Remember, the stuff I was doing was strictly routine—practice. It's not like what Dave does with his research, where they are trying new procedures all the time."

Elizabeth squinted, recalling something he had just said that had caught her attention. "You said the board members are *appointed* by the Director of Animal Resources? Isn't that kinda like letting the fox watch the henhouse?"

"What do you mean?"

"I mean, geez, is the *Director* of *Research* really going to appoint someone who is going to seriously challenge the status quo?"

"No," Bill said, shaking his head. "You're assuming the worst. Everyone wants to see good research, and that means keeping the animals as stress-free as possible. That only makes sense."

"Unless," Elizabeth rejoined, "your object is to *produce* stress."

"There *are* going to be times when stress is unavoidable, or even desirable, in order to obtain a certain result."

"How do I find out about this board?"

"Go to the Animal Resources Department and ask them."

Elizabeth chewed her bottom lip and considered. She already harbored grave suspicions of this "appointed" board.

"What made *this* dog stand out? You see dozens every day, don't you?"

"Yeah, hundreds I think, some days. I don't know." She paused and then went on, shrugging her shoulders. "I guess I really couldn't tell you why. I just like the way he's so serious, he's not goofy. He *knows* where he is, and what's going on. He *knows* who he is. He's *somebody*. Does that make any sense?"

Bill watched her face. He saw her thoughtfulness as she struggled to express her kinship with the dog. He was remembering Bea, his wife of thirty years, and how she had loved animals. But Bea had shut her mind to the practice surgeries he had to do as a thoracic surgeon, and they had simply never spoken of it. In Elizabeth, as he watched her profile while she pondered her problem, he saw Bea's passion and Dave's resoluteness.

"Life is full of difficult choices, El. Some are devilishly hard, and you're facing a choice right now. *Right now* you need to come to terms with the fact that in order to succeed in your chosen profession, you are going to be using dogs in research. At least the dogs we use are dogs which are just going to die anyway, it's not like colony-bred dogs that are born for the purpose of research, understand? These dogs are going to be destroyed at an animal shelter, so we just make use of them, so that at least their death has meaning."

Elizabeth listened to the voice that had always spoken truth to her. She did not feel the usual relief and sense of easement she felt after talking something over with her grandfather. Instead she felt, sitting in the sweltering late-afternoon sun, a coldness inside. For the first time in her life, Bill's words rang hollow. She could find no comfort in them, no solution to the questions that plagued her. And yet she knew that what he said was true; this use of animals was in her future. *She* would be the one using a "Damien" soon, using a dog's body like a living practice sketch, and then tossing it away when she was done.

"You're not going to do anything foolish, are you?" Bill asked her seriously.

She thought about that, then Elizabeth shook her head slowly. "No. No, I don't think I am," she said sadly.

The next day she went to the office of the Director of Animal Resources to investigate the AUIC. The office secretary handed her a shiny pamphlet which boldly proclaimed across the front that "animal welfare is a primary concern" at the University and that "animal use is balanced with the needs of research." A large rat on the back of the pamphlet had the words "Our Heartfelt Thanks For Your Contribution" over his head. Below him was a paragraph describing the scientific community's deep appreciation for the sacrifice of lab animals everywhere.

Let's see, she thought dryly, *just how grateful they really are—let's see what kind of people they have watching out for you. . . .*

She leaned her book bag against the counter and opened the pamphlet. Inside was what she was looking for; the listing of the board members. The chairman was listed first; David Barton, Ph.D., Department of Physiology, School of Medicine.

She continued down the list; Annetta Lawson, Director of Animal Care and Control, representing animal welfare concerns, it said. Elizabeth grimaced—everyone knew the local animal "shelter" was in bed with the University, and made plenty of revenue by selling pet dogs into research.

She squinted, as if in pain, at the rest of the list. There were more doctors, more researchers, and then a name, second from the bottom, leapt out at her like it was her own. *Dr. Joseph Seville.*

Elizabeth almost laughed out loud. What could be better? Not only was she contemplating bringing charges of improper conduct against a senior and well-respected staff member of the University, but now an Animal Use Investigation Committee *member* as well.

She set the pamphlet back down on the counter. She had learned a valuable lesson today about "appropriate channels." What Seville did to Damien was so carefully protected behind layer upon layer of bureaucratic red tape, she would never be able to penetrate to a meaningful level. She picked up her book bag and gave the woman behind the counter a knowing smile.

"I don't think this is the way for me to go. Thanks," she said.

The woman could sense Elizabeth's disgruntled attitude and wasn't sure she liked it. She remained silent in frosty disapproval of any possible criticism of her office.

Hurrying to her summer class in the sweltering heat, Elizabeth regrouped her thoughts. The committee—what with Seville being a member—was out, that was for sure, but what about going *above* the committee? Elizabeth shared with most people the belief that you could always go *up*. Even if the whole committee was dirty there would be someone in authority farther up who would be appalled at her report. The higher you went, the more just the person, right? She just had to find that person.

The logical place to start her search was within the committee itself. Who was its ranking member, and then who was that person's superior? David Barton, the pamphlet had said, was the chairman, and he was head of the Department of Physiology, School of Medicine. Would he be concerned? Without any real justification to back up the opinion, she couldn't help feeling that anyone interested in physiology would not be of much help to her. Besides, outside of the context of the committee, Seville's use of the dog did not fall under Barton's jurisdiction.

She stepped into the foyer of the large hall where her class was. The committee, she ruminated, was run out of the office of the Director of Animal Resources. The director, she remembered, was not on the Animal Use committee, and that sounded promising. And no matter what kind of work Seville was doing, his protocols with the dog would fall under the jurisdiction of the office of Animal Resources. As Elizabeth passed with the other students through the doorway and up the slight ramp to the curving rows of seating, she resolved to make an appointment to speak to the director immediately after class.

She left her information with the same receptionist whose earlier suspicious disapproval of her blossomed into triumphant disdain when she learned that Elizabeth wished to speak to the director concerning a complaint.

"The nature of the complaint, ma'am?" The woman stared at her smugly, pen poised above paper.

"Oh. Well, I want to speak to the director about the treatment of an animal here, at the University."

"Of course, I just need a few more details at this point. Who, specifically is the complaint being lodged against?"

"Well, I never said I was actually lodging a complaint, I just want to talk to her about something I saw."

"Of course, but who is the party concerned? We need a name, or we won't be able to go any further."

Elizabeth, annoyed by the receptionist's use of the royal "we," was uncomfortable giving this girl her information, but she realized she probably had no choice. "Dr. Joseph Seville."

The girl stared at her, dark eyes wide. After a moment, they narrowed. "Dr. Seville is an AUIC committee member."

"I know that."

After another long moment the girl's pen finally dropped to the paper. Without looking up the receptionist said, "What is the nature of your complaint?"

"I told you, I want to speak with the director about this. I have concerns about humane treatment. That's all."

The girl lifted her head then, and tilted it, looking at her sideways out of still-narrowed eyes. "Concerns about Dr. *Joseph* Seville."

"Yeah, that's right."

"What's your name and daytime phone?"

"Elizabeth Fletcher, 912-3354, that's my cell number. When will I hear back?"

The receptionist gave her a queer look. "Oh, I would think within twenty-four hours."

"Thanks."

The call came in less than three. "Can you be at the office early, at eight, to meet with Dr. Novak?" the receptionist wanted to know.

"Sure."

"All right, Dr. Novak will see you tomorrow then."

Elizabeth felt a fierce enthusiasm—perhaps it boded well that the director would see her that quickly.

The next morning, sitting in the Animal Resources office waiting room under the continuing lukewarm hostility of the receptionist, Elizabeth watched the various comings and goings. Several young, professional-looking persons moved about behind the glass-and-fabric partitions, speaking quietly, and occasionally glancing at her. The door which led to the director's private office opened and she drew in a sharp breath, afraid this was it. But a sharply dressed young man exited the room laughing with affected cheerfulness, nodding to the receptionist with a wink and a smile as he walked out. Having spent so much time at her father's work Elizabeth instantly tagged him as a drug or equipment sales rep—she knew the type.

But now she was shaken; she knew that when she tried to explain to the director what she had seen at Seville's lab it would sound weak and pointless. What words could paint an accurate picture of Damien's pathetic anticipation of each upcoming shock? And what words of hers could describe the *pointlessness* of it all?

But she must.

If she failed, if she left this office without having convinced the director that what one of the University's researchers was doing was unconscionable, Damien would continue to be tortured. There was no other word for it. At that moment she realized she no longer wondered *why* she was so concerned about the dog. His fate *was* of interest to her, their lives now intertwined.

The door opened again and an impeccably dressed woman in her forties with a face Elizabeth would have described as "plastic" beckoned to her. "Come in."

This is it.

Elizabeth rose and followed. As she came through the door she noticed she was quite a bit taller than the director. Katharine Novak settled the silk scarf about her neck at the same time she settled herself in her chair, and then they regarded each other across the desk.

"Elizabeth Fletcher, isn't it?"

"Yes."

"Are you a student here, Elizabeth?"

"Yes, I am."

"What program?"

"Premed."

"Really? You *know* that's what you want?"

"My father and grandfather are both cardiac surgeons. I guess I've got to be the son my father never had." She had meant it as a small joke, to help break her tension, but it sounded flat and complaining to her ears.

"You don't sound very pleased about the idea. Are you?"

"Oh, no. I guess I am."

"I see." Novak smiled very carefully. "Are they *here*? Your father and grandfather?"

"Yeah, my dad's over at The Med—my grandfather's retired."

"Your father, does he work in surgery or R&D?"

"He works primarily in research."

There was a pause while the petite woman looked her over with a critical air. Elizabeth wondered if her blouse had a button undone.

"So your visit here today, Elizabeth, your concerns regarding Dr. Seville, what do they consist of?"

"They're about the treatment of a dog I saw."

"You *saw* this dog, how? Where were you?" She had a way of speaking that made Elizabeth question the validity of her own statements. She wondered for a split second if she actually *had* seen Damien.

"I was in Dr. Seville's office, over at . . ."

"In what *capacity* were you there?"

"Oh, I'm a handler."

"A handler. I see."

Elizabeth's gut contracted sharply; she didn't like Novak's tone.

"You are familiar, I would *think*, with research? You're familiar with your father's work?"

"Well, yes . . ."

"So now, tell me, what was it you saw at Dr. Seville's office that caused you concern?"

"I saw dogs being shocked—repeatedly—in small metal cages; they couldn't escape at all. No one was even there watching or anything. They were just there, being shocked, and they were terrified out of their minds. It was a horrible thing to see. I mean they were *literally* crazy from fear."

Novak said nothing.

"I mean, it's just not right."

The woman across the desk from her exhaled and sat back. Rose perfume, applied too liberally, wafted across the desk to Elizabeth.

"Did you inquire as to why electrical stimulation was being applied?"

"There wasn't anyone there to ask. I went into the office by mistake, you see, and just saw that."

"So you really have no idea what the experimental protocol is? You have no idea if it *is* being violated?"

"If what is being violated?"

"An established and approved experimental protocol."

"Well, no. I mean really though, is this a matter of protocol? Can he just do that—shock them like that, with no one even around? It seems so cruel, I thought . . ." She trailed off. This woman would not help. Then slow, rising anger began to come to Elizabeth. This was ridiculous. How could what Seville did to dogs possibly be legal? If someone on the street did something like this to a dog they would lock them up and throw away the key.

I'll go to the press. Damn it all, I will!

Though she was seated, she felt herself rise an inch or two, and her shoulders square up. She cleared her throat, preparing to tell the Director of Animal Resources what she thought of her, of Seville, of the whole situation. But Novak had never taken her eyes off of her, and now the woman steepled her hands and nodded, appearing rather judicious. "Would you, Elizabeth," she said suddenly, "be willing to put your concerns on paper for me? It would be most helpful in any investigation—and I do think this should be looked into."

It was as if there was suddenly a different person seated across from her. Elizabeth sat blinking. "I . . . Well, yes, I . . ."

"Will you give me some time to look into this—after you give me your report—will you give me some time to investigate this?"

Elizabeth was taken aback. She must have misread the woman. "Well, sure, yeah." Her voice rose with her growing hope.

"*Thank* you, Elizabeth, for bringing this forward. You understand, I'm sure, that we maintain the strictest research protocols here at this University, and any concerns regarding them are taken quite seriously. Of course, Dr. Seville is a very respected member of this faculty, and allegations such as this are also quite serious." Novak leaned forward, confidentially. "Because Joseph Seville is an AUIC member, I will not be assigning this to my staff. I will personally look into this matter. Now, you get me that report, as quickly as possible, and I'll contact you when I have something to report to you, all right?"

Elizabeth stood. "Yes, thanks, that's great." Her voice again betrayed her hope. "I'll get something in here this afternoon. Thanks so much for seeing me—and for your help."

Novak stood and saw her to the door. Though the scent of rose perfume was still strong enough to gag her, Elizabeth found she did not mind it nearly so much now. "You did the right thing coming *here*," Novak continued. "If you have other concerns, I want you to feel free to call or stop by anytime. I'll get Lydia to give you my direct number, all right?"

"Sure." Elizabeth stammered, overwhelmed by the woman's sudden concern. "That's great. Thank you."

"It's my pleasure, Elizabeth. I'll give this my attention as soon as I have something from you in writing."

Elizabeth left the office, walking out into the bright whiteness of the concrete courtyard. She felt dazed; Novak was concerned. She had a possible ally, and a powerful one at that. As she walked to her car she was smiling to herself.

CHAPTER FIVE

The Soul Selects Her Own Society

I've known her from an ample nation
Choose one;
Then close the valves of her attention
Like stone.

—EMILY DICKINSON

Stoic and resilient creature that he was, Damien still approached the edge of madness. Even had he been treated kindly by the men, simply confining the young bulldog to a cage and depriving him of the hard work necessary to exercise his formidable body and mind was unspeakably cruel. However, Damien was not treated kindly; yet neither was he treated with intentional cruelty. He was simply used. Used with dispassion, for he was a tool, and the men did not think in terms of his use, nor the use of any other implement in the lab, as being kind or cruel. Damien was in a place where the study of behavior was reduced to its most elemental aspect. In this place the scientist only needed, and could only see, the animal's biochemical reactions to the stressors they applied. In this place Damien himself, the rugged brindle pit bulldog who possessed humor, patience, courage and depth of character, ceased, as a whole entity, to exist.

Here an animal's behavior could be manipulated, monitored, measured, described and the results published. Grant money was readily available to those with the inclination and imagination necessary to come up with new and innovative projects. Done right, basic research made a decorous livelihood. It was a comfortable world—for the researchers. For Damien, as a subject in those experiments, it was not so comfortable. He lived now in a world constructed on tenets of madness. He no longer could rely upon the cage floor to simply be a cage floor. In this place it had become a bitter enemy, attacking him constantly, and there was nothing he could do about it. He could bite at the floor—and he had—but it accomplished nothing. He could scream and climb the corner of the steel cage whimpering in terror and confusion—and he had—but that accomplished nothing. He could rage and snarl, biting at the bars of his cage door—and he had—but had only broken teeth.

In this place he discovered that fight or flight were *not* the only two choices when faced with fearful stimuli from which you could not escape. Here the rules of the universe were different. Here there was a third choice. The once-proud bulldog learned to give up, a thing that did not come easily to his kind. He learned to submit and give in to the helplessness that came from inescapable torment. And still the random shocks came. He couldn't know for sure *when* the shocks were coming and that made it all the worse. Sometimes a tone sounded to warn him, sometimes it didn't. Sometimes it sounded and then nothing happened, and that was the worst of all. Sometimes loud, frightening noise, very painful to the ears, was produced without any reason or warning, to further disorientate the canine inmates as they were methodically pushed toward madness.

But there was a method to the madness which surrounded Damien. The researchers needed his terror and hopelessness; they carefully cultivated it. The grant money involved—a very considerable sum—depended on their producing in dogs, over and over, the mindless, disturbed stereotyped behavior associated with frustration, hopelessness and madness in many species. These men, and countless hundreds of other scientists had been doing it for years. Over and over again.

Through it all, Damien did not become vicious. The genetic instructions of countless thousands of ancestors demanded he give his submission to these men. Acknowledging their superiority, he never resisted Seville or the other men who worked there. He was a bulldog, a true working bulldog, and a bulldog did not turn on men because of pain. It was a harsh and unyielding obedience that his blood demanded, but its logic was age-old. Dogs of his bloodline were possessed of shocking courage, taking their death in the pit, destroyed in the grinding, hellish jaws of an opponent, or under the horns and hooves of an enraged bull. They died, tails gallantly wagging, glancing up at their owner's face to see if in their last moments they had pleased. Because of this, Damien, as long as he could hold on to his sanity, would take his death without lashing out at these humans. For that reason, and for one reason more; he perceived that what happened in these rooms was the *will* of the terrible dark-haired man in the white coat, the alpha to all the others that worked in these rooms. Damien's dread of this man knew no bounds.

It had happened as a coincidence. The first time the electronic floor grid had shocked Damien, Seville had just approached his cage, and was standing, watching. Seville spoke to an unseen person as he pointed to the cage floor. The dog had perceived that the man was pointing at him at the moment of the intensely frightening shock. That moment of startle had developed into a strongly conditioned, unconsciously developed fear that increased every time the random shocks of his electronic floor coincided with the random appearance of Seville. The man might approach his cage, and the floor would shock him. He might hear the man's voice in the other room, and the floor would shock him. The man's scent, or the scent of the cigarettes he smoked, might drift to him, and the pain would come, sharp, instant, hard. It was unintentional but nonetheless effective conditioning—something Seville was not even aware of.

So when the door to the outer room was left open Damien watched Seville closely, feverishly, obsessed with attempting to predict the man's actions. He ached to understand, to be able to predict what transgression of his caused what he perceived as punishment. Despite the chauvinistic and patronizing tenets put forth by many learned behaviorists stating otherwise, the concept of punishment was as easily understood by the dog as by any penitent human. Punishment, guilt and forgiveness were as central to the dog's view of the world—as hardwired into his soul—as that of any prostrating monk. Damien began watching the door, waiting for a glimpse of Seville. Waiting, also, with pathetic fervor, for a chance to please, for a chance to reduce the odious punishment that the man saw fit to inflict for reasons that remained, to Damien, unknowable. There are dogs that don't care to please—spoiled dogs, and dogs bred for a churlish indifference to their owners' wishes, often mistakenly called "nobility"—but Damien and his kind did care. The pit bull was convinced; if he could just somehow please this unappeasable alpha, things would be better. He tried at every opportunity.

The tempo of the "aversive stimuli" delivered to the subject animals increased as the study progressed. Electrical stimulation originating in the floor grids was joined by electrical shock applied through the food and water dispensers. When driven to desperation by hunger and thirst, Damien would approach the receptacles, weighing the possibility of a shocked tongue against his insistent need. Most of the time his anxiety was needless, but randomly—always randomly—he would receive a shock on his sensitive tongue and recoil grunting to the far end of the cage until his hunger or thirst drove him forward again.

The hellish existence took its toll. Damien and the other dogs began to exhibit the stereotypic movements the men had worked to produce. Damien weaved in his small cage, pacing rhythmically back and forth, creating for himself, by his repeated actions, a world of mercifully predictable movement, predictable pattern, predictable sensory input.

Having produced the desired behavior they needed for their study, the scientists now began injecting the dogs with a variety of psychostimulant drugs, testing their effectiveness in reducing the induced stereotyped behavior. At times the effect of the mind-altering drugs reduced the subject's natural inhibitions, and Damien lost control of his reactions. At those times, when the men needed to handle the bulldog while gathering samples or administering pharmaceuticals, they used great caution. The dog had never actually bitten or even attempted to bite a human, yet because of his appearance he had developed an undeserved reputation for "fierceness" which followed him to each new location. When the psychostimulants entered his bloodstream however, the results were dramatic and unpredictable, and twice he descended into a mindless rage which lasted several minutes. For Damien the experience had a surreal quality to it, and finding himself growling at the white-coated gods—even biting at them—was confusing and frightening. It felt so wrong when he resisted and lashed out at these men that, while he recovered from the effects of the injected chemicals, he would lie blinking up at the scientists, deeply ashamed and quivering with conflict.

Chase, a favored grad student of Seville's, objected to the use of the pit bull for any reason. "He's going to kill someone—look at that," he shouted from across the room as Seville and Tom struggled with the animal during one of his drug-induced frenzies. They were trying to draw blood from a vein in the front leg, and Damien, glassy-eyed in his confusion and fright was struggling on the end of the noose stick held by Tom. "It's a freakin' *pit bull*, for God's sake."

"Shut up, Chase," Seville said conversationally. "Hand me that syringe—*if* you're not afraid to come over here." He had grabbed the dog's front leg and was applying the tourniquet. Chase swore under his breath and edged closer.

"Well, I don't have Divine Protection like Tommy, and I don't have your damn good luck, that's all. Here." He handed the syringe to Seville, who took it, deftly slid it into the bucking dog's vein and slowly withdrew the blood. When it was filled he held the syringe in place with one hand as he undid the clamp holding the tourniquet with the other.

"No, you don't have my good luck." Seville slid the syringe out and pinched off the injection site for a moment. "Or my good looks." Finished, he stepped back as Tom wrestled the dog back into the cage. "You just stick to the electronics, leave the dangerous work to Tom and me." His tone was mocking, and Chase shot a glance at Tom to make sure he wasn't smiling at the exchange.

"Yeah, and someday while you and Tommy-boy are out and about, that bastard gets his cage door open. Then you're out one good programmer, right? Is it worth it?"

Seville attended to his sample. "Are you really that worried about it?" he said without turning around.

"*Yeah*, I'm that freakin' worried about it. That freakin' dog is crazy. He gets out, we're toast. I don't think it's that far-fetched, do you? Say Tom didn't shut the door just right? I just don't see the point, you know, of having a dog like *that*."

Seville glanced over at the dog. The scientist knew the dog was really only frightened and disorientated; had it wanted to bite him or Tom, it certainly could have many times over the past weeks. He considered the dog for several moments, sensing the real concern on the part of his grad student, and amused by the thought that Chase was larger and more than likely stronger than either he or Tom, yet he was the one frightened by dogs. A tiny smile played on his lips. He wondered if Tom, who despised the grad student, *had* ever been tempted to leave the gate ajar. Certainly Chase was thinking about the possibility.

There was no question the dog would stay; it was a small favor requested by his friend, Viktor Hoffman. "The dog stays, Chase. In the meantime, if I were you, I wouldn't piss Tom off quite so often, uhm?"

Later that afternoon Seville forgot about the conversation, distracted by an unexpected uprising on the part of August D. Kotch, his nemesis from Ohio State University, in the form of the unforeseen publishing of a paper in the *Journal of Experimental Psychology: Animal Behavior Processes.*

"Oh Jesus, look at this," Seville complained to no one in particular, slapping the journal he held aloft. He took the journals primarily to skim them, keeping an eye open for any sign of his Ohio nemesis. "You *know* Kotch is going to make a bid for the Netherlands with *this*. He stopped, too disgusted evidently to finish his thought. Taking a drag on his cigarette, he stood contemplating the journal and shaking his head.

"What's he saying now?" Chase asked from where he was working at a computer.

"It's more of his usual bullshit. How can this stuff be 'peer reviewed'? How does he get this stuff into a *scientific* journal?"

"Maybe he's sleeping with the editor," Chase offered helpfully. "Well, what's it going to be this time? Are you going to get out the poison pen, or take more direct action? He's thrown down a glove, and if he gets to that symposium, and you don't, it's not going to set well with you—you know that."

Seville didn't answer but crossed to a desk and sat against its edge, looking out into the room with an expression half thoughtful, half disgusted. "No, it won't," he said to himself quietly. "No, it won't." His rivalry with August Kotch had developed years before, when the youthful Seville's flippant rebuttal to a statement put forth by the senior investigator in the prestigious *Journal of Behavior* had sparked a strong, swift, and unforgivably condescending response from Kotch. Much to the amusement of their fellow journal readers, the two men had assailed each other mercilessly for half a year. Since that time, neither man missed an opportunity to throw the harpoon at the first sight of the other's bared flesh.

The point of contention between the two men was trivial, unimportant to any but the most academic of behavioral researchers. For Seville, the larger issue was Kotch's perceived impertinence manifested in his dogged continuance of the running dispute and the manner in which he went out of his way to ridicule Seville's views. Very few things were as important to Joseph

Seville as getting the last word, so his being invited to the Netherlands was not nearly as important as Kotch's not going. If it wasn't for Kotch, he wouldn't even bother to apply. Now though, he reflected with grim humor, he must get there, or perish in the attempt.

It was time to divert some time and energy into an appropriate response. He really couldn't think of anything he had going that was more pressing than keeping Kotch from being insufferable at a symposium.

For the most part, Seville did as he pleased, influenced by very few people. As the only son of a New York real estate millionaire, money was simply not a factor in what he did or did not do in life. He had earned his degrees simply because he wanted them (his now deceased father having called the dozen year effort—accurately—a "whim"), and then, having obtained them, he felt not in the least like applying his skills to the dry arena of clinical practice.

Having discovered early on a certain flair for grant writing, Seville quickly found a comfortable and satisfying niche in the world of research. Armed with a strong ego and a sharp wit, he cared little for advancing his rank, for his goals were quite different from many of his peers. So long as he was surrounded by subordinates he was content. As long as the venue of behavioral research gave him an opportunity to exercise his formidable mind and his passion for the manipulation of behavior, he had no further demands of his profession. He viewed with disdain the efforts of his less affluent peers to struggle eternally for increased status and funding, or even more preposterously, their quests for that one earth shattering breakthrough moment of "pure science" which they spoke of as if it hovered before them like a shimmering Grail. It was easier and much more enjoyable his way.

He did as he liked within his domain, a world insulated by special privilege from the ordinary standards of the real world. With federal law exempting research facilities from normal accountability where animal cruelty is concerned, his work could be as imaginative as he could make it and still go uninterrupted. Having taken the Director of Animal Resources as his lover, he had availed himself of an additional layer of protection.

"Sir, don't forget you told Dr. Novak you would meet her at four o'clock." Tom spoke up from where he was preparing to leave. "And you might want to look over the order on your desk from Plusco, so I can send it out in the morning." Tom hesitated. "And, remember it's Christina's birthday on Tuesday."

Stirred from his brooding, Seville glanced at his watch and gave a non-committal grunt as answer. "Where are you going?" Chase asked in a tone which implied, as always, that he assumed Tom's leaving was some sort of scam.

"I'm going to pick up the AL600 from the shop. Would you mind feeding and cleaning up the dogs tonight?"

Chase frowned. By making the request in front of Seville, Tom had definitely trapped him. What irked Chase was knowing that despite the innocent expression, Tom *knew* he had trapped him. There was nothing now but to make a brave face of it, and not let the aide know how annoyed he was.

"Sure Tom, you know I will."

What Tom knew, as he exited a few moments after Seville, was that the dogs would more likely than not go without any food that night.

Months had passed, and it seemed to Damien that his life had never consisted of anything but this time, this place, these people and this madness. Then, suddenly, mercifully, the shocks, injections and blood draws all stopped. The study was over, but Damien could not know that. He knew only that the other dogs were taken away and he was now the lone occupant of the dog room. It is doubtful whether Damien should have felt gratitude toward Viktor Hoffman for his desire to keep him alive, thus discharging the man's perceived debt. The ethologist had not been by to see Damien since his transfer to Seville's lab; he had, however, asked after him several times, reassured that Damien was finding equitable treatment in his friend's hands.

Damien's soul quivered with exhaustion. His sleep was always troubled, for even though the floor had stopped its sharp and frightening shocks, it was still not to be trusted. Damien sat in his metal world, forty inches by thirty inches, while days went by.

He waited for The One.

She would come soon, he had only to wait.

Damien was left alone now, attended to only morning and evening by Tom, who fed him and cleaned his cage without a word. The men in the lab were preoccupied with their upcoming fall vacations. There being no real work to do in the last few days before they left, researchers from other labs dropped by to visit, sitting on stools and smoking (against building regulations) and drinking coffee while Tom cleaned and repaired equipment and smiled politely at their witticisms.

Seville left for his annual autumn dove-hunting trip to Mexico, accompanied by the Director of Animal Resources, who had Elizabeth Fletcher's written allegations against the researcher tucked away in her briefcase. Chase and his girlfriend left to windsurf the frigid waters of the Columbia River gorge. Tom, as usual, said nothing of his plans. A place for the dog had to be found, and Seville's aide received permission to temporarily house Damien in the main kennel, until the men returned.

Back in the main kennel ward again, Damien hunched up at the rear of the dog run and waited. His days were filled with waiting. He waited for The One. He waited for Seville. Seville was the alpha, the leader, the dominant being in his world now, and it was natural that the dog's thoughts revolved around him. Damien's pack instinct demanded he find and obey the dominance hierarchy of his world, and he was trying. But he thought about the girl too, most often when a distant door opened or some other sound made his ears prick up and his eyes raise in hopeful and patient expectation. She would come. He was unable to doubt.

He ate little and he began to chew his front foot. He had to do something, some work, some motion, some *thing.* That was all that was left now; all his drive, all his energy and life force, all his intelligence and curiosity, all the splendid power of the young bulldog was denied a useful outlet, and yet it *must* come out. So he chewed his left front foot, whimpering softly sometimes at the pain, until the techs came and put a large plastic cone collar around his neck, and then even *that* was denied him. No one noticed he could no longer access his automatic water device because the large cone collar kept his square muzzle too far back from the nozzle. Damien, finding nothing unusual in this deprivation, stoically hunched up in his corner. He waited through days filled only with his thirst and the incessant barking of the other inmates.

By the sixth day, with the cone on his head and no ability to drink water, Damien no longer sat upright in his corner. He slouched down limply into a little heap and waited patiently in that position. The barking of the dogs around him was now a strangely soothing background noise. A technician, noticing his uneaten food, checked the dog over but found nothing obviously amiss. Observing that the animal was under an admin-hold authorized by the director, she shrugged and went her way.

The next morning when the kennel door was pulled open he did not hear it. When he saw a dark shadow loom beside him through the side of the white plastic cone that obscured his vision, he pulled back weakly. As a hand reached out, hesitantly, and touched him, he flinched away without meaning too. It would be Seville or Tom, and he wistfully hoped they would take the irksome cone off his head. He hoped they gave him some water.

The hands were touching him gently but he couldn't stop his skin from twitching and anxiously pulling away out of habit. The hands took the cone off, and he was grateful for that. Then suddenly—he couldn't trust his hot, dry nose—he turned his head and saw, kneeling beside him, the familiar form of the girl. He crawled into her lap then and buried his broad head in her stomach, whimpering like a cur dog in his delight. His cries grew in strength while Elizabeth crushed him to her, gently trying to hush him while wiping at her own eyes and nose.

He knocked Elizabeth over and trampled her as she struggled to rise. For the first time in his life he turned upside down and wriggled like a puppy in front of her. She rubbed his chest, grabbed at his wildly flailing legs, and kissed him again and again when his head happened to come anywhere near her. Then, very quickly, Damien was exhausted. He lay, grunting with pure pleasure, with his head in her lap and his eyes on her face.

"She got you moved, Buddy! That is *so* awesome." She gave his neck a little squeeze and he responded with a backward tipping of his head. "It pays to have friends in high places, huh?" She wished long life and blessings on Dr. Novak and all her generations. "You're a sight, though. Look at you; you're almost as thin as when you first got here. What are these techs *thinking* of?" At the anger in her voice the dog thumped his tail on the kennel floor and writhed, discomforted by her tone, but knowing it wasn't directed at him. They sat like that for a while; Damien dozed in contentment and exhaustion, his head still in her lap while her hand lay on his broad head. Then the girl stood up, suddenly, forcefully.

"I'll be right back, Damie, I'm going to get you some food."

The pit bull struggled up and crept along behind her as she went to the kennel door. He pushed at her legs, trying desperately to exit the cage with her.

"No, Damien, I'm sorry, you stay here, I promise I'll I be right back. *I promise.*"

Damien didn't stop, he struggled against her, pushing and twisting in his effort to get out the kennel door.

"God, Damien, *please* stop. Don't make this any harder. I *can't* let you out. I'll be *right* back."

Stricken, Damien fell back on his side of the gate and looked up at her with pleading eyes.

She was gone over half an hour, but when she came back she smuggled in an astounding variety of goods under her coat. As she sat down she took a bag from under her coat and looked with concern at several spots of watery vomitus on the kennel floor that hadn't been there when she left.

"Here, this is what you need." She unwrapped a gigantic cheeseburger and broke it into small pieces, offering it to Damien. The dog sniffed it warily, but then seemed unsure what to do.

"Come on, eat it," she prompted while Damien looked at the food hungerly. He wanted it, but it seemed an awful risk to reach for it. There was no telling what might happen. He had been shocked so many times in connection with food or drink he never did either now without great deliberation.

Damien reached out gently and took the offered food.

"*Good* dog. That's it."

When he finished the first burger, she produced a second. "This one's a *bacon* cheeseburger," she told him significantly. He ate that too. "You're probably thirsty too—check this out!" She proudly produced, from under the same coat, a small vanilla shake. "You're going to *love* this." With his plastic collar removed, Damien had slaked his thirst during Elizabeth's absence. He had thrown up the water repeatedly until his stomach settled, but now he was better prepared for the creamy shake, and lapped it up as quickly as she could pour it into the top of the cardboard container the cheeseburger had come in.

"For dessert, sir!" Elizabeth produced a NuttyGooie bar and several sticks of beef jerky. She held them out for the dog to see. Damien snatched the candy bar from her hand.

"Hey! Where's your Emily Post?" She leaned forward to take it back, and then paused. She watched with interest as the dog carefully unwrapped the candy bar using his teeth and paws. "You're pretty smart," she said with respect. When there was nothing left to eat she cleaned up the mess and, taking off her coat, stashed the wrappers under it by the cage door. She sat down beside him again and picked up his front foot. Damien went rigid and turned his head away.

"This is really bad. *Why* are you doing this? You're hurting yourself." She tapped his foot with her finger. "Now you *stop that*, do you hear me? It's *bad*," she said severely. Damien's eyes jumped about guiltily, his little dog eyebrows shifting with them, and he flattened his ears. He understood that she was angry about his foot and he felt burning shame. He kept shooting guilty glances from the foot in her hand, then straight ahead, to sideways at her eyes until she set the foot down and laughed. "God, you're so silly."

Her forgiveness made Damien ache with pleasure. The presence of The One here, treating him gently, speaking to him and laying her hand on his head; his contentment was monumental.

When Elizabeth got up to leave Damien struggled up and again tried to push out the gate along with her. She scolded him, promised to return with more food and, taking the plastic cone collar with her, she left.

She was faithful in her visitations. She came every day, and every day she brought him food. He watched expectantly as she produced an astonishing variety of contraband from under her coat. She brought him raw liver, packets of raw hamburger, chewable dog vitamin tablets, plastic containers of cottage cheese and always a NuttyGooie bar. Her presence revived his flagging spirits, and the food he accepted from her revived his body. Waiting for The One to come each day became his obsession, his work. He would sit now at the front of the kennel, leaning into the gate trying to watch down the hall in the direction she came from. He no longer gnawed his foot—he was too busy watching for her. He reluctantly retreated before the cleaning hoses morning and night, the only abandonment of his post. He even lay, in the middle of his brightly lit night, with his head upon his outstretched paws, waiting for a glimpse of her arrival.

With Dr. Novak away on leave, Elizabeth was unable to ask her about the future plans for the dog. In the meantime, she came as often as she could that week, sitting in the harsh din of the incessant barking with the dog's head on her thigh. Sometimes she read her lessons to him, more often she just stroked him gently and wondered where he would be going next.

Tom arrived early the following Monday morning and, slipping a lead over Damien's head, returned the dog to Joseph Seville's laboratory. It was no surprise that Dr. Katharine Novak's investigation, conducted poolside with follow-up in various hotel rooms in Mexico, had turned up no breach of protocol.

CHAPTER SIX

No one suspects the days to be gods.
—EMERSON

H i, Daddy."
Seville turned around quickly, a look of genuine pleasure crossing his ascetic face. "How's my little Ninky?" he said, nodding a dismissal to Tom standing in the doorway behind her. His aide had gone down to meet her at the security desk where her mother dropped her off on the third Friday of every month, and had brought her up to the lab. In an arrangement which worked well for everyone, Seville would drop his daughter off at her private school on Monday morning, the two parents tactfully not having to meet.

Tom disappeared—he was let off early on these Fridays—and the little girl skipped into the room without a backward glance. "Fine," she answered her father in her piping seven-year-old's voice. She came to where Seville was standing beside his desk, looking narrow-eyed at the latest edition of the *Journal of Experimental Psychology*, which included a strongly supportive letter from Tufts University commenting on Kotch's previous article. Seville's name was mentioned, and not in a capacity of particular respect. It was insufferable. Seville heaved a long sigh directed at the journal in his hand and then reached down, hugging his daughter to his leg with his free arm as she looked up at him brightly. She had his startling light gray eyes. "What are you doing?" she asked.

"Working." He held her out at arm's length with his hand on her shiny brown hair and inspected her.

"I got my ears pierced."

"Yes you did. It makes you look very grown up."

"It hurt."

"I imagine it did. Piercing body parts with sharp objects usually does. Did you cry?"

"I don't know," she said evasively. She thrust her right hand out, palm down, fingers spread. "I got a ring too." An inexpensive child's ring was on her middle finger.

"Uhm. Who gave that to you?"

"Bob."

"Bob, huh?"

"Yes—and he said he's going to get me a kitten too."

Seville tossed the magazine down on his desk. He felt assailed from all sides. "That's nice," he said dryly. "Now look, I've got to go next door and start a backup and take care of some equipment. I want you to sit right here, on this stool, and wait for me. I'll be back in just a minute. Will you do that for me?"

"OK." She climbed up on the stool and sat down.

"Now I mean it, Christina. You stay right there till I get back. Right in this *room.*" He deftly changed the terms to something he felt was more obtainable.

"Uh huh." There was less commitment than he would have liked to have heard in her voice. He left the room, glancing back over his shoulder. His daughter sat on the stool, angelic, her bright, intelligent eyes already moving about the room. The moment the door shut behind him Christina hopped off the stool and walked along the counter, exploring everything. She noticed several instruments at the end of the counter, clustered around a large surge-protector strip. She looked at the electronic equipment, her eyes drawn to all the switches and toggles. She reached out and hit a few of the toggles. She did it again. When she had seen everything on the table she turned and saw before her the doors that led to the two animal rooms. She crossed the room and looked through the narrow window in the near door. Inside she could see dogs. Delighted, she hurried into the room.

Her father was very strict about letting her see his dogs and it annoyed her. She loved animals and yet he refused to even let her enter the rooms where they were kept. She did so now with clear determination; she wanted to pet the dogs.

She approached the first metal cage and looked at the gold and black striped pit bull standing in the stainless-steel box he lived in.

"Hi," she said.

Damien was frozen in place. His whole existence centered on the people who came through that door. The men who came into this room came for the purpose of doing *something* to him. He knew all the men, and the very occasional women who came, and what they were likely to do to him. But here was someone new. Someone strange and puzzling. She was so small and very strange in manner. He did not remember children from the time before he was lost in the forest. He had seen none since.

Christina wanted to pet the dog. She slipped her small hand through the bars but Damien retreated to the back of the cage. He was reluctant to allow any human, in this place, to touch him. Undaunted, Christina quickly figured out the cage latch and swung the door open.

"Hi," she said again.

Her scent came to the dog in a wave.

Seville.

This little human was his—was *of* him. The dog tried to back further away in growing alarm as Christina crawled into the cage with him. Damien knew nothing of the special shared sense of fun between dogs and kids, he knew only that The Voice was telling him that this young thing, like a puppy, could not be harmed.

Having crawled inside the cage, Christina sat up beside the dog and began to stroke his neck and powerful shoulders. She liked the feel of his warm, sleek fur and she was unaware of Damien tensing beneath her touch. Inside the small metal cage the girl was very close and Damien felt trapped and uncertain. Yet still, he felt no real fear. After several moments of uncertainty, the dog relaxed enough to lower his head and sniff her face and hair in curiosity.

"That tickles!" Christina cried, pushing his broad head away with her hand. "Don't!" But she laughed and kept petting him. Damien's mouth pulled back in a dog's grin, and he sat quietly, enduring her attention with a thoughtful and patient expression on his grim face. The child pleased him.

The door to the room jerked open and both the dog and the child startled at the sound. Seville stood looking in, his eyes wide with alarm. At the sight of his daughter in the cage with the pit bull, crowded up against the dog, forcing her attention on him, the color left his face.

"Christina," he breathed. He lunged forward and jerked the child free of the cage by her upper arm. The sight had badly frightened him, and his fear made him angry. *"What do you think you're doing?"* he said in a loud and angry tone, shaking the girl by the arm.

Christina was scared. Her father rarely raised his voice to her, but she knew from experience that his temper could be sudden and severe. His intense emotion frightened her and she pulled back, bursting into abrupt tears. He continued to hold her upper arm and he bent his face near hers. *"What were you thinking?* Do you want to get bitten—or *worse?"* he persisted in a loud and angry tone at the sobbing child.

Damien had shrunk back at the sudden appearance of the man in the doorway. Now, however, the sight of the angry man handling the child in such a manner touched him deeply in his soul and a visceral reaction raised him to his feet. The Voice allowed no hesitation, no time to consider *what* he was doing, nor to *whom,* and Damien came forward in the cage, teeth bared savagely. He stopped at the edge of the open cage door, warning the man to release his aggressive hold on the child.

"Jesus!" With one quick motion Seville swept the cage door shut against the dog's rigid form, and made fast the latch. He hurried from the room, his daughter in his arms. Once he was in the outer office he set the crying child down. The man's chest was rising and falling rapidly beneath his shirt. The grim vision of the dog snarling from the cage stayed with him. Though nothing *had* happened, he did not feel gratitude; he only felt lucky that he had gotten there in time. He thought of the dog's powerful, wide jaws and short, heavy neck. In a flash his clinical mind saw what *could* have happened—what he *thought* had nearly happened but for his intervention. Seville's paternal instinct rose up against the animal, against his image of the dog's teeth flashing after his daughter's soft flesh as he pulled her to safety. Something horrible could have happened so easily—because of the dog. Chase had been correct, the dog was far too dangerous to have in the lab. Angrily, and in vengeance for the fear he felt, he swore to himself he would have the dog destroyed.

Seville knelt down and held his daughter at arm's length before him. "That was very, *very* close, Christina." He tousled her hair, thinking about what Lori, his ex-wife, would say if she found out he had left the child unattended in the lab. "Come on, don't cry, he didn't get you. You're safe; but you understand *now* why I tell you to stay away from these dogs?" The girl's crying was dwindling down to sniffling broken by an occasional sob. "Come on, Ninky, let's go home." Standing up, he piloted his daughter out of the office door and pulled it tight behind him.

In his metal cage, Damien watched the door for several moments and then lay down with a deep sigh. He was surprised at himself. He had growled at the alpha. He felt unsettled and uneasy and lay, his head on his paws, watching the door long after the sounds of the man and child leaving had faded.

After dropping his daughter off at her school on Monday, Joseph Seville walked into his lab and into the inner workroom that contained the dog cages. Staring at the brindle pit bull's broad head and powerful shoulders, he again experienced the sharp stab of anxiety he had felt when he perceived his daughter to be at the mercy of this dog. He never thought about his research animals outside of the context of the experiments in which they were utilized, but the image of this dog had haunted him all weekend. His phone conversation with Viktor Hoffman on Saturday had not given him the satisfaction he desired.

"Bastard," Seville said quietly through gritted teeth and turned away. In the outer office he addressed Tom. "I want that dog out of the lab—*stat*—Hoffman's pit bull." He pointed toward the dog room with his chin. "Viktor doesn't want the damn thing dead, so figure out where he wants it put. Do it *now*." He crossed to the hall door and opened it, nearly running into Chase, who was trying to back into the room while carrying a monstrous latte cup with a maple bar balanced on top in one hand, and a shoe box full of computer discs in the other. Seville stormed past him, leaving Chase swearing in his wake.

"What's his freaking problem this morning?" he asked Tom.

Tom let out his breath then shrugged. "I'm not really sure. He wants the pit bull gone."

"'Bout time! Did he get bit?"

"I don't know. He just told me to move it. I don't know what happened."

"Well some*thing* did, huh? He's going to be a pisser all day, that's for sure." Chase moved off, smiling wickedly to himself. He went into the computer room and slammed the door shut behind him.

Tom stood for a moment, unsure what to do. Seville appeared to be gone, and he couldn't begin to guess when he would return. He had no idea where to take the dog, but his boss had been explicit—the dog was to be removed *now*.

He crossed to the dog room and took a lead down from the rack on the wall. He would just get the dog out and then try to find either Professor Hoffman or Dr. Novak. He slipped the lead over the dog's head and stepped back with a wary expression as the animal exited the cage. He didn't trust the dog and he walked stiffly, his arm holding the lead out straight and rigid in case the dog lunged for him, and headed for Viktor Hoffman's office.

I expected you, Thomas, come in son, come in." Hoffman waved him to the chair, quickly moving a few items from the seat before he seated himself again. "Joe called me on Saturday and said the dog went after his daughter." Addressing the dog he added, "I guess we need to find another place for you, eh boy?" He snapped his fingers at the pit bull, who stood alone between the two men, unwilling to respond to the friendly overture. The time for trust, and any possible friendship between the two, was past. "Surprises me what an unfriendly cuss he's turned out to be; just won't warm up. Well, never mind, I can find a place for him to live out his life. Joe's pretty hot at me for not letting him euthanize the dog, but I don't think that's necessary, do you? I mean if we can put the dog somewhere safely, I would just feel better about it. So let's try that, why don't we?"

While Tom and the dog waited, Hoffman called Novak's office. She was in and they were to come right over. It caused a bit of a scene when they entered with the dog. Novak stepped out of her office to wave them in.

"I'm sorry Viktor, I've been on the phone and I didn't have time to let the staff know you were coming. Come right in." Hoffman entered and seated himself, while Tom remained standing by the door with the dog. Novak glanced at the dog while she seated herself at the desk. "This is obviously the dog Joe spoke of this weekend. What do you have in mind, Viktor?"

"I need a place to put the dog for now, long-term really, until I can come up with other arrangements. It didn't work out in my colony. I just need time to come up with some student project that he could be utilized in, or find some other staff member that would take him. So for now, I'm looking to place him in some kind of facility where he would be out of the way."

Novak nodded and looked again at the dog standing beside Tom.

"Joe says the dog attacked his daughter."

"That's right. I understand the child entered the dog's cage. She wasn't bitten, however."

"Joe was very upset. Wouldn't it be better in the long run to just euthanize it?"

Hoffman's nod had in it both reluctant consent and steadfast resistance. "Yes, it would. I have a reason for not wanting to euthanize the animal if at all feasible. Obviously, if there were to be another incident I would, of course, destroy the dog myself."

"I see. Well, by the look of things this morning you need a place rather urgently, don't you? I was rather surprised to hear the dog was still around, to be honest with you. After speaking with Joe I assumed it wouldn't be leaving his lab alive." She smiled at this observation of her lover's disposition.

"Joe's a good guy—I had asked him specifically not to terminate the dog for any reason, and he honored his word. Understand, if the dog had actually bitten the child, I wouldn't have hesitated to let Joe euthanize it. But I think perhaps this was a case of an undersocialized dog being exposed to a precocious child with predictable results. I'm not excusing the actions of the animal, but I'd like to give Damien one more chance before we look at termination as an option."

"Tom, did you see what happened?" Novak asked.

"No, ma'am."

"Did Joe mention any details to you?"

"No, ma'am. I didn't even know what I just heard you say."

"Well Viktor, certainly I can accommodate you somehow. Let me think." She picked up her phone and dialed. She had a one-sided conversation while the men listened and Damien curled up in a ball at Tom's feet with a sigh.

"Gloria, I need a kennel for a dog, something long-term and out of the way. Yes. Yes, that will do. All right, I'm sending an aide down with the dog now; meet him and show him where you want it. All right." She hung up. "If Tom will take the dog to the Long Term Holding facility, Gloria will meet you there. Do you know where that's located? There are three separate buildings there. Gloria will meet you in the center building." She turned to Hoffman. "He'll be fine there for as long as you need. If you have any problems, ask for Gloria, she'll be able to help you."

Viktor stood to go. "Thank you, Katharine."

Novak stood up and moved with him toward the door. She stopped short of Tom and the dog, staring at Damien intently. "Viktor, is this the dog that a girl named Elizabeth Fletcher was interested in?"

Hoffman was surprised. "Why, yes. This is the same dog. How do you know about that?"

"The girl came here, asking about him."

"Asking about him? Asking what?"

"She wanted to see the dog. I told her no."

"Really?" He nodded, taken aback. "Well, she's formed an excessive fondness for the dog and I had to warn her to stay away from him. She can be a little impetuous."

"Well, she's not staying away from the dog, she is actively looking for it. I told her that I was not going to disclose the dog's location because of what had happened when the dog was in your possession. When Joe and I discussed this, he informed me about what happened at your enclosure." She directed her next question to Tom. "Has she been hanging around Joe's lab? Have you seen her there?"

"Just once, a while ago. I've not seen her back."

"If you see her Tom, you let me know. It's important."

"I will."

"Well," Viktor said, "I doubt she'll find the dog over in Long Term. And even if she does, there really isn't any harm done, I just thought it best to discourage that kind of attachment to a research animal. It's for her own good, really, she's a medical student."

"I think she may be more trouble than you think, Viktor. She is intent on interfering. If there's any more trouble, I'll pull her as a handler."

"Even if she did find the dog over in Long Term, she'll just fade away in time. What can she complain about?"

"Perhaps you're right, Viktor. Tom, you know where you're going? Fine, then I think this is settled."

The Long Term facilities were located in three brick buildings set side by side, each housing forty-four kennels along one wall. Here dogs used in long-term studies were held until they either died or were "sacrificed" according to research protocol. The dogs in the building Tom and Gloria entered were all victims of toxicology, oncology and nuclear medicine research, a quiet bunch; many hardly looked up as the three passed by. Some of the dogs in this building would stay in their kennels for months; some would stay for years. None would leave except by death.

They walked down the cement hallway to the very last kennel and Tom guided the pit bull into it. Gloria closed the kennel door, posted his kennel card and a red caution sign next to it, and then they left. Both the sides and back of his kennel were cinder block that had once been painted white, but which were now darkened with untold years of use. The gate was chain link, misshapen and coated with hair and filth. An empty food bowl sat in a holder by the door, and an automatic watering nozzle, like the one in the main kennel ward, hung at the back of the kennel. Damien eyed it critically. He was not sufficiently thirsty to risk trying it yet. He cat footed to the rear of the cage. The floor was cement, not a metal grid, but so traumatized had he been by the random floor shocks he had received, he no longer trusted any floor. After a moment he gingerly lay down.

Moving only his eyes, Damien remained still for several hours. The kennel cleaner came and for an hour there was that to occupy his mind, then the cleaner left and it was night. This kennel block had no windows, and the lights were turned off at night.

He awoke abruptly in the early morning with a frightened grunt. In his dream he was still at the veterinarian's lab and Seville had been approaching from the outer office, coming for him. The dog could hear his steady tread. The very sound of the man's approaching footsteps had frozen Damien's soul. There was sufficient terror in the nightmare to wake the dog, and Damien raised his head in the absolute silence and darkness of the hallway, scenting and listening. There was no suggestion of Seville in this room. No sound of his approach, no lingering odor of his cigarettes. Damien laid his head back down again, waiting for the light and activity that signaled morning.

The next day Damien learned the entire routine for his kennel block. The cleaner came at seven, worked for an hour, then moved to another block. The young man wore headphones while he worked and hardly glanced at the dogs. After he left, nothing else happened. Unlike the main kennel, this one was rarely visited. On his first day there no one came until seven P.M., when the cleaner came again. The day was made of waiting. The inmates lacked even changing light and weather to mark the time. It was always either lit, or black. It was always sixty-nine degrees. It was monumentally tedious. Damien spent most of the first day getting up the nerve to touch the food bowl and water nozzle. Later, the cleaner came again, finished his cleaning and left. The lights went off and it was night again.

The director had been sympathetic but firm. Reassuring Elizabeth that the dog was removed from Seville's use, Novak had steadfastly refused to discuss or provide any information on its location or utilization. Elizabeth had Novak's own word that the animal was being treated according to the University's—and her own strict personal—standards of care. Reluctantly, Elizabeth let herself be reassured.

As to Dr. Joseph Seville, Dr. Novak had further assured Elizabeth that she would continue to take a personal role in the monitoring of all his research, assuring that his work was within the University's protocol standards. Novak had thanked her graciously for bringing "all this" to her attention, and then she had sent her on her way.

Elizabeth was appreciative, and quite impressed with the level of consideration shown to her complaint, but she knew a dismissal when she heard one. The woman had done her a huge favor, seeing to it herself that the dog was removed from Seville's use. Elizabeth vowed to return to her studies with a clear and focused mind; removed from Seville's lab, Damien no longer needed her help.

But there was a nag in the back of her mind.

Where on the University grounds, in what research capacity, would Damien really be "all right"? Try as she might, she could only see Damien as she had recently found him, hungry and lonely in the main kennel. Was *that* the kind of care Novak was guaranteeing?

She worked desperately to convince herself that she had stepped in and saved Damien from use in a uniquely abusive situation. Once removed from that particular circumstance, wasn't it unlikely that he would end up somewhere like *that* again?

Wasn't it?

She thought a lot about resigning as a handler. Every day that she went to the ARC building brought the question of Damien's welfare to her mind. If the truth be told, she *could* use the extra time to study. This was her third year of premed, and things were getting tough. Her physics class was proving to be the most difficult challenge of her academic career. Instead of quitting her handler job, however, she cut her schedule way back, maintaining the minimum hours allowed, and spending that time in the main kennel only. She had happened upon Damien there before, and it still seemed the most likely place to run into the dog again.

The Thanksgiving holiday came, and Dave invited Tony to dinner. Elizabeth shrugged at the news, leaving Dave blinking in her wake, shaking his head as a father will. She spent hours decorating the house the night before, and in the morning she came out of the kitchen only long enough to hand out refreshed bowls of snacks or to place items on the dining room table. Wisely, the men opted to use the wet bar in the living room rather than seek to penetrate her kitchen at this critical time.

When she called them to the table her father remarked as an aside to Tony that she looked rather like an obstetrician who had just delivered their first breech baby, but the table that awaited them was spectacular and the men were impressed.

After the meal, when she had cleared the dishes and squared away the kitchen, Elizabeth joined them in the living room, where the gas fire had been lit, and the buzzing sound of a football post-game show turned low on the television gave the room a comfortable feel. As she entered she was the object of much admiration and praise.

"Well, well! That was your best yet," Bill asserted as she came to sit beside him. She was wearing a simple royal blue dress, and she slipped off her shoes and pulled her feet up under her.

"Thanks, Bill. But remember, you picked that turkey out."

"Ah, yes! That took great skill!"

Tony admonished her. "Don't be so modest, you cook *very* well. You'll make someone a great little wife slash heart surgeon someday!"

"Thanks Tone." She *was* pleased. She knew the dinner had turned out well and she enjoyed the compliments on what indeed had been quite a feat. Even though she enjoyed cooking, it was always more enjoyable to cook for those who appreciated it. Surrounded by such capable and gifted men, it felt good to know that they admired her for her own particular talent. She couldn't help but wonder if someday they would admire her as much for her work as a cardiac surgeon.

Tony took courage at her unusually gentle tone. Never sure which Elizabeth he would encounter any more—the one who was impatient with him or the one that was gentle and kind, he made a move calculated to gain favor. "Did Elizabeth tell you about her grade point average in physics?"

Dave shook his head. "No. What is it?"

Beaming, Tony reported the news as if by the telling, he was somehow at least partially responsible for Elizabeth's grade point. "She's holding on to a perfect 4.0 this quarter. She's really been applying herself, and it's paid off. No one else in the class is touching her. In physics!"

"Tony!" Elizabeth was embarrassed, but obviously pleased. She had not mentioned it to her father or grandfather, but everyone present knew that she found physics difficult.

"That's wonderful Elizabeth, I *am* pleased. You were having trouble with that, weren't you?" Dave asked.

"A little, yes." His praise made her face warm, and she looked down, fiddling with a nonexistent spot on her dress. Her father's praise had always made her feel like a five-year-old child and she fervently hoped that someday it would not. "I just tried a little harder, that's all," she said more firmly.

"A change of heart?" Bill asked gently, giving her arm a little squeeze. She gave a tiny nod. "Yes, a little. I'm a little more focused, you know, on the end result than I think I was. It helps."

"One more year—think of it, Bill—and she'll be in medical school. Hard to believe eh?" Her father studied her keenly then tipped his glass in her direction. "Here's to *Dr.* Elizabeth Fletcher, third-generation cardiac surgeon." The other two men murmured assent, raised their glasses and ducked their heads in her direction. Uncomfortable to be the continuing focus of so much attention and praise, Elizabeth blushed again harder and looked down, pleased beyond words. At that moment she knew the comfortable feeling that comes from the contemplation of repaying in full a debt of gratitude. In another five years, on the day she handed her father her diploma, she felt she would at last be able to give him tangible evidence of that gratitude.

Curled up on the couch, her arm through her grandfather's arm, she was content to let the talk drift to medical matters again, leaving her to her own quiet thoughtfulness. Using her memory of the scanty photographic evidence left extant by her father, she tried to picture what her mother would look like, sitting across the room, beside her husband. Failing that, Elizabeth then wondered what advice a mother would give a daughter at this time in her life.

On the following Monday Bill was hanging around the door as she came in from school. Dave wouldn't be home for another hour and a half so, moving into the kitchen, Elizabeth stood staring into the refrigerator questing for the perfect before-dinner snack.

Bill sat down at the kitchen's island and folded his hands. Elizabeth glanced at him as she pulled some cheddar out and put it on the cutting board. *"What?"* she asked with mock exasperation and her grandfather, tickled by her perception, smiled.

"I've been wondering about something, but I'm not sure if it's any of my business."

"Does it have to do with me?"

"Yes."

"Well then of course it's your business. We haven't any secrets, right? What is it you want to know, grandpa?" She bent down out of sight a moment, rummaging for the crackers. "Do I love Tony?" Her voice came to him. "I can answer that; no. Have I ever smoked pot? No. Have I had an abortion? No. Do I *need* an abortion? No." She popped back up, crackers in hand.

"Do you really want to be a physician?"

The unexpected directness of the question killed any glib remark on her tongue. "Wow. What made you ask that?"

"You haven't answered."

No, she hadn't. So that was it; he *was* perceptive, and he had seen her hesitation, the quiet reluctance with which she embraced her chosen profession. Evidently he was going to call her on it. She stood for a moment, staring at him, and then she came to sit across from him. "I don't want you to worry about this. I *do* want to be the third Doctor Fletcher. I've thought about it a lot lately, I think you know that. And I won't tell you I haven't had my doubts, I'll bet you had some when you were in school. I bet dad did too. It's probably natural," she shrugged, "but I've thought it through—hard—the last few weeks, and I know this is right. I think I'll connect more as time goes on. Right now actually earning the degree seems sorta ethereal. It's a long way off."

"Shorter than you know, El. Time goes so much faster, the older you get. For me, it will seem like six months from now, and you'll be Dr. Elizabeth Fletcher, a cardiac surgeon, with your own practice, or maybe doing R&D with Dave, whatever you decide, but living your adult life, married maybe, and I'll be just sitting here, unchanged really, and seeing you in my mind's eye as a ten-year-old, or a fourteen-year-old, but never as what you are—a grown woman and a practicing physician."

"Geez, it's scary when you put it that way. I don't feel ready for that kind of responsibility. Someone's *life!* How do you ever get there?"

He shook his head dismissively. "It's steps. Small steps. And really knowing your field. You'll find that when you know the material, when you've seen cause and effect a few times, you start feeling more comfortable with making decisions on your own. But believe me kid, there is always self-doubt." He smiled wickedly and leaned his head toward hers, whispering conspiratorially, "Except for your father. There is never any doubt there." He shook his head. "Never was."

They laughed a little at that.

"I *was* kinda wavering, I'll tell you that. But I've thought about it and this is what I want. I can't wait to present a picture to dad of the three of us all standing in a row, all M.D.s. That will really make his day."

"Will it please *you*, that's all I'm asking. Your father wants you to be happy. You have to live your own life, and I just want to make sure that medicine is where your heart lies."

"I think so. I mean I don't *know* yet, I haven't really gotten into it yet. Maybe after I'm actually working in it I'll know more about how I feel."

"You have to know, Elizabeth. It's a huge commitment of time and energy. Six years into it is not a good time to change your mind. You've been around the R&D end of it for years. You know the work."

Elizabeth looked down. She knew that better than anyone. Her grandfather couldn't know the depth of her doubts, her hesitation about her commitment to medicine. But she was sure about one thing—her commitment to the two men who had raised her. "I won't change my mind. This is what I want."

She sat, looking at her place mat, pretending to be resolved while Bill sat staring at her, pretending to be convinced.

As Christmas approached, bringing with it the added pressures of finals, she could spare very little time to look for the brindle bulldog. Preparation for the dreaded physics final took up her evenings, and weekends she went shopping with Tony or worked on the house decorations. Bill was vowing to reach the 25,000 mark on individual lights outside—he was in fact, considering planting an additional tree in the front yard for no other reason than to cover it in lights—and Elizabeth wanted the interior to match the grandeur of the exterior.

The Pacific Northwest lowland climate, moderated by the warming influence of salt water, was far too mild to support frequent snowfall. Rarely occurring more than once or twice a year, snow was an event either much anticipated by those who delighted in it, or dreaded by those who loathed it. Some years passed altogether snowless, leaving children feeling cheated, and cautious drivers feeling blessed. When snow occurred near Christmas, it was an extraordinary event. The thought of snow *on* Christmas—an actual, official, White Christmas—was unimaginable.

Then the week before Christmas it snowed. Sunday night it began as a light sprinkling of tiny, icy pellets, and by midnight the fervent prayers of thousands of children were answered. The wind switched to the north, the temperature dropped low enough to freeze water and turn the ground iron-hard, and the precipitation turned to large, slow flakes that meant business. By morning the familiar landscape was transformed. The meanest streets were now glittering lanes, every rough edge smoothed by a twenty-inch blanket of snow.

In a climate where a dusting of snow caused school closures, this epic event shut the community down. Last-minute Christmas shoppers as well as store owners awoke to panic, children to absolute bliss, while everyone else agreed that while it *was* inconvenient, it did add to the Christmas spirit, and ventured out to enjoy the novelty.

Elizabeth set out to walk around the block. She was struck by the sense of community the snow brought. Neighbors who had never spoken to her waved. As she passed by, children shyly included her in their games of snowball, delighted when she fired back. She smiled at the unusual sight of cross-country skiers gliding silently down the street. Sleds, and the plastic disks which passed for sleds these days, were everywhere, but in her relatively level neighborhood they were useless. When an older kid appeared on a sputtering snowmobile, willing to tow the sleds, the morning peace was shattered. Elizabeth turned for home.

Nearing her front walk she saw something which made her hesitate. It was a man and a dog, coming toward her. She had seen the pair several times before in the neighborhood but never given them much thought. Now something about them stopped her, and held her. She watched them approach.

It was the most common-looking dog in the world, about fifty pounds, black, old and stilted in its walk. It had the look of a Labrador retriever crossed with a spaniel or perhaps a sheepdog. Its owner was equally common, an older man in dark overcoat and hat, stepping along with care, keeping to the shoveled portions of the sidewalk as much as possible. The two came on, slowly, carefully, and every fifteen or twenty feet the dog would glance up at the man's face, and she could see that he would glance back. There was an empathy between the two, visible even at a distance.

As they approached, Elizabeth knelt down to the dog by way of greeting to them both. She smiled and put out her hand. "Hi, how old is your dog?" she asked.

The man stopped, and the dog, caught off guard by this break in routine, continued on a step or two, then swung about to face his owner, curious to see why he had stopped. "Bear is fifteen years old," the man said proudly. The voice was stronger than she had expected from the man's figure, so she glanced up, really seeing him for the first time. He was probably in his sixties, but he looked far older. She could see that he had once been powerfully built but that his frame now appeared to be diminished by disease. In the gaunt, pale face, his eyes were kind. "I got him when he was just a pup."

"You've taken good care of him, then, to live this long."

Elizabeth reached out and patted the dog's broad back, and it turned its head civilly in her direction. It was the polite but impersonal "How do you do?" of strangers meeting on the street.

"He's been good for me. I have cancer you know," he said in the matter-of-fact fashion of those who live with the disease, "and he gets me out, every day, no matter what. I don't know what I would do without him."

Momentarily discomforted by the man's frankness, Elizabeth searched for something to say. She had been touched by what she had seen between the dog and the man—their need for each other. For these two beings, the whole world had condensed down to each other's company.

"Do you have a dog?" the man asked in a friendly fashion.

Elizabeth straightened up and to her absolute horror felt her eyes begin to fill. It was such a simple, straightforward question, calling for a simple, straightforward reply and yet she hesitated. She paused so long she saw the man give her a curious look, which made it worse. And yet she could still not articulate what she felt.

To disavow Damien now seemed so cheap, so unworthy, and yet he *was not* her dog.

Or was he?

Was she denying something that was, or was she trying to be realistic about something that was not? Her mouth opened and shut, but still no words came to her. The man nodded.

"You've lost your pet recently, haven't you, dear? I can tell. No need to answer, I know the feeling." He reached out, a man who wanted to comfort but too courteous to impose, and touched her arm gently; a vestige of the hug he would have liked to have shared. "Don't be sad. Your dog is in a better place, and he's waiting for you." He nodded again, a man at peace with his mortality, and passed on his way, the old dog moving off with him, glad that the interruption of their walk was over.

Elizabeth stood in his wake, devastated. Why had he said that?

He's in a better place, the man had said, *and he's waiting for you.* The words hurt.

She had not even bothered to make sure Damien was in a better place, and yes, he would be waiting for her, more than likely in a stainless-steel prison.

How he would love this snow. Wherever he is, he doesn't even know it's snowed.

She had been content to let his memory slip away; to ignore his plight because he was "just a dog." Shame swept her, drying her eyes and making her mouth thin-lipped and grim. She was revitalized by the specter of the man and his companion, true friendship in the flesh.

Damien, she thought in the chill air. *Hang in there. It may take me some time, but I'll make sure you're OK, buddy.* She *would* find her friend.

CHAPTER SEVEN

The fidelity of a dog is a precious gift demanding no less binding moral responsibilities than the friendship of a human being. The bond with a true dog is as lasting as the ties of this earth can be.

—KONRAD LORENZ

Elizabeth knew that what she needed was help, additional eyes and ears working for her as she began trying to locate a single dog within the vast University complex in earnest. Her inability to approach the people most likely to have information concerning his whereabouts made it infinitely more difficult.

With studied indifference she began to mention to fellow handlers and a few of the techs she had become friendly with that she was wondering about the fate of a specific dog. She spoke about it in the most casual fashion possible, saying she was simply curious about where he had ultimately ended up. If anyone saw a brindle pit bull type dog with little ears, they might mention it to her.

Handlers and animal technicians were required to attend quarterly meetings at which rules, regulations, accident reports and safety considerations were reviewed. Elizabeth took advantage of the new year's meeting to circulate, gently reminding and questioning her fellow handlers about the dog, working to keep any trace of real interest or impatience out of her voice and demeanor. Elizabeth had become friendly with the plump animal technician who had helped her on the day she had first seen Damien, and they sat together at the meetings. During a particularly boring portion of the January meeting, Elizabeth leaned her head in Patty's direction and whispered, "Have you seen that pit bull I'm looking for lately?"

"Oh!" The girl exclaimed loudly enough that several heads turned in her direction. "That's right, I was supposed to tell you! Jessie says she thinks she saw your dog." The girl turned toward Elizabeth, her round, pleasant face quite animated at the sudden remembrance. "I meant to tell you—I'm sorry—she said she saw one over in the long-term kennel, you know, the one clear over on the east side of the campus? She thought it was him, kind of a gold, with stripes, right?"

Elizabeth kept her eyes straight ahead and her tone light. "Did she say he had really small ears?"

"I don't remember that, but she said she sure thought it could be the one you were talking about."

Elizabeth nodded, still staring straight ahead. "What are the long-term kennels used for?"

"Mostly terminal studies. You know, where they put . . ." the technician paused, seeing the consequence of what she was about to explain. If one were looking for a dog one had any concern about, finding it in the long-term kennels would not be promising.

"Terminal." Elizabeth said softly, with no emotion. "Terminal studies?"

"Well, mostly. They *might* put a dog there for some other reason, you know . . ." The girl's voice trailed away, knowing full well that dogs did not go there for other reasons. "Maybe you should go check, you know, it *might* not be the one you're looking for."

Elizabeth stared straight ahead, trying to process the information she had just received.

Damien has been infected with some deadly disease or had some terminal procedure done to him—because of me. Because I went to the dog pen and started that dogfight. If it wasn't for me, he'd be in that enclosure yet. Hoffman said he was only good as a research dog, that he was not a pet. They ran out of places for him so the bastards used him, and now he's in the long-term kennel, waiting to die.

Because of me.

Guilt uncurled inside her stomach. "I'll check it out, thanks," she said faintly.

Damien was standing in his kennel, waiting for her. All these weeks he had waited in patient expectation for her arrival, and as Elizabeth moved down the hall, her eyes jerking from kennel to kennel, the pit bull's ears had pricked at the sound of her tread and he had risen, meeting her at the gate as if she had only been away a matter of hours. Elizabeth knelt down and, with her arms around the dancing, twisting dog, buried her face in his sturdy neck. She found she was crying a little, tears from an unnamable emotion forcing their way past her natural reserve. She wondered at it, at the force of the relief she felt at the sight of Damien's rugged, golden face. She clung to Damien while he grunted and snuffled and tried his hardest to reassure her that now everything was fine. He struggled to get past her arms and lick her face, ducking and swaying like a boxer trying to find a way through her guard.

This time Elizabeth didn't hesitate. Taking a kennel lead from a rack on the wall near the door, she slipped it over Damien's head. Seeing him here in this place of death, surrounded by silent, gaunt-eyed dogs, and thinking that he too would soon join them in their fate, she thought, *the least I can do is give him one last day outside.* They sprinted down the hallway and out the door.

It was a bitterly cold morning, far below freezing, and the air made itself felt in her nose and lungs. The sun shone bravely from its distant position on the southern horizon but all its effort did nothing to warm the air. The lawn beneath their feet was hard as stone. Instinctively she headed toward a tree line which lay across the access road in front of her.

The dog went wild. He couldn't decide what rich earth scent to pull into his deprived nose first, so he skipped along looking for all the world like a dog gone mad. He grabbed at brown, straggling grass blades while he ran past, tried to dig up frozen mouse holes without pausing at them, pulled with violent jerks toward trees which needed marking, all the while trying to jump up on Elizabeth. At a drunken, weaving run they reached the tree line and slipped into the protective shadows of the evergreens. Here, under the cover of the trees, the ground was not nearly so solidly frozen, and Damien snuffled through the woody odors, his tail thrashing from side to side in un-spoken testimony to his glee. Ahead of them, through the short span of ma-ture Douglas fir in which they were standing, Elizabeth could see a very large field. Reaching down, she slipped the lead from the dog's neck.

Beside her the dog hesitated for a heartbeat then, eyes glittering with de-light, he sprang away down a path only he could see through the tree trunks. Immediately Elizabeth sobered. Hoffman had said the dog was a wild dog. Maybe this open space would be too much like "home" and he *would* run off and not come back. If he did, she had just stolen a research animal—a felony. She considered that fact, watching Damien disappear into the tangled underbrush, surprised to find she felt nothing. No elation at his freedom, no fear at the thought of the serious consequences of her action. Her overriding emotion was still the numbness which had arrived with the news that Damien was being housed in a terminal ward. The bitter thought came to her that Damien could afford to be happy, unaware as he was of his future.

As they exited the backside of the tree line the two found themselves standing on the edge of a curious ditch. It sloped away from their feet, dropping down at least twelve feet and was the same distance across, then rose at the same angle on the other side. Looking across the ditch at the field, Elizabeth was surprised to find it was planted with row upon row of tiny fir tree seedlings. This must be where the little trees were "hatched" for the forestry department.

No one was visible working in the field, and if she and Damien walked along the bottom of the large dry ditch, no one not actually standing on the edge would be able to see them. It was perfect. A flimsy field fence blocked their way so she pushed the top down a bit and cautiously straddled it. When she called to Damien to jump it, he eyed her dubiously. He was searching for his own way through when she thought to grab the bottom of the wire and pull it up. This created a passage big enough for Damien to crawl through, and when she called his attention to it he quickly joined her.

Somehow, being on the other side of that rickety fence from the University made her feel quite strange. Here she was, a felon, skipping class, yet she felt unfettered, as if everything *back there* was really unimportant and the only things that mattered, the only things which were real, were on *this* side of the fence.

Why do I feel this way?

Standing above the ditch in the bright winter sunlight, she knew she was not an "outdoorsy" person. She had spent far too much of her young life preparing for the academic challenges ahead of her.

I've spent more time looking at a computer screen and textbooks than looking up at the sky.

It was a sobering thought.

Why, then, do I feel so comfortable here?

This was just a homely ditch covered in short, dead, tan-colored grass. Frost gleamed from the shady spots, and Scotch broom, that singular, primitive plant, unchanged by any season save spring, quietly blended into the background as if trying very hard not to call attention to itself

Angling down the ditch wall, Elizabeth put herself in the dog's place; how must it feel to be allowed outside for the first time in such a long while? Down the track ahead of them, she and Damien spotted a cock pheasant pacing quickly away. The dog sprinted after the bird and with a strange, startling cry it lifted, angling away with its long tail streaming. Elizabeth grinned in pure pleasure at the sight—she had never seen a pheasant in the wild before.

Quickly giving up on the bird, Damien circled back, running in a determined fashion. With his ears pressed back out of sight, his tail tucked tight between his legs and his mouth open wide in a grin that was foolish but nonetheless showed all his formidable teeth, he ran straight for her. Disconcerted for a beat, Elizabeth stopped and held her ground as long as she could. Dodging out of his way at the very last moment, she was unsure what he was doing. The dog seemed delighted when she lost her nerve and squealed without meaning to as he passed by.

"Hey, stop that!" she shouted at his retreating form, but he was circling, and coming back.

"He's strafing me!" Elizabeth whispered in revelation. "You're strafing me!" Like Patton with his pearl-handled revolvers in hand, she determined to hold her ground. Ready for him this time, she instinctively ducked her head and neck into her shoulders in a hunting predator posture and waited, hands outstretched like talons. Damien saw that he had assumed the role of prey so, switching duties easily, he zigzagged to avoid her. She jumped at him as he passed, for good measure. Damien seemed to enjoy that immensely, and he baited her into rushing him several more times. They played for several minutes, changing roles quickly and smoothly according to rules of a game they both understood. On a final rush the dog closed on her, grabbing the girl's jacket sleeve in his wide jaws and tugging her in helpless circles. With absolute care as to the strength of his bite, he never applied any but the gentlest of pressure, even when Elizabeth struck playfully at his head, cursing him as he kept her off balance. He turned her about until she tripped backwards over a hummock and sat down hard.

"You win!" she conceded. "You big bully."

They sat for a while, down in the ditch, protected from the chill breeze on the plain above, warm from their exertion. After a while Elizabeth broke the silence. "Well, I think you might be in for it, Damien, that's why you're in the terminal ward." Silence for a moment, and then she went on. "But *maybe* they didn't inject or infect you with a disease. *Maybe* you're just part of a study where they just expose you to something—or don't expose you to something—you know, like that, and then they do a necropsy on you later. It *could* be. I need to find out, I mean you could be OK. You *look* OK." She leaned back, propped up on her elbows. "But what am I going to do with you? I sure as hell can't take you home—you can't even imagine how much I can't take you home."

With a little sigh she leaned back even farther, staring up at the cloudless sky. "I'm in for it now too, Damien. I'm missing class right now. I'm *skipping* class. You don't hold the kind of grade point average I'm holding and skip class, buddy. Not to mention the fact that stealing you was a *felony*." She was amused by the thought of Tony's consternation if he were to see her right now, a felon skipping class. That helped a little.

She had to decide what to do. This was getting ridiculous. Damien settling his chin on his front paws, sighed heavily, and closed his eyes.

You're putting your whole career at jeopardy.

You need to get this right.

She turned her eyes to the pit bulldog.

She reached out, touched Damien's side, and left her hand there. With her hand on him, he seemed so real—not an intellectual question at all.

Do I take you back?

She sighed so hard the dog lifted his head and regarded her steadily, concerned. She returned his look with a little wan smile. "It's OK," she whispered, and patted him reassuringly. "It's OK."

Is it?

She had no choice. She had to take him back today, and ask Patty to find out why he was in long-term kenneling. She needed more time. She could not just dump Damien somewhere, hoping he could escape the fate of most stray dogs, destruction at the wheels of an automobile or what awaited him at the animal shelter. Additionally, there was the chance he might have been infected with some disease that would cause a lingering death. No, she must leave him for now.

They rose and Damien, determining her direction of travel, started off, his tail up and gently waving as he trotted along, his body swaying in the slightly reptilian manner of a barrel-chested pit bull. She envied him his innocent view of life. He could drop all the baggage of the past months and simply enjoy *now.*

Given the opportunity, Damien, it seemed, would always enjoy life to its fullest *at that moment.* She thought it a fine way to live, though certainly nothing she was destined for. Her happiness, it seemed, was always a distant goal, something to be worked toward. Something to be earned.

Why has my life all been preparation? Why can't it be about now?

She started down the ditch slowly, lost in thoughtful contemplation of the pit bull's resilience. Damien had come through months of undeniable torture with his grace, his dignity and his humor intact.

Is it because he's stupid, and doesn't know his circumstances, or is it because dogs have wondrous souls and simply live a better way?

She admired him at that moment.

It was a fateful decision she made that day to skip not one, but all her classes. It just seemed more important to walk along the bottom of that sunny ditch, watching birds and rabbits, throwing sticks for the dog and, in a narrow spot made shady by the overhanging firs, to run and slide on a long frozen puddle. Slipping the lead over the dog's head, they left the ditch and walked the side streets for a time, coming to a large park where they spent the remainder of that short winter afternoon. Elizabeth played that day, for the first time in many years, a student to the dog's wise teachings.

Patty, her "inside source" as she thought of her now, proved to be worth her considerable weight in gold. She reported back in less than twenty-four hours that the pit bull was not being used in a terminal study after all, but was simply being warehoused there for the time being by order of the Director of Animal Resources. Elizabeth breathed a prayer of thanks in the direction of Novak's office.

Deciding she could at least take an active role in improving the quality of Damien's daily existence, Elizabeth devised a plan for liberating the dog that did not necessitate her lying to Bill or Dave about what she was doing. She simply told them that she had taken an interest in running, and found the very early morning the most convenient time. Dave, never supportive of anything which took time and energy away from her studies, pronounced the whole thing dangerous. A woman running around the campus in the predawn dark, she was sure to get into trouble. To that she had an honest answer—she would be perfectly safe, she was running with a male friend.

Though Elizabeth had always been something of a morning person, morning had meant studying books in bed or conversation at the kitchen table while her father got ready for work and Bill fixed breakfast for them all. It had never occurred to her to go outside the house before the sun rose. Now, when she must combine the challenge of getting Damien out of the kennel block at least once each day with the reality of her hectic schedule, inspiration came in the form of an early-morning trip to her bedroom window. Awaking before dawn she was drawn to the hint of brightness behind her filmy curtain, and stood leaning against the sill entranced by the softness of the scene before her. Through the partially open window she saw, even though it was still late winter, a half dozen robins spread out across the dim, gray lawn like tiny sentinels. She put her face to the open window and breathed in deeply. It was the clear, intoxicating air, she was sure, that gave her the mad idea of dressing and going out into the morning. Slipping from the house, she drove to the University, let herself into the kennel block with her handler's keycard and found Damien standing ready at his cage door, expecting her. Together they ran across the campus lawns in the gray dawn, playing like children. She did it the next day, and the next. She derived a real pleasure in waking before light, slipping from the house, and setting Damien loose as the eastern edge of the world brightened. As days became weeks, it became *their* time, for at that early hour she and the dog shared the new day with only a few other hardy souls.

Next to the grassy ditch, the arboretum, with its huge maples and oaks, became their favorite place. While exploring the arboretum's furthest reaches, Damien experienced a mishap which offered Elizabeth proof of what she had suspected for quite a while. Turned loose in a formal lawn area, the galloping dog was glancing back over his shoulder toward her when he failed to notice a square pond, the rim of which was level with the lawn. The green of water vegetation hid the pool from his sight until it was too late, and he disappeared under the water, reemerging a few moments later completely coated in clinging algae and duckweed. He was a green dog. Bent over with laughter, Elizabeth met him at the edge of the pool where he was pulling himself out. His look of absolute chagrin surprised her. With his lips pulled back in a wry and sheepish grin, he stood taking her laughter while his tail slowly wagged. It was so clear that he *understood* he looked foolish, that he had embarrassed himself, and that he saw the humor in it all. At that moment she knew in her heart that her friendship with the dog did indeed include the shared emotions of humor, camaraderie and affection.

Now, for the first time in her life, Elizabeth began to notice Nature. She looked and saw the sky. Having spent so much of her life under the cover of a roof, she discovered that the day was *made up* of weather; of shifting light patterns and changing temperature and a thousand other evidences of the sun's certain advance across the sky. She was surprised by the loveliness of what she saw and it filled her with gentle regret; here was beauty in its purest form, free for the taking, had she only looked up from the trappings of civilization to see it. Back in class, her eyes strayed more often now, leaving the pages of her books or her computer screen to visit a window. She learned that, though given freely, Nature's beauty waited for no one. Each moment transformed it, and if she missed a flush of red above the mountain, or the beauty of a heron, moving with slow deliberation across her path, that precise moment was gone forever. For Elizabeth, the effect was to make her a miser of the moments she and Damien shared. Walking their secret ditch or trotting through the arboretum with the dog at her side, Elizabeth felt honored to be witness to each sunrise.

Following cloudless nights the rising sun often caused a wet, white fog to form. Some mornings it lay thick and well-defined in only one valley, looking like a startling, prehistoric glacier which had arrived overnight. Other times it lay low and all-encompassing, draped over the seedling farm while the tops of the tall, dark fir trees which ringed the field stuck up out of the whiteness, looking like a partially erased pencil drawing. She came to think of that year's predawn time as a special gift—from whom she had no idea— to herself and the dog. While everyone else slept, waiting for mundane daylight to start their day, she and a handful of joggers seemed to be the only ones to witness the daily birth of the sun. When the sun finally rose, bathing the fog within which they walked with light, the beauty was indescribable, and Elizabeth would reach down and pat the dog in gratitude, knowing it was only because of him that she was privy to such wonder.

For all that she was helping Damien by releasing him from his sterile cage to enjoy the morning, he gave to her as well. She came to recognize within herself a confidence and feeling of comfortable security that came from being so well accompanied. Several times when figures emerged out of the gray dawn and she found herself face to face with strange men, she couldn't help but appreciate the muscular and watchful dog at her side. While she had no particular fear of walking alone, she instinctively felt a slight prick of concern when approached by men in isolated areas of the arboretum. Damien seemed to sense that, and he always came close at those moments, walking before her with his tail and head raised in an attitude that left no doubt that he considered her protection his province.

From the top step of the long stairway running down the side of the hill to the arboretum below, Elizabeth could watch the sky over the Cascade mountain range and farther to the south the huge, surreal form of fourteen-thousand-foot Mount Rainier, turning peach and purple as the sun came on. Damien had discovered ground squirrels living in the soft dirt beside the stairs, so he generally left the sightseeing to her. At times, however, he did join her, sitting quietly at her side, his fierce eyes turned out over the same view she enjoyed. Elizabeth had heard the theories asserting dogs could not see color, and she wondered what Damien *did* see as he sat beside her. She wondered why he should see so differently from herself. Why shouldn't he see color? She knew about rods and cones, but it still didn't make sense to her.

Having come into the relationship with very few preconceived ideas about dog behavior, outside of the usual myths, she interpreted his behavior the only way she could—as if he thought in a manner very similar to her own. She learned to recognize happiness, regret, trepidation, curiosity, fear, and affection in the dog, and he in her. Those early mornings revealed more than a rising sun to the two companions as they came to understand each other and the significance of a smile, a wag, a grin, a scowl, a quick stare at the horizon, a play bow or a finger put to a lip. Elizabeth and Damien came to have perfect communion based on body language and the looks which passed between them.

With her mornings devoted to Damien, her evenings by necessity became devoted only to study. To be fair to Tony she knew she must honestly confront him about the idea of "breaking up." It seemed the wrong term. They had been seeing each other, that much was true, but she simply wanted him to understand that she needed to move on, and while they could remain friends, realistically she had very little time for a friendship with him. She had never loved Tony, though at times she had liked him. Now he was simply an annoyance.

She called him and asked to meet at lunch. He agreed, but with a tone that left her wondering if he had the gift of foresight. Then again, she admitted, it probably didn't take much foresight at all.

Tony was graduating from medical school that spring, and he carried that information in his walk. She shook her head with sad affection as he approached her table. He was such a doofus. After they ordered Tony sat giving her *that* look, so she started.

"I want to be really honest with you, Tone. We've had a lot of fun *(that's not exactly an accurate statement)* these past months but you're getting ready to graduate, and then into your postdoctoral program, and I'm entering medical school, *(God help me)* and I think we need to think about our plans. *(Lord, that sounds like you want to marry him, hurry!)* I just think that maybe we . . ." She hoped he would jump in and help her, but of course, being Tony, he didn't. He was sitting there enjoying her discomfiture with a look of long-suffering patience that was maddening.

She thought briefly of lying and saying she was seeing someone else, but Tony being Tony, he would run to Dave and that kind of tangled web she would just as soon not weave. "I think you need to find someone who . . . can spend more time with you. You know?"

"No, I don't know. I thought we had a relationship?" She knew Tony was just being difficult. Tony knew damn good and well their "relationship" hadn't been much to write home about for months.

"Tone, I don't want a 'relationship,' you know? When I fall in love, I'm just old-fashioned enough to want it to be 'romance.' We don't have that, *you* know that."

"Whatever, Elizabeth. What are you *actually* trying to say? That you don't want to see me anymore?" He began staring straight ahead, suddenly uncomfortable with the idea that he might be the one getting dumped.

"Yeah, I guess so, but it's important that you not think it's like, that I don't enjoy you—I do—I'm just so busy now, and so are you, and I really think, if we're honest, we both know it isn't like this relationship is going to go anywhere." *(Welcome to Dumpsville, baby. Population: You.)*

"OK. So now we're 'just friends,' right?"

"Yeah. *(Hopefully, not even that.)* Are you OK with that?" She could see he wasn't, and that frustrated her even more. He didn't really want her, she knew that, but still, now, when she was trying to resolve the thing between them, he would balk just to be difficult.

"I guess I have to be, don't I?"

148

"Geez Tony, what's the problem? We aren't Romeo and Juliet, OK? I'm just making it official."

"Why? Why now? What prompted—this?"

"Nothing 'prompted' this." *Well*, she was tempted to say, *to be honest I would rather spend my time with a dog than you!* "I just see how busy you are, and, you know, I wanted to be up front about it, and let you know I'm going to be really busy now, and if I didn't return your calls right away I wanted you to know why, and know it's nothing personal. We're adults, Tone, I just think this is what I need to do, and I'd like to stay friends."

The waiter arrived, the plates were set down, and then it was simply a matter of trying to get through lunch. She supposed Tony felt the same way about it.

They talked a little, about classes, grades, the usual, and then, in a parting gesture that was obviously important to him (and unfathomable to her) Tony paid for both their lunches and walked away. She sat at the table a while longer, wishing the waitress would reheat her coffee and trying to feel, if not guilty, at least a little bad. She felt only relief. Tony was simply not the kind of man she was looking for.

The notorious unrelenting rains of the Pacific Northwest, which had mercifully but most uncharacteristically held off so far that year, came now to stay. Slashing rains driven before the wind would be interspersed with fine, misty rain which would fall unabated for days. On the first day of the monsoons, Elizabeth blew into the long-term kennel on time, but with no intention of going back outside. She greeted each of the other inmates as was her custom now, then opened Damien's kennel and let him out.

"Want *out*? OK, but we're not going anywhere today, buddy. No way. We'll have to stay in here." She had neglected to bring a toy of any sort, so she decided to take a stab at training the dog to do some tricks. Without the benefit of collar, leash or any reward other than her praise she began, in an extremely haphazard fashion, to teach him the basic commands of sit, down and stay. The dog was thrilled. He relished any attention at all, even a glance from her, but Elizabeth's words of praise, directed so effusively at him when he managed to understand what she wanted, pleased and embarrassed him beyond measure. He strained to understand and she strained to make herself understood, and when at last the moment came when he *understood* that she wanted him to sit down as she made the "sit" sound, both of them went wild. They danced about, he because she was pleased, she because he was so clever.

"Ah, you're *very* good, Damie, very good. I have to go now, so you have to go back in. Come on now."

Damien pulled back, his expression stricken. Before she had taken him for long runs and he had been willing enough to obey her command to return to the kennel. But now, now she wanted him to return and she had not taken him out. Worse, she wanted to stop the *work*.

"I know you want out, I'm sorry. You have to stay. I'll let you out tomorrow, I promise. Now come on." He could not disobey. Head drooping, he slunk into the kennel. "Sorry buddy. I'll let you out tomorrow. You be good now."

Desolate, the normally quiet pit bull whined from deep inside his chest. *Don't leave!*

He ached for her to understand.

Take me with you!

Elizabeth turned and retreated down the hall. When she reached the hall door Damien cried out sharply, a strange, high sobbing cry that stopped Elizabeth in her tracks.

"Oooooooouuuuwwwwwww."

"Damien, *stop* that! I'll be back tomorrow. I can't take you out into this rain, OK? I know you want out—I promise I'll get you out again tomorrow. Now, *stop* it."

Obediently Damien fell quiet, and she shut the door behind her.

The next day was worse than the day before. Hard, cold, driving rain slashed her window when she woke at four-thirty, and for a moment she considered just turning off the alarm and not going—just this once. Then she sighed. Damien would be waiting. Her visit was the only relief to his otherwise grim existence, and she couldn't let him down just because she was lazy. She rose and dressed warmly, hoping against hope that spring would come early this year.

She had stopped the night before at a variety store and picked up some tennis balls, and by throwing them down the hall, she provided Damien with a half hour of relatively hard exercise. The dog chunked the balls happily between his jaws, his eyes bright with prey drive when she raised her arm to throw. She wanted to leave one with him when she left but was afraid it would raise questions as to how it got there. Were Viktor Hoffman to see it, he might guess. Again, as she walked away, the dog's haunting cries of misery followed her down the hallway and out the door.

The rain persisted, nothing unusual for the Pacific Northwest. Gray mornings became gray afternoons which simply faded into a darker and darker evening. Worms rose drowning to the surface, easy prey for miserably wet robins who fluffed themselves repeatedly, trying to stave off the dangerous moisture. Elizabeth had no choice but to exercise the dog as best she could within the confines of the kennel, working on his training, and leaving without a trace before the kennel cleaners arrived at seven A.M.

She could tell Damien was frustrated at not being allowed outside, and bored. Having started the dog on the elements of sit, down and stay, Elizabeth began training the dog tricks, shaking hands, and speaking on command. Bringing two NuttieGooie bars to be doled out as a reward for performing correctly, she approached Damien's kennel gate and showed him the candy. Obviously, since he howled and barked to be let out of his kennel, this would be the ideal situation to use in teaching him to "speak" on command. She unwrapped the candy bar, broke off a piece, and showed it to him.

"OK, you want out, right? Well, today you've gotta ask." She waved the candy back and forth before the wire but he ignored it, just excited to see her. "Come on now, speak! Speak, Damien. Speak." She held the candy up, chest high. "You want *out*? Speak! Speak!"

Elizabeth had never hesitated to open the cage, this was new, and Damien didn't like it. He wanted out, and he knew that the word "out" signified as much. Normally a very quiet dog, he now vented his frustration in a short vocalization.

"Oooouuwwhh," he said, tipping his head back in his effort. "Oooo-uuuwwhh."

"*Good* dog!" Elizabeth yelled, delighted at his quickness. "Good dog. That was good." She handed him a sliver of candy and he accepted it, pleased that she was pleased. "Do it again, now. Speak!" She teased him with the remaining candy, and again he voiced his frustration.

"Ooouwwhht."

"*Very* good. You're very clever Damien. Here you go." She opened the gate and he swarmed out, taking the entire candy bar from her hand and swallowing it in three gigantic gulps.

"Geez, you eat like a shark." She showed him her empty hands, holding them out, palms open toward him. "See, no more. No more." The dog understood, and he relaxed.

She threw the ball until her arm hurt, then she ordered him back into the kennel.

"Sorry Damie, it's that time. I'll be back tomorrow. Hopefully we'll be able to go out then."

She turned to go and the dog's expression changed instantly. He jumped up on the wire and made a horrid, choking, pleading sound that made Elizabeth wince.

She turned resolutely away and started down the hall.

Damien cried, desolate, and clawed at the wire. Elizabeth turned back, shocked again at his unusual behavior. He was such a quiet dog normally; his desperate outbursts dumbfounded her. "No, Damien. Now I mean it, don't make me feel worse than I do. I know you want out." She started down the hall again.

Damien did not—could not—question Elizabeth's actions. It is not the way of a dog to wonder why she did not take him out, or why she left him behind when she went away. But he could know that he *did* want to go with her, that he could change her actions. There are few more master manipulators than members of the canine race, and Damien had learned that vocalizing the word "out" pleased her. She had released him from his odious confinement once when he had performed that behavior, so he was willing to try again.

"Ooouwhht." His mouth snapped shut, he had almost perfected That Sound. If only . . .

Elizabeth had stopped and turned to face him, her face difficult to read. Damien wiggled, hoping she could see how tired he was of waiting patiently through long, tedious days.

"Ooouwhht," Damien growled hopefully. He saw her eyes go wide, and took that as reinforcement. Her renewed attention rewarded Damien's efforts and he tried again. "Oouwht." His head rocked back with the effort.

"*Cheese and crackers,*" Elizabeth said weakly, "it almost sounded like you said, '*out.*'"

"Out!" Damien snapped his teeth together in his excitement. The word came out in a strange, sharp bark, but the utterance was clear. She understood him perfectly.

Elizabeth came to the front of the cage slowly, staring at the dog. He writhed in pleasure at having recaptured her attention, and grinned fool-ishly, sure now that, having made the sound that pleased her, the gate would be opened.

"What the *hell*," Elizabeth said softly, staring at the dog out of the side of her eyes, "did you just say? Damien, did you *say* out? Is that what you *said*? Go on, speak! Say 'out' again."

"Out!" he said promptly at her cue, satisfied again that *this* behavior would definitely keep her from leaving.

"You gotta be kidding me, right?" Elizabeth stepped back from the ken-nel. Her face was white as the wall she reached for behind her. She looked around, thinking perhaps someone was playing a trick on her. But she had seen the dog's muzzle move when the sound came out. Damien had articu-lated that word, clearly, and it frightened her.

The dog sat back and looked at her hopefully. It occurred to Elizabeth she *should* let him out, after all, that is what he'd asked for. She put her hand on the cage door latch. "Do you—want *out*?" she asked again.

"Out," Damien said, rising and wagging his tail. The word was very clear, despite the strange, deep, rumbling "accent."

"This can't be happening," Elizabeth whispered as she pulled the door open. Damien rushed out into the aisle way, tail lashing. He ran to the end of the hall and stood expectantly at the door to the outside. Elizabeth stared down the hallway at him, her hand still on the cage door.

I guess I'm going out in the rain.

She could not deny him now, that was for sure. She walked down the hall and put her hand on the doorknob. She cocked her eye at the dog.

"Out!" he said happily.

She felt ridiculous. She opened the door and the happy dog raced out into the somber, rainy morning.

CHAPTER EIGHT

How dreadful knowledge of the truth can be,
When there's no help in truth.
—SOPHOCLES

She let Damien run about in the pouring rain while she stood in the doorway staring after him, eyes which had been wide with wonder now narrowed in disbelief. After a few minutes, feet muddy and fur dripping, the dog came in of his own accord and Elizabeth took him back to his kennel and shut the gate. She stood a moment, staring at him still, and even through her amazement it occurred to her that it had been foolish to let him out. Surely when the kennel cleaners arrived they would notice his sopping-wet fur. There was nothing to do about it now.

She needed to go, but hesitated, transfixed by the idea that perhaps Damien was some sort of . . . well, somehow different from other dogs. But there was Damien, shaking himself off, and when he sat down and scratched behind one ear she felt reasonably sure he wasn't some supernatural being. Damien watched her go without protest.

The next morning the rain still fell. She stood before Damien's kennel with a package of dog treats. "OK, let's see what you can really do, Bucko." She held a treat in her hand and cocked her head at him. "Do you want *out?*"

"Out!" the dog snapped, his teeth clacking at the end of the word. She understood him clearly—it was *not* a bark.

"Oh man," she said weakly. "That's pretty good." That was an understatement. She glanced down, surprised to find that her hands were trembling.

My God!

"OK, you can come out." He ran to the hall door which led outside. "Out!" he snapped again, his nose to the door, feet dancing in anticipation.

"Oh, now, hey, Damien, *listen* to me, you can't just talk like that—somebody might hear you. Do you understand?" But Damien was crowding and pushing the door in his eagerness to get out. He did not understand, and she hadn't a clue how to tell him. "You're not going out. I'm sorry, but if you're wet every morning, somebody's going to tell a supervisor, and they're going to contact Hoffman, and then *he's* going to come down here or something, and *then* we're in for it. Trust me on this."

She was eager to try and teach him another word, to see if the sound he made *coincidentally* sounded like the word "out" and was nothing more than a fluke. She thought for a moment, her mouth moving soundlessly, about which sounds would come the easiest out of a dog's muzzle (that struck her as a very odd thought) and what would have meaning to Damien. "Food" seemed a difficult word, so she decided on "eat." It was very close to "out."

"Do you want something to *eat?* Eat. Speak! Say that, say *eat.*" Damien stared at her, his head cocked to one side. "Come on now, if you can say *out,* you can say *eat.*"

"Out!"

"That's great, I like that one, but I want you to say *eat.* Eat! Speak, Damien, speak. Say *eeeeeat.*" She held a dog treat before his nose. He lunged for it and she drew it away. "No! If you want it, you have to say *eat.* This is *eat.* Well, it's food, really, but for you, it's eat. Say that. *Eat.*"

She had never felt so stupid in her life. *You Tarzan, me Jane,* she thought wryly.

She tossed the biscuit alluringly and caught it before his nose. "This sure looks good—good enough to *eat.*"

"Eat."

"*Son* of a bitch!" Elizabeth straightened up, her face pale beneath her dark hair. "You *said* that! You said that word." Damien's ears went flat and she saw, with a perception that was growing every day, that the dog was confused at her harsh exclamation. "No, no, it's OK, Damie. You did good, *real* good, you just freaked me out, that's all."

She couldn't get straight in her mind how Damien had articulated the words. She had heard it said that chimpanzees, even though they resembled humans closely, could not articulate speech because of subtle differences in head and throat anatomy. But then again, she thought, that argument didn't hold water—look at parrots. She knew African Gray parrots, for example, could not only mimic human sounds exactly, but could answer questions and solve problems. All that from an animal whose head structure was radically different from a human being's, and which had a brain the size of a pea to boot. So much, she thought grimly, for brain size and throat structure theories.

Excited, she worked the dog for several minutes, letting him in and out of the kennel on the "out" cue, and rewarding him with a treat when he identified the biscuit she held up before him as "eat." Damien performed happily, thrilled with her attention, and quickly grasping the association between the words and the object or action it was paired with. "Out" got him out of the kennel, "eat" got him a treat; it was a simple exercise for a dog.

"I *have* to go, Damie. I wish I knew how to make you understand that you shouldn't do that in front of the kennel staff. In front of anyone! Man, I wish I could make you understand. If you say *anything* we're doomed." She held her finger up in front of her lip, a signal the dog was familiar with. He knew it to mean he must not bark, or must stop barking. She had taught it to him on their walks. She did it now and whispered, "No talk, no talk." Damien yawned and thumped his tail at her.

"Oh brother," Elizabeth worried, "I need a miracle; I have the world's dumbest talking dog. . . . Just don't talk, OK? Till I get back."

Don't ask the kennel staff to let you out, please, please, please!

All that day Elizabeth's mind was racing. She kept arguing with herself, insisting she had heard words clearly spoken, and arguing the impossibility of that very statement. She wondered if she should tell someone. She wanted in the worst way to tell Bill, and to bring him with her to see the dog. Bill was one of the cleverest people she knew. Once shown the dog, he would have to see the importance of the situation. Then again, she mused, Damien's natural reticence around strangers might preclude his speaking in Bill's, or anyone else's, presence. If that happened, they'd lock her up for a loony.

You know what you heard.

Even if she had heard words, Damien wasn't really *speaking*. It was more like a parrot, he was just making a sound he had heard in association with the gate being opened. He was simply mimicking her sounds in association with an item she showed him or the action associated with the word.

Yeah, so? That's how I would learn a foreign language. What's the diff?

Now she really wanted to talk with Bill.

Hey, Tom," Chase called with disarming innocence when Tom appeared, crossing through the room on his way to one of the workrooms at the back of the lab. "Whatcha doing this weekend, buddy?"

No one present, including Chase's current lover, Mandy, who had seated herself comfortably on a counter near the graduate student's workstation, could have mistaken his tone for anything but what it was, the preamble to another round of provocation. Chase, having been caught unawares on the phone by a collection agency earlier in the day, was in a foul mood. It didn't help that Seville was being closemouthed about the immediate future. His graduate student, sitting idle, made his own entertainment.

Tom did not stop his forward progress or turn to face Chase. "Oh, the usual."

"Why don't you come snowboarding with us? There'll be girls there—lots of beer. Whad'ya say? It's the end of the season Bud, come on, it'll be a good time."

"I have plans, thanks anyway."

"Come on Tom, you gotta have fun *some* time. You know? Trying to be your buddy here. It's just not normal to never unwind. Have you ever been snowboarding? Have you?"

Tom stopped at the doorway and turned to face him. "Thank you anyway, Chase. I have plans."

"You don't have any plans, come on—admit it!"

Tom turned away, his face set, leaving the room.

"Well it's *your* loss friend—I'm just trying to help, you know? You're getting kinda old to be a virgin."

Chase noted with satisfaction that he had registered a hit. Tom's gait faltered for just a moment, as if he was going to hesitate, and then he disappeared into the workroom.

Seville looked up from where he was reclining far back at his desk, a folded journal held up in one hand. "You need to ease up on him."

"He's a toady," Chase responded dismissively.

"He's *my* toady."

To that, Chase had no ready answer.

"Well, what *does* he do for fun?"

"That's not your concern. Just ease up."

Chase shook his head as if Seville's research assistant was a sad, and ultimately doomed, case. "He's one sorry dude. He doesn't *want* to have any fun. Is he a Mormon or something?"

"Maybe he is. He's punctual and he suits me, and he doesn't sneak off every time there is 'radical' powder or the waves are just so, okay?"

Chase shrugged, rubbed his nose, frowned and shook his head. He was antsy and bored. "Come on, Mandy." He snapped his fingers at her and she slid off the counter and followed him into the computer room, leaving Seville—after he watched the girl's backside leave the room—to return to contemplation of the journal he held aloft.

August D. Kotch of Ohio State University, having had just about enough of Joseph Seville's nonsense, had fired a salvo intended to tear a sizable hole in the aft section of the Seville battleship, effectively sinking it once and for all. A written defiance in response to Seville's latest reply, penned in the blunt, Ohio straightforwardness that he found so infuriating, challenged him to "put up or shut up" on the matter between them. Flushed by the support that had come his way after the last round of publications, due more to the readership's dislike of Seville's arrogant style than any real support of Kotch, the Ohio professor nonetheless was in rare form.

Seville, knowing all eyes were upon him, and that the ball was most firmly in his court, would not be baited into a precipitous response. Kotch could wait. Seville rather enjoyed the thought of Kotch waiting in eager expectation for a reply and, not receiving one immediately, wondering if that boded well or ill for himself. The important thing, the all-important thing, was getting a paper—any paper—invited to the Netherlands, and doing everything possible to see that Kotch did not.

So Seville pondered the question of what to *do* to insure his invite to Europe. The deadline for submission was fast approaching. He needed something flashy yet sound. Very sound. At this moment, he could hardly afford to present something insubstantial. He set the magazine down with a sigh, pulled out a cigarette and stared at it, lost in thought.

Bill?"

"In here."

She walked in to where he was sitting, a beer balanced on the arm of his chair, channel surfing on the television. "Dave would kill you if he saw that beer."

"I know it." He grinned at her and muted the TV sound. "Don't tell on me, OK?"

"I won't tell if you don't tell—how about that? I kinda want to talk with you about something."

He waved his hand toward the couch, almost hitting the beer can, which he grabbed with a guilty lunge. "Let's talk."

Elizabeth set her coat over the back of the couch and eased herself down in the corner.

Where to start?

This was not going to be easy. Not by any stretch of the imagination. She decided to take the first hurdle at a dead run.

"Grandpa, I'm going to tell you something that is going to sound crazy, but I want you to listen to me, OK?"

"OK." Guarded.

"I know you're going to think I was foolish, but I've continued working at the ARC as a handler, all this time. Remember the dog that I was concerned about? The one I asked you about that night in the kitchen? Well, he's still at the University, still a research dog." Bill's eyes raised up to meet hers, his expression grim. Elizabeth saw it, but gamely struggled on. "And I might as well tell you one other thing—when I leave in the morning to go running, it's with that dog." She waited for a reply, and getting only his silent stare, she continued. "We're *friends*, I don't know how else to explain it, and I'm not sure I should try and explain it any other way."

She stopped, looking, hoping for some encouraging sign from her grandfather but received none. She drew in a breath and started again. "I *know* what you're thinking, and I guess I don't blame you, but that's only because you don't *know* Damien. God, it's so hard to explain how all this happened. . . . OK, now something, well something rather unique—to put it mildly—has happened, and I need your advice. In fact, I need to take you to see the dog. . . ."

159

"No," Bill said, "stop right there."

Elizabeth stopped, shocked at his tone.

"Elizabeth, I won't be a party to this kind of thing. I . . . ."

"What kind of thing?" she shot back, more warmly than she meant to.

Bill was an intelligent man and he had seen the implications lightning fast. "Are your activities with this animal clandestine to the University staff as well as your family?"

That hurt. "Well, yes, but . . . ."

"All right, and where do you suppose it will stop? Are you going to end up stealing the animal? Maybe you could just join the AFF and steal them all? What are you *doing,* Elizabeth?"

"I'm being careful and I'm *not* doing any harm. I simply take the dog out for a run in the morning, what harm can that do? I think it makes me a better person. I don't want to be the kind of person that could just ignore that dog's suffering."

"Evidently you somehow manage to ignore all the rest. How many dogs are up there, Ellie, how many are in your father's program alone? Why are those dogs any different?"

"I don't *know* why you become friends with someone, and not someone else!" She was almost shouting, struggling to hold back the frustration of the past months. She drew in a breath and lowered her voice; she would not raise her voice to Bill. "If I betrayed Damien's trust, if I walked away, would that make me the kind of person you want me to be?"

"You're a young woman headed for a promising career in medicine. That's what I want you to be. You're going to help thousands of people in your career, save thousands of lives. If you go into R&D it's conceivable you could contribute to a procedure or a piece of equipment that could ultimately save millions of *people.* That's the big picture Elizabeth. That's what I see. I think *you're* just seeing one pet dog right now, that's fun to play with, and which you don't see as seriously jeopardizing your career. Becoming a physician takes *discipline,* it's hard work, but look at the end result. Are you going to throw that away and jeopardize your position at this University by sneaking around with a lab animal that you've become fond of? I think you're smarter than that, myself."

Running her hands through her hair, Elizabeth regrouped. "I asked you to hear me out. Will you do that?"

"There's nothing you can tell me that will change the basics of what I just said, is there? Is there something you can tell me that will reassure me that you aren't going to continue a foolish course of action? If so, I'll listen. However, if you're simply going to attempt to justify, by whatever means, your ongoing errant and, quite frankly, deviant actions, I'm not sure there would be a point to this conversation."

Deviant actions? Was that what helping Damien was? More importantly, was that how someone in her position *should* view it? Her respect for Bill was immense; she had always wanted to be like him, so capable, so intelligent, saving lives each day as casually as others drank coffee. But was he *right*?

"I'm sorry you feel so strongly about this. I feel strongly too. When I take Damien out each morning, it may be clandestine, and that may be devious, but let me tell you one thing I do know. It's *not* wrong. It is the *right* thing to do." Her frustration was complete and she felt herself losing control. Eyes brimming she fled the room. Fletchers did not cry. At least not in public.

Bill did not bring up the subject again and neither did she. As had always seemed to be the case, she and Damien were on their own. She began considering whom she could approach. Professor Hoffman, the dog's original benefactor, seemed a likely choice, but his friendship with Seville troubled her. While she weighed her options, she began to seriously school Damien, endeavoring to teach him words, lots of words, so that she could, sometime soon, present him to *someone* who would help. If she could not remove Damien from the research environment, she was at least going to help him gain mercy.

Looking up dog behavior on the net, she was shocked to find dogs were not considered all that clever. That seemed strange to her, for Damien struck her, sans his recently acquired vocalization, as being a pretty normal dog, able to understand what she wanted perfectly well. She became increasingly indignant at each smug rejection of canine reason.

Spurred on by a fierce pride in her student, Elizabeth never missed a morning's lesson. She brought a towel to hide the evidence of his freedom, and she set Damien free each wet, warm morning, letting him range ahead as they made their way to the ditch that doubled as their classroom. The pit bull ran madly, circling, buzzing her, coming and dropping sticks at her feet then stepping back with laughing eyes and inviting her to try and throw them as far as she could.

She began by trying to teach him a multisyllable word, just to see if he could do it. She chose her name, feeling more like Tarzan's Jane all the time. It took three days for her to realize what Damien had known all along; he could not manage multiple syllable words. His words came out sharply, somewhat like a bark would, with a distinct pause between them. She had thought perhaps he could "growl" a word—like dogs on late-night TV shows who were purported to say things like "I love you" and "mama"—but the mechanism by which Damien attempted human speech was entirely different. Her name proved far too much for him, and they finally settled on "Lux," the dog's shortened and harshly guttural best attempt.

Having established that, she began to teach the dog "good" and "bad," concepts she assumed would be simple enough for a dog. She quickly learned, however, that while Damien understood clearly enough when *he*, or more precisely his behavior, merited the title of good or bad, assigning that quality to an object was formidable indeed. She very nearly gave up, more than once, and the only thing that kept her going was the certain knowledge that it was not Damien's lack of willingness or intelligence which was the hindrance, but rather her inability to make clear the lesson.

Teaching "good" and "bad" had given her another idea, one which she felt might be useful to Damien in whatever future awaited him. She wanted to teach him words which might touch the hearts of those around him. Using her hands, she taught the dog "pet" and "pain." Gently stroking the dog, she would repeat, "Pet." When she stopped, Damien, who knew that by repeating the words correctly he would be rewarded, would nudge her hand with his nose and repeat, "Pet." After he correctly identified that action, she struck at his back, giving him a mild slap, startling him, and saying "Pain" in a harsh tone. She was thankful that he learned that particular word quickly. He was loath to use it though, and often confused it with "bad."

Elizabeth's grades were slipping. She found herself spending more and more time concentrating on how to teach the dog words, and less on her classwork. There was a tension in the house, caused, she knew, by her insistence on continuing the morning lessons. Bill she knew, would not have mentioned the dog to Dave, and he continued his silence to her on the subject as well. Dave, unaware of the real issue, continued to voice concerns about her ability to concentrate on school while spending so much time "running," to which she had no reply. Her graduation, and her matriculation into medical school, was inevitable. She felt a sense of urgency in her work with the dog.

Though she was making good headway with Damien she decided it would be much easier, though less showy, to teach object names rather than concept words. As for the pit bull, he was an eager and attentive student; not because of any desire on his part to learn—he'd much rather chase a tennis ball—but because he found his actions delighted her so. By trying to repeat the sounds she made, and learning to pair them with the visual cues she gave him, he could earn her praise and approval. For the bulldog there was a new and profound pleasure in pleasing this human, and if this was the work which The One desired of him, then he would do it with good will. He did not, however, *chat* with her. He did not converse. As a canine he was primarily a nonverbal animal; it was not a skill for which he was particularly well hardwired. It was rare that he initiated speech, and when he did, it was generally to request something or to comment on something of importance to him, most often something he wished to draw Elizabeth's attention to. However, the bulk of their real communication continued to be in the almost constant eye contact established between the two friends.

Compared to teaching concept words, object words were simple. Damien had only to remember the name associated with the object, and speak it on the prompt, "What's this?" Using laminated construction paper (because of the dampness of the environment in which they worked) she made a series of colored squares. She simply refused to believe that Damien could not see the world as she did. Well, perhaps he didn't see it *exactly* the way she did, after all, she didn't *smell* the world exactly the way he did, but she thought it unlikely that he was as severely color-blind as science seemed to think.

Running her own primitive color test, she taught Damien words for black, white and gray. When he fully associated which word went with which square, she asked him to name them correctly and when he did, she knew that not only could he differentiate between colors (in some fashion) but she felt the unsettling knowledge that the dog was not simply mimicking her words—he understood perfectly that he was to answer a question. Feeling vindicated, she moved on to other colors, giving them short, one syllable words she could remember. Yellow became "yell," orange became "hot," and purple became "perp." Flushed with her easy color victory, she moved on to shapes, teaching "box" for square, "dot" for circle and "tri" for triangle.

Spring arrived at last. The rain did not stop, but became noticeably softer, and warmer. As she worked with her willing student, Elizabeth solidified her own plans on how best to present the dog, and more importantly, to whom. Hoffman had seemed the logical choice, and yet she could not shake a reluctance to trust him. Novak seemed the other possible and better choice.

One horrid, nagging apprehension kept rearing its ugly head; Damien did not belong to her. She had, in fact, no claim to him at all. She could only hope that when the time came to show what he could do, whoever was in authority would see that it was fitting to let her stay on as the dog's caretaker and teacher. She denied with cold determination to even consider the implications behind refusal of that request. There *was* another alternative, and grimly she made herself consider it. She had to consider relinquishing his care and training to another—if she could be assured that Damien would be treated with great care and kindness. It seemed possible that once the true value of his special skill was recognized, some patient and kind animal trainer could take over, leaving her to finish her family obligation with Damien safely away from any possible fate as a victim of medical research.

But that was nearly impossible for Elizabeth to picture. Would they take Damien out to run on deserted dewy lawns? Would they know that he didn't mind the soft summer rain and that he loved to drop a rock into a mud puddle and then dig at it until he was black? Would they know that he loved to play in water, but would cringe like a cur when a hose was trickled over him in an effort to clean him up? Would they play "peekaboo" with his head while they toweled him off, until he grabbed the towel and shook it out of their hands? She had the sense to know that once anyone knew about his talking, the morning runs would end. Things would change. She could only hope fervently for the better. The only thing she felt sure of was that the way things were now—Damien sitting all day in the death ward, forgotten but with the possibility of further use before him, put him at far greater risk than going forward with her plan.

While she prepared him for presentation, she stressed constantly, in every way possible, that Damien was not to speak to anyone else. She had no way of knowing if he understood her. The best she could do was to teach him to stop barking or speaking instantly if she raised her finger to her lips. Damien, however, often mistook the signal for the raised finger she used to signal one, and would happily respond with a loud "one," instead of hushing. (He was no genius at math, but he could distinguish between one finger and two.) She would laugh at his mistake, but it worried her. If he spoke now in front of anyone it could spell disaster.

Elizabeth struggled to find the rhyme or reason as to why he could learn some words and not others, or why he could not speak all the words she knew he understood. He certainly responded to many commands, knew places, names and actions, but he never used those words in speaking. With only one exception, he used only the words that she taught him specifically to say. That exception was "sgo," his pronunciation of "let's go," and an entreaty he used often to lead her afield. This word he taught himself.

A soft, warm, dripping spring now hummed and chirped outside the walls of the University's grim buildings. Brave little tree buds swelled outward tentatively, the ground fuzzed with tender new growth and soft rain fell almost every day. Tiny green tree frogs were to be found everywhere, calling to each other in excited, vibrant voices, feeling that the whole warm, wet world had been recreated just for them.

Lying in his cement world within the long-term kennel, Damien knew it was spring. Waiting through the tedious hours of his day, waiting for The One, the compelling ache of its Ancient Voice beat against his never-ending confinement, vexing him more than any discomfort imposed by humans. Spring was the ancient time of resurrection; and The Voice which compelled the frozen, buried, soggy acorn to put forth a noble young oak, or the tender blade of grass to push its way through a concrete sidewalk, filled its other subjects with the same mad, magic energy that came only at this time of year. Young things ran, frolicked, fought or mated as opportunity presented itself. Older, wiser things felt it also, and became, if not as effusive as the younger generation, at least restless and preoccupied. The Voice told them all to run, to move, to chase, to play, to mate. To *live* after months of huddling against the dark and cold. Everywhere there was movement; the gusty wind sent white clouds scuttling, geese arrowed to the north, sap rose, plants stretched upward, the deer moved back up the hills, the sun moved higher in the sky and the Earth turned its face toward the growing warmth. Everywhere, female looked for male, pollen looked for pistol. It was an exciting and heady time, a grand and hedonistic party for Nature's players who had survived another harsh and deadly winter.

It was a time to move, to *do*, and Elizabeth felt it too. On a warm, humid, still gray morning she forwent the lessons. She took the dog across "their" ditch and out onto the now fallow end of the one-hundred-acre seedling farm. It was very early, the sun still below the horizon, and Elizabeth's mind wandered far from the restrictive confines of the textbook facts she had memorized the night before. She thought the serious, fleeting, ephemeral thoughts of youth while contemplating the three-quarter moon poised above the western horizon with one bright star standing vigil alongside. The moon, she decided, was much more beautiful and significant in the dawn sky than in the evening's. Though its beauty gave way before the masculine and more powerful sun, she admired the fact that the moon seemed possessed of a special grace, leaving quietly and with serene beauty. *She withdraws with dignity,* Elizabeth thought at such times. *Her strength is not as apparent, yet it is just as real.* She decided she liked the moon.

Beside her the brindle pit bull stalked along, staying quite near and glancing up at her face from time to time. She stopped and knelt down, and Damien came crowding against her, nuzzling her and pressing against her knees.

"What is it, Damien? What's the matter?" She expected no reply to her question and she got none. Damien just leaned against her, wanting the comfort of her touch. The dog sensed her unease and, doglike, he wanted to comfort her. "It's OK, buddy. It's going to be OK." Elizabeth said this more to convince herself than him. Today she had a three o'clock appointment with the Director of Animal Resources and there she would disclose the dog's unique abilities. What happened after that was anybody's guess, but at least *something* would happen, and that would be better than this continuing limbo. She would be starting medical school in the fall, and when that happened there would be no more time for Damien. She had only a short time in which to get all her ducks in a row. She had to make sure that Damien was appreciated and therefore safe and well cared for. She had come to terms with the fact that it was highly unlikely the dog, as valuable as researchers would find him, would be allowed the kind of liberty she allowed him. But Damien would be safe. That was the payoff. And that was what this had really always been about; watching out for each other. This then, she thought, must be what the dog was sensing; the finality of this last morning's walk together.

Still kneeling, still cradling the dog to her, she found herself hugging the pit bull's solidness, her cheek against the soft, warm flat top of his skull. Damien held perfectly still in her embrace, in perfect sympathy with her sense of unease.

Elizabeth showed up at Dr. Novak's office with the pit bull's leash in one hand and her bag full of props in the other. She couldn't help but notice the unease the animal's presence produced, the growing murmur paired with heads popping up, over and around cubicle walls, staring at them. She was glad of the dog's sturdy presence beside her and her hand stole down to rest on his head. The simple action soothed her.

The personal assistant to Dr. Novak was sent for and secured and, watched by a half dozen other staffers, she came forward to challenge the dog's presence. The woman brushed at her dress as she approached, as if dog hair had already gotten on it. She had dark hair and eyes and a naturally sober expression, and she frowned at the dog before addressing Elizabeth. "How may I help you?"

"I'm here for a three o'clock with Dr. Novak." Feeling the need to justify the dog's presence (having intentionally failed to mention Damien when making the appointment) she added, "She's to see this dog."

"I don't think . . ."

The director's office door opened and Novak's head appeared. She stared at Damien for a split second before commanding, "Lydia, send her in."

Elizabeth stepped past the scowling assistant, took a deep breath at the threshold and passed into the director's office.

Novak was waiting for her, standing beside her desk, her expression one of disapproving impatience. She did not ask Elizabeth to sit down. "What is this?" she said.

"I have to talk to you about something very important. Please, I want you to understand this is *really* quite important. I didn't know who else to go to. I brought Damien because it has to do with him." Here she reached down, needing more than ever the support of his presence, and stroked his neck. The dog however, was busy sniffing the air, the end of his nose quivering and his head wavering slightly as he sought the source of an odor only he could smell.

"Does this have to do with your past complaints against Dr. Seville?"

"Oh no, no, not really, uh-uh. I mean this *is* the dog that he was, you know, being so cruel to, but no, this doesn't really have to do with him."

"Well, what is it? What's so important?" The director moved around behind her desk and sat down, her manner none too encouraging.

"If I were to just *tell* you what the dog can do you would never believe me, so I'm going to show you. I'm not even going to try and explain, OK? But before I do, may I please ask one thing?"

Novak waved her hand impatiently.

"I think that what you're going to see will make Damien quite important to scientists in general and to this University in particular. I know someone important is going to be put in charge of him and I'd like some kind of assurance that whatever happens, I can have at least some say in how he is treated. I mean, you know, I don't want him to end up in the hands of someone *like* Seville."

"Elizabeth, please realize that what you're saying makes absolutely no sense whatsoever. How can I offer you any assurances when I have no idea of what you're asking? Obviously you've trusted me enough to come here today; can't you extend that trust a little further, to include whatever possible actions I would deem appropriate for—whatever this is?"

Elizabeth dropped her eyes. "I'm sorry, I didn't mean to imply I didn't trust you. I do. You don't know how I've agonized over who to come to. See, the honest truth is I have no claim to this dog—no legal claim—and I *am* putting all my trust in you. I just, I just wanted to try and make you understand how important this is to me." Damien suddenly pressed against her legs as if uneasy. Reaching down she stroked him again and murmured, "It's OK, boy, you're all right." Damien shot her a quick glance. He seemed distracted by something on the far wall. "Give me one moment, please," she said to the director. "I need to get a few things." She fumbled with her bag of props while Damien, still concerned about the far wall, came around her and sat down, his tail tucked and his ears flat to his head.

"White," the dog snapped. Novak's head jerked but her face remained expressionless. She sat, hard eyes narrowed, scrutinizing the dog. Elizabeth laughed nervously.

"Damie, take it easy. Wait till I get the cards out." The dog was rushing and that was strange.

Taking out the color cards she tried to step out in front of the dog. Damien, however, hung on her every move, and there was an awkward moment while she tried to get the dog to stay at a working distance from her. She smiled apologetically at the director. "I'm sorry—he's nervous too, I guess."

Novak remained expressionless. "Show me," she said.

Mentally, Elizabeth blew out her breath.

Cripes, she means business.

At that moment Elizabeth decided she had made the right decision; Damien needed *this* person on his side. Elizabeth sensed that if the powerfully positioned Katharine Novak took this dog in hand, he would be as safe as she chose to make him. It was up to her to show Novak that Damien was worth protecting.

"Sorry." She turned to the dog and raised her eyebrows to him in a private facial shrug. There was no turning back now, and all she could do was hope for the best. The fate of the two friends sat squarely from this moment on with Dr. Novak. "OK, Damien, stay there now, stay right there, we have to work. I want you to say 'hello.' Say 'hello.'"

A faint scent in the room stirred unpleasant memories and the dog's eyes moved about restlessly. "White," he said again with a sharp clack of his teeth, trying in the only way he could to alert Elizabeth to the lingering odor of Seville's presence. He had recently been in this room, and the only word Damien knew that he could relate to Seville was the color of the man's lab coat. Seville had been *white* when he had stood before Damien's cage.

"No, now stop it, say '*hello*.'"

The dog's ears stayed flattened out unhappily on either side of his broad head. He looked up at the girl's face, and she encouraged him with a quick lift of her chin. *"Hello,"* she mouthed the word to him.

"Hello," he said reluctantly but obediently. The word was clearly pronounced.

Novak's face went white and her lips were tight. There was a silence in which the only sound was the soft patter of the dog's feet as he stood and turned in a tight circle, unsettled by the tension in the room. She watched the woman slowly recover from her initial shock enough to take a deep breath and compose herself. Her face took on a hard cast; she did not believe. Not yet.

"It knows more words?" Novak said quietly, as if she were looking at something of mild importance, and Elizabeth had to admit she admired the woman's professionalism. Novak was tougher than her petite form led one to believe. Elizabeth stroked the dog's back proudly and Damien glanced up at her, his tail giving a half wag. She shrugged modestly. "Yes, he knows quite a bit, colors and things."

"*Colors?* Show me."

She wasn't sure why, but Elizabeth felt relief sweeping through her. She certainly had the attention of the director. "Sure." She turned and faced the dog. "OK, buddy, we've got to *work* now. Colors first."

She took the little pile of worn and dirty laminated cues and held them up, asking the dog to name each one. Damien, with a last wary glance about, settled into the work, answering quickly and correctly.

"What's this?"

"Blue."

"What's this?"

"Black."

"Yeah, that's good. What's this?"

"Brown."

"Good. Now what is *this*?"

"Hot."

"That's his word for orange, sorry, I forgot to explain he can't really say more than one syllable, and some words are just too difficult for him, so we kinda made up words for the hard ones."

Novak nodded, as if in a trance.

"He does shapes too, here, I'll . . ." As she reached for the shape cues Damien swung about sharply, then retreated to her opposite side. Annoyed at the strange and persistent nervousness he had shown since entering the room, she began to castigate him, "Damien, come on now . . ."

"White Pain." It was the first time she had ever heard him put two words together, a feat she had decided he was probably not capable of. But "white" and "pain"? She turned to look where Damien was staring, his ears flat and tail tucked.

Dr. Joseph Seville stood, as if he had appeared out of thin air, in the middle of the room. She saw in her shock that he had stepped out of a small side room, the door of which had been cracked open. She froze, hoping he had not heard the dog's voice, but ascertaining instantly by his expression that he had. Beside her, with a dog's quick perception, Damien had marked Seville's tight lips, ashen face and narrowed eyes. During their months together, the pit bull had seen Seville impatient, displeased, angry—but never like *this*— this eerie intensity directed *at* him. Elizabeth had dropped the leash while they worked and Damien was free to bolt for the door. Reaching it, he pushed his nose against the crack, hard, then turned back with a quick look of appeal to Elizabeth. "Out!" he pleaded. "Out. Sgo."

Completely bewildered, Elizabeth walked to the door in the eerie silence which followed Damien's outburst and collected the dog. She pulled him back and stood, waiting for Novak to act. Besides being terribly startled, she was afraid of the way the scientist was staring at Damien. The man and woman exchanged a meaningful glance and she suddenly felt very, very wary. What was going on? Why *was* Seville here?

"I should tell you," Novak said quietly, as if making a conscious effort to control her voice, "I asked Dr. Seville here today, because I thought you were going to bring further accusations against him, and I wanted him to hear them himself. You should know I found no breach of conduct, no violation of protocol in any of Dr. Seville's work. I thought the best course of action, if you persisted, was for him to speak with you himself and clear up any misunderstandings. It would be unfortunate to your forthcoming medical career if you were found to be making accusations against senior University staff which were easily proven false, and you were not given the opportunity to see that you were incorrect. But now, this."

Seville scrubbed his chin with his hand and seemed to come out of a trance.

"Elizabeth," he said, "why don't you sit down. I think we should talk about what we've just seen."

Elizabeth's face flushed deeply. By what right did this man tell her what to do? She had come to see the Director of Animal Resources—not him. She turned toward Novak.

"I brought the dog to see *you*, Doctor, not him." But Novak didn't answer, she let Seville address her again.

"I'm not your enemy, don't make me out to be. I've done nothing to you—we don't even know each other. You've jumped to some wrong conclusions about whatever it is you think you saw when you entered my lab and I'm more than willing to explain the protocol behind anything you question. *Right now*, I think the thing we should be talking about is this animal. Please, sit down, we're all friends here."

"Look at the dog—he *knows* you. He's terrified of you. Your *protocol* did that to him."

Seville stopped her with a sharp movement of his hand. "*You* question *my* use of animals? You're drawing some pretty fine distinctions for a *medical* student. Do you suppose you will never use animals—some quite ruthlessly—in the course of your studies? You seem a bright young lady, and I think you know better than that. My use of that dog was SOP all the way, so suppose we set aside the finger pointing, hand wringing and fist shaking and discuss this like adults?"

Elizabeth felt sick. Why was Novak letting this happen? She looked behind her, found a chair and sat in it, pulling Damien close to her. The dog, glad for the physical comfort in the presence of a man who filled him with such dread, climbed into her lap and leaned against her, panting with stress. He was shaking, small gold hairs falling from him onto the black leather of the chair. Elizabeth had no idea what to do.

Seville and Novak exchanged another glance.

These two know each other very well. They're working together. Elizabeth clutched Damien's neck, hugging him to her.

What have I done?

Novak got up and came around the desk. "You must understand, what you've shown us is most extraordinary. *Most* extraordinary. This must be handled carefully, and with great discretion. It *may be* that Dr. Seville will be the best qualified person, able to manage this in the most appropriate fashion. Right now we need to all work together. All of us want to see this dog handled in the best possible way, wouldn't you agree?"

"*I've* taught him all these words, he trusts *me*," Elizabeth shot back. "I'm telling you, he's not going to work for some hotshot researcher he doesn't like. You can't just take him away from me—that's so wrong! I'm *begging* you, Dr. Novak, to simply let me make sure he goes to someone who will treat him well, and understands him."

Novak laughed lightly though there was no mirth in her manner. "Your concerns continue to be unfounded. This animal presents a unique research opportunity. *Absolutely* unique. Rest assured the animal will be treated kindly and handled with the soundest scientific principles. And obviously, yes, we'd welcome your cooperation in this effort. May we count on it?"

"We? Who we? Who are these people going to be?"

Seville interjected. "I think we're getting a little bit ahead of ourselves, and I don't think Elizabeth sees clearly her position as it relates to the dog. Let me ask you a question, Elizabeth. Earlier this morning, before you came here, where was the dog?"

"In the long-term kennels."

"The dog is still University property?"

Elizabeth swallowed. "Yes."

"So, technically," Seville continued, "by removing the dog from the kennel without authorization—I assume you did not have authorization, correct me if I'm wrong—by removing the dog, your actions could be misconstrued as theft or attempted theft."

"No, I don't think so, I brought the dog *here*. What's wrong with that?"

"You were absolutely correct," he said smoothly, "to do just that—to bring it to Dr. Novak's attention. The dog is under *her* jurisdiction as head of the department, to do with as she sees fit. Do you understand my point?"

She did. Why didn't Novak say something? Her confusion was complete. She turned to Novak, making another attempt to force the woman to deal with *her*. "I brought Damien here because I *trusted* you. You seemed concerned. Will you help me now?"

"What is it that you want, specifically, Elizabeth?" Novak asked. "You're asking for something in relation to concerns which are not founded. That makes it difficult for me to see, exactly, what it is I can do for you."

"I want to protect Damien from exploitation and abuse." She shot a meaningful glance at the researcher. "That's why I came here today—I don't want to just hand Damien over to somebody, you know? He *trusts* me to protect him." She dribbled to a stop, feeling trapped and foolish and betrayed.

"That's what *we* would like as well, Elizabeth. So why the fuss?" Seville said, crouching down on his heels a few feet from the dog. Damien buried his head in Elizabeth's chest and she patted him, as one comforts a baby. "Why don't you show us what else you taught him?" His tone was so pleasant, his stance so disarming, Elizabeth chewed her bottom lip.

What else can I do, really? What are my options?

She wasn't coming up with any.

Argument would only result in termination of *any* effort on her part to help Damien. She couldn't even go to the press. If anyone did believe her—and that was rather dubious—the Animal Resources Department would simply and officially deny any knowledge of a "talking" dog as laughable. She had no proof. She hadn't thought to make a video for which she cursed herself roundly. For now, she must go along with them.

"OK," she said with reluctance. "But you need to stand back, he's afraid of you."

"I understand."

She eased Damien to the floor and stood up. Novak reseated herself behind her desk, while Seville crossed the room and stood leaning against the wall, his arms folded.

She tried, really tried, but Damien had shut down. It was obvious he understood what she wanted, but panting, pacing and circling at the end of the lead, he was too distressed to respond to the cues. Seville's sudden appearance, the unfamiliar environment of Novak's office, and Elizabeth's tension and anger had all combined to unnerve the dog. Elizabeth recognized the situation for what it was and turned to Novak. "I'm really sorry, but he's too upset now. I can't *force* him to do it, you know. I'm sorry, maybe we could give him a little break, maybe bring him back to . . ."

Seville interrupted. "Katharine and I will step out for a moment. Settle him down and we'll try again." He gestured to the door with his arm, and Novak rose as bidden. Elizabeth sensed he was anxious to get Novak out the door. She stood, watching them leave, knowing she had no choice but to go along, accepting whatever scraps they threw her way. Bitter anger toward Novak stung between her eyes like an ice-cream headache. In a few moments, when they returned, it would be to take Damien away from her.

Damien watched the man leave with a tremendous sense of relief. Seville's sudden appearance had spooked him, even though his nose had warned him the man was near. Now the pit bull wanted out of this place and could think of nothing else. Elizabeth soothed him with her hands, and tried to reassure him, but he knew better.

"Sgo," he said, pulling sharply toward the door. The leash held him; the girl seemed unaware that leaving would be Good. It seemed the simplest thing in the world to the dog.

Then The One did a strange thing. She squatted down in front of him and took his face in her hands and held him with a grip so strong it was uncomfortable. She spoke to him, the kind of words he could not understand, but he felt her emotion.

His dog's heart ached to comfort her.

Then Elizabeth said, "Be a good boy," in a quiet, strained voice and stood up. The door opened and Seville and Novak came back in. The way Seville kept looking at him *felt* Bad. As Seville approached his scent set off vague, whispered warnings in the dog's mind, and stirred associations with some of his more unpleasant spells as a "basic model." Somewhere the man's clothing had picked up the horrid bitter smell of anesthetics, the rich smell of blood and, faintly, the odor of fear.

Damien stepped back, trying again to retreat, but the leash held him captive. Above him, Seville spoke.

"Let's see him work now."

Elizabeth pulled out a color card, and held it listlessly in front of the dog. "Damien, what is this?"

But Seville stood too close and Damien, throwing the girl an imploring look, crowded her legs and invoked her divine protection.

But Elizabeth looked down, caught his glance and only said tersely, "It's OK," in a tone which assured him it was anything but OK. Seville crossed his arms and stared at the dog. Damien returned his stare as long as he dared, fur prickling at what he saw there, then Elizabeth looked down at him again and spoke. "We need to do this, Buddy."

Damien could not put a name or a reason to his dread, but the thought of Seville reaching out to touch him was unimaginably unsettling. Keeping his eyes on the man and his ears on the girl he stood beside her, wanting to work, wanting to please, but unable to. Hypnotized by his dread of the scientist, he ignored her repeated requests to name the objects in her hands.

"I'm sorry, he can't work right now. You can see he's stressed out. He needs to get away from him." Here Elizabeth pointed with her chin at Seville.

"Have a seat then, Elizabeth, we need to discuss some details," Seville said.

Elizabeth did as she was told, her posture drooping with resignation. Novak spoke first. "I'm going to be very straightforward with you. I think you understand your position concerning the ownership of the animal. The dog, very simply put, belongs to the University, specifically the Department of Animal Resources, placing him under my direct responsibility. I think you understand that I am, by necessity, compelled to assign the dog to a senior investigator with the experience and facilities to handle a project of this significance."

Elizabeth sat, her hands clutching the loose skin on the dog's neck. She did not respond to Novak's pause.

"There are many considerations here, Elizabeth, besides your sensibilities. However, Dr. Seville and I both feel it would be beneficial to allow you on the research team, but understand, it is contingent on your willingness to abide by project protocol. You understand?"

"Do you *really* understand what we're offering you?" Seville said.

Elizabeth's eyes rose to his. "Oh, I understand what I'm being offered, all right. *You're* to be the senior investigator Damien will be turned over to."

Seville continued, "I invite your cooperation but I want the following assurances: that you understand the strict discipline inherent in any investigative team, that you understand you are not to question my judgment or actions at any time. I'll ask you for your suggestions or comments when I require them."

Damien grunted in pain as Elizabeth's fingers tightened involuntarily into the skin of his neck.

"I understand."

Damien looked up into her face and the girl glanced down, giving him a quick, brave, private smile.

"Who knows about this?" Seville asked.

"No one. I didn't know who I could trust, so I kept it to myself."

Novak spoke up from where she sat. "You've done the right thing, Elizabeth. You may have concerns about Dr. Seville's techniques, but you'll quickly feel much better after you've become better acquainted with the work he does."

"Elizabeth," Seville said. "The single most important consideration for this project is confidentiality. Nothing will be served by this being broken before we're ready. If you speak to *anyone* about this, you're off the project, just that fast, and what that means is this—you'll be denied access to the animal from that point on. I think that's clear, don't you?"

The girl nodded.

"All right, I'd like to meet with you tomorrow, say at ten o'clock."

"I have a class then."

Silence. Then Elizabeth said "I'll be there. Where?"

"I understand you know the location of my office?"

"Yes."

Seville enjoyed her discomfiture, a slight revenge. "I'll see you there."

Elizabeth remained seated. It was not possible that Dr. Novak would ask her to walk away, leaving Damien behind in Seville's care. It was not possible.

"Thank you, Elizabeth." Novak moved toward the door, put her hand on the knob. "You may leave the dog with Dr. Seville."

Slowly she rose, numb, unable to even comprehend how she felt. Damien nosed her hand, affected by her sudden despondency. Somehow the leash left her hand. As he realized she was leaving him, the dog, stricken, crowded her knees, trying to leave with her. Seville pulled up on the lead, restraining the dog firmly beside him.

She spoke, unaware of what she was saying. "No, Damie, you stay, I promise I'll be back—I promise." At the door Elizabeth shot one last look back at the dog. Damien's leash was wrapped firmly around the man's hand, holding the dog's head tightly to his side. Damien had stopped struggling and as he watched her leave, the expression in his eyes pierced Elizabeth's heart.

"Lux. Stay," she heard him say, and then the door shut behind her.

CHAPTER NINE

The god of dog is man.
—BURNS

Elizabeth walked slowly out of the building into a late afternoon of rare Pacific Northwest sunshine. Walled off by a curtain of grief from the between-class rush of students which swarmed around her, she simply kept walking. Without conscious thought her steps led her to the tree farm, where she sat on the edge of the grassy ditch and cried from pure wretchedness.

She had delivered Damien into the hands of Joseph Seville. She herself, through her own choices and actions. She railed at herself that she should have done *something* differently. She should have stolen the dog. She should have known Novak was untrustworthy. She should have gone to Viktor Hoffman. She should have done *anything* but what she had.

She dreaded to go home. No matter how hard she tried to hide it, her grandfather would see her desolation. With their always close relationship strained over the subject of the dog, she knew Bill would not ask her what was wrong, but she bet he would make assumptions about her grief, one of them being that perhaps at last something had happened to Damien and the dog would no longer be a distraction to her. She could not stand the thought of any satisfaction coming to anyone from that idea.

She roused herself only when the long shadows which had crept toward her all afternoon finally crossed the ditch and darkened her feet. She rose, grief making her movements wooden, and stood looking down the ditch. It was lush now with early summer grass and along its flanks Scotch broom was in bloom, the mass of bright yellow flowers filling the depression with a strong, sweet fragrance. The orange of California poppies and the blue of lupine dotted the slopes. Elizabeth, standing alone now on its edge, saw only an ugly, empty ditch bereft of life.

Ten o'clock the next morning she ascended the stairs to the second floor of the Behavioral Sciences building. Standing outside Seville's door, she took deep breaths to calm and steady herself before entering. She had no idea what she would find within. She had no idea how Damien would be housed or treated here now. No matter how soul-satisfying it might be, she would accomplish *nothing* by blowing up at Seville or causing a scene. If she made one wrong move it would give the scientist the excuse he was surely looking for to boot her off the project and get rid of her once and for all. Because of that, she, like Damien, must simply endure until she could think of what to do.

Unsure of this particular lab's etiquette, she hesitated before entering. Of course at her father's workplace she walked right in, but this man's lab? She hesitated a moment longer and then knocked lightly. The door was opened by Tom, his face, as always, set in a polite, noncommunicative expression. He nodded by way of greeting as she passed him.

Oh, Damien, you won't get much help from him, Elizabeth thought, already sizing up Seville's staff as those who could potentially be helpful or an impediment to her cause.

Seville was at his desk, on the computer. She stood, ignored, in the middle of the lab until Tom nodded toward a stool and asked her in his soft drawl to sit down. She sat, telling herself not to be bothered by the behaviorist's little mind games.

It was one thing to tell herself to disregard his conduct, it was quite another to actually do so. She was seething when, a quarter of an hour late, Seville looked up from his screen and said, "Let's go." She followed Seville and his aide down the hallway and down the stairs, angry and bewildered.

Once outside Seville spoke. "The dog is at my home for security reasons. I assume you have no problem with working in that location?"

"Ah, no."

"Fine. We'll drive you today, I want to talk to you on the way over."

Dave was an aficionado of sport and luxury cars and Elizabeth had grown up around them. She found herself, against her will, admiring the understated black sedan they approached. She knew it to be truly expensive.

He has family money. He didn't get this on what he earns here.

She was surprised to see Tom get into the driver's seat after he opened a back door for her. Seville sat down beside him and turned to face her.

"I want you to show me what words he knows already, and how you taught them. I need to get this on tape before going any further. It's an incalculable loss not to have had tape from the inception. It was unbelievably thoughtless on your part not to have brought it to the attention of someone before now." He stared at her for a moment and Elizabeth was sure it was calculated to make her uncomfortable so she stared back.

"We'll be doing quite a bit of work with the dog over the next few weeks, and since he is already accustomed to working with you, obviously you're the best choice as instructor, for now. Are you prepared to arrange your schedule to accommodate this? I appreciate it will cause some inconvenience, however, it's also apparent that you are aware of the significance of this project."

In her disgust she found it easy to return his stare. *You had your chance, didn't you? Now he won't have anything to do with you and you'll never get him to work for you. You think you're pretty hot stuff, but the dog works for me, not you.*

She checked herself. "Certainly," she said softly. "Certainly I'll come whenever you need the dog worked. I'm graduating this quarter. I planned on having the summer off before starting medical school this fall."

"That's fine. I'm sure I won't have to take up too much of your time, certainly not clear into next fall. I appreciate your concerns about the dog's welfare. Obviously you've become quite attached to him and that's understandable. However, you really have nothing to be concerned about. I grew up with dogs, my father trained and trialed English pointers as a hobby and I trialed a few myself when I was in my teens. I still go pheasant hunting every fall, and we use dogs. I *know* dogs, both on a personal and professional level. I don't want you to be concerned, however, understand that in the course of my work with this dog, I may use techniques that you're unfamiliar with. This is where we need to understand each other—clearly. I'm offering you the opportunity to continue with this dog, contingent on your attitude and cooperation, as I said yesterday. This is important, so I want to mention it again to be fair to you, because frankly I think it's possible your retention of facts from yesterday's meeting could be incomplete. Obviously you were upset; you feel strongly enough about me—for whatever reason— that you went to Dr. Novak with a complaint. I'm trying to be fair here; if you have a problem with me, now's your time to air it. If you don't think you can work with me, now's the time to tell me."

Elizabeth considered his words. She had no illusions about the fact that the arrogant scientist would want her off the project as quickly as he could manage it. Her presence stood between him and his desire to assume ultimate responsibility for the dog's abilities. He might need her right now while he discovered how to compel this genie in a bottle, but she had no doubts about what he would do as soon as he succeeded in making the dog work for him. She must be very, very careful. She wanted to give him no such excuse.

"You just need to let me know what you want, and I'll try and do it. I don't want to cause trouble, that was never my intention."

Seville gave her a small smile. "I'm glad to hear that. We'll get along fine. There's only a few things I require from my staff. I'll repeat them for your benefit. First, you must not question—while we are working—any action I might take. *Any* of my actions, including those with this dog. I don't tolerate it from my staff, and I *won't* tolerate it from you. I don't get along well with people I have to explain myself to, understand? Second, there has to be an element of trust. If you do *have* a question on anything you see involving my work, at an appropriate time you bring it to *me*, not someone outside the project."

"Do you trust me, Dr. Seville?"

"You haven't given me much opportunity to do so. For now, until we get to know each other better, what I have is the assumption that you have the animal's best interests at heart. *His* best interests will be served by keeping him calm and compliant, don't you think? Encouraging or allowing inappropriate behavior of any sort will certainly result in unpleasantness for Damien and excusal for you. If you work for me, Elizabeth, you'll do what I say, when I say it. You may not always understand what you are seeing, but any hesitation or defiance on your part could set back or destroy valuable work with the dog. You *cannot* question me. You must understand that. Do you?"

Elizabeth nodded slowly. They finished the rest of the ride in silence, each of the three people deep in their own thoughts.

Seville's home was in a gated community catering to management-level personnel from the University and nearby business parks. Each lot was two acres, and the entire area was heavily wooded with second-growth Douglas fir and cedar trees. Ferns, salal and huckleberry bushes made an impenetrable ground cover. With her knowledge of medical field incomes, Elizabeth confirmed her earlier suspicion that Joseph Seville must have money through his family, for he surely didn't live here on his research income alone.

Tom pulled the car past the front, around the left side of the house and down to a side door at the lower level of the two-story structure. She caught herself just in time from saying "thank you" to Tom when he again held the car door for her. She'd be damned if she'd thank anyone who worked for this jerk. She watched with growing curiosity as Tom, not Seville, unlocked the house door and deactivated the security alarm. The researcher stood by, hands in his pants pocket, watching. Squaring her shoulders, she summoned the strength to face the difficult task of seeing Damien in Seville's hands again.

She was distracted from her thoughts by Tom's polite "This way, ma'am." To her best recollection, she had never been called ma'am before. Tom must be from the South, as his faint accent indicated. She wondered at Seville's quiet aide. He seemed to be much more than an undergrad or grad student, more like a personal secretary or assistant.

She followed the men down a hallway and into what she recognized, from the acoustic material on the roof, as a former music room now converted to a home office, surprising in its resemblance to a very small lab. It was apparent Seville could keep animals here, and perform work here, away from the University. Looking about, Elizabeth was surprised and disgusted.

My God, doesn't he get his fill of this sort of thing at work?

She looked for Damien but could not see him. She felt her heart rate increasing and she made a conscious effort to calm it.

To her left was a counter with cupboards above. Against the wall was an ominous-looking V-shaped animal surgery table, covered now with boxes and a thin layer of dust. She couldn't help wondering what use he had had for something like that. To her right was a work desk, facing forward toward a strange little room. She craned her neck, staring at what was obviously a rebuilt recording booth, the front wall of which was now clear Plexiglas from roof to floor. The side which faced into the rest of the room was solid, with a door and a small one-way observation window. A video camera was pointed into the room through the window, and a control panel, evidently for the video equipment, sat beneath the window. The observation room was white, and very bright.

What kind of person has something like this *in their basement?*

This was getting weird. She had a fleeting concern that she had been lured into the basement of some sexual deviant but then, with grim humor, thought, *I wish it were that simple.*

Seville got right to the point. "First I'll send you in alone and I want you to just interact with him normally, the way you would on any visitation."

"Like what? What do you want, exactly?"

"Just normal interaction. I have no idea what your normal interaction with him would be. Just let us get some film."

"OK. Uhm, where is he?"

Seville walked over to the video control panel and hit a switch. He opened the door and she stepped in to be confronted by a second security door directly in front of her, the type typical to aviaries. It was solid, and it took her a moment to realize she would need a key to get in. She turned back to Seville and he was holding out the key to her.

"Oh." She felt self-conscious, knowing the two men were watching her every move. Seville shut the outer door, and she opened the inner door and entered the small, bare, harshly lit room. Looking out through the Plexiglas window she could make out Seville's empty desk, now looking as if it were in shadow. The little observation window appeared to be a mirror from the inside.

My God, what does he keep in here—and what does he do to them?

Her stomach contracted sharply. Damien was lying up against the wall, under the observation window, which was why she had not seen him when she had glanced in. As the room was soundproof, he had no way of knowing she had been in the lab, and her entrance was a total surprise to him. He scrambled to his feet squinting and writhing in an ecstasy of joy.

"Hey, D, how's it going?" They met in the middle of the bare room, and as she knelt down his wild rush caught her off balance and she went to the floor. Struggled to fend off his tongue and trampling paws she ducked her head this way and that, avoiding his wild kisses. "OK, now, OK, take it easy!"

This overexuberant greeting told her plainer than words that the dog was attempting to relieve a high level of stress. She stroked him calmly, whispering in soothing tones, and at last he lay down across her, his hind legs stretched out froglike behind him, grinning. She hugged his strong shoulders to her and sighed. "Man, oh man, Damie, we do get in some weird predicaments, don't we? This place gives me the creeps." Glancing up at the small one-way window, she remembered Seville was recording their every move and sound.

Whoops.

She sat back, considering the likelihood of Damien working in such an unfamiliar and inimicable environment. "Dang, I forgot to bring a toy, I'm sorry. Here!" With sudden inspiration she removed her tennis shoe and pulled her sock off. Turning it in on itself it made a neat, soft little ball. "Look!" She waved it before the dog. "Get it!" She tossed it across the room and Damien bounded after it, thrilled. Pouncing on it he shook it violently, then teased her with it until she grabbed his neck and took it from him. She threw that sock every way she could think of in an attempt to entertain the captive dog. Damien, growing weary, finally lay down across the room from her and, holding the sock firmly between his paws, quickly shredded it.

"Oh, I can't believe you just did that, you punk!" Elizabeth let him, pitying him for having no toys in the sterile white room.

Elizabeth was anxious to try working the dog for she feared he would fail to respond to her in this environment. If Damien did fail to respond, that would be the single worst thing possible. The dog *must* work for her, otherwise she was of no value to Seville and he would not hesitate to remove her from the "project." "OK, Damien," she called to the dog, "we gotta talk. You need to understand this: we *have* to work. It's important. We need to work *here*, now." The dog grinned his pit bull grin but remained mute. She watched Damien's eyes shift nervously to the door, then to the Plexiglas wall. Seville, backed by Tom, stood beside the desk, his arms folded across his chest, watching. For just a moment the dog lifted its head, scenting strongly in the direction of the two men, then turned, sheepishly, back to Elizabeth and smiled. His tail wagged slowly back and forth, an obvious apology.

"What's the matter, Buddy? I know you're scared but it's OK. They aren't going to hurt you—not while I'm here. You just need to pay attention to me, Damie, and *work*. OK?" She settled herself on the cement floor next to the pit bull and began to stroke him very gently on his neck and shoulders. Sighing happily, he sat in her lap. He groaned with pleasure when she began to massage the muscles on either side of his spine. "It's OK, it's OK, Damien," she murmured. The dog was trembling ever so slightly. "Poor thing, you're scared to death," she said under her breath.

She looked out at the two men and wondered if they had been in here, earlier, badgering the dog, trying to discover how to make their magic goose lay its golden egg.

What have they been doing, I wonder?

As he did so much of the time, Damien simply gazed at The One, watching every nuance of her expression, trying with painstaking effort to determine her will. She, like other humans, often puzzled him—they were a perplexing species—and right now he was confused. She seemed to want him to make the noises, here, in this place which The Voice warned was very, very Bad. She had taught him, better than she knew, that he was not to speak before others. He had broken that rule yesterday, because it had felt right to do so. She had wanted him to work so desperately, and so he had. In direct response, as Damien perceived it, Seville had made an abrupt and terrifying appearance, the girl had become very upset, and within minutes White Pain had taken him away from The One. In canine fashion, he saw the correlation between his act and the resulting unpleasant action. He understood that now, and would not do it again. The One was back with him, which was Good. If he worked with White Pain present, Damien knew with a dog's simple wisdom that the researcher would take him away again. Resolutely, he maintained his silence.

If Damien won't work, Seville will throw me out. God alone knows what they'll do to him then.

A rising fear grew in Elizabeth. She *must* make Damien respond. The door opened and Seville stepped in. He held out her laminated cue cards. "Here." He waggled them at her. "Take these; when you get him working, show me everything he knows."

She rose to take them and Damien, his expression suddenly anxious and drawn, stood with her, taking a few nervous steps backwards. Seeing the change, Elizabeth called out quickly, "It's OK, Damie, he won't hurt you."

Unconvinced, Damien turned his head away from the specter of the man, staring into the middle space with tense resignation apparent in his every line. Both genetics and circumstances dictated that he could neither run from nor fight this man, therefore he must endure—but as a dog he could dread future expectation the same as any man.

Elizabeth took the prompts and waited for Seville to exit. To her dismay the researcher closed the door and remained, arms crossed, leaning against the wall.

"I'm sorry but I'll never get him to work with you in here. He's just too frightened of you. He's so stressed he can't concentrate on what he's doing."

Seville nodded, affably enough it seemed, but his words chilled her. "I understand, but it's imperative that he get used to working around people. This behavior can't be studied properly if he is capricious in his responses. In the future he's going to be asked to emit these behaviors, on cue, in the presence of strangers.

"This is a potential issue, Elizabeth, and *you* have an opportunity to address it immediately." He stepped into the middle of the small room, arms still folded across his chest, and sighed. "Here's the problem, you see, with positive reinforcement," he said, pointing at the dog with his chin. "Positive relies on the animal *wanting* to produce the behaviors, or work, as you call it. But what if he doesn't want to? Like Damien here. What if you don't happen to have a high-enough ranking reinforcer handy? What if he isn't hungry or in the mood for a pat?" He smiled at her and Elizabeth felt the cold fear in her stomach spread outwards into her limbs. "Negative, on the other hand, relies on the always—excuse me, I should really say almost always—predictable desire to avoid unpleasant stimuli. It removes all the problems inherent in the 'pet relationship'; the kinds of issues you have with dogs that you wouldn't have, say, with mice or monkeys." For a moment he said nothing, just ran his eyes over the dog.

"I'll give you every opportunity to get him responding to cues consistently with your methods. But to be fair, I think you need to realize that I cannot, and will not, wait forever. For now, do what you will, but either I or Tom will always be present, and he's going to have to respond, from the very start, under those conditions. I think you can do it. I have all the confidence in the world in your ability."

It was on her tongue to reply when she remembered herself. Was he baiting her already? Was he serious, did he really think it fair to ask the dog to work with him present, or was he trying to force her to a confrontation and be done with her here and now? Either way she must accept his rules.

"This is important, Damien," she said low, as if the dog understood her every word. "You must do this for me *now*! White Pain wants to hear you. *I* want to hear you. You'll be a *good dog* if you *work*."

Damien shifted uncomfortably, finding it impossible to submit to the trust that she required. What she was asking felt wrong. He was devoted to her but she was asking him for something unimaginable. Elizabeth did not, could not, know all that had passed between the researcher and the dog. Up until now, the single strongest emotion the dog had ever experienced was his fear for this man. The fear born of months of systematic torture could only be displaced by something stronger even than that fear. Within Damien The Voice rose in intensity, screaming now, and the sound of it was louder than the sound of Elizabeth's voice.

White Pain is here. Lie still.

Damien crouched and lay quietly, obedient to The Voice of his experience.

"Damien, listen to me, it's OK. He's not going to hurt you. I *promise* you that." The quiet fierceness of Elizabeth's vow broke through the sound of the dog's fear. "You must *trust me*."

Damien did not understand all the words, but he understood the tone. It touched the ache he had carried in his soul as a stray dog. The ache which had brought him to Professor Hoffman's fire. The ache which had caused him to come to the front of his kennel in response to the girl's overtures. The ache which, sitting forgotten and alone in a recovery cage, or in a lab, or in the long-term kennels had been worse than the physical pain endured as a research animal. In dire conflict with his instincts, he felt compelled to listen to her, trust her. To do as *she* willed, ignoring the commands of his own soul.

Damien could not understand why The One asked him to speak, when so obviously White Pain stood poised to move against him if he did. Nor did he try too hard to understand, for it is not in the nature of a dog to ponder the reason behind what a human asked him to do. He *did* want to please her—as much as he did not want to rouse to action the powerful and frightening alpha who stood across the small room.

Elizabeth reached out gently and put her hand on his head, a simple gesture, and he began to tremble again. This trembling was different, however, from the nervous tension his fear of the man produced. It was far beyond

Damien's reasoning power to understand why The One had this effect on him or why he felt such loyalty to a member of a different species. The bond between them, the girl and the dog, was of an immense antiquity, forged when their respective ancestors became allies against a harsh and unforgiving environment. Absolute trust had come hard for those wild men and even wilder dogs, but trust did come—complete trust. Home, hearth and even children, all eventually entrusted to the care of the carnivorous animal formerly looked upon as a deadly enemy. Damien's love for Elizabeth was becoming the pure love of a good dog for The One it chooses to follow. It came from a clean, deep, desperate place in his soul, and it burned like a physical thing.

From where he leaned against the wall, Seville shifted his weight, causing Damien to start in apprehension. That was all. Damien glanced at Elizabeth. He glanced at Seville. The Voice was loud and insistent:

White Pain is here.

Feels Bad.

Lie still.

Yet Elizabeth's soul was calling quietly to him, and like an elusive scent on a sharp breeze, he could just catch it, faint but true. Elizabeth's hand stroked his head and he raised his eyes to hers. Damien whined uncomfortably for his constraining fear of Seville was being excised by a stronger emotion, and it hurt.

"Do this for *me*, Buddy. We've got to get through this, *together*," she whispered.

And then the pit bull locked eyes with her and it was done. At that instant he became her dog, and she became his god. She was his to protect, his to serve. In his veins ran the blood of the most resolute and faithful dogs of history, and it was like a coming home for him, this realization that his duty was to this other creature, and no longer to himself. This strange partnership, this wonderful thing, flew in the face of conventional survival instinct. Willing to die for her, he would face any privation at her side. The girl gently reached out again to Damien and the dog stepped under her hand. Her touch held him in place. "You've *got* to trust me on this one, Damie, we've come this far together." As Elizabeth picked up the cue card Damien glanced at the man, back at her, then back to the man again.

"Don't look at him, look at *me*. It's you and me, Buddy," she said slowly, carefully. "You and me, just like it's always been. Now." She held the yellow card before the dog. "What is this?"

Damien writhed. Elizabeth wanted him to speak, and there was something desperate in her tone. He sensed her frustration. If Seville did something Bad to him because of it, it was still what The One required of him. Damien, the dog who had grown up alone, desiring but never knowing human leadership, found contentment now came from the fusing of his will with hers.

"Yel." It was a hoarse whisper, spoken for her alone. Damien would take Seville's wrath for her; from now on he could deny her nothing. The dog squinted, waiting for Seville to act.

Nothing happened.

Elizabeth reached out, stroked him, her eyes shining, her eyelids blinking a little too often. "*Good!*" she whispered to him fiercely. "*Good.*" She grabbed the sides of his strong cheeks and tousled his head back and forth gently. He had pleased her, and Damien basked in the feeling, his tail slowly thumping out his contentment. The deep, pleasurable ache of her approval was worth whatever came of it. He had neither pride nor philosophy to hinder his contentment at that moment.

"You see," Seville said, "that wasn't so difficult."

She could have strangled him at that moment.

Thomas Owen, fourth of eight children born and raised in a trailer park tucked back in the scraggly pines lining a nondescript rural state highway, had, while still in his youth, developed two unshakable tenets by which he lived. The first, that if he was good and pleased God, he would be deserving of a glorious reward in the by and by. This faith he had inherited from his mother, as rugged and resilient a creature as had ever endured beneath the oppressive southern-Louisiana sun. Earthly things pass away, the mother counseled her silent son, and the temporal world was filled with afflictions to test and try one's faith.

Her profound and simple faith appealed to the boy looking for ways to make sense of his world. The stark realities of their existence could not feasibly be hidden from the younger inhabitants of the single-wide trailer, and Thomas watched, with eyes too grave for one his age, how his mother coped with the often-overwhelming trials of her life. Her willingness to quietly endure life's afflictions caused certain of her children to ridicule what they considered her weakness. The older children abandoned her as quickly as they could, disgusted by what they saw as betrayal when she failed to defend herself or them from the savage abuses of their father on his rare visits home. Young Thomas *knew*, however, with the faith of a loyal child, that she *did* care, that her stout heart failed to break only because she *was* so strong. She was his hero and he never thought to question her obedience to the difficult and often unfair dogmas of her religion.

The second tenet of faith was more a matter of genetics than environment. Thomas Owen's ancestors had been the stout, shock-headed Saxons that had swarmed over southern England, settling in and joining the general population of the feudal island. Stoic and fiercely loyal, his ancestors had served a variety of lords while passing on the traits which had made sturdy yeomen, faithful men-at-arms and trusted stewards. To the marrow of his bones, Thomas Owen was monumentally true.

Having had no opportunity to partake of the higher education he longed for, Thomas had jumped at the opportunity to become employed by an actual University staff member, someone with multiple titles, well known and well connected within the world of research. Tom could not help but hold Dr. Joseph Seville in awe, and having come to terms with the fact that, due to family commitments, there would be no formal schooling in his future, Tom was content to learn what he could through this lucky association and energetic study on the side. Gratefully, and with Seville's inattentive blessing, he availed himself of the sea of educational material which surrounded him. Quick and eager to learn, he rapidly began to hold his own when the conversations turned technical. Being so nearly the medical education he had longed for, the situation was ideal. Because of that, Tom, with a patience developed in his stark childhood, struggled through the often difficult realities of life with a moody and demanding employer.

Seville's students were another problem. He felt awkward and ill at ease when they would stare at him, unsure of his position but reasonably sure he wasn't a grad student. Once his true position became known—that he was simply an assistant to the doctor and not a student—they treated him differently. Seville rarely ran interference for him, however the job paid well and had, for the past six years, provided the steady employment his obligations necessitated.

This girl was going to be no different. Tom thought about her as he drove out to Seville's house, having been sent ahead when the doctor was detained at the University. She had been coming out every afternoon for a week, and would be waiting for him there now. She *seemed* nice enough, but there was an undeniable hostility in her eyes. He saw it, but he couldn't really blame her. Seville was being hard on her—it wasn't clear yet why—and it bothered him to see any woman treated that way. Tom was smart enough to understand that the expression she turned on him arose from her sentiments about his employer. What he couldn't understand was why she put herself through so much trouble for a soulless animal.

When he pulled up she was standing by the side door, obviously confused at their absence. He nodded to her and unlocked the door.

"Doctor will be along directly. You're to come in." He led the way down the hall and into the little makeshift workroom.

"May I go in with him?" she asked.

Tom shook his head. "I'm sorry, Doctor said to have you wait until he got here. You understand?"

"No, I don't," she said quite strongly, surprising him. "I don't understand any of this. I don't understand how you guys can keep Damien locked up like this, in a little room, in a basement. It's wrong."

The girl went to the front of the Plexiglas and knelt down. The dog was resting and, the room being soundproof, he hadn't heard their arrival or Elizabeth's words. She tapped the glass softly, but the dog remained curled up, oblivious to her presence.

"I'm sorry," was all he could think to say. "I can see you're fond of him."

She gave him a withering look then reluctantly seated herself on a stool.

Ten minutes went by, in which they both sat, trying to avoid each other's eyes. At last the girl fidgeted mightily and then asked.

"You have an accent. Where are you from?"

Tom was surprised at the question. "Louisiana."

"Uhm."

There was another long pause. Tom looked at his watch. The girl looked at her nails.

"Have you lived up here long?"

"My mother moved us up here some years ago." He hoped she didn't ask why. He could not lie and did not want to admit the remaining family had been moved here to be closer to their father's latest prison.

"Your mom, what does she do?"

"Do?" He frowned, unsure what she meant.

"Do. You know, did she move up here on business?"

"No, ma'am. She raised us kids. That was work enough for her."

"Are you close?"

Tom swung around to face her. He had expected arrogance from this girl. After all, her daddy was a heart surgeon and she herself was going into medical school. Tom tried to imagine what it must feel like to be accepted and simply waiting to start *medical school* in the fall. He wondered if she knew how lucky she was.

"We were very close. She went on home seven months ago."

"Back to Louisiana, huh?"

"She passed on."

"Oh, God, I'm sorry. I misunderstood you."

He shook his head to show it was all right. "No, it's my fault. That's an expression we use back home. I don't think its common up here."

"You're right. It's not. But I am sorry."

He nodded and they were silent again. He was relieved to hear Seville open the back door and come down the hall. " 'Scuse me." He nodded at the girl and quickly let himself into the dog's room to clean up before the upcoming work session.

Good afternoon," Seville said as he entered the room. "Where's Tom?"

"In the room with Damien."

"You haven't gone in there?"

"No."

"All right, let's get to work." He set his briefcase on the desk and shrugged out of his jacket. As he rolled up his shirtsleeves he walked to the video equipment on the shelf outside the little room and activated it. Tom, coming from the dog room, handed the keys necessary to open the inner door to his boss. "Bring that." Seville indicated a small metal pouch lying on the counter. Inside it were pellets of dog food. Elizabeth fetched it and the small box of props and followed him into the room.

"His DFI is going to be coming from what you have in your hand," Seville explained as he unlocked the inner door and held it open for her. "It will benefit him if you become more regular in your presentation of the positive."

"What's a DFI?"

"Daily Food Intake. What manner of reinforcer have you been using, and on what schedule?"

"He just wants to please me. He likes to learn. I'm not sure . . ."

"When he approximates a response, how do you reinforce it?"

"I don't know what you mean. If he does good, I tell him he's good." She shrugged. "Or I pet him or something. I don't use food that often."

Seville nodded. "That's what I'm endeavoring to point out. We need to standardize his reinforcer. Starting today, give him a pellet as the reinforcer, on the schedule with which you have been verbally praising him. That's how he's going to be earning his food, Elizabeth. If you don't dispense his DFI during the session, he won't eat today."

"Oh." Elizabeth couldn't think of anything else to say.

After a wary glance in the man's direction, Damien rose and hurried to Elizabeth. Seville took his usual position, leaning against the wall a half dozen feet away. Elizabeth knelt down, her arms around the dog's neck, and they greeted. Damien nosed at the container in her hand.

"Here you go." She picked up a food pellet, inspecting it, and held it out to the dog who took it. "Gawd, you *like* these things?" She held out another. "Well, I guess you don't have a lot of choice, do you?"

Seville interrupted, stepping forward. "What behavior, just now, were you reinforcing?"

"Who did I what?"

"Just now you reinforced a behavior by offering the reinforcer—I'm not clear on what the target behavior was."

"Uh, I don't think I was doing what you just said. I just gave him a pel-let . . . I'm sorry, am I doing something wrong?"

Seville made a dismissive gesture. "It's apparent the dog has been able to learn *despite* you," he said, stepping back.

Elizabeth shrugged and turned back to the dog.

Damien was panting. "Drink," he said.

"You want some water? Is that what you want?"

"Drink."

Elizabeth turned to seek permission from Seville. He shook his head.

She turned back to Damien. "Uh, no drink right now. I'm sorry, I'll get you some later." She frowned; Seville's action struck her as odd. What pos-sible harm could it cause to let the dog have some water? If he was thirsty it would distract him from his work.

God, he's a jerk. A bully and a jerk.

"How many words can he learn, and retain, in a day?"

"Just two," Elizabeth lied quickly as she stood. Damien had once learned three words in one extraordinary day, but she didn't want Seville to know that. The man would undoubtedly push the dog.

"And why only two? What limits his learning?"

"Well, he gets tired. Bored. I mean this is rather hard for him; it's not natural. He really has to focus, and he gets distracted after a while. I don't see the point in pushing him—it's so amazing what he can do just as it is."

Seville considered them both. "Teach him a word now, and use the food reward. I'll remind you that you're causing him to go hungry by not rewarding his responses." He came to stand before the dog, who had gone rigid and turned his head away in avoidance.

"Regardless of how I feel about many of your actions with this dog, I'd like to say I think you've done a nice bit of work here, Elizabeth."

"Well, thanks . . ." She couldn't help feeling wary, and thinking, *what's the bastard up to now*? But Seville was genuinely impressed. This young woman had done something extraordinary. It was the most amazing thing he had ever seen, and it had been placed into his hands at a most fortuitous time. He *did* feel gratitude to the woman responsible.

Taking advantage of his rare good humor, Elizabeth decided to make hay while the sun shone. As respectfully as she could and steeling herself for disappointment, she said, "Doctor, may I spend a little 'unstructured' time with him, please? It would mean a lot to both of us. Please."

Seville regarded her for several long moments. His light gray eyes were expressionless, impossible for her to read. She made herself hold his gaze, and wondered at his inner self. What *was* in there? Was he even *capable* of feeling the least regard for the animal, in any form? Was he a "bad person" or simply ignorant of a dog's nature? She truly didn't know.

"I don't see why not," he said. "As soon as we're done working here. And you are not to feed him outside of monitored training situations."

"Wow. Thank you. *Thank you.*"

They worked for two hours. Damien began asking again and again for water and it tore at Elizabeth. It was clear that his thirst was both a distraction and a discomfort. She didn't want to push the water issue with Seville, especially now when he was being decent to her. As she worked, she wondered how to get water to the dog. Finally she asked for a break. "I really need something to drink and to use the rest room," she said. Seville obliged, coming out into the main room with her and asking Tom to help her find her way. When she returned, sipping a cup of water, she was thinking she could sort of sneak the cup into the room, and give it to Damien. The dog needed water, how could Seville object to that? Seville was not in the outer office when she returned, so she went to the Plexiglas wall to see if he had gone back in with Damien. She was surprised to see Seville inside the observation room, crouched down, holding a dish of water in one hand. She sat on the edge of the desk, watching. Seville was two feet from Damien, holding the dish out invitingly. Neither moved. Seville remained still, the dish extended, his expression neutral. Damien was crowded into the far corner of the room, his head turned away from the man, but his eyes darting little tentative glances at the dish in the scientist's hand. After a moment Seville rose and left the room, taking the dish of water with him. Elizabeth met him at the outer door and he offered no explanation for his action. He held out his hand to take her cup as she passed him. "That doesn't go in."

"Why are you making him go thirsty?" she asked in frustration.

"I'm shaping approach behavior. You needn't worry, and you needn't question me on what I do with the animal. Understood?"

"Yes."

"Go ahead and spend your time with him now. Just call when you want out, I'll have the audio on." He took the food container and the water cup and secured the door behind her.

"I hope there's a special hell for people like that," Elizabeth said under her breath. This time was precious—more so because she knew it was only a matter of time until Seville no longer needed her to work the dog. She began pulling the fur away from the pressure sores the dog was developing on his legs and sides from the hard floor. When she was finished, Elizabeth leaned back against the wall, holding the dog's head in her lap.

"You *have* to be good, Damien, and mind White Pain. It's important."

"Out," he said forlornly.

"I know. I'm sorry. Things are kinda iffy right now. Out of my control. I can't take you out. I wish I could but I can't. I'll try and bring you some toys though." She glanced sidelong at the one-way mirror on the wall across from her. "Not that he'll let me give them to you," she said under her breath. A bone was what the dog needed, to pass the endless hours of isolation. A nice juicy bone. She knew *that* was out of the question. She could just hear Seville: *bones will endanger him, he'll puncture his gastrointestinal tract, he'll fracture his carnassials.*

"You're a good boy though. You know that? You're a good, *good* boy!"

She rubbed him briskly up and down his spine, and the dog responded by rolling onto his back, pawing playfully at her. She feinted gently and deliberately at each front paw in turn, in a game they had developed. He pulled each paw back as she reached for it, snapping with mock aggression at her hand. The game was a natural extension of their perfect trust and easy familiarity, and it ended when Elizabeth was finally able to grab Damien by the throat, right under his chin, and pretend to throttle him. Flipping back onto his stomach, he growled fiercely, struggling to get her hand into his powerful jaws. Finally she pretended her grip slipped and he quickly caught up her hand in his wide, powerful jaws, mouthing it gently, then licking it, finally laying his head down with a sigh, eyes cocked to her face, content to simply stare at the object of his worship.

Outside the observation room, Seville considered his options. Time was running out. If he was going to present the dog at the Netherlands (and oh, how sweet that would be) he must submit an abstract very shortly. The dog *must* work for him, and the dog must work perfectly. And, before much longer, he must rid himself of the girl. Seville sat and smoked and watched.

CHAPTER TEN

The belief in Science is the superstition of our time.
—M. WANDT

Joseph Seville continued sitting up smoking and thinking well past midnight. He thought about how he could arrange his schedule to allocate more time to the dog without exciting curiosity in his department and among his staff. He had told no one but Tom. He thought about how his life would change after his triumphant presentation of the dog and with a small, unconscious smile, he thought about the look that would be on Kotch's face. There was a tremendous amount of work to be organized and carried out, no doubt about that, but it would be interesting, exciting work. He wished fleetingly he could share it with longtime friend Viktor Hoffman, but he would tell no one until the dog worked for *him.* The sharp irony of having in his possession the single greatest behavioral breakthrough in centuries and being unable to utilize the animal, contributed greatly to his insomnia. He was determined to remedy the situation as quickly as possible.

Before him lay the seemingly mundane feat of eliciting a response to a given stimulus, in this case his commands, then putting the response under stimulus control. Simply put, putting the dog's verbal behaviors on cue. First-year student stuff. But the dog was not reacting in the usual fashion. The simplest approach behaviors were nearly impossible to achieve, and the animal's severe avoidance behavior was precluding any actual work on the verbal behaviors.

The dog disliked him.

It was a gut reaction, not a scientific observation. But his gut told him also that, try as he might, it would take months to sweet-talk the animal into working for him, and he didn't have months. Conditioning the dog through the use of positive reinforcement would have been his preferred method, but with his time constraints it was no longer feasible. He knew he was running out of time, both before he must submit a paper for inclusion in the Netherlands symposium, and before that erratic girl did something stupid.

Seville considered the problem of Elizabeth Fletcher. For now he saw no reason to stop her visits. Besides continuing to be dumbfounded by the behaviors he witnessed the girl evoking from the animal, he was shrewd enough to know that if he denied her access to the dog, she would have nothing to lose by going to the press or causing some other type of scene. Which got back to the fact once again, that if word of the dog got out now, when he was unable to make it function correctly on cue, it would be a screwup of unimaginable consequences. As a compromise between his desire to be done with her and the knowledge that he had to keep her quiet and content, he decided to allow daily visits to the dog, but with strict instructions that she was no longer to engage the animal in any form of verbal communication. He would explain that formal conditioning had begun and unstructured work would interfere and cause confusion to the animal.

Sitting in the dark, watching the slowly fading glow on the end of his cigarette, Seville remembered the chill autumn days spent out in tan fields edged with brilliant hardwoods, assisting his father in force-breaking their English pointer dogs. Joe Senior, had been a businessman with little time for his hobby, but he persisted in trying, placing at a few of the smaller trials. The pointers, sleek, sturdy dogs of the Elhew line, were sent away to trainers in the Southeast for most of the year so that their master could have the pleasure of trialing them without the inconvenience of putting in hours of training time. Sent home for the trial season, ultimately the dogs' unfamiliarity with their handler caused the animals to respond erratically, prompting Joe Sr. to fire each year's trainers and attempt, with his son's help, to rehabilitate the dogs' "training problems" on his own. The pattern would always be the same; the dogs, reasonably well trained and willing at the start, would soon be evidencing problems within weeks. Merciless application of the electric shock collar by Joe Junior and Senior would result in abjectly obedient animals no longer capable of stylish trialing. The dogs would be discarded by his father as "no account," and the next young prospect sent off to join a new trainer's string of hopefuls.

As a teenager Seville had enjoyed the guns, the shooting, and the feeling that came from controlling his father's dogs with the push of a button. He found trials boring however and was content to act as the gun for his father, killing pheasants over the dogs. His memory was vivid, however, on the techniques used by his father and other trainers to compel pointers to perform fast and accurate retrieves. A pointer, by nature, is a specialist. The instinct to freeze on scenting game has been so strongly set in the breed that tiny puppies will smash into stylish points at the scent of a game-bird wing. Their delicate nose and machinelike bodies are perfected for fast searching, location and indication of game. What a pointer does *not* want to do is have business with game once it is dead. They are disdainful of the warm, still bodies of their dead quarry, and often extreme measures are taken to try to convince a pointer that he must retrieve the bird to hand.

Using this memory as well as an intensive knowledge of the principles of positive and negative reinforcement, Seville now prepared to train the dog to be as fast and obedient with his verbal responses as his father's pointers had been with their retrieving. It shouldn't take long—some pointers had been force-broke to retrieve in one afternoon's session. Contemplating the successful completion of Damien's conditioning, the researcher's mouth pulled up in a wry grin. Put mildly, he was about to rock the behavioral world.

All right, partner," Seville said, "here we go." It was the next morning and the doctor was standing before the dog, which was secured to a new staple in the wall, installed moments before as a safety precaution for the trainer. A twelve-inch-long piece of half-inch steel cable kept the dog in position.

Conspicuously missing were the food pellets with which he had bribed the dog in earlier attempts. He had swapped the treats for the electric shock collar with which he could produce a negative stimulus the animal could control by its responses. A correct response stopped the negative stimulus. A slow or incorrect response, or a lack of a response, would result in the noxious stimulus persisting or increasing. It was straightforward negative reinforcement, and it was all Seville had left. If the dog wouldn't work for him to earn food or his praise, nor out of any sense of respect or affection for him, it *would* work to make the pain stop.

The man took up the electric shock collar's transmitter, a black, foot-long handheld cylinder from which a six-inch plastic-coated antenna protruded. From the table beside him he held up the black color card. "Damien," he said, speaking in a loud, clear voice, "what *color*?"

The bulldog stared in honest incomprehension. He knew the sound to make for that color, but it never occurred to him to say it now, to this man. He had never spoken to anyone but Elizabeth. He was nervous and puzzled by the restraint. He backed up carefully, testing the limit of the cable that restrained him to the wall. His pulse quickened automatically in fearful anticipation of *something*, and he felt this gut pull up into his rib cage.

Seville depressed a stud on the remote and held it down. It produced low-level electrical stimulation in a continuous mode to the underside of the dog's throat. Startled, Damien jerked and grunted in surprise. Unlike the momentary shocks he had experienced in Seville's lab, this didn't stop. At this level of intensity, the sensation was not extremely painful, more of a frightening, unpleasant and persistent sharp tingle. Damien bucked and struggled, instinctively trying to get away from the pain. There was nowhere to go and he couldn't even turn around. As the stimulation continued he shrugged and fought, trying to get his jaws on the collar around his own neck. He wanted to fight it, to rip it off, but his stocky bulldog neck would not allow his powerful jaws to reach it. As the sharp bite continued without letup, he sat down in total confusion and voiced his rising anxiety in a series of short, high-pitched grunts.

"What *color*?"

Damien heard him but was unable to focus on the man or what he was saying. He was concentrating on the frightening sensation. Taken so completely by surprise, he reacted on a purely defensive level, unaware of why he was being shocked, unaware even if it was punishment or simple circumstance. To make the pain go away he would have done *anything*, if he could only figure out what was required. The pain stopped momentarily, then returned, a little sharper. Now Damien panicked. He was not being stubborn, he honestly did not understand what was required of him.

Standing implacably before him, Seville was satisfied that the dog *did* indeed understand what he was to do and why he was being shocked. How could he not, when he responded perfectly to the same commands when issued by the girl? Seville was not trying to train a behavior here—Damien knew the correct response but simply refused to give it—so he felt no sympathy for the dog. He was convinced the collar's sharp bite would induce Damien in short order to comply with his commands. The dog must understand who was his master now. This was no different, Seville recalled, than a few ugly afternoon sessions he had spent with bull-headed pointers who refused to retrieve to hand.

More from instinct than reason, Damien frantically tried a behavior which Elizabeth had taught him. He threw himself to the floor of the cage, in the "down" position, but the twitching, jerking, biting low-level stimulation continued implacably. He cowered there, his confusion complete.

The stimulation continued and he could not stay still. He sat upright and threw an imploring look at the man before him.

"What color?" Seville asked again calmly. The dog stared at him, shaking with stress. The answer to making the pain go away lay there, with the man. But what did the man want? What *command* was he giving? The man was saying "color." What color? Was he to speak? Is *that* what the man wanted? He would try anything to make the collar stop. Even something as implausible as making the word-noises for White Pain.

"Red," the dog gasped, the first thing that came to his tormented mind. The power went off, the stimulation stopped, and Damien stood wild-eyed and spraddle-legged, panting and confused.

"Good," Seville praised the dog's proximation to the desired behavior. This was the big step—the first word Damien had uttered for him. Once he got the animal responding in any fashion, he could shape the correct answer easily.

"OK," Seville showed the dog the black card again, "what color?" The power came back on. The dog jerked and flinched again, his mind preoccupied by the sharp jolting, unable to think clearly.

"Red."

"Good," Seville said again, letting his finger off the button. The amount of time it had taken the dog to respond had decreased significantly. He was making excellent progress. He dropped the level of stimulation back down a notch.

"This is *black*," Seville prompted him, showing him the card again. "What color?"

The power back on, Damien blinked as the stimulation jerked him, but he never took his eyes off the man. "Black," he said quickly.

"Uhm, *very* good." The power came off. He held up the next card. Before he even gave the command, he depressed the stud, turning the collar on. This, Seville knew, built "motivation" to perform quickly, and was a standard electric collar training procedure.

"What color?"

The dog's eyes flicked to the card then back to the man. "Blue."

"Yes. Good." The dog had answered both instantly and correctly.

As Seville moved to reach for the next card, Damien went wild, trying to spin within the confines of the short cable. In anticipation of the forthcoming stimulation he was panicking, knowing it was coming. Unlike the senseless shocks which had pushed him toward the phenomenon of learned helplessness in Seville's lab, this stimulation he could control himself. He *would* learn that absolute compliance to his master's whims would cause the pain to cease, but as yet that process had not been completed. He fought it yet, unwilling and unable to trust the man who was hurting him. Seville ignored his struggles, aware that this was a normal stage and a predictable development with electric-shock training. Damien must work through his panic and fear, coming to accept the electrical stimulations as part of his everyday life. It was the way to simple, mindless cooperation. For the dog, obedience and communication were now only acts with which to cause the cessation of the electrical stimulation to his body. Nothing more.

Seville activated the collar at a low level and held up the next card, which was green. "What col . . ."

"Blue," Damien, rushing to answer, panicked and responded incorrectly. Seville ignored the reply.

"What color?"

"Blue, blue." Damien struggled wildly. He now knew what the man wanted, but something deep inside of him resisted. He did not *want* to obey this man; his very soul rebelled against it. Damien would work for The One to please her, but now, with this man, he only wanted away. An uncharacteristic feeling of rebellion arose within the dog. He did not like this man and he wanted nothing to do with him. Both body and mind twisting with conflict, he fought against what was being forced upon him.

His will was strong but the man knew how to break that will, had the tools to do it, and had a strong impetus to refashion the dog's soul to his own purposes.

Damien could not fight the frightening, implacable force of the collar. "Green."

"Yes." The power went off. "Very good."

The dog was panting heavily, unnerved and overheated. He stood staring listlessly at Seville, his sides heaving, while the behaviorist turned away, finished. Seville was pleased but not surprised that his choice of methods had worked so quickly and effectively; the collar was a tool commonly employed by certain types of dog trainers unable to gain compliance from their pupils any other way.

Seville's edict concerning her visitation rights with the dog filled Elizabeth with an uneasiness that made her want to stick close to Damien, to keep her hand protectively upon his brindle neck. She had a tight, ominous feeling that things were going to change drastically, and very soon. Realistically, she had assumed her days with the dog were numbered, so that afternoon, when Tom let her in, she was content to just sit in the little room with the bulldog, stroking him, and watching him sleep. Was it her imagination, or did he look particularly gaunt and tired this afternoon? Elizabeth fingered the black box on his collar and wondered at its purpose. Damien, missing her touch upon him, nudged his nose under her hand, asking her to simply replace it upon his neck.

She thought about how their mutual friendship had developed from tenuous tolerance to an affection so strong that it could cause such pain. To her father and grandfather, dogs were "basic models," research equipment to be ordered and purchased, used and discarded. Because of Damien, she knew, she had been spared that mind-set.

As the afternoon passed into evening for the two inmates of the observation room, Elizabeth marveled at Damien's attitude toward her race. Most dogs—really the entire canid family—were cowards when facing a confident human. Recalling Damien's reaction to the approach of strange men on their walks, she wondered about protective dogs. What about Damien? What about a dog who could walk among people with good grace, and even humor, and yet was capable of overpowering any one of them if need be, in defense of his human friend? Elizabeth had a strange feeling that it made him in some ways an equal to members of her own race. He was their match, and he knew it—yet he did not abuse his power, which was all the more remarkable considering how cruelly he had been used. To the contrary, he gave his submission and obedience to those he respected, and seemed willing to harm people only in defense of *other humans*.

Why didn't Damien simply bite people whenever *he* felt threatened? He was eager enough to attack in her defense, yet he would turn his head away rather than bite Seville. She wondered at the strange and strict code of ethics this bulldog appeared to live by. Just then the dog's eyes opened and he searched her face. *Is all well?* the look said. Having determined from her face that nothing was amiss, he let out a sigh and closed his eyes again. Without having said a word, he had as much as spoken. She smiled to herself.

Makes no difference to us, Seville, if you won't let us use words! We've never needed them.

Elizabeth's mind wandered, and she found herself pondering the idea of "humanity." She had heard religious and scientific speakers alike, describing the unique and special quality of being human. Somehow, no matter how terrible a person you were, you were more worthy than an animal by virtue of your species. She thought about Damien and what he would do for her if need be. He would give his life for her, she had no doubt. How many humans would do that? Her mind toyed with the idea of Seville and the dog standing on the edge of a raging river. If both fell in, who would she save? Who *should* she save? And by *whose* standards? What did her heart say? Was Seville's life somehow more important than Damien's—just because of his species? Or did loyalty and *friendship* mean more? Another scenario jumped before her—what if Seville was replaced by a human child? What then? Would Damien, she thought wryly, jump in the river to save a strange puppy and let *her* drown? Her mind, long disciplined to thoughts of human sanctity, drew back from the thought.

Elizabeth stared up at the acoustical material on the ceiling, wondering for the thousandth time how she and Damien had gotten into this situation, and where it was all leading. She would be cut out of the picture, that was a given. There would be no room for her simple love of the dog in the high-tech research world which would soon envelop Damien. Only the very biggest of the Big Boys would have direct access to the animal, and Seville would be right there, getting the glory that was important to him, never caring for a moment if the dog was tired or hungry or frightened or lonely. And the dog would probably come to work for Seville because that was his nature. The dog would, when she was gone, work his heart out for a word of praise from the man, no matter how Seville treated him. Observers would probably even think that the dog was happy, that he liked Seville. It was maddening.

The distinguished scientists who came to see Dr. Joseph Seville's famous "talking dog" would see a shadow of the real Damien—*her* Damien. They would draw conclusions about his intelligence, his ability to reason, his *soul*, all based upon what they saw in Seville's laboratory. They would never know—would never even suspect—that the real Damien was a dog who skimmed with his nose to the ground across a frozen meadow, leaving powdery ice crystals swirling back to the frozen grass behind him in the pink, predawn light. They would never appreciate the real Damien, who slept with his head in her lap, raising his eyes to hers in a silent communion far more powerful than any words he might be taught. And she knew with bitter certainty they would never recognize that Damien laughed as surely as she did at the little jokes they played on one another, that he loved to play hide and seek, and that he would run, zigzagging crazily with his mouth pulled back in a wide grin, because he loved to be chased.

Her revelry was abruptly disrupted by Tom, who opened the inner door and leaned his head in. "Doctor wants you to come out now, please."

Elizabeth nodded. "All right, Tom, what's this thing?" She touched the shock collar's box, snugged up against the dog's throat.

Tom hesitated, obviously uncertain what to say. Elizabeth picked up on it and sat up straighter. "What is it, Tom? What does it do?"

"It's . . . a training device. Doctor uses it to help with the dog's training."

"That's not telling me anything. *How* does it help? What does it do? Is it some kind of a recorder?"

"No ma'am. You'll have to ask . . . ."

"Seville? That jerk won't let me ask him anything," she said, forgetting for a moment that Seville, out in the office, could hear every word through the intercom. "You know that. I'm asking *you*. What does it do?"

"I'm sorry. You need to come on now."

Abruptly Seville appeared behind Tom, pushed the door open and came into the little room, his expression tight. Elizabeth swallowed, realizing he had heard what she had said.

"It's called an e-collar, Elizabeth. It delivers electrical stimulation when I depress these buttons." He held up the transmitter for her to see. "It's an established and humane method of applying either punishment or, in this case, negative stimulation which the dog learns to control by his responses. Does that answer your question?"

Elizabeth stared at the ugly black wand in his hand. "Electrical stimulation?" There was a pause. "You're *shocking* him? For what *purpose*? To *teach* him something?"

In all her life Elizabeth Fletcher had never been *this* angry. It was beyond angry. It was the sudden, fierce, roiling temper of her Celtic ancestors come to life. This man was applying electric shock to an animal with which she not only shared her deepest friendship, but which, in its helplessness and innocence, roused her maternal instincts as well.

Her eyes, filled with cold hate, moved slowly from Seville, to his aide, and down to the dog's collar. Tom was taking in the scene with what could almost be called concern. He tried to catch her glance with an expression she couldn't read, but she ignored him.

"No." Her head shook slowly. "No, you're not going to do that. You're *not*."

"I have and I will." Seville's voice matched her own. His gray eyes, hooded now, held hers. Beside her, the dog stood up, tense, watching the men.

She reached down and grabbed the collar, turning it, looking with deliberation for the buckle to remove it.

"Tom, get her out," Seville said sharply.

The aide stepped forward, trying to take her by the arm. She was strong and she was furious, and Elizabeth shook him off. She found the buckle and began to slip the strap through. Quickly Tom was back, this time using more force, and he grabbed her from behind. Elizabeth swore and struggled viciously to get loose. The dog's eyes widened, then narrowed to slits. He had a strong, natural taboo against biting these gods. However, when he saw the girl's distress coupled with the man's aggressive actions toward her, he advanced, silently, in the manner of his bullbaiting ancestors.

"Get her out, Tom." That was easier said than done. Elizabeth was pissed and had no compunction about taking it out on Seville's henchman.

"The *door*," Tom gasped at Seville. He was busy trying to control the woman while keeping a wary eye on the bulldog which was closing in on him. "The door!" It took a key to get the primate-proof inner door open. Tom began turning in a circle, keeping Elizabeth's body between himself and the dog.

"Get *off* me!" Elizabeth nearly broke loose again, and Tom was bleeding from his nose. Seville, appalled at the turn of events, took a deep breath and cursed his own temper. Determined to pick up the pieces as best he could, he placed himself where Elizabeth, struggling with Tom, could see him. "Elizabeth, *you're* going to make it harder on the dog." He said it quietly, but his words came through to her. He held up the transmitter in a meaningful fashion.

"You bastard!" she panted, then she glanced down. "No! Damien, *NO!*" she screamed at the dog. Damien had found an opening and he sunk his teeth into the aide's leg, shaking it savagely. Tom groaned painfully but maintained his grip on her. Elizabeth was shouting at the dog but Damien heard only The Voice, egging him on. Damien held on grimly while Seville adjusted the collar setting to the highest level and applied it continuously until at last the dog fell back with a strangled yelp. Tom grunted as the residual effects of the shock to the dog came through his leg. He half reached for his leg and at that moment Elizabeth wrenched free.

"Damien, *stop!*" Elizabeth hurried to the dog, grabbing him around the chest. "Get out, Tom, hurry!" she shouted. Tom looked questioningly toward Seville who, grim-faced, unlocked the door and let him out. Damien leaned after Tom's retreating form, pulling against Elizabeth's restraint. His eyes glittered with excited aggression.

"Damien, *no!* Stop! Calm down." She jerked on him, trying to get his attention. She looked up at where Seville stood, the transmitter in hand, obviously considering his next move. "Please, *please* don't shock him again. Leave him alone, he was just trying to protect me. It's *my* fault he did that."

"Yes, it is." Seville's anger which had flashed so hot and quick was subsiding, being replaced by cooler calculation. "This is very serious, Elizabeth. I think you and I are going to meet, later, and discuss your future on this project. I can assure you it is in jeopardy right now, but I'm not going to make any decisions while my aide is bleeding all over my floor. Go on, you know the way out. Expect my call."

Elizabeth didn't wait for the call. Assuming she would now be denied access to Damien indefinitely, she was waiting outside Hoffman's office the next afternoon. He glanced at her as he locked the door, and then turned to face her.

"What is it now, Elizabeth?"

"I'm really sorry, Professor," she said. "But I need you to listen to me. I need to ask you a question—it's very important."

Hoffman, impressed with the candor of her tone, tipped his head in an impatient affirmative. Elizabeth took a deep breath, held it, then spoke. "Do you know about Damien? About the talking?"

Hoffman began walking away. "Do you mind talking while we walk? I have an engagement." Elizabeth caught up beside him and asked again. "Has he told you? About the talking?"

"What are you referring to?"

"You don't know? He hasn't told you?"

"Who?"

"Seville."

"Told me what? What are you talking about?"

"About Damien, about what he can do."

They were walking through the trees to a parking lot visible in the distance. She had very little time.

"I haven't a clue what you're talking about."

He doesn't know!

Elizabeth felt a tiny sense of relief. If Hoffman did *not* know, then perhaps . . . She stepped in front of him, halting him in his tracks. "You *have* to listen to me. You're my last hope. *Please* give me five minutes of your time, and if what I say doesn't interest you, then, well, then believe me when I say I won't ever bother you again."

"It's the dog, right? You think he's being mistreated again?"

"You make it sound so trivial! I just don't understand. Why did you help Damien at all if you were going to simply abandon him to this fate? He would have been better off dead in the forest than this. I don't know why you've let the things happen to him that you have, but right now I'm going to appeal to whatever feeling you ever . . . ."

Hoffman cut her off with an uncharacteristic sharpness. "Look, I've scrutinized what I did with that dog to a fare-thee-well. I was foolish to try and help the dog to the detriment of my research. It was the lapse of an old and sentimental field biologist and I had no business interfering with nature and abandoning project protocol, but I did, and I wish now I hadn't. The animal is not appropriate as a pet, which you don't seem willing to accept. Why can't you let this go? Why are you so obsessed with this dog?"

"We're *friends*, Professor Hoffman, friends. Do you know what that means? That means I don't walk away when he needs me. Damien's done the same for me. Please just let me explain what has happened; you have no idea what's going on."

Hoffman sighed, and stepped around her, continuing toward his car. "Well, what is it? What's going on?"

"Look, what I'm going to tell you you're not going to believe. That's OK. All I ask is that you check it out. Go see for yourself. I'm asking you because I can't help him. No one will listen to me. Let me ask you a question. Do you know where Damien is right now?"

"I believe he's in the long-term kennel complex."

"He's not, Professor Hoffman. He's at Dr. Seville's *house*." She let that sink in, and she could see that despite himself her statement intrigued him. "Would you like to know *why* he's there?"

Hoffman glanced at her disapprovingly as he shifted his battered briefcase to his other hand. "It's none of my business what another investigator does."

"Yeah, there you go! That's the problem—nobody at this University cares. Damien is being *tortured* over at that man's house, and everybody thinks it's 'protocol.' Well . . ."

"It *that's* how you see research, Elizabeth, then you have no business enrolled *here*, in medical school. You belong with those sorry individuals standing around with "Stop Animal Research" signs outside the Life Sciences building. You belong on the fringe, with the humaniacs, not as a responsible member of the medical or scientific community. But I think you're smarter than that, Elizabeth."

"I taught Damien how to say some words. Quite a few words. Not *just* say them, he knows what they mean. He can actually talk like a person. Seville found out about it and he stole the dog from me. He wants all the credit, and you know what? I could care less about that. I *tried* to work with him so that he could *get* his precious credit, be a big shot though he has had nothing to do with anything, if he would just treat Damien all right. But then he . . ."

Hoffman tipped her a patronizing look.

"I know what you're thinking. Go see for yourself! Damien can name colors, shapes, ask for things, lots of stuff. I taught him, and now that bastard took him and . . ."

Hoffman stopped abruptly. "What are you trying to pull here, Elizabeth? I don't . . ."

"Go *see* for yourself! Go up there and see for yourself! Ask him! Make him show you. You have to believe me because it's all true."

Elizabeth waited, watching his eyes. Hoffman shook his head.

"He *speaks?*"

"Yes he does."

"*You* taught him this?"

"Yes."

"And *what* does he say?"

"He can name colors, shapes, ask for things, all sorts of things."

The professor sighed and started toward his car again.

"Do it. Please! Go see him. But *please*, you can't tell Seville that I spoke to you. You *can't*. He's probably never going to let me near Damien again, but he'd *never* let me around again if you do. Then Damien will have no one looking out for him. You can't even believe what that man is doing to Damien. He couldn't get Damie to work for him any other way, so now he's put this collar on him that shocks him with electricity. That dog is the most willing animal in the world, and he's put *that* collar on him." Elizabeth's voice broke and, ashamed, she stopped and composed herself. Out of pity for the very real emotion he could see she was experiencing, Hoffman hesitated beside her.

"I've known Joe Seville for years, and I've never known him to be less than professional in his handling of animals."

"I saw with my own eyes what he was doing. If that is professional, then the word means nothing. Professional means you *know* what you're doing. When you have to use electric shock—a form of torture—to get an animal to work for you, you don't know what you're doing. That's pretty obvious I would think. The poor dog is so freaked out—you should see him! It's just like the Stockholm Syndrome—you know your psychology—he's put so much stress on Damien that the dog will do *anything* to appease him now."

They started walking again and they reached the man's car. He stopped, set his briefcase on the hood, and fumbled for his keys. "I'm having a hard time believing your story, of course." He sighed. "I can see that one way or the other, this issue needs to be resolved so we can all get some peace. I'll go see Joe. No matter what I find, if for some reason I feel the dog's treatment is inappropriate, I'll say something to Joe. Will that satisfy you?"

"Thank you, Professor, *thank you* very much. That's all I'm asking. Go see Damien. See what it's like for him there." She lifted her eyes to him. "I pissed him off yesterday, and he's never going to let me see Damien again. I know that much. Damien will be completely alone with a man who will do *anything* to force the dog to work for him. I'd like to think he has at least you there, watching out for him. Please."

Hoffman made a dismissive gesture. "This is quite a story you've told me, young lady. I know Joe and I'm confident Damien is getting nothing but the finest care in his hands. *Nobody* wants to see him ill-treated, Elizabeth, and I don't know what gives you that idea." He raised his hand to stave off her further comment. "I'll speak to Joe. I'll check on Damien."

"You won't mention me? Please."

Hoffman threw his briefcase in the car and got in. "I've got to go. Please don't worry. If there is a problem, I'll deal with it. Please trust my judgment."

His car pulled away leaving Elizabeth to tread her way, deep in thought, through the maple-lined walkways. She was considering what Hoffman had said. *Did* she belong with the animal-rights extremists? It was disconcerting. In another month or so she would be a medical student, beginning the rigorous journey toward the knowledge and prestige of an MD degree. She saw nothing she had done so far as seriously jeopardizing that goal. She was simply trying to save one dog from a particularly inhumane situation.

People who fought for animal-rights issues were the kind of people who would try to shut her father's lab down. Disrupt valuable research.

The enemy.

Or are they? Why hadn't she thought of this before? The humaniacs might help her get Damien away from Seville. She couldn't see how, but she knew at least *they* would see the why. Would they help her? The thought of gaining powerful allies against Seville thrilled her.

But the idea was too radical. Too many years of seeing those people as the enemy made the taste of their help bitter in her mouth. She would wait and see what Hoffman did before she even considered allying herself with the animal-rights movement.

Viktor Hoffman stepped out of his car and crossed the driveway, noticing as he did that one of Seville's cars was parked on the lower level, near the side door. A frequent visitor to his friend's home, he walked down the sloping stairs to the side door and knocked to announce his arrival. He was not expected. Receiving no answer but loath to walk all the way around to the front of the house again, he tried the door, which was unlocked.

"Hello? Joe? Tom?" There was no reply. He stepped inside. "Joe?" He walked ahead to the workroom and poked his head in the door. The brindle dog was in a shipping crate near Seville's desk. No one was in the room. A hose snaked across the floor from a sink through a door into the small room which Hoffman remembered as having housed a primate some years before. From behind the partially opened door came the faint sounds of spraying water.

He stepped up near the crate to peek in the Plexiglas wall and see who was inside the small room. As he passed the crate he greeted the dog. "Hello, Damien."

"Hello."

The biologist froze. "Tom?" It hadn't sounded like Tom. It hadn't sounded—*right*. He stepped back to the lab door and glanced down the hall. It was still empty. The sound of hosing and the scent of bleach still came from the cracked door.

"Out."

He turned back to the room slowly. The dog in the crate met his stare. "Out," the animal said hopefully.

Hoffman staggered back, feeling for the counter behind him and, finding it, stood there staring at the dog, his expression one of utter shock. *"Jesus."*

Tom appeared from out of the animal's room, dragging the hose. Steam from the hot water used to clean the room followed him out, swirling and dissipating into the cooler air of the room.

"What," Hoffman said pointing at the dog, "what in God's name is going on, Tom? Tell me!"

The aide paled. "What do you mean, sir?"

"That animal just *spoke* to me! So help me, Tom, it did. Plainly—*in English.*"

"Oh," Tom said quietly.

"Oh?" Hoffman swung to face the young man. "I tell you this *animal* just *spoke* to me, in plain English, and all you can say is 'oh'?"

Tom swallowed. "Uhm . . ."

Hoffman dropped to one knee before the crate. "She said he could . . . I didn't believe her—not for a moment. Would you? No, no one would." He tore his eyes from the dog and looked up at Tom. "What I heard is not possible, it's just not possible." He threw his hands up and turned back to the dog. "This is *not* possible. What *actually* is going on here?"

Damien spoke again, hoping this man would let him out. "Out. Now. Sgo."

Hoffman stared, eyes bulging. Tom groaned softly. "Dr. Hoffman, he's going to *kill* me. He didn't want anyone to see this right now. He wanted . . ."

Hoffman was bright red, and his head was shaking. "Tom, how can this be? What am I seeing? How was this done?"

When Tom didn't answer, Hoffman turned around and saw him standing there, and he understood the look on his face.

"For God's sake, Tom, don't worry about him. It's not your fault I walked in here. But *this*," he stood slowly, shaking his head, "*this* is not possible. How, in the name of little green apples, did he do this? How? It's not possible, it's just not *possible*."

Tom's austere features managed a grimace. "I'll go get him. I think it would be better if you talked to him."

"Oh, I'll *talk* to him, all right. Is he upstairs?" he said with some heat, then he turned around and continued to stare at the dog and shake his head. He felt unable to do anything else, and he knew he looked like a fool. "This just isn't possible," he muttered.

"I'll go find him." Tom slunk from the room like a dog to a whipping. Hoffman knelt before the crate again, bending down till his face was inches from the dog. "Speak! Go on now, speak!"

"Hello," it replied in a strangely rushed, forced manner. Then it hesitated and said plaintively, "Out."

"*Amazing!*" Hoffman whispered. The dog and the man stared at each other, waiting for Seville.

Seville came into the room with Tom at his heels. "Ah, Viktor," he said, and his voice was cold. Hoffman stood his ground, looking at the younger scientist over his half glasses. "Well, Joseph?"

There was a long, tense silence, which was broken when Seville looked down, shook his head and grinned. "I was going to tell you soon . . ." he said ruefully. "You can understand my desire to perfect it first?"

"*Perfect?* Joe, the thing speaks clearly—I mean . . ." He stopped. He was speechless. He couldn't stop grinning. He couldn't even think of what questions to ask.

Seville glanced at Damien with a trace of pride. "It *is* getting fairly good."

After the first sharp flash of anger, Seville realized he was deeply relieved to share this extraordinary event with his oldest and closest friend. "Think I'll shut Kotch up with this one?" he finally said with a smirk.

Hoffman burst out laughing. "Oh, Jesus, Joe, I need a drink. Right now. Are you going to try for the Netherlands?"

Seville called Tom, who had been putting the hose away as unobtrusively as possible. "Tom, run upstairs and get Viktor a scotch." He waved Hoffman to a stool. "Bring the bottle," he called after him. "And two glasses." They sat. "Oh yes, I'll get in. No one knows about this, Viktor, no one. They'll think I've gone insane, expect to see me make a fool of myself. And then, this. What would you give to be there at *that* moment, eh?"

"Jesus, Joe, you better have a crash cart handy. For Kotch, I mean it."

Seville laughed a short, harsh laugh. Hoffman's mind began, slowly, to work again. "How in the world did this start? Jesus, Joe . . ."

"When I asked Tom, he said you mentioned Elizabeth. Did she tell you about this?"

"She came and asked me to check it out, yes. She's still worried about the dog. She's concerned about what you might do if you find out she approached me though, so go easy on her. She seems a nice kid, just undisciplined."

"What did she tell you?"

"Not much—nothing about how all this started. She claims she taught the dog to speak, and that you took it away from her." Hoffman saw a muscle twitch in the other man's cheek and hastened to add, "She's just an emotional girl, Joe. She wants the dog treated like a pet. She won't listen to reason. She's never going to go away if we just ignore her. I told her I'd come look. I know you, I know you wouldn't be doing anything unethical. I'll tell her that. It was the only thing I could think of. But what *did* happen?"

Seville was quiet for a moment before he spoke and Hoffman, who knew the man well, let him alone. After a moment Seville exhaled, smiled darkly and said, "Well, I guess my schedule has been moved up for me. I'm glad though, Vic, for whatever reason, that you're on board now. You're not going to believe what you see because I still don't really believe it. What occurred was some kind of spontaneous vocal behavior that just happened to end up being accidentally reinforced in an appropriate fashion. Once that happened, evidently the behavior was quite easily shaped. I know that's a little hard to swallow, but there," he pointed to the dog in the crate, "it is." He shrugged his shoulders.

Hoffman tipped his head. "He just started talking one fine day. You don't expect me to believe *that*?" The men shared a small laugh as Tom came in and the men took their glasses. Tom set the bottle on the counter between them, taking in their expressions out of the corner of one eye.

"Would you like the dog back in the room?" he asked.

"No, he's fine there. I'll be working him in a moment. Go ahead and take off, Tom. I'll see you out here tomorrow at eight."

Tom nodded politely to both men and left without a word.

Seville grinned at Hoffman's first swallow. "Somehow the kid got the dog to respond to some cue cards, and she shaped the beginning of some rudimentary vocal behaviors. I happened to be over at Katharine's office when the kid brings the dog in and yes, Katharine put the project in my hands."

Viktor shrugged.

"This kid has these cards, little cards—you're not going to believe this story—she gets these little cards and with the dog standing there in Katharine's office, says 'OK, what's this?' The damn thing says 'green' or something. Can you imagine?"

Hoffman held up his hand suddenly. "Stop! Not another word, wait . . ." He reached for the Scotch, poured his shot glass full, leaned over and filled Seville's. "All right, I'm ready," he said as he set the bottle back on the counter.

"That moment took five years off my life span," Seville said. "Of course I knew immediately that my life—my very destiny," here he grinned wickedly, "involved that dog, the Netherlands and our boy August D. Kotch." Hoffman blinked. Seville shrugged. "The rest is history. I moved him here and I've had a shit job shaping any kind of reliable performance. This girl just reinforced him willy-nilly, which made it difficult. She spoiled him and made him sullen. However, he's working well now, and it *is* absolutely amazing." Seville looked into his glass. "You won't believe what he can do, actually. It amazes me, Viktor, every day. By the way," he said as he took the last of his drink, "what did he say to you? Just now?"

"What *did* he say? Jesus, I was so shocked, I . . . I think he said . . . You know, I don't have any idea!"

The two men stared at each other. After a moment Seville grinned. "You want to see him work, don't you?" He got up a trifle unsteadily. Hoffman didn't even answer. He poured out two more drinks and then sat, arms folded on his chest, an excited grin on his face. "Jesus, Joe . . ."

Seville rummaged around and found his flash cards. He was taking an awful chance working the dog like this, before the conditioning was farther along, but he wanted to show off. He pulled the dog from the crate and placed him on his chain against the wall. He took up the shock collar remote in his hand. "OK, dog, it's show time."

Seville and Damien ran through the color cards flawlessly. "Well?" He turned toward Hoffman. Hoffman's exhalation was audible across the room.

"Unbelievable, *unbelievable.* I can't even think what to say."

Seville went to stand beside Damien, who pulled away to the furthest limits of his short tie. "You know, it's even more amazing than what you're seeing here. This dog can actually *talk.* Carry on a conversation of sorts, not just name objects. I've seen it; he can initiate contact, put words together to make new 'words.' It's absolutely amazing. He won't do it well for me yet— I've just started the process—but we're working on it, aren't we, Buddy? And he will. He will."

Hours later, the two men came out of the lab together. They went, rather unsteadily, down the hall and Hoffman went out the door, calling back to Seville that he was "too much," and calling him "Dr. Doolittle." Seville had a lopsided grin, and shook his head as he shut the door behind his friend.

Seville took the dog from his training position and placed him back inside his room, where the dog relieved his bladder and then made his usual inspection of the small, bare room, ever hopeful of finding a food or water bowl. At the sound of the door opening again Damien looked up expectantly. He knew he had done well and pleased Seville, and that felt Good. He didn't like the man, but he had learned through harsh repetition that it was far better to please the alpha than to displease him. The man had not praised or rewarded him for his effort. Just a word would have done. Like all dogs, Damien had a well-developed sense of justice, and the unfairness of the man's failure to praise him was an unpleasant twinge. And there was guilt. Damien was sure he had done well—but perhaps he *had* done something wrong? He was a working dog—his soul ached for a human's approval.

Seville did not enter the room this time, he only opened the door wide enough to step in, holding the door open with his left leg. He gestured to Damien with a food and water bowl, one in each hand.

"Here you go, Buddy." The smell of alcohol reached Damien, who noticed the man was unsteady. As Seville leaned over to set the bowls on the floor, he took an involuntary step forward to steady himself. The door shut behind him with a quiet but firm click. Seville straightened up and turned around. On the other side of the door, the key was still in the lock. He stared at the door.

"Oh, *damn it!*"

Tom would not come again till morning. He was locked in.

Damien watched with growing interest as the researcher turned back around to face him. He wasn't sure what was going on, but he could tell that the man was discomposed. Damien eyed the water bowl; his thirst was a persistent ache at this point and he wanted the water at Seville's feet badly. Humans had a strange and unnerving way of insisting subordinates such as he *approach* the alpha and *take* food and water *from* them. This, of course, was the most incorrect thing possible, and dangerous—The Voice told him so each time he did it.

The dog came forward, hesitating at every step, his eyes on Seville. The man stared back, a strange expression on his face. Damien hesitated, unsure what to do. He knew Seville would insist he come forward and drink at his feet—that was the way it had been for weeks now—but he was put off by the man's unfamiliar and disquieting body language. Something was *frightening* the man. From six feet away, the dog stared straight at Seville, his eyes riveted to the man's eyes, searching for clues to his strange behavior. Like summer thunder, The Voice rumbled low and distant—*something's not right.* The dog's hair rose involuntarily as he became increasingly spooked. The doctor took a step back, then another, until his back was against the door.

"Jesus," the man said, his voice tight.

The dog looked at the water bowl. *Water.* His need was imperious, and he took another step forward.

"*Get back!*" Seville shouted, pointing his finger at him, and Damien jerked to a halt. Unsure what he had done wrong, and increasingly agitated over the strange turn of events, he retreated to the Plexiglas front of the room. Damien watched as Seville moved away from the food and water bowls, carefully edging along the opposite wall, toward the Plexiglas window at the front of the room. When the man reached the halfway point, as if by mutual consent, they swapped sides, the dog scooting hurriedly past him to the back of the cage and the water, Seville moving to the window. Damien stooped to drink, his eyes never leaving Seville's face.

Seville looked about him at the small, bare room. There was nothing with which to protect himself should the dog attack; there wasn't even anywhere to sit, and he needed to sit down.

"Damn it!" Seville said again, angrily. He ran his hands through his hair and then slowly removed his lab jacket. Never taking his eyes off the dog, he wadded it up and set it on the floor, then sat upon it and leaned up against the Plexiglas wall with a grunt.

Damien finished the water but was far too troubled to eat. He began pacing a U-shaped pattern which kept him from having to pass by the human, while Seville watched him uneasily from his seat on the floor.

The dog had never seen Seville sitting on the floor before, and he found it unsettling. It didn't feel right to have the alpha in such an unaccustomed, inappropriate and powerless position. The dog became increasingly agitated at the *wrongness* of it. Seeing the man's uneasiness, the dog wondered why Seville was doing *nothing* about whatever it was that was frightening him. The sudden lack of the strong command and leadership which had been a consistent hallmark of Seville's relationship with the dog made Damien uncomfortable. Within a canine social structure, there can be only one undisputed and assertive alpha. The alternative is constant conflict and destructive infighting. The fairer and more assertive the alpha, the more pacific life within the group is. The need to keep cohesion and clear rank order among the members is an overwhelming drive for this reason, and at no time is cohesion as a pack more important than when danger threatens.

The disquieting effect of the entire situation made the dog's hair rise and fall over his shoulders, as waves of uneasiness passed over him. Why *didn't* Seville rise, why *didn't* he handle whatever was bothering him as an alpha should? *What* was he afraid of, and why couldn't Damien smell it or see it? The dog felt keenly his obligation to help the man, but hadn't the vaguest idea what the threat was. If it frightened his formidable master, it must be dreadful indeed. Damien listened hard, and stared into Seville's face, and tested the air, but he could not perceive the danger.

Damien could stand it no longer. His alpha was troubled, and he, personally, had the horrible unsettled feeling that came with not knowing where he stood with his master. Why had the man told him to go away? What had he done wrong? He had pleased the man earlier, he was sure of it. He had done his best, and now the man rejected him and sent him away.

Having given his heart to Elizabeth, Damien's soul now ached for the leadership of a human. It was the most basic component of his domestic canine nature. Not having her, Damien could not help but turn to the only human available for that leadership. Damien did not like Seville, but he was a man, and the dog looked to him for direction. The uncertainty of the situation felt Bad. He *must* do something.

Avoiding direct eye contact, the dog slunk forward toward Seville, appeasement written into every line of his body. The Voice urged him to confirm his allegiance with his alpha, in an effort to maintain "pack" cohesion. Seville remained silent and still as the dog crept up the last few feet, eyes squinted and tail down. The pit bull was unsure how the man would tolerate his approach, so he crouched beside him, not presuming to be too familiar, and respectfully laid just the tip of his muzzle on Seville's thigh. The man was stiff, unmoving, and Damien waited in an agony of expectation for his reaction. Would he be rebuffed again, or would Seville accept his subordination and affirm their allegiance, as man and dog, as they faced this unknown threat? Worse, would the man continue this horrid *nothingness*?

After what seemed an eternity to the waiting dog, Seville's hand descended cautiously onto his broad head, and stayed there. Damien thrilled to the alpha's acceptance, and his relief was exquisite. Now, no matter what fearful thing faced them, they were a "pack," and they would face it together. It had been thus, with the two species, for untold thousands of years. The dog lay all night beside the man, vigilant and watchful, protecting the scientist as he slept.

The next morning Tom came into the office and, not seeing his boss, looked for him. Thinking Seville might already be in the dog's room he glanced in the window. Seville was slumped against the Plexiglas wall, asleep. Beside him the dog lay curled up, asleep also. The doctor's hand was resting on the dog's head, the animal's chin on his thigh.

Tom's eyebrows climbed an inch. He walked back to the outer door, opened it and saw the key stuck in the inner door. One side of his mouth twisted up.

At the sound of the door opening, the dog rose to his feet. When Tom poked his head in, Damien charged, bristling and growling in fury, and Tom slammed the door shut.

Seville scrambled to his feet, swearing and clutching his head. He looked about, squinting. "Damn it! Be quiet, do you want to kill me with that barking?" He walked toward the door. "Tom? Is that you?" The dog had his nose to the crack under the door, inhaling deeply and loudly. His hair was erect all along his back. The door opened a fraction, and a key was tossed in, landing to the dog's left. Damien darted after it, smelled it, then went back to his vigil at the door. Seville picked up the key with a small groan, holding his back. "That's enough! Get back," he said to the dog, and Damien fell back, watching with anxious protectiveness as Seville let himself out.

CHAPTER ELEVEN

What creature that, so fierce so bold
That springs and scorns to leave his hold?
It is the Bulldog, matchless, brave—
Like Briton on the swelling wave.

—PIERCE EGAN

Viktor Hoffman knew that all he had to do was wait. He knew Elizabeth would seek him out. The question was, what exactly was he going to do about her? Nothing he had witnessed at Seville's house had caused him the least concern for the safety or well-being of the animal.

Hoffman set down his coffee with a sigh; nothing short of Joe feeding the dog bonbons while it lay on a velvet couch would satisfy the girl. She was naive to the extreme, seeing the dog only as a pet when the reality was that Joe Seville had taken a half-wild and fully unpredictable animal and turned it into a scientific phenomenon. He felt for the sentimental premed student; she seemed a decent sort, just caught up in the single-minded preoccupation with ill-advised ventures which seem to be a hallmark of youth. For whatever reason, she continued to look to him for affirmation of her fears concerning the dog's treatment, a concern he simply did not share. He pondered the safest way to proceed.

The problem was exacerbated by Seville's legitimate concern about withholding information regarding his project until the time was right. They both knew that even the slightest whiff of "talking dog" would open Seville up to untold heights of ridicule and professional derision. Leaked out the wrong way, without the strong and steady keel of sound, dignified, scientific presentation, even the ultimately credible presentation which Seville was capable of would never be free of the taint of pop science. That, he knew, Seville could never tolerate. The girl must be kept silent.

Seville had finally agreed to allow him to act as moderator, but it was unlikely that the girl would simply accept his assurance that all was well with the dog. Hoffman sighed again. If only peace could somehow be restored to the situation, Joe could get on with his project, Elizabeth could return to her studies with her mind—hopefully—at ease, while he, Viktor, could sip his coffee and smoke his pipe in relative peace. He left a large note taped to the sliding door of his office advising the girl to call for an appointment. And then he waited.

It was late when Tom appeared at his upstairs study door. Seville had forgotten the young man was still on the premises, working late looking up references, obscure or otherwise, on acquisition of language in any animal species. Tom often came and went, catlike, without Seville even noticing.

"Is there anything you need before I leave, sir?"

"Oh, Thomas." Seville waved with his cigarette toward the aide, "How's the leg?"

"Fine, thanks." Tom had, in fact, received three sutures in a nasty laceration and had two deep punctures cleaned out. Other than the time it took to actually stitch him up, Tom had not missed a moment of work, which was why Seville valued him so highly. He was the right sort. "Professor Hoffman called. The girl will be at his office tomorrow at 2:30. He'd like you to come."

"Wouldn't miss it." Seville took a drag on his cigarette. "Not for the world," he said as he exhaled.

"The way you've got that dog working now, I can't imagine what people are going to say when they find out about it."

"Oh, it's going to be beautiful. *Absolutely* beautiful. I'm considering the feasibility of submitting the paper by the end of the month. It's a gamble and it's rushing, something I damn well didn't want to have to do, but I'm not sure I have an alternative—that crazy girl could do anything at any time." He shook his head. "Jesus, we know that now, don't we?"

"I'll get here early tomorrow, sir, we'll get it done. Chase can manage at the office."

Seville nodded. "Call Chase tomorrow and tell him I'm not coming in for a few days—that'll make him happy. Tell him to hold off on the Cornell thing, that can wait. And try to get across to him that I better not be called at home every thirty minutes with petty personnel problems. Tell him to just handle it. Everything.

"Also, call Johnston, you know, the department head, and better ask Katharine to help you get in touch with—what's his name—you know, the dean of . . ."

"Dr. Pritchard, sir."

"Pritchard. Right, I better do him too. Tell them we need to talk. I suppose I should get some of these guys on board, or it'll be my ass when this blows. I better call Pritchard myself—you call Johnston." He hesitated, thinking. "And Tom, I hate to do this to you, but would you call the ex and tell her I can't take Christina this weekend? Better you than me, Buddy."

"No problem, sir. Anything else?"

"I think we got it, son. We just have to get our ducks in a row and get that paper in."

"Well, good night then, see you tomorrow. I'll let myself in, probably around seven?"

"Fine. Good night, Tom."

Below Seville, in the basement, Damien slept curled on the floor of the stark, white room. As he slept he dreamed, and besides the usual nightmares featuring Seville, the dog dreamed joyful dreams, the dreams of a bulldog. In his most pleasant dreams there was always a man, a man much like himself, and they understood each other. The man was large, barrel-chested and bald, and he wore a dirty leather apron. In life, Damien had never seen such a man, but in the strange sleeping memory of his genetic makeup he was ever present. Man and dog sat before a little ever-present fire, and the bulldog's world was perfect when the man would glance at him. They would get up, the man and the dog, and leave the little hut and work together all day alongside other rough men, among cattle.

Cattle. The mix of dust and bovine legs swirling before him intoxicated the dog. Their rank scent filled his nose and their cries his ears. The men killed the cattle, and cut them up. Sometimes, when the dream was at its best, the man would nod to Damien and point at a bellowing, resisting bull. Then Damien would be allowed to rush among the beasts, and slam into the one indicated. The beast would try to crush the life out of him, but he would hold, and the dream was so real Damien could smell the bull's sweet breath snorting from the snout he held so firmly. Then—and here Damien would twitch and moan in a bulldog's ecstasy—then, while he gripped the twisting, bellowing, murderous animal, the man would come close and kill it. He and the man, together, killed the beast. The man alone could not control the savage bull, making the bulldog that followed at his heels invaluable. Working together in dust and danger, man and bulldog melded together into a single entity, a single link in an ageless chain binding the two species together. It was rough, dangerous work, and there was no other type of dog on earth that dared it.

Then Damien would wake, and find himself imprisoned still in a small, sterile, white room, where there was a scientist instead of a butcher, and no real work for him to do. He would sigh then, the long, sad sigh of a patiently waiting dog, and continue his steadfast vigil for Elizabeth.

Elizabeth's hands gripped the steering wheel too tightly as she drove along, her arms pushing her stiffly back into the seat of the little truck. She was so tense and knotted up it felt good on her back to be pressed into the seat, and she flexed a little, hoping to relieve the muscle ache she had been living with for the past few days.

Today she was meeting with Hoffman. What would he say? It was no longer inconceivable for her to imagine someone *not* thinking Seville's treatment of the dog cruel, so the real question which needed answering was what would she do if he refused to help her? The dog was willing to protect her, without giving it a second thought, evidently. Would she hesitate when it came time to act in his behalf? If she failed to act she would be betraying such innocence that the thought of it made her wince. She frowned, finding fault with herself. The Voice within her mind, quiet and low, said only, *he would never forsake you.*

"What would you have me do?" she shouted angrily into the truck cab, but The Voice was gone, leaving her alone with her doubts. Before she reached the University she knew it was up to her to find a way to save her dog.

Elizabeth seated herself in the plain, straight-backed chair that was the only other piece of furniture in Hoffman's cubicle besides his metal desk and duct-taped chair. Sitting grim-faced while Hoffman shored up a tower of files on his desk that were threatening to tumble over, she was not surprised to see Seville's form appear at the sliding glass door, open it, and walk in.

So Hoffman had betrayed her.

She guessed she wasn't really surprised after all. Bitter disgust for the biologist welled up in her soul as she watched him make a show of offering the new arrival his seat. "I'll stand," Seville said and, folding his arms, took up a position near the door, to the left of Elizabeth.

She sat, resolved now. She had made up her mind on the drive over that she must save Damien. At Seville's arrival she had made up her mind what she had to do next. Now this meeting was simply a formality. Nothing these men could offer would satisfy her. How could it, when she would accept nothing less than Damien's removal from the control of Dr. Seville?

"How are you this afternoon, Elizabeth?" Hoffman, uncomfortable, wanted to begin.

"You tell me, Professor Hoffman."

The older man seemed taken aback by her uncustomary rudeness and Seville addressed her. "Professor Hoffman has gone through some trouble to arrange this meeting, Elizabeth. It's not something either he or I particularly need. He set this up as a kindness for you, so perhaps you'd give him the courtesy of being civil."

Unable to think of anything clever or defiant to say, Elizabeth remained silent. Hoffman, more uncomfortable than ever, tried again. "We understand this is difficult for you; that's why Joe and I wanted to set this meeting up, so we could all sit down and resolve the issues between us."

Seville's cell phone rang, and he shut the ringer off without looking at it.

Hoffman started again. "Realistically, Elizabeth, how do you see us resolving your concerns?"

"I guess I don't see that happening, Professor. Dr. Seville told me that if I went to anybody but him with my concerns he would deny me access to Damien. Well, obviously he now knows I asked you to go look for yourself how he was treating the dog. He's not going to let me back with Damien, and I'm relatively certain you're going to tell me you didn't find anything wrong with what he was doing. So . . ." She raised both hands in a questioning gesture.

"Nothing could be resolved by my being furtive, and I don't work that way. You asked me to see what Joe was doing and I did. I asked you to trust my judgment, and I hoped you would. My judgment is that the only way we will ever resolve this is to meet and discuss it openly.

"I sympathize with the fact that you'd like to see the dog treated as a pet. The simple truth is, it cannot be. I've known Joe for over twenty years now. I've never had reason to question his ethics in all that time, and I don't see any reason to now. You have to understand, Elizabeth, the man's a veterinarian, he has a Ph.D. in behavior—he *understands* how to handle dogs. If the truth be told, he has many more years experience than you do.

"We're all grateful to you for bringing the dog's exceptional behaviors to our attention, but now is the time for you to step back and let Joe show the animal off to its full potential. He is uniq—"

"How can you say full potential? He has to shock Damien with electricity to get him to do *anything*. I didn't. There are probably other people out there that Damien would work with—all I've ever asked is that the dog be treated within *normal* humane standards."

She didn't see what Seville did beside her, but Hoffman held up a restraining finger to him and went on. "You have an unfair bias against a conditioning method you are unfamiliar with. Try to believe me when I tell you that using an e-collar actually makes it easier for the dog to learn. Damien quickly learned how to control the mild negative stimulus by his own actions. That in itself gives dogs confidence. We don't expect you to understand the intricacies of shaping behavior, but we do expect you to understand that both Joe and I have the dog's best interests at heart."

What in the world do they expect me to say to something like that?

She sat for several long moments, unsure what to say or do next. The men seemed content to force her to make the next move.

"So," she turned and addressed herself to Seville. "*Will* you let me see him?" It seemed the only issue with the remotest chance of being negotiated. She expected Hoffman had suggested to his friend that he show some clemency toward her as a concession to keep her quiet.

Seville regarded her for some time before he spoke. "Tom required stitches as a result of your last visit. You placed yourself, myself and my aide in danger. You attempted to interfere, by physical force, with the training of the dog," he tolled off her crimes. "Then, you went against our agreement by coming to Viktor with your continued complaints against me. Despite all that, I *am* willing to consider allowing you access to the animal. However, I think you would agree that I am justified in having certain concerns regarding you."

She raised her eyebrows in a small defiant affirmative which he, but not Hoffman, could see.

"What I am willing to consider is a continuation of your visits after a one-month probation. If you can show me that you are willing to cooperate fully and act responsibly, then I will reconsider. This is a one-time offer, Elizabeth, you blow this and you're gone. If you behave yourself, I'll give consideration to your return to the project."

A small smile played about Elizabeth's tight lips. "OK," she said softly, "that sounds fair. I guess that's as good as I'll get."

Seville and Hoffman glanced at each other, and she saw it. It made no difference, really, what she said or agreed to. She knew she was naive in many areas, and she knew she had been duped by almost everyone involved with Damien so far. She knew she was naive, but she knew something else.

Seville was lying.

It was Hoffman, actually, who had given her the idea when he had referred to the kids on campus who took action for "animal rights." She had grown up in a home where the acts of such people were openly compared to those of willful vandals and the kind of people who shot abortion providers. Locally, animal activists concentrated their efforts on mink farming and fast-food chains that served beef and pork. There were far more candlelight vigils than direct actions, and that was fine with the University staff. Vigils were easily ignored.

Elizabeth was more than a little chagrined to think that even though she was putting her entire career on the line for one research animal, she did not know anything about the "animal rights movement." The whole idea of the issue confused her now, because suddenly she seemed awfully close to being "one of them." She didn't know if what she was fighting for was Damien's "rights" or not. It didn't really feel like that. She just wanted to get her friend out of harm's way. But now, knowing she could not help Damien on her own, she was about to turn to the same people she had always viewed with disdain. It felt very strange. Could she lead the "enemy" against her own kind?

She got on the internet and searched for local contacts. She knew that the underground organizations which performed direct action would not be listed. They had "cover" groups, with legitimate faces, which supported them. She looked, however, for the most radical listings she could find. She needed shock troops, not philosophers.

She e-mailed the site which offered the most damning display directed toward animal-based medical and psychological research. They were called Animal Freedom Fighters, and they looked like any researcher's nightmare. She wondered what they could do for her. At the very least, having their kind of attention turned on Seville and his work with the dog could not hurt. At the best, they would help her free Damien, and maybe even help her get him to safety.

She sobered at the thought of turning Damien over to anyone, even an animal lover. She was desperate however.

She had a reply the next morning, asking her to come to their "head-quarters," which was a small shop-front near the University. The director was *very* interested, the letter indicated, and most eager to meet with some-one from "the inside." That statement made Elizabeth sigh.

They met the following morning, a Saturday, at nine. Taking a deep breath, and with a furtive glance around the street behind her, Elizabeth walked through the hazy glass door and into the headquarters of the Animal Freedom Fighters. The first thing that met her eyes was a gigantic poster of a skinned cow, shivering, it seemed, from its lack of coat as it dripped blood all about and looked at her with accusing eyes. "ARE YOU WEARING MY SKIN?" the poster screamed. Startled, Elizabeth looked down to make sure she wasn't wearing leather shoes. She wasn't.

Thank God for that.

A woman came through a hanging curtain at the back of the office. In her late fifties at least, she was older than Elizabeth had assumed the people here would be. She had a complexion hardened by weather and her straight brown hair was styled more for convenience than fashion. She fixed a steady and not altogether friendly stare on Elizabeth. She was followed by three much younger people, who were more what Elizabeth had expected in age and appearance, complete with accompanying billows of patchouli oil. A slim boy about twenty sported blond dreadlocks, a tank top and baggy cargo pants, while the two girls were fashionably ragged. Elizabeth, trying to repress an attitude concerning animal rights activists shaped over a lifetime spent in a home supported by medical research, could not help one last sneering comparison of the older woman to Dickens' Fagin—the master-mind who used youngsters to do his dirty work.

She forced herself to stop thinking of them as adversaries. They were, truly, her last hope. After this she had no more ideas. And, she allowed the thought to surface unchallenged for the first time, I guess these guys love an-imals—they're on Damien's side. It was a strange but thrilling concept.

She began. "Morning. I'm Elizabeth Fletcher. I e-mailed you?"

"Good morning Elizabeth. I'm Margo Goings. Come over here and have a seat, we're all very interested to hear what you have to say. Your e-mail in-trigued us very much. It's not often, of course, that we have someone actu-ally *working* in the labs come here to us."

Elizabeth hated her already. She pictured the woman directing a break-in into her father's lab, destroying things, spraying slogans on the walls.

Stop it! Get over it. This is for Damien.

She forced a smile and seated herself.

"This is Jon, and JoyNoel and Jas." She offered no other explanation for their presence, but other than the nauseating patchouli odor wafting from their direction they weren't bothering Elizabeth nearly as much as the older woman. She didn't know why. She just disliked her. "So you are aware of an-imal cruelty taking place at the University? And you're willing to work with us?"

"Well, it *was* at the University. Now the dog is over at the researcher's house. He's keeping him there—maybe because what he is doing is against University policy," she lied, then added, to pique their interests, "Though after what I saw him doing there I find that hard to believe."

"What did you see?"

"At the University? The guy was keeping dogs in metal cages and shock-ing them over and over until they went crazy. It was pretty bad." The woman turned around and gave a significant look to the three people behind her and they murmured and shook their heads. Elizabeth was encouraged. She felt a slight twinge of guilt for not telling these people about Damien's abil-ity to speak, but they didn't need to know. She was simply here to get their help in getting the dog out, after that they would go their separate ways. "But here's what I want to talk to you about. What goes on at the University is bad, but I'm not sure there is a lot we can do about that, and besides, as far as I know it isn't happening anymore. But one of the dogs needs help, badly. He took a dog to his house. This guy is shocking him with a shock collar. I know anything goes at the University, but I guess my question is, can he do something like that in a private home situation?"

Margo nodded gravely. "He can. Anyone—any kind of person—can purchase a shock collar and there's no training or certification required to put one on an animal. It's disgraceful. But I'm more interested in what is going on at the University than in a private home. We can . . ."

"But the dog *we* need to help is in this home. I'm here to ask you—beg you—to help me get him away from this guy. Either legally, or break him out."

"We're a legal organization, Elizabeth. We don't 'break animals out'."

"Whatever. Someone does. Put me in touch with them."

Marg waved her hand dismissively. "The animal rights movement is not about smash and grab operations. It's about lots of work. Lots of educating. We can rarely save individual animals . . ."

"But I *have* to. This dog needs our help. He's trapped up there."

"You see the small picture, Elizabeth. You want to save one dog, but we want to save millions. Your information might help us do that. But you need to work with us. Education is what this is all about."

Elizabeth shook her head in frustration. "Damien is trusting me to come get him. I always have, and I always *will*."

"Is Damien a beagle?" Jay asked from behind Margo, in an attempt, Elizabeth thought, to break the tension.

"Damien? No, he's a pit bull." Elizabeth saw Margo visibly stiffen and the kids behind her exchange a knowing look among themselves.

"Even if AFF members did do direct action," she said with close to a sniff, "we would not be able to do anything about one animal in a private home. That's just not in the scope of what we do. You understand, of course?"

Elizabeth sat staring for fifteen seconds before she answered. The four people sat across from her, staring back. "You won't help?" she managed at last.

"You have to understand, Elizabeth, there are things we can do, and things we can't do. The kind of help you ask for—breaking into a home and stealing a dog—we simply don't do that sort of thing."

Elizabeth could see that the interview was over; Margo Goings's body language stated that plainly. Something had gone wrong, and she did not know how to make it better. She wasn't even sure what the problem was.

What had she said wrong? Frustration made her want to lash out, to force these people to understand.

Margo Goings drew a deep breath, evidently rethinking her handling of the situation. She made one more attempt to salvage the meeting. "I think we need to return to the big picture. Are you interested in helping us infiltrate this man's lab? That's the reason we're meeting today. It's possible we can do great good with your help. I'm sorry, however, that we would be unable to help you with a pit bull being kept in a private home. I think you understand."

Elizabeth stood up, her voice frozen calm. "I don't understand. You say you love animals, but you won't get your hands dirty to save one. You won't wear leather from some cow that died for food, but you'll refuse to help me help Damien." She glared around at them all. "I came here today because I thought I could find people who loved animals—all animals—and who would help me. But I've come to the wrong place, haven't I?"

She glared at them all again and banged out the door. She began to cry, her frustration absolute. Halfway to her car she heard a soft sound behind her and turned to see the girl, Jas, hurrying to catch up.

"Wait, please. I want to talk to you."

Elizabeth stopped and wiped at her tears, angry that this girl should see her crying. "What?" she said savagely.

"I'm sorry about that, back there. About Margo. There's some stuff going on with her that you don't know about. She's OK, really, but she wouldn't help you with this. But we, me and Jon, and JoyNoel too, we want you to know that we'll help. Give me your phone number, I'll call you, and we can meet. Jon and I have done some stuff, we might be able to help, you know?"

"What's Margo's problem?" Elizabeth was breathless with hope.

"Oh. She's afraid of pit bulls; thinks the breed should be eliminated. It's just a weird thing with her, she got bit once, or something stupid like that, I dunno. It's crazy, but when you said 'pit bull,' boy, that was it. We all knew it, but nobody else here is like that, you know? We'll help you, we just have to do it without Margo knowing. Everybody else is cool."

"Jas, I need you to know how important this is. I simply can't let him down. I won't. But you guys were my last hope. I'm out of ideas and every day my dog suffers, can you understand that?"

"Sure. We'll help. We, I mean Jon and JoyNoel and I, we have to be careful though. I mean, we don't know you, you know? You work there—you're 'one of them,' so to speak. We don't know you're not undercover or something. We have to be really careful. So don't think we're giving you the runaround if it seems like we're vague sometimes. We have to be."

Jas, Jon and Jon's friend Rob met her outside the Stat Snack cafeteria at The Med two days later. Ordering only drinks, they headed out onto the wide University lawns, where they could speak in privacy. They listened to the story of Damien's plight again, with added detail, but still without any mention of his talking. Elizabeth knew mentioning that little fact would just gum things up.

She was surprised and ultimately pleased to hear their level of commitment to helping an animal they had never met. They hinted around that they had been involved in several direct actions that she had read about. Politely Elizabeth did not press for details. They agreed to take a look at the location where the dog was kept, but for security reasons they would never let Elizabeth know when or how they would be operating. She agreed to the condition, thankful they were ready to act so quickly. They discussed at length the arrangement of Seville's house, the security system as far as she understood it and people they could expect to be there at any given time. They reassured her that no one would be hurt.

"That's not our style." Jas had a serious smile and Elizabeth was surprised to find that she really liked this girl who, until so recently, she would have considered "the enemy." "We don't want to harm anything. We want to *stop* things from being harmed."

"Tom is likely to be there anytime, night or day, or at least that's the way it seemed. Tom is doing all kinds of research for him, most likely preparation for the paper Seville's going to present on the dog. My best advice would be—and I'm not telling you guys how to work or anything—but if it were me, I'd try and go when only Tom was there. He doesn't seem like a real aggressive guy."

"We'd like to go, obviously, when no one is there, but if that is not feasible, then yes, we'll try for just one person."

"If we can get this guy to let us in, then we don't have to deal with security," Rob observed.

Jas and Jon nodded thoughtfully.

"Are you sure I can't come along?"

"Absolutely. It's for our protection and yours. If either of these guys recognizes you, where would that leave you? And if they get you, they may eventually get us." She left the implication of Elizabeth cutting a deal with authorities unspoken. "We'll get the dog and call you. It'll be OK."

Elizabeth shook her head, unwilling for the moment to trust her voice. At last she said, "After I earn my M.D. you guys can count on free health care the rest of your lives, eh?"

This was met with laughter and thanks. "We need to meet with you again, after we scope this place out. Give us the address and we'll be back in touch." As a precaution, they always called her, and she did not know any of their last names. Jas turned to Jon. "I think we better talk with Ed, being as there may be people involved."

"Yeah, you're right."

Jas turned back to Elizabeth. "We'll call you."

Damien looked up to see Seville standing in the observation room's doorway with a leash in his hand. "Let's go," the man said.

Damien rose hurriedly and stood, hopefully, with his tail softly wagging at the idea. Leaving this room, even with Seville, was an appealing prospect. Slowly, memories battling expectation, the dog came to the man. In the days since Seville had been locked in the observation room with him, a subtle but complete shift in their relationship had occurred. Damien was a working dog, with a heritage strongly compelling him to serve man. Elizabeth had been taken from him, and while he deeply grieved her absence and remained ever hopeful of her return, the business of living must go on. The business of living, The Voice told him, was to serve and please his master within the capacities of his breed. For now the only master he had was Seville.

The selective breeding of untold thousands of generations of his ancestors had prepared him for a life of rugged work, spent at the side of an equally rugged master who had need of his services. But here, in the sterile scientific environment, there were no bulls to hold, nothing to defend, no real work at all. Seville had tasks for him but it was not really *work*, and it did nothing to fulfill his inborn drives.

When Damien reached Seville, the man placed the lead over his head and reassured himself as to the snug fit of the electric collar. Out in the workroom waited Dr. Katharine Novak as well as the head of the Psychology Department and the dean of the Arts and Sciences department. Seville had told neither of them what he would be showing them this day, and both men, thinking his request peculiar, waited expectantly.

In a brief moment of sympathy, Seville rested his hand on the dog's broad head. "You get me through this, Buddy, and I'll buy you a damn steak." The dog felt a thrill at the man's gentle touch. Damien responded to the kind tone of his voice by pressing against the veterinarian's leg in a quick show of gratitude. Seville moved aside in annoyance. "Here, stop that! Don't get hair all over me." He brushed at his pant leg.

The man brought him out into the workroom and Damien was surprised to see three people seated on stools, all watching him closely. Noticeably absent was Tom, for after his "attack" on Elizabeth, the man's mere presence sent the dog into a rage. Damien recognized only one of the strangers so he stopped short, trying to use his nose to tell him more about the two men he did not know. Seville pulled sharply on the lead and Damien followed him to the cable setup where he was used to working. As the man secured him in place, he continued to draw in the scent of the two men, curious about them.

Seville gave him little time to wonder. He produced the color cards and held the first one up.

"Damien, what color?"

"Green."

The man had not used the shock, though his finger was hovering near the button. Damien had answered quickly and accurately, and now the three people were exclaiming and talking amongst themselves. Seville hushed them and produced another card.

"Damien, what color?"

"Black."

"Damien, what color?"

"Red."

They continued through the colors. Damien shot furtive glances at the strangers between cards. There was a tension in the room which was palpable to him. Suddenly they were done and Seville whisked him back into the little room and locked him in. The people came and stood at the Plexiglas wall, staring in at him, and Damien sat down at the other end of the room and stared back.

The little group of animal liberators met with Elizabeth one more time. They brought Ed, a large man in his late twenties who did not, in any way, appear to belong with the other three. He looked, to Elizabeth, like someone who should be on the Green Bay Packers' front line. His haircut and manner of holding himself affirmed his ex-military status. Ed, evidently, was held in reserve for just such occasions. It was obvious he was there because Jas had asked him to come. Ed's eyes rarely left her face. Elizabeth smiled to herself and shook her head.

My evil army!

Ed was induced to look away from Jas long enough to question Elizabeth very specifically about the house, the access, the two men who might be present and the exact location of the dog. They had driven by, he mentioned, and were pleased at the long, heavily wooded driveway. It was Ed's studied opinion that it would be "apple pie."

They separated. The group, for their own security, would not tell her when they planned the action. They would call her when they had the dog.

At a quick honk from the street below, the little band of animal liberators moved out of the apartment and filed down the stairs to the waiting green van, sticky marks on its window indicating where once a plethora of windsurfing and "Deadhead" stickers had held sway. Jas swung into the passenger's seat across from Rob while Ed and Jon squeezed into the back with JoyNoel and the dog crate. JoyNoel handed Ed a dark ski mask, but he waved it away; he had brought his own. The van pulled out, swaying slightly from poor shocks, and the two women and three men were quiet, each thinking about the mission.

The team members carried no weapons but Ed had brought a large roll of duct tape. They were planning on the aide's presence—they were counting on him to get them into the house without having to disarm the alarm system. Seville's movements had proven so erratic that they knew they would just have to deal with him as best they could at the time. He might be there, he might not. That was what Ed was for.

Jas turned in her seat and gave the final instructions. "I had Elizabeth call yesterday evening, about this time, and his aide answered. She asked him if she could visit the dog and he refused, of course, but that tells us that he does stay late, and that the dog is still there. We get the dog, but while we're in there, if everything is smooth, we might as well look for tapes, disks, anything we can use against him. If the guy shows, Ed will handle him. Don't anybody get hurt."

The van pulled just far enough into the driveway so as to not attract the attention of any passing police, but not far enough up to alert the occupants of the house. Covered in plain black clothing and ski masks and armed only with a crowbar and duct tape, they carefully filed up the driveway and grouped around the side door. For one split second they were all in position and there was a soundless pause, and then, outside the basement door, one hooded figure knocked lightly. Ed waited flattened against the wall, out of sight. Their plan called for the researcher or his aide to answer the door, and it couldn't have gone better. In a few moments they heard the locks being worked, the door opened, and Tom stood looking at them. Ed moved into action, clapping one large hand over Tom's mouth, and pulling him down. Taken so completely by surprise, he was easily overpowered, and in less than thirty seconds he was gagged and bound hand and foot with duct tape. He did not resist them and he made no sound. He simply watched them passively. Ed and Jas gave each other a silent high five. They entered the hallway, followed by other shadowy figures.

They quickly found the workroom door, which Tom had left open. Though security forbid them to speak while on a raid, there was an audible sound of disappointment as the first glance around the room revealed no dog. One figure went quickly to the back and opened the doors into the storage closets. Then, their heads turning as one, the four other raiders noticed the Plexiglas wall to their right. Cautiously they approached and saw a dog, lying curled up inside on the bare floor. Their movement caught the dog's eye and his head lifted. He stared straight at them and they, in their black ski masks, stared back. The dog's room was soundproof and they could not hear the loud, deep growl emanating from the animal's chest. The animal was wearing an electric shock collar. The liberators waited to see no more. They quickly moved to the side of the observation room, locating the doors in. With swift movements they began prying the doors open.

Upstairs in his study Seville cocked his head. He had heard a strange sound, one he couldn't put a name to. He was putting the finishing touches on the abstract outlining his project. He reached over to the phone to inter-com Tom. Getting no reply, he immediately left the room.

The bulldog was waiting to see what came through the door before he re-acted. He had awakened to the alarming sight of strange black-hooded fig-ures staring in at him. Startled, he experienced a moment of intense fear. Now he stood defiantly to see what was tearing at the door to his room. Hateful as it was, it was his room, in his basement, which belonged to his hu-man, and he would defend them to the death. He snuffed deeply at the widening crack and growled again. He didn't know these people.

In the next moment, the door was kicked open. The aggressive entrance of the strange and threatening hooded strangers made the decision easy for Damien—they were Bad People and they had no business here in his hu-man's place. He would have been justified in attacking them as a bulldog should, silently and without hesitation as violent intruders into his master's domain, yet something made him temper his action. He growled, showing his formidable teeth, warning these people to leave. He didn't want to hurt them but he did feel strongly they must be repelled. He lunged forward, challenging these unwelcomed intruders to his master's domain boldly as the door fell away from Rob's foot.

"Get back!" Rob screamed, pushing back against the other raiders com-ing in behind him. Damien pressed forward. The intruders' fear fed the dog's conviction they were Bad; their retreat fed his lust to chase and rout them. The masked figures scrambled out the destroyed double doorway into the workroom with Damien at their heels. Breaking every possible credo the AFF went by, Rob was swearing and swinging a chair at the dog they had come to rescue. Jas was backed up against a counter, watching the dog's en-thusiastic defense of its home and realizing now that the dog saw them as vi-olent intruders, not saviors.

Things couldn't be going much better, she thought grimly, when something made her look up at the door which led to the hall. The researcher, Dr. Joseph Seville, was standing in the doorway, an expression of absolute out-rage on his face. She straightened up, a shot of adrenaline causing her stom-ach to contract sharply. For a moment their eyes locked, and outrage matched outrage. She was suddenly, fiercely sorry they would not now have time to vandalize his office, violate it, ruin years of records, steal valuable video. In short, make him feel the anguish she felt every time she read between the lines of the research papers he and his kind wrote. In that brief moment they were united across the space which separated them by the depth of the despise they felt for each other's point of view.

Jas had to do something. The situation was chaotic. Rob, the chair and the dog passed in front of her, intent on each other like bizarre dance partners. She signaled frantically to Ed, who was intently watching Rob and the dog with his back to the doctor, to turn and do his job. He turned, saw Seville and lunged. The scientist had no chance against the 260-pound former hand-to-hand combat expert and in a moment Ed had the doctor's arm twisted up behind his back in a pain compliance hold while Seville struggled furiously.

"I'll break it!" Ed hissed in his ear, so Jas wouldn't hear.

"You sons of bitches!" Seville spat back in contempt, gasping from the pain. Ed whistled shrilly through his teeth and a raider broke away from the melee to put duct tape across the furiously struggling doctor's mouth. Ed dragged the man out the door and down the hallway several feet, slamming him down, while another hooded figure bound his arms and ankles. Ed leaned all his weight onto his knee, which was placed on the small of the researcher's back.

There was a commotion at the lab door and Ed looked up. The liberators were fleeing down the hallway toward the open outside door. Rob came last, doing a "lion tamer" routine with a chair, the silent dog still intent on him.

The ex-marine was a gentle man, but when Seville began struggling again, Ed punched him in the kidney area, as a reminder to behave. The dog saw the motion and swung about. Damien saw *his* human, his *responsibility*, writhing on the ground, the Bad Person kneeling aggressively over Seville. The intruder had just struck his man. Damien didn't hesitate. He charged Ed, furious, his paws skidding and slipping on the slick floor. Rob ran down the hall without a backward glance.

Damien's impact took Ed over backwards, the man's left arm, which he had thrown up instinctively, in the dog's jaws. Even though he outweighed the dog by 195 pounds, Ed began to feel panic. The dog's attack had been so direct, so forthright, not at all what he expected a dog attack to be like. He had figured at worst the animal would dart in and out, nipping at him. He didn't realize he had crossed swords with an animal bred to bring an 1800-pound bull to its knees. For several furious moments they fought over the top of Seville's bound figure. Ed was brave, and Ed was strong, but all his human hand-to-hand commando training was useless against his canine opponent. His hardest blows only made the dog shake its head harder, its teeth grinding into his flesh. The harder he fought, the harder the dog fought. When he hesitated, the dog simply maintained its grip, squinting at him curiously, as if sizing him up as an opponent. With sudden inspiration Ed used his size and strength to drag the dog to the lab door, positioned the dog inside the lab, and began slamming the door on the dog's head and muzzle. Over and over he slammed the door as hard as he could.

"Let go you bastard!" he said through gritted teeth. But Damien was listening with half-closed eyes to another Voice.

Hold your bull, dog, holdfast! the Ancient Voice praised him.

It felt so Good. All he had to do was hold his grip, the rest of his body was just along for the ride. What this intruder could do to him was no worse than a maddened bull, and unless commanded by his master, only death could make Damien let go now. Through the pain his tail wagged gently. He was a good dog. He would hold until his man came and took control. There was pain, but there was glory. He felt it. This moment was written in his blood. At last, he was working.

Ed's adrenaline was flowing and he abandoned the door as a bad idea. He hadn't wanted to harm the dog, but to save himself Ed might have to kill the animal. His survival training kicked in and he began to fight in earnest. He tried to choke the dog with one hand, but the bulldog was sleek and twisted out of harm's way while bearing down harder with his jaws. The dog grunted now with each kick. The violent abuse was taking its toll, but still he held, in defense of his master.

A figure glided back into the room and approached them. Jas had found a small fire extinguisher hanging on the wall, and she began to reluctantly hit the dog on the head with it.

Ed, however, had seen something which gave him an idea. On the desk to his right was a marble pen holder. He dragged the dog over to the desk and grabbed a long, black pen. He stabbed it at the dog's head, penetrating its left eye. Like a scene from a nightmare the dog did not let go. It simply groaned and shook its head harder.

"Shit!" Ed screamed. Defending himself, the dog shook its head while Ed stabbed wildly, the pen skidding off Damien's skull. The dog's powerful shaking knocked Ed off balance and he dropped to his knees. In another moment he was on the floor. That spooked him. The dog was shaking and

dragging him around like a mauled cat, and he struck out with the pen he still held, going for a vital organ. As the pen sunk into his abdomen the dog grunted sharply. Without releasing his hold, the dog paused, looking straight into Ed's eyes.

Jas had been standing, gaping at the terrible scene before her. Now she righted the extinguisher and activated it, covering the dog's head with fine white powder. She directed the spray up the dog's nose and into its mouth. In a few moments, the powder had the desired effect, blinding the dog and choking his breath. Unable to breath or see, he was forced to fall back, gasping for air. In a flash Jas had Ed up and they were running down the hall.

The dog continued to back up, pawing at his face in an attempt to remove the foam. By the time he could see out of his one good eye, the Bad People were gone.

He had won.

He had successfully defended his home and his man. He felt immensely proud, but he also felt ill. Damien snuffled and sneezed around the workroom, his tail held stiffly up in victory, bristling at the intruders' scent. As his nose cleared he caught another scent that stopped him in his tracks.

Outside!

It was unmistakable. He went to the door and hesitantly stepped out into the hall. Seville was lying on the floor to his right. The fresh air came from the left.

Reeling with growing pain and nausea, the dog could not ignore the prostrate figure of Seville. He could smell the man's injuries, and it felt *very* wrong for the man to be on the floor like that. Why didn't he get up? Gore from the dog's ruined eye dripped onto the floor, mixing with blood from the hole in his side. The dog's back was arched and his stomach contracted sharply against the pain he felt there. Squinting against the discomfort, the dog advanced cautiously, unsure what to do. One front leg had a bone cracked near the paw from one of Ed's sharp kicks. It hurt to walk on it and he stopped, licked at it, then, limping, started down the hall again. The man was watching him, holding very still. The dog smelled him cautiously, ready to jump away at the first sound or movement. He couldn't understand why Seville was like *this*, and he knew it wasn't right. A wave of nausea brought on by the violent beating his skull had taken broke over the dog, and he lay down with a groan beside the doctor. Seville's hand had hit the doorjamb in the struggle, resulting in a small abrasion which had seeped some blood.

The dog sniffed it, then licked it carefully, tenderly. Seville jerked away, and the dog struggled upright, his tail wagging tentatively in apology.

Forgive me.

After a moment he lay down again and, because the man would not allow him to attend to his wounds, began licking his own terrible injuries. The man began to wriggle and twist and, alarmed, the dog struggled up again and stepped aside. Damien retreated a few paces. Seville became more animated, making muffled sounds at him through the duct tape. The dog stared, uncertain what to do. Then the outside air hit him again, and with it the memory of someone more important even than Seville. In the heat of the battle he had forgotten. He turned to face the doorway and the breeze. Seville was agitated now, wriggling and making strange, unintelligible sounds. The dog swung his head back and looked at the man. Seville had not given him a command, and The Voice said, "*Find her!*" so he limped down the hall without a backward glance.

At the back door he pulled up at the sight of Tom trussed up like Seville, lying in the driveway. The dog's one useful eye grew hard at the sight, and he limped over to where the helpless man lay. Tom shut his eyes and prayed while the dog sniffed him critically. The Voice told him he could not attack a defenseless, submissive victim like this. But there was one thing the dog *could* do. A simple, everyday gesture of dominance the battle-weary dog could use to show his contempt. Balancing on three wavering legs, the dog urinated on Tom and then disappeared into the dark.

CHAPTER TWELVE

Doubtless, when man shares with his dog the toils of a pro-
fession and the pleasures of an art, as with the shepherd or
the poacher, the affection warms and strengthens till it fills
the soul.

—ROBERT LOUIS STEVENSON

The moment Elizabeth stepped into the shower the next morning, Jas
had called, leaving a terse message on her cell phone. The dog had become aggressive, Jas reported, and because of that their mission had failed.
They had done what they could. She left no call-back number. Elizabeth
glanced at her phone as she sat down to breakfast, saw the message and left
the room to listen to it. Rushing back through the kitchen on her way out,
she could not even make a pretense that nothing was wrong, and swept Bill
and Dave with anguished eyes in response to their questions. Telling them
not to worry, she raced out the door, headed for Seville's home. The horrid
uncertainty made her feel faint. What had happened at Seville's? What had
happened to her dog?

Her anxiety, as she raced to the scene of the botched rescue, continued as
a painful, physical throb. Things were spiraling out of control. Now more
than ever she wished she had someone she could talk with about the dog.
Someone to give her advice. But there was no one. Not even Bill, with whom
she shared almost everything else. How many times had Bill laughed or
joked as he worked over the bodies of dogs, dogs which minutes before had
gazed at him with trusting eyes? Was it possible he did not realize just what
it was he had his hands thrust into? How could he be so careless with a re-
ceptacle which held a soul such as Damien's?

Before she had come to know Damien she had not given a thought to the comfort or well-being of the research dogs used by her father and grandfather. She was as bad as they were—only Damien had changed her, and for that she could take no credit. It was with increasing shame she realized that Damien had always been Damien—even before he spoke. His speech had changed nothing, only made it easier for her, in her blindness, to *see* him. Staring mutely out at her from behind the wire at the Center, before she had known him, he had been the same dog she held so dear now. What about all the other dogs? Did they possess the same qualities of loyalty, good nature and humorous intelligence? Did they possess similar desires and fears? She knew the answer to that, and it was hard to face.

She came to the gate of Seville's neighborhood and punched in the pass number, the same one she had given to the AFF members. She knew that by nightfall it would be changed. If Damien was within this neighborhood, she must find him now. She pulled slowly past Seville's driveway, looking for anything that would tell her what had happened.

There was nothing.

Steeling her nerve she pulled slowly up the drive, trying desperately to think of what she would say if Seville or his aide appeared. She could think of nothing but it didn't stop her. She pulled slowly up to the house.

She hadn't been sure what Jas had meant, exactly, by "mission had failed," and not knowing made her fears rampant, but every scenario she had imagined could not have prepared her for the sight of a body lying in the driveway.

"Oh, my God," she breathed. It was Tom, lying bound and gagged by the door.

What have I done?

She sat in her truck, craning her neck, undecided between leaving immediately and going forward to see if he was alive. Her horror that he might be dead overruled her fear and she slid from the vehicle and crept cautiously to the body. The man was facing away from her, duct tape around his ankles and his wrists bound behind him. Cat stepping like a cautious deer, she moved around to Tom's front, and at that moment his head lifted and he looked up at her. She actually screamed, something she had only done as a child, and then only when being chased—a thing she disliked intensely—in games of tag. Tom gestured to her with his head.

She knelt beside him with overwhelming relief. She tried to be careful, but her shaking hands made the job more difficult, and she winced more than Tom did as she pulled the tape away from his face.

"Seville," he said.

"*He* did this?" she said incredulously, her eyes going wide.

"No. Check inside. He may be hurt."

"To hell with him! I'm not going in there. I'll find the start of this, hang on. Quit moving." She searched his wrists for the start of the tape, found it and began unwrapping. In a moment she had his hands free and watched as he picked at the tape around his ankles. There had been a heavy dew overnight, and Tom was soaked. There were marks on his skin where the rocks had pressed into his flesh. He looked cold and miserable, and she wondered how long he had been lying there.

"What happened, Tom? Are you all right?" She couldn't believe this. It seemed unreal, like something you saw on TV.

"I think it was animal rights people, they came last night. They got me, I don't know about him." He nodded toward the house door. "As far as I could hear, it sounded like the dog attacked them. The dog was badly injured. They all ran out, and then the dog came out and—ran off."

"*What?*" If Damien was injured it was her fault. She had sent these people here. She felt light and cold, almost as if she were floating.

"Come on." He tore the last of the tape from his ankles and stood, wincing at the pain of a night spent lying on gravel.

It seemed natural to follow Tom into the open doorway and down the hall to the workroom. Seville had inched his way into the room, but had been unable to find a way to cut the tape. He had spent the night leaning up against the wall.

When Elizabeth entered the room behind Tom, the expression in his cold, gray eyes froze her in the doorway. From across the room his furious glare singled her out, its accusation plain above the gray tape that covered the lower half of his face. Tom looked from one to the other, and then went to a drawer to retrieve a scalpel. He knelt beside the man and, hesitating just a moment, looked back at Elizabeth.

"I think you should go," he said very quietly.

She understood. She could not be here when he freed Seville. Backing away, she turned and fled.

She was torn between the gut feeling that she should put as much distance between herself and Seville as possible, and the desperate need to search for the dog in the immediate area around the house. She wished Tom had told her which way the dog had gone. As she hurried to her car she wondered, would the dog go up the driveway, or straight into the woods? Injured, he would probably take the route of least resistance. As quickly as she could she scouted the woods on either side of the drive; then, hearing Seville's raised voice coming from the open basement door, she ran to her truck and got in. She hit her clenched hand on the steering wheel. She didn't know exactly how to feel—but her overwhelming emotion was relief that Damien was away from Seville. He was injured, but she had only to find him. If he was anywhere near, and she called him, he would come. She pulled down the drive and into the street, calling the dog's name loudly.

Driving down the quiet road for several minutes her hopes began to sink. How do you find a dog? Would Damien be trying to go back to the wilderness he had originally come from? Or would he just be running scared in traffic? Was he too badly injured to travel far? Was he lying somewhere, curled up under a bush, dying? Tom had said he was badly injured. By the AFF? Why would *they* do that? Then she remembered Tom's words. The dog had attacked them. She could almost see the scene. They had treated Seville the way they had Tom, and no doubt Damien had reacted to defend him. A sob caught in her throat. Damien had been injured, perhaps seriously, defending the very man he was to have been rescued from.

It was late afternoon when she arrived back at her home. She had composed herself as best she could before pulling into the drive, but Bill, puttering in the last vestiges of this summer's beloved tomato plants, straightened up in concern at the sight of her. Elizabeth walked over and sat on the retaining wall near him. The late summer sun was brassy and diffuse, the air having the unmistakable hazy feel of autumn to it. School was starting in less than two weeks.

"What's going on, Ellie?"

Elizabeth sighed deeply from where she slumped. "In a nutshell? I'll tell you if you want." Her voice had a strained edge to it that made Bill think it best to let her talk. He knew before she began what it would concern.

"Damien was broken out of Seville's house last night by AFF members. I sent them there. When they roughed up Seville, Damien attacked them, defending that . . ." She paused, then continued, fighting to keep her tone as neutral as possible. She didn't need to add emphasis, the story spoke for itself. "Now I can't find him. I've looked everywhere. I think maybe he's dead. I don't know." She stared at the ground before her. "I just don't know."

Bill's face was expressionless. Knowing that his granddaughter had developed a strong attachment to another man's lab animal, the salient point to him was that if Elizabeth did indeed find the animal, she did not intend to give it back. If the dog was found in her possession, that would be real trouble. Elizabeth had never told him what the dog was being used for but something made it of personal interest to Seville. And now his granddaughter had moved from annoying the man with petty meddling to setting animal activists on him. He turned back and continued cultivating around the drying vines, still heavy with ripe tomatoes. Hornets, stirred by his movements, rose and resettled, too busy feasting to be annoyed at the disturbance.

"I know what you're thinking, Grandpa, and I don't have an answer for you. I've only done what I thought was right. I still am. But I have no one to talk to. Not even you."

She watched his shoulders stop their motion and freeze. "Elizabeth," he said without turning around. "You had the AFF go to his home? Break into his home to try and steal the dog?"

"Yes."

He turned around then, and she saw in his eyes bewilderment and distress, emotions she understood she had put there. She looked down, unable to face it.

"Oh, Ellie," Bill came slowly to her side and sat down. Around them the warm dirt put off a sweet smell. "You *should* have talked to me. You should have . . ."

"I tried, remember? You wouldn't listen to me. You told me nothing I could say would change your mind. I just did what I thought was the only way to get my dog out of there."

"*Your* dog?"

"As far as that dog is concerned, I'm his 'owner.' You understand? He's counting on me. He's *waiting* for me. Somewhere, in this town, if he's still alive, Damien is counting on me to help him. You know what that does to my guts? I'm not going to walk away from him because I know *he* wouldn't walk away from me."

Bill ached to put his arm around his granddaughter but he refrained. "Will this man know that you were behind this action?"

"Oh, he knows."

"Have you considered the consequences? To your life, your career?"

"To my life? Yes. To my career, no, not as much. I hope someday you can understand why I felt I had no choice. It's not *just* about Damien. It's about me too."

"I'm having a real hard time with that one, Ellie. You have not done yourself any favors here. I wouldn't be surprised if you've thrown away your medical degree. I just don't know."

Elizabeth turned her face to him. "Grandpa, please just be there for me. Please just wait, and let this play out, but *be there* for me, like you always have." She covered her face with her hands and bowed forward, racked with silent sobs. Bill had no choice but to hug her to him and hold her, as he had always done. "My little girl," he murmured, rocking her and shaking his head in despair. "What have you done?"

Elizabeth called the paper and found they would run a small lost ad for free, starting the next morning. She simply put: *"LOST! Striped pit bull. Injured. Much loved. Reward,"* and her cell phone number. Using Styrofoam plates, she made up some signs which said the same thing and she went out, armed with a staple gun, to plaster the area around Seville's home. She returned at dinnertime, and came into the house prepared for the worst if Bill had said anything to Dave. Evidently he had not, for dinner was pacific.

"Elizabeth, come in here." It was Bill calling to her softly, from the kitchen. She and Dave were watching a movie in the study, but she rose and went to the kitchen. He was watching the news on the small kitchen television while he finished up the dishes. As she approached her attention was caught by the word "dog" coming from the newscast. By the time she entered the room the story was over, and she looked at Bill. He muted the TV.

"They just had rather extensive coverage about the dog. Seville is offering a twenty-five-thousand-dollar reward for his return, and one thousand dollars just for information about locations where he might have been sighted.

They said he'd been badly injured by the animal rights whackos, and they're advising everyone to stay away from him, and just report any sightings. They said he can be very dangerous, and that he very nearly killed the animal rights nut who tried to take him." His tone let her know he questioned her judgment dealing with such an animal. "They didn't mention your name, but they pretty well vilified you nonetheless. They made Seville look pretty good—a combination Nobel Peace Prize winner and bereaved dog owner."

Elizabeth was pacing up and down the kitchen. In one brief moment, her feelings of hope had been destroyed. Seville, his status and his money were now aligned against her. He had the press, he had money, and he would lie like a rug in order to manipulate people into helping him. Bitterly she ridiculed herself for thinking her paper-plate signs had been such a good idea!

The next day the news reported numerous "sightings." Animal Control reported they had received several calls the day the dog escaped, describing the dog as having been either walking or lying by the side of the interstate. It appeared he had been trying to cross the freeway, the Director of Animal Control told reporters, but later he had been reported just lying along the side of the road. By the time an officer arrived, the dog had disappeared. Elizabeth raced to the scene of the report, and came face to face with the reality of just what a twenty-five-thousand-dollar reward could do for Seville. The place was a circus. State Patrol officers were chasing dog hunters off the freeway shoulder. News helicopters circled above. At least a dozen people were looking over the embankment where the dog had been spotted, several were wading through the grass, searching. Elizabeth surveyed the scene grimly. Seville had played his cards well, offering the cash and getting the media involved. She not only had to find the dog before Seville, now she had to find the dog before *everyone* else. With his reward he had mobilized the entire city into a frantic hunt. She turned away, knowing exactly what her odds were.

After running only one day, Seville was able to get her "lost" ad in the paper canceled. Someone removed all her signs. She became just one of hundreds of "bounty hunters," as the news reporters called them, driving aimlessly around, searching for a sign of the dog.

By the end of the third day, she had given up. It was pointless to drive around. How could she hope to find the dog when hundreds of eager searchers couldn't turn him up? She hoped he had died quickly, not suffering in a ditch somewhere, alone.

Alone.

It was more than she could bear. She locked herself in her room, trying not to hear the murmur of her grandfather's voice in conversation with Dave. School started in less than a week. She wondered what Bill would tell him.

The morning of the fourth day, she didn't bother to get out of her robe. After Dave left she came out into the kitchen for coffee. She tried to come to terms with the fact that Damien was gone, but it just didn't *feel* right. She knew she would be able to *feel* his absence.

The doorbell rang and she ignored it. It was probably a package and she looked horrible; they could leave it on the porch. Suddenly she heard her grandfather's voice, rising in pitch, angry. She ran into the entranceway, sliding in her socks on the slate floor. In the doorway were a male and female police officer, politely insisting on something, and the woman officer raised her chin at the sight of Elizabeth and called out over Bill, "We'd like to speak with you, Ms. Fletcher."

Elizabeth came to stand beside Bill.

"I'm Officer Johnson with the police department. Are you Elizabeth Fletcher? Is he your father? Grandfather? Does he live here also?"

"He's my grandfather, yeah we live here. Can you . . ."

"I understand you are familiar with Dr. Joseph Seville. Could you tell me how you know him?

"He . . . He." What could she say? What was he to her? The man who had taken her dog, except the dog had never been hers. "He and I have worked on training a dog together." That seemed safe.

"The dog, would you describe it please?" Officer Johnson looked at her notes, written on a tiny spiral-bound notepad.

"Damien is a brindle pit bull. A male."

"When is the last time you saw Damien?"

"A couple of weeks ago I guess. A while. What is this all about? Why are you here?"

Officer Johnson looked at her notes again and then adjusted her heavily loaded duty belt. "Is that your brown Toyota, ma'am?"

"Yes."

"We have reason to believe that you may have picked up the brendle pit bull in question off the freeway about nine A.M. on Tuesday morning. We have reports of a woman in a brown pickup truck matching the description of your vehicle picking the dog up. Did this in fact, happen?"

"Are you kidding? Someone's got him? Someone picked him up?"

"Are you the one who picked him up, ma'am?"

Elizabeth reached out, touching the arm of the female officer. "When did you say this was? When was he picked up? How long ago?"

The officer pulled back. "Ma'am, please relax. Could you answer my question? Did you pick up the dog in question at any time?"

"Of course not. I've been looking for him for days."

"Do you have here, on this property, a brendled pit bull?"

"Of course not."

"Well, we have reason to believe the dog may be here. Do you mind if we look around?"

Bill straightened up. "Yes, I mind. You're not coming in here looking for a dog. The dog is not here, and my granddaughter has no idea where it is. She wasn't responsible for it being taken, so why would she know where it is now?"

The heavyset male officer put his hand up. "We just want to make sure the dog isn't here. That's all."

"That's more than you'll do. The dog is not here and you have no warrant. I'm sorry, but I'm going to have to ask you to leave if you're through with your investigation."

"Dr. Seville had his home burglarized and was assaulted. The first person on the scene after the assailants fled was your granddaughter. This leads me to believe she has knowledge of the facts which led up to that event. This also makes her a person of interest."

Elizabeth broke in. "Please, believe me, the dog isn't here. You don't need to come in. I'll answer any questions you have, but the dog is not here. Please don't bring my family into this." She was having a hard time concentrating on the scene before her. She didn't know whether to laugh or cry. Someone had Damien. But why hadn't they turned him in for the reward?

The police gracefully backed down. With much taking down of full names and handing out of cards, the police left the porch. The revelation that Damien had been picked up by a stranger left Elizabeth quiet and thoughtful. Where was her dog? Who had him, what were they doing with him and why hadn't they come forward for the twenty-five-thousand-dollar reward?

The call came at eleven P.M. and Elizabeth grabbed at her phone on the bed stand. There was a long pause on the other end of the line and Elizabeth nearly hung up.

"I'm looking for *Lux*," a female voice said, with an Australian accent so strong it took Elizabeth a moment to make out what she had said. Lying there in bed the color left her face—she understood perfectly.

"Oh God! Oh, God!" Elizabeth moaned. She rocked back and forth, clutching the phone. To her the revelation was stunning. Damien was alive, he had spoken, and the person the dog had spoken to was on the phone with her right now.

"Is he *OK?*"

There was another, longer pause.

"Is this *Lux?*"

"Yes, yes! Is he alive—is he OK?"

Another pause. "He's asking for you, but tell me, why *should* I give 'im back?" The tone held accusation.

"Because the most important thing in the world to me right now is to find him and keep him away from that man who wants him back."

"Why'd you let 'im get *there* in the first place?"

"I . . . I found him there, please, I'm trying to help him!"

"Why would you even *be* in such a place?"

"Oh, I know what you're thinking—that I'm one of *them*, well I'm not. Not anymore. You *have to* understand."

"Then tell me *this*: why in bleedin' 'ell did that dog have a shock collar on? Why? Who's the bastard put that on 'im?"

"The man—the researcher at the University that had him—he's scared of Damien, that's why. I tried taking it off, but that's the only way he could get Damien to obey him. I *hate* the thing, please believe me!"

There was an even longer pause. "I saw your ad in the paper, the first day. *Your* dog is the one they're looking for?"

"Yes! That's *him*. Please, tell me if he's OK, *please.*"

"Look, I need to sort this out before I commit myself. Where *I come from*, we don't sell our mates out for money."

"Damn it, all I'm trying to do is get him away from those people. I don't have twenty-five thousand dollars to give you, but that's my dog—my friend . . ." She trailed off, knowing how unconvincing she sounded.

The caller blew out her breath, as if very undecided what to do. "Who are you? Are you the person they said in the papers, prob'ly tried to have 'im broken out?"

251

"Yes, that's me. If you let him see me, you would *know.* That would convince you how he feels about me. Can't I see him, please?"

There was a long pause. "Listen. The reason I called you is this; it's funny, but now I have to trust *you*, I need *your* help. Here's the deal, do you know any medical stuff? It said in the papers you *worked* for those researchers, so I was thinkin' maybe you might. The dog is really bloody crook, and I can't help 'im anymore, and I sure as 'ell can't take 'im to a vet. Can *you* help 'im?"

Elizabeth didn't hesitate. "I'll bring someone who can. What's wrong?"

"One eye is poked out and it's infected. I think he might have a broken front leg too. He's going to need some type of surgery for his eye, to clean it out. And strong antibiotics or something."

"God! Is he all right? Where can we meet you?"

"You know where Try-N-Save is? Westside?"

"Yeah." *Funny, everyone in town uses that same nickname for that store.*

"Well, it's twenty-four-hour. So go to Try-N-Save, they have that huge car park. Park pretty far out, but not so far out it's obvious. Park at the west end. What sorta car do you have?"

"A brown Toyota pickup."

"Oh, yeah? Huh, Coincidence. What's the rego?"

"What's the *what?*"

"What's the plate number?"

"The license plate number—Jesus, how would I know? I never look at it."

The voice chuckled. "You seem OK, mate. More importantly, the dog seems to think you are. I hope to 'ell you are what you say you are. See you there in twenty minutes."

"Thank you! God, thank you *so* much. Why are you doing this? Why not go get the money?"

The strange woman answered with some heat. "Don't you get it? I don't sell out me mates, and if you know 'im like you say you do, I'm surprised you'd even ask that."

Elizabeth pulled on her clothes, swore horribly while she searched for her shoes, and then darted down to Bill's room. She knocked lightly on the door.

"Bill!"

She heard him turn over in bed, could visualize his face as he sat up in the darkness, startled.

"What?"

"I gotta come in, OK?"

"All right."

She closed the door behind her quietly. Bill had turned on his bed light. He sat up, his white T-shirt showing his stocky, still-powerful physique beneath it. A tuft of silver hair showed over the top of his shirt. Elizabeth sat on the edge of his bed, speaking in a whisper. It would be a disaster if they woke Dave right now.

"Bill, remember what I said about being there for me? Well, this is it. I need your help and no one but you can help me. It's that simple."

Bill was rubbing his eyes with his fingers. He froze, dropped his hand and stared at her.

"What's the matter, Elizabeth?"

"I don't have time to explain it to you right now. I need you to come with me somewhere right now. You're absolutely the only person that can help me. The *only* one."

He considered her and her request for a moment. "You want me to become involved with the dog." It was a statement, not a question.

"Yes."

Elizabeth watched his face. He seemed to be thinking of far more things than her immediate request. The girl knew the pattern of her life hinged on this moment.

"Can I get dressed?"

Elizabeth leaned forward and hugged him to her tightly, silently.

Bill mumbled and complained, but he dressed swiftly and they eased down the hallway. Reaching the kitchen, Elizabeth whispered to him, "You'll need some instruments. You may have to do a little surgery. And antibiotics. Stuff like that."

"I'll go look at what you want to show me—that's all. I'm not doing any surgery tonight."

Elizabeth was so relieved to have him even look at the injured dog, she wasn't going to argue. If Bill was willing to commit this far, she could convince him to do whatever was necessary. He was a highly skilled surgeon and her faith in his ability to repair the dog was absolute.

"Well, just get some stuff, you know, emergency-type stuff. Antibiotics. I guess he really needs 'em."

Bill disappeared down the hallway and she went out to warm up the truck. He got in beside her a few minutes later, carrying a small sports bag.

"It's not like I'm a family doctor, you know. I don't keep that kind of stuff around the house. I got what I could. I hope you know what you're doing, Elizabeth."

"Oh, I do. And you'll understand why in a few minutes. Hang on, I'm going to drive kinda funky to make sure we aren't being followed."

"Followed, are you kidding?"

They sat in the Try-N-Save lot for over twenty minutes. It struck Elizabeth as ironically amusing that whoever had Damien did not trust *her.* All she wanted was her dog back. But what would this woman want? What could she want *more* than twenty-five thousand dollars. That part didn't make sense. It occurred to her she could be being set up somehow, though to what purpose she could not imagine.

"Bill, I want to try and explain this to you. I wouldn't put you at risk of getting in trouble if it wasn't *this* important. The dog is badly injured, and obviously I can't take him to a veterinarian. I don't know *how* bad it is, but it sounds pretty bad. You're a doctor, and that's what he needs. I know right now you have no desire to do this for him, and that you even think this is wrong, so I want you to do it for me, OK?"

"I said I would look at it, Elizabeth, and I'll look. But I'm not a veterinarian. I don't . . ."

"For God's sake, Bill, you've worked on dogs all your life!" Her tone was hard and she instantly regretted it. "I mean," she said more gently, "I know you've used a lot of dogs in your work, practice surgeries, things like that. You know how to anesthetize a dog, how to do surgery on one."

Bill didn't answer. He was staring out the front window at a figure approaching the truck. Elizabeth followed his line of sight and saw the person too. "Oh my God, here she comes." Elizabeth scrambled from the car.

The woman was tall and dark-featured, thirty-, maybe even forty-something. She was wearing an old green army jacket and faded blue jeans. She eyed Elizabeth thoughtfully.

"He wants to see you," she said simply.

Tears ran silently down Elizabeth's face. She couldn't stop them. She wasn't crying; she wasn't making a sound, she just couldn't stop the tears. As they walked to her vehicle the woman jerked her head at Bill. "Who's this?"

"My grandfather."

"Are you a vet then?"

"I'm a thoracic surgeon."

"Bloody 'ell!" The woman stopped in her tracks. "A thoracic surgeon—he's OK?" She stared evenly at Bill, but her question was directed to his granddaughter.

"Yes, he is. He'll help us. I give you my word." She understood instinctively the woman's concerns.

The woman shrugged with her eyebrows, as if the idea was plausible, but just barely, and walked on. They came to a large van which had no windows in the rear section. "I had to borrow this," the woman explained, "but it's perfect."

Elizabeth wanted to tear the metal door off. She ached to call to him and hear an answering bark, to reassure him she was near and trying to get to him.

The woman opened the side door and Elizabeth saw Damien, lying on the carpeted floor looking straight at her. One of his eyes was destroyed. Without a sound she dropped to her knees next to him and grabbed him around the neck. Her grandfather and the mysterious Australian forgotten, she hugged and hugged him, tears continuing to run steadily down her cheeks.

Damien.

She had never thought to see him again, so she sat, rocking him, stroking his head over and over. The dog was too weak to stand, but he twisted this way and that, trying desperately to lick her tear-streaked face. At that moment, Elizabeth realized how unnecessary speech really was.

The dog's hard, solid body wriggled with his delight as she held him to her, unable to let go. Even though grievously injured, Damien was alive and away from Seville.

"Let us in," the woman said with urgency, "we need to shut this door."

Elizabeth moved to the back of the van and Damien crawled along beside her. The woman climbed in, turned and gestured at Bill.

Bill hesitated. "Are you sure it's safe? They said the dog was dangerous."

The Aussie gestured into the van with her head. "Yeah, obviously," she said dryly. "Come on, I trust the dog to do the right thing."

Bill stepped hesitantly into the van, and the door slammed shut behind him.

The exertion of the joyous reunion soon took its toll on the injured dog and, with a huge sigh, he settled down near Elizabeth with his head stretched out between his front paws, his eyes on the girl's face. Elizabeth half sat, half lay up against the van's back doors, one arm flung over her dog's shoulders. She felt she could never let go of him again.

"Thank you," she said to the woman, her sincerity absolute.

"I'm doing this for 'im, mate." She indicated the dog with a nod of her head. "By the way, I'm Barbara."

Bill put out his hand. "Bill Fletcher, my granddaughter Elizabeth."

The woman shook his hand but cocked a questioning look at Elizabeth. "Well then, who's Lux?"

Elizabeth smiled. "That's what *he* calls me."

"Who?" asked Bill.

Barbara gestured for Bill to sit in the passenger's seat, then settled herself against the van's side wall. "He doesn't know? What's the story here? How did those blokes teach 'im to talk?"

"Wait! The dog *talks*?" Bill interjected. "What are you saying?"

Elizabeth held up her finger to Bill, bidding him wait just one moment. "*They* didn't do anything. No one did a thing, he just wanted out of his cage really bad, and I guess he tried to make the sound that he associated with it. Other than that, I can't give you any kind of explanation." Then she turned to her grandfather. "That's what he does, Bill. That's why Seville wants him back so badly."

Bill addressed Barbara. "You *heard* the dog speak?"

The dog's reaction to Elizabeth having more than proven that, at least as far as the dog was concerned, she was OK, Barbara felt confident to tell her story. "I saw 'im lying on the side of the freeway—this was in the morning before anything was on the news. I'm a pit bull person," she said proudly, with a touch of something akin to defiance. "You know, *real* bulldogs, not your bloody show mongrels." She looked at Bill and Elizabeth for a moment as if she dared them to comment on her declaration. "So I see a bulldog lying on the side of the freeway, a *real* bulldog, mind you, I'm gonna stop. In this day and age, if a bulldog person doesn't help a bulldog, no one will. Everyone runs screamin' to lock the children up and call animal control, and they kill the dog." She shook her head in disgust.

"Anyway, I see a pit bull, and he looks so bloody much like . . . well, he was injured, so there's no way I'm going to be able to drive by. When I walked up to 'im I could see he was *really* bloody crook. He was obviously in a lot of pain, but, bein' what he is, he never growled, he just stared at me, and then sniffed me hand when I held it out for 'im. At first I thought maybe some fool had fought 'im and dumped 'im, but the injuries were wrong—no bite wounds—so a blue was out. His eye was dripping all down the front of 'im, and he couldn't get to his feet. He just sat there, looking at me so steadily, so proudly, waiting to see what I would do. Just waiting to see if I *would* help. That really got me, so I said 'come on mate, we're going home, and I'll sort you out there,' and he understood.

"I coaxed him into rising, and first thing, I throw that bleedin' shock collar as far as I can into the woods." Here she muttered under her breath, "*bastards*," and then continued. "I had to pick 'im up and carry 'im to my ute. Well, he's sitting in the passenger seat, his poor head drooping down, and he's so tired and buggered, that I reach over and put my hand on his head and tell him he's a 'good boy.' So he looks over at me—so grateful it broke my heart—and touches my hand with his nose. Then he lies down across the seat, putting his head in my lap, and rolls his good eye up at my face. Then he says, just as clear as I'm talking to you, he says 'pet.' Well, that really threw me for six! Not so much what he says, as how *clear* it is. That *dog* speaks better bleedin' English than I do!"

Bill was staring at the tall Australian woman and Elizabeth laughed at his expression. He looked at Elizabeth. He looked at the dog. "It's *true*, Bill," Elizabeth laughed. "I taught him all kinds of words, he's *so* smart you wouldn't believe it." She looked down at the dog, who was watching her face with utter contentment. "Damien, this is my grandpa, and he's *good.*" She laid her hand on her grandfather's forearm. "He's going to help you. Bill is *good.* Why don't you say hello to him. Go on, say hello."

The dog cocked his head so his good eye was on the man, and his head wavered slightly as he searched Bill's scent for clues to his character. Coming from the bag the man held in his hand were unmistakably, the same scents which, in the dog's mind, affirmed his status as one of the kind of people who did things to him. That felt Bad. But his scent told Damien another thing also. This man was *Elizabeth's.* So wonderful was the dog's sense of smell, that he could discern that Bill and Elizabeth were related, and that they lived in the same home. In the short time they had all been together in the van, the dog had already noted that Elizabeth was subordinate to Bill, and that she liked him. Damien was both wary and skeptical but for now he would reluctantly accept him, because it was Elizabeth's will that he do so.

"Hello," the dog finally said, his teeth snapping together audibly at the end of the word, as was his style. Elizabeth laughed out loud. "You've been formally introduced, Bill."

She had to smile at the scene; if there had ever been two beings which doubted each other's intentions, it was the retired surgeon and the escaped laboratory dog. Bill was staring, eyes wide, mouth gaping. The dog returned his gaze warily. She let them have a moment, and then reminded Bill of his urgent mission.

"You need to look at his eye."

Bill slowly turned to face his granddaughter. He shook his head. "I had no idea," was all he said.

"Come on, he's not going to hurt you."

Bill still hesitated. "Talking or no talking, I'm a little uncomfortable with this. Do we have a muzzle for him? It's kind of close quarters in here to be examining the dog—I may cause him some discomfort."

Damien, with the extraordinarily observant eye of a dog, had already determined the man's intent to examine him. An experienced research subject, he knew the subtle moves and sounds a man would make before using him. With growing apprehension he looked to Elizabeth. "Pain?" he said anxiously.

Barbara shook her head with a small smile, amazed by what she was seeing. She caught Elizabeth's eye. "He's afraid of him," she said. "Can you reassure him?"

"It's all right, Damien," Elizabeth said quickly. "He's a *good doctor.* He has to look at your eye because it's hurt very badly. He's *good*, OK? He'll be nice, don't worry." She longed to tell the dog how relieved she was to have a doctor here. The dog remained wary. "It's *OK*. You *have* to let him look at you. It may hurt. Trust me, though, we have to do this. I'll be right here." She fancied both Bill and the dog looked at her like she was mad. "Bill, come on, just ease over here and it'll be OK."

Bill sighed and cautiously scooted toward the dog. He looked at his hands, whole and undamaged for what he figured was the last time. *At least I'm retired and don't need 'em anymore.* As he reached out the dog pulled back, ducking his head away.

"Damien!" Elizabeth warned in a stern voice, "so help me, now stop it! Hold still. It's *OK*."

The doctor reached out again, tentatively touching the top of the dog's head as if he were testing an iron to see if it was hot. The dog squinted up at him, but held steady. The doctor took the blocky head in his hands and tipped it up toward the light.

The eye was a mess. Shreds of tissue and oozing puss were all that were apparent. The damaged eye was obviously blind, and a putrid odor came from the socket.

"Check his mouth too, it's really crook," said Barbara.

Bill sighed. *Great. The mouth.* There was nothing he could do about the eye at this time. It would take enucleation. He gently lifted one lip and saw nothing amiss. His eye lingered on the long fangs.

"Other side."

"Oh." He gently shifted the dog's head and noticed immediately that the entire side of the dog's muzzle was swollen. He lifted the other lip. The tissue in the area of the canine tooth was red, swollen and strangely crushed and torn.

"How did this happen?" he asked Barbara.

"Blowed if I know—this is how I found him. It said somethin' in the paper about him havin' a go at the people who broke him out."

"Damien attacked the people who tried to break him out, in defense of the man who put that shock collar on him. All this must have happened then."

Barbara, with her innate knowledge of dogs spoke first. "The people came, and they grabbed his man and he whooped them good. Huh boy?" Damien's tail thumped once, weakly, at her voice. "I bet," Barbara continued, "he had a pretty good punch-up with whoever broke in. He was protecting his home and his master." She put her hand on the dog's head. "Good boy!" she praised the dog warmly. "You were *very good.*" The dog thumped his tail in gratitude.

Bill was shaking his head. "I hear it, but I don't believe it—not for a minute."

Elizabeth's head was shaking slowly as well. "Imagine that, will you? He got all *this*, trying to protect that *bastard.*" The image, and her part in it, haunted her still.

Bill had grown bolder and was examining the dog's body. Damien was sore all over from his pummeling, and when the man picked up his swollen right front leg, the dog jerked it back with a grunt. Startled, Bill jerked away too. "Sorry," he said to the dog before he caught himself.

"Well," Bill said, "here's what I can do for him tonight. He should be started on fluids and penicillin. It should be a drip, but I don't have that. I do have some erythromycin with me, and that will have to do for now. I don't like his color, and his abdomen is distended and tender, so there's internal bleeding, and we're going to have to deal with that soon. And, of course, the eye has to come out. His right front leg appears broken or sprained at the wrist. I'm not touching it until he's muzzled. His mouth *looks* bad but it will heal." There was only a slight hesitation before he continued. "I suggest we set something up to work on him tomorrow. It's going to take some time to get what I need. I don't have anesthetics around the house," he said in response to Elizabeth's disappointed look.

Barbara flexed her sore back. "Tomorrow at 10:00 A.M.?"

Bill shrugged. "Where are we going to meet? All this cloak and dagger seems unnecessary now."

Elizabeth shook her head. "I'm sure they're watching the house at least part of the time. We were lucky tonight. I bet we wouldn't have been if we had left any earlier. Seville wants Damien back, *bad*." She turned to Barbara. "They already had the police over to the house."

"Fair dinkum?" Barbara was impressed.

"They're a lot less likely to follow if *you* go out alone, Bill. If I wasn't with you, I doubt they would bother. It's me they want to follow." She looked at Barbara. "If Bill leaves alone in the morning, they're a lot more likely to think I'm still in the house. And, I'll be honest with you, I couldn't walk away from him now, I just couldn't."

Barbara smiled and shook her head. "He needs you now, mate. You stay with 'im. Bill, I'll meet you here tomorrow at 10:00, OK?"

"OK. Here, let me give him something which will help until tomorrow. I wish . . . Well, I have to get all that stuff tomorrow." He rummaged around in his bag, came up with a syringe and a bottle. While the dog watched anxiously, he drew up the dose, leaned forward and smoothly injected it in the animal's thigh. Putting away his things he reached for the van's door. "OK. I won't be driving this truck tomorrow, I'll be in a blue Lincoln."

"Oh, my God, Bill—what are you going to tell Dave?" Elizabeth said suddenly.

Bill was staring at the dog. "I'll think of something," he said, stepped out, and shut the van door.

CHAPTER THIRTEEN

To sit alone with my conscience
Will be judgment enough for me.

—CHARLES WILLIAMS STUBBS

So intent was Barbara in contemplating the events of the past few days, the Australian was pulling into her driveway before she realized she had been driving in silence for some time. The conversation with the stranger in the back of the van had dwindled, and then stopped all together a few miles back. She couldn't see into the dark interior of the van, but her suspicions were confirmed when she got out and pulled open the van's side door. The girl was sound asleep, lying on her side with her face buried in the dog's solid neck, one arm still flung protectively over his shoulders. Weak as he was, the dog raised his head and gazed steadily at Barbara.

"I know mate, I know," she soothed. "It's OK. Nobody's gonna hurt your friend. You're both safe here." Barbara knew that perilous as his own hold on life was at that moment, the dog's one concern was for the girl's safety.

"Lizzy, hey, wake up, we're here."

They persuaded the dog to stand, but they had to carry the pit bull into the house. Elizabeth was concerned, for his eye injury, though serious, would not produce this degree of weakness. She could only hope the internal injuries her grandfather suspected weren't too severe. As they went in the front door, Barbara whistled shrilly at the barking coming from behind the house and it fell silent. Inside they were met by a small, red dachshund

which bayed an unfriendly alarm at Elizabeth, while at the same time dancing with delight at seeing Barbara. The little dog sniffed critically at Damien,
then went back to baying at Elizabeth and leaping up on Barbara's knees.

"That 'uns a snake. Watch out for her," Barbara said with a laugh. "Let
her come to you—don't try and pick her up. You've been warned."

Elizabeth looked at the little dog. She weighed less than ten pounds, had
flyaway ears and a sharp pointed nose. About the only thing to identify her
as "mostly dachshund" was the fact that she was three times longer than she
was tall.

"Somehow I figured you'd have . . . big dogs."

"Oh, I got some bigger than this. But this one runs the place."

One look at Elizabeth sitting on the edge of the couch, yawning and trying to keep her eyes open, and it was plain to Barbara that they wouldn't be
talking much that evening. Barbara wondered if the kid had gotten any sleep
while her dog was missing. The woman walked out of the room and came
back with a large black-and-red plaid dog bed, which she placed beside the
couch. Barbara left the room again and came back with blankets and a pillow.

"Here, let's get 'im on the bed, then you stay here with 'im tonight." Together they encouraged and helped the dog crawl onto the bed, where he
settled with a deep sigh. Barbara covered him with a light blanket. "You
sleep right here, next to 'im. He's been kippin' next to me bed, but I think
he'd be happier here with you. Bathroom's right around there. I'm going to
leave my dogs outside tonight, it won't kill them, though they're going to
think it is, because we don't need a blue—ah, fight, you know—tonight.
Whatever you do, don't get up in the middle of the night and let 'im out the
back door. He hasn't been eating, so he shouldn't have to go. I've got to get
up at sparrow's . . . I mean, rather early, and return the van to a mate, so if
I'm not here when you wake up, just make yourself at home and I'll be back.
I'll take a sickie at work tomorrow, so I'll see you in the morning, we can talk
then, OK?"

Elizabeth shook her head. "I don't understand why you're doing this. No
one would. *Anyone* would take the twenty-five thousand dollars. Anyone."

"Would *you*?" Barbara said sharply, a hint of irritation in her voice.

"Well, no, but I . . ."

"Maybe you're not the *only* person in the world thinks mates are more
important than money."

"Yeah, I guess." Elizabeth's incredulity showed in her voice. She collapsed on the couch and put her hand on her dog's back, just wanting to feel him, to know he was really there, and to let him know she was near. She was proud of that one thing; she *had* finally come for him.

Barbara, standing in the doorway, looked from Elizabeth to the dog. Her face changed, a strange expression that reminded Elizabeth of the way shadows and light play across a field when clouds pass across the sun. "I had my own 'Damien,'" she said quietly, "I know how it feels. I know what it's worth. And that's why I know twenty-five thousand dollars is meaningless. G'night."

The next morning, at the same moment her eyes opened, Elizabeth truly realized that she had entered—not particularly willingly—into a whole new world, very distinct from her comfortable and routine past. She couldn't go home; not with the dog. It looked distinctly like she was going to be a non-starter for her medical degree. Her father would probably have her committed if he ran across her. She'd tried so hard to avoid all this chaos, yet it had happened all the same, and she found it terrifying. Since the time of her mother's desertion she had grown up in and around the University medical center and environs, spending more time there than at her father's home. Weekends she had colored with her crayons, or blown up surgical gloves for balloons, waiting for Bill or Dave to finish up their projects and take her home. The people she had grown up around and knew best, the arrogant, brilliant researchers, and hectic techs and aides had all suddenly been replaced by a forty-something woman who would refuse twenty-five thousand dollars for the sake of a stray dog. The Med's bright white walls, long hallways with polished floors, and constant background murmur of voices, phones, pagers, faxes, monitors and lab equipment, had been replaced by a small, quiet, rural house with paw prints on the kitchen floor and pictures of dogs lined up on the mantel like relatives. Elizabeth hugged her dog.

We're not in Kansas anymore, Toto.

She was disappointed to find that she had no joy at the prospect of being on the run. She was even more disappointed to find that she was actually a little frightened.

I thought it was supposed to be romantic and glamorous to be a fugitive. Where's the glamour?

She scratched her foot through her sock. There were only uncertainty, concern for her grievously injured dog and the uneasy feeling that comes from knowing you are tampering with your career.

She stretched muscles which were complaining about a night on a couch that smelled more than lightly of dog. When she heard Barbara come into the house, the Australian woman was singing to herself:

> *Once upon a hill we sat beneath the willow tree,*
> *counting all the stars and waiting for the dawn.*
> *But that was once upon a time, now the tree is gone.*

The tune and words were sad, but Elizabeth couldn't help smiling at the woman's strong Australian accent, and what it did to the song. She sat up on the couch and quickly assessed her current status. She was dirty, sore, unemployed, most likely soon to be expelled, homeless, tired, hungry, in trouble with the law, and sleeping on a stranger's couch. Not too shabby for 7 A.M. in the morning on the first day of the rest of her life.

Barbara came into the room and handed her a cocoa and a sack with a lukewarm egg sandwich and hashbrown in it. "Here, I figured you'd be starved."

Elizabeth found Barbara to be what her father would call "unvarnished." She seemed to be intelligent enough in a rough-and-ready sort of way, rustic and totally without pretense. She was friendly, and willing to help, but there was a confidence and reserve that indicated she was a private person, and not overly concerned with what Elizabeth thought of her. Her brown eyes were striking; laughing and lazy and keen all at the same time. Elizabeth had never known anyone like her before, and found it amusing to think of Seville trying to take Damien away from the Aussie.

"How's your mate?" Barbara asked. The dachshund was sniffing Damien's back leg and drawing no reaction.

"He's really weak," Elizabeth replied. "I can't help but think there's something else wrong, something we're not seeing." Ten o'clock seemed like an eternity to wait for Bill's help.

You're the daughter and the granddaughter of brilliant medical men, how can you know so little about medicine?

She felt a dull shame, as if she should have been paying more attention to her family's work, as if she knew little in this world about anything. "Is there something we can do while we wait?" she asked miserably.

"I have him on antibiotics, the strongest I have. I think he should have fluids, myself," Barbara said. "I have the stuff here, if you want. It's your call."

"You *know* how to do that? Really? Yeah, fluids would be good."

Barbara shrugged as she stood up to go. "Yeah, I've got an IV setup. I'll get it." She left, leaving Elizabeth to wonder why she would have such a thing around the house.

When Barbara came back, Elizabeth asked her just that. "This stuff? I just keep it around. You never know when it might be handy. Where I grew up—in the outback—we didn't fool with vets and such. This is pretty basic stuff, stuff you needed to know." While talking, she had set up the IV. She knelt down in front of the dog and he regarded her with his one good eye half closed. She squinted back at him.

"He does look bloody awful. Did he get up at all last night?"

"No. He hasn't moved."

"I think we've got internal bleeding. Bloody 'ell. It makes sense though, if someone kicked the shit outta him or something during the fight. He's got internal injuries all right. Well, we'll get this fluid into 'im; that'll help until that doctor gets here. Here, I need you to hold off his vein on his leg, like this . . ."

The dog, with complete trust in the two women, watched without emotion as the IV needle was slipped into a vein in his front leg, and taped in place. Elizabeth sat back to watch the fluids drip into her dog. "What did you mean, Barbara, that you had your own 'Damien'?"

"Wait a sec." Barbara went into the kitchen, got a fresh cup of coffee. "Want some?" she called.

"No thanks, got my cocoa."

Elizabeth heard the refrigerator door open, the sound of milk being poured into coffee, and the door slamming shut. Barbara came back in and sat down. She pointed to a large grouping of photos on the wall over the TV set. They were all of the same dog.

"He came along five years before I married, and left me four years af-ter . . ." She stopped, obviously unwilling to finish the sentence, then went on. "We went through a lot together. He was me best mate. In Australia, where, I guess, you may have figured out I'm from, 'mateship' is a very important part of life. It implies a much stronger bond, I would say, than just the word 'friendship,' you know? Your mate's your mate, and you don't ever let 'em down. You've got your work mates, and your sports mates and, well, it *is* hard to describe, exactly, but if I was in Australia, and I said to someone, 'Damie and Liz are best mates,' they would know that I meant you were more than just 'friends,' that you had a strong tie, and that you would always be there for each other.

"That one," she indicated the pictures with her chin, "that one was me best mate—and as true as steel." She turned to Elizabeth. "I think *you* would know; to be in the company of such a strong and magical animal, and then to go out into the bush, or forest, and share your love of Nature with another creature, another *species*—for whom Nature is also a great passion—what a *gift* that is. Spending a day in the bush together, and never having to say a word, because you each know what the other is thinking. Only those people, Elizabeth, that have had both a really great dog, *and* the capacity to experience it, can begin to understand. Those people that *'ave* experienced it—they *know*. That's how you feel about Damien, and that's how I felt about that dog."

Elizabeth stared up at the photographs. The dog was a brindle pit bull with ears cut short and pointed, and a white chest and chin, startling in his resemblance to Damien. She wondered if that was the reason the Aussie had stopped on the side of the road for Damien. In the largest photo the dog stared straight at the camera, calmly looking into Elizabeth's eyes. "Yeah," she said under her breath. She was remembering the first time she had looked into Damien's eyes, as he lay on the floor at Seville's feet, starved and injured, and she had been repulsed by his condition. She remembered that when the creature had lifted its eyes to hers, there had been a moment of shock, of recognition, of comprehension, for she had seen his soul, and their two souls had somehow recognized each other, though they were not yet friends. Here, again, she saw a presence which could not be ignored, even though the strange dog stared at her only from a photograph. This dog had been *somebody.*

How like Damien, she thought.

"Why didn't I act sooner?" She said it quietly, almost to herself, but the Australian understood the cryptic reference.

"Not many bloody people *ever* do see, mate. Don't be so hard on yourself. How many people would see *him*, even if he did speak perfect English to them? How many people see their own bloody dog? Come on, you know the answer to that."

Elizabeth rested her hand on Damien's head, and he raised his remaining eye to her face. His tail thumped once, weakly, and then his eye shut again. Elizabeth looked up at the older woman, and Barbara frowned at her troubled expression. "I don't really quite understand," the girl began, as if unsure of what she was trying to ask, "I mean, I guess I'm not sure how come people feel affection for a *dog*? And how come some can, and some can't?"

Barbara started to laugh, then stopped short, realizing how seriously the question had been asked by the stranger. Whatever her background, she was feeling guilty, or uncomfortable, about the strength of her commitment to the dog. She had evidently never before been exposed to kinship with other species. Someone had taught her that it was wrong. Barbara suspected she knew who, and she hesitated a moment before answering. "You're grandfather, Bill, he said he was a what? A chest doctor?"

Elizabeth was surprised at the question, but answered willingly. "He's a thoracic surgeon. He did a lot of valve work."

"Uh-huh. A heart surgeon." Her tone, again like the night they had met, seemed less than approving. "And your father—what does he do?"

"Uhm, he does R&D. Research, you know."

"On what?"

"Oh, the heart, transplantation, mostly."

Barbara looked at her sharply. "He does heart research—practices on dogs, maybe?"

"Yes, but . . ." Elizabeth instinctively moved to defend her father's work but stopped with her mouth still open. Barbara watched keenly while she waited for Elizabeth's reply. But there was no reply—Elizabeth's mouth shut and she remained silent. She now knew that her father's work with dogs was indefensible. "Your mum work?"

"No."

"Did your father ever keep dogs?"

"We've never had a dog. I've never actually had a pet of any kind. It's not something my father would want around the house."

Seeing how it was, Barbara nodded and sighed. "I think you're *very* lucky mate, that you're able to feel what you do for Damien. That's all I can say about that. Very lucky." After a moment she spoke again. "If you raise a member of either species—dog or human—in isolation, you get one screwed-up bloke. Why do humans have friends?" She shrugged. "That's probably the same reason dogs have friends. We're social animals, both of us, eh?

"The way I see it, there's all kinds of love. There's the strong attraction and commitment between husband and wife which is essential to raising healthy, happy kids. You love your man in a desperate, strong, real way, but does that mean you love your mum and pop less? No. How 'bout the love for a little sister or brother? For grandparents? Some people think," Barbara continued, warming to the subject, "it's wrong to love a good dog so much. The same people who say *that* are often the ones who don't even value their own kids enough to stay home and raise them. Women who pop out kids because they selfishly want 'em, then ship them off every morning to daycare and preschool so someone else can raise them. Not because they have to, but because they want a *career*. Like there's a career out there more important than raising good human beings! You know yourself, don't you, in your heart, that you love Damien more than many folks love their own spouse, or even their own children, right? Are you and Damien ever going to go through a messy divorce? Ever call each other names? Sue each other? You ever going to abuse or neglect 'im, like so many people do their own little children?" She shrugged again, as if the vagaries of human emotion were disgusting to her.

"People are embarrassed by that fact, and don't want to accept it, and some try and deny the depth of feeling that exists between man and dog. Others, like your dad and granddad, if you don't mind my saying so, simply aren't capable of it, and don't even know of its existence. Maybe there's some part of their soul missing that makes kinship possible? I don't know, mate. But you, Liz, you can't help but love a soul like Damien's. As for *my* dog," she said with a tender fierceness, "there was more nobility, more kindness, more patience, more *worth* in that dog than in most people I've ever known." She shrugged and put her head to one side.

"Try to look at it this way, Liz; Damien is a very religious fellow. Devout, submissive and ever hopeful of good things coming from his god. You must realize you're Damien's god, and never forget that." Here Barbara smiled gently, and a little sadly. "How you treat your dog says a lot about what kind of god you are, doesn't it? Are you a vengeful god? A god obsessed with rules and obedience to your will? A god of love? Interesting to contemplate, isn't it?

"A *good* dog is incapable of treachery—so we need to make sure we're reasonable and fair to 'em. But even when we aren't, they still love us. It is religion. If you want to know something about love, put down the Bible and observe a good dog. It's our 'Trust in God' all over again. Some people renounce their religion when things get rough, and dogs put us all to shame there. They stick it out. Do you think Damien ever gave up on you?"

"No. I know he didn't. Ever. And that's why Damien won't attack Seville," Elizabeth said, more to herself than to Barbara. "He's his god too."

Barbara nodded, remembering Seville's name from the news reports. "Yes, I'd say he's not a god of love, eh?"

Elizabeth shook her head, as if a spell had been broken. "I don't know what that man's problem is. It's weird to hear you talk like this. I've never . . . Well, no one I know has ever really, you know, loved a dog." Elizabeth looked away, troubled. "I feel so guilty, now, about the others. The dogs, right now, in my father's lab. They are all going to die, horribly. The other day I dropped by, and there was this dog, a sweet yellow dog, like a retriever I guess, and it was lying there in the cage, watching me, and its eyes were so friendly—it wanted me to come over and speak to it. It just wanted a word from me, so badly, so I did, I went over, and they had put another dog's heart, a second heart, in its neck, to see how long it would retain it, and when it rejects, it will die, horribly, and I . . ." Elizabeth stopped, the image of the dog before her. Her remorse hurt like a physical wound. It choked her and she squeezed her eyes shut. After a moment she opened them and said, "What made Damien special, why did he stand out, and not the others?"

Barbara was watching Elizabeth intently. She was curious about her, but too polite to pry. "That's a question that can't be answered. Whatever it is, it's the same things that makes you like some people and not others. Dogs and people aren't really that different. Think of all the people you meet; lots of 'em are great people, but how many become lifelong mates? How many become lovers? And yet you meet heaps of people—so is that to say there is something *wrong* with all those other people? No. It just shows how special, and unique, how magical a *true* friendship is when it happens, be it with a human or a dog."

Barbara stood up, glanced at the empty fluid bag and removed the IV line from Damien. "As to why some people can look at a dog and see a wonderful fellow creature and others cannot, that's the way of life." She grinned. "It's that way for people too. How many times have you looked at a married bloke and wondered, 'What in bloody 'ell did she see in 'im?' You know what I mean?"

Elizabeth thought of Seville and Novak and grinned. "Oh, yeah. I sure do."

269

"I need to see to my dogs, would you like to meet them? Damien will be fine here."

"Sure." Elizabeth patted Damien, assured him she would be right back, and tried to follow Barbara. But the pit bull, at seeing her rise to leave, whimpered and began to pull himself after her. Elizabeth dropped to her knees, distraught, and hugged him, reassuring him for several moments that she would be right back. When she rose again, Damien watched anxiously but stayed on his bed. With several glances backward, Elizabeth finally followed the woman out the back door and into the brisk early autumn morning.

The property was large, fifty acres spreading up behind the house on a slight rise. There were meadows among the trees, and morning sunlight shot through apple trees, firs and maples, lighting the golden grass at their feet. Elizabeth saw the glimmer of a pond on the rise ahead of them. A vegetable garden to their left showed pumpkins among the drying corn stalks. Before them, three pit bulls lunged at the end of their chains, making strange crying and gurgling sounds. Tails whipping madly, they were twisting with delight at the approach of the humans.

"Oh, they're pit bulls! Are they friendly?" Elizabeth asked.

"What in bleedin' 'ell do you think Damien is?" Barbara said over her shoulder. Then she added, "Do they *look* friendly?"

"Well, yeah. But I've always heard . . ."

Barbara stopped and turned, giving her a withering look. "I won't tell you what I've *always* heard about people who work at the Research Center."

Elizabeth grinned. "Yeah, OK."

Elizabeth was amazed to see that the dogs seemed to be as happy to see her as they were to see their owner. They twisted and reared up and smiled and wagged and flipped onto their backs, waving their paws at her, just like they did to Barbara.

"Watch this."

Barbara unhooked one struggling dog and took it out of the fenced area they were tied in. Holding the dog by the collar she walked it toward what looked to Elizabeth like a hangman's gallows with a rope dangling from the outer edge. The dog was screaming in excitement, and walking on its hind legs, nearly choking itself in the process. Elizabeth couldn't see what the dog was so excited about. Suddenly Barbara let the dog loose, and it flew, straight as an arrow, to the dangling rope. The dog left the ground ten feet back, and hit the rope hard and true, five feet from the ground. The rope was long enough that the dog swung back and forth as if on a swing, shaking its head and neck and hanging suspended in the air the whole time.

Elizabeth cried out with astonishment. Barbara was grinning, and the other dogs screamed louder in their frenzy to get their turn on the rope.

"Why is she doing that?" Elizabeth shouted over the din.

"She's a *bulldog*!" Barbara shouted back, as if that answered the question definitively.

One by one Barbara took the dogs from their cables and allowed them several minutes on the rope, the whole time telling them they were "brilliant," and "clever dogs," and that it was "well done!" When they were finished, she put them back on their cables, and the dogs all relaxed, lying stretched out on the tops of their doghouses, one lying in one of the small plastic wading pools which were beside each doghouse.

"Come meet them!" Barbara said. "This brindle one is Thriller, I don't know her breeding—she was a rescue dog. Got her out of a pound where they said she was 'vicious.' They wouldn't adopt out pit bulls, so I just said she was mine and paid the fines. She loves everyone, and isn't even dog aggressive. She's a gentle soul, loves other animals, loves kids.

"This one," she pointed to the dog lying in the pool, "is Beltane Fire. She's a rednose red, see the color of her nose? She's a well-bred little dog, high drive, a little simple sometimes, but that's OK." Beltane Fire was panting happily at them from her pool, her hind legs stretched out froglike behind her. She was a beautiful brick red all over, with gold eyes and toenails.

"And this little girl is Cobra, see those yellow snake eyes? She's just a pup, another rednose red—she's my baby! Come, Cobra, let's have a bit of a cuddle up!"

When they were done petting and admiring the dogs, Barbara gave them all fresh water and brought out frozen knucklebones the size of cantaloupes for each dog. "Sorry mates," she called to the pit bulls, "but we got a bulldog in the house needs us today. I'll see you all later."

Elizabeth noticed each dog was tied by a shade tree. "This seems like a nice setup for them. But doesn't keeping them tied up make them mean?"

"I repeat, do they look mean? A dog's temperament is not *so* very flexible. A sound dog stays sound, even in bad conditions—just like people. Don't blame a chain for a dog's grotty temperament. Look at your own dog, he's been through bloody 'ell and back, and he's still sound. And if you were a dog, would you rather be tied out on a day like this, or stuck in a shipping crate in some house or garage, or stuck in a small kennel with a hard cement floor, or stuck in the house all day? Me, I'd rather be able to roll in the grass and watch the interesting things which go on around here."

Elizabeth was anxious to get back to Damien so they returned to the house and talked of the dog's experiences until Barbara left for her rendezvous with Bill. Elizabeth sat with Damien, waiting, frightened now that the dog was truly dying. His gums were very pale and he wouldn't or couldn't lift his head. He lay staring straight ahead, waiting also, it seemed. Elizabeth thought she saw the beginnings of a strange fear in his eye. Was he aware that he was truly in danger of dying? Did he understand the concept of death? She didn't need Damien to speak to understand that the dog was, indeed, experiencing anxiety about his condition. His one eye looked searchingly at her face, wanting to know the answer to a question he was unable to ask.

"Damien," she said, stroking his head, "you're going to be OK. *Bill* is coming. Bill's going to fix you up, make you better. He'll be here any time now. In fact, any minute."

Damien sighed deeply. She watched the dog's sides rising and falling with his shallow, rapid breaths, and knew their time was running out.

She heard Barbara's truck, followed by another vehicle, pulling up outside and she hurried to the door. What she saw froze her in her tracks. Bill and Dave were stepping out of the car, her father glancing around with a tight expression.

Ohmygod! Dave here? God help me!

She let out a deep breath and walked out to meet them. She was awfully glad Barbara had had the foresight to lock the dachshund away.

"Hi."

What did one say at a time like this? This was not something she could have foreseen.

"Elizabeth." She noted he didn't sound great. How in the world—*why* in the world—had Bill talked him into coming here—to help with *this*? He was risking everything to be here with the "stolen" dog. Why *had* he come?

Bill and Barbara were pulling equipment out of Bill's car and Elizabeth walked over to help carry it into the house. She glanced at Barbara and registered the Aussie's grim expression. She had vouched for Bill, but her father? She truly didn't know what to think.

Oh boy.

Walking into the house through waves of tense silence, Elizabeth felt awkward; her father and Damien inhabited two entirely different worlds for her. She found their sudden and unexpected juxtaposition unsettling.

She looked over at Bill as he contemplated the kitchen as an operating theater. Elizabeth knew her grandfather was critical of Dave's parenting skills. The truth was, Bill had always been more of a father to her than Dave. She wondered with awe at the content of the conversation which must have transpired that morning between the two men. Whatever had occurred, it had had the near miraculous effect of getting her father here, presumably to help with the surgery. She was grateful for that—Dave was a consummate surgeon, and obviously they could get the work done in half the time with two men working. She knew Bill had been concerned about keeping the weakened dog under the less than ideal IV anesthetic they would have to use for the duration of two procedures.

"This will have to do," Dave said suddenly, rubbing his chin. He exhaled as he glanced about the room; it was well lit, and the kitchen table was a good height for an operating surface. At least, Elizabeth noted with relief, there was not going to be any further debate at this point on the subject of Dave's involvement.

Bill nodded. "You girls prepare the table by spreading a sheet or something as clean as possible on it. This is going to be very messy, and we'll need newspapers spread under the table to protect the floor. Dave, I'm going to start laying everything out; why don't you go examine the dog, see what you think."

"The dog's in here . . . doctor," Barbara said, hesitating slightly at the title. The three of them walked into the living room and stopped. The dog bed was empty.

"Damien!" Elizabeth ran forward, swinging wildly around, looking, "Oh no, he , . . Oh *shit*, I *told* him someone was coming for him. He must think someone is coming to take him again. Could he have gotten out?"

"No," Barbara said, "he's in here, he must be down the hall." They found the dog sprawled on the floor halfway down the hall. He had tried to escape when he heard the men enter the house. The once-proud bulldog had his tail between his legs, and he was shaking in abject terror. The scent of the men and their equipment drifting in to him had confirmed his fears. These men smelled like Seville and they had come for him. His fear, though simple, was profound.

"Oh Jesus, Damien," Elizabeth said, "you scared me to death. I told you it's OK, they're *good* doctors, remember?"

The dog glanced back at the man standing behind him, and in an instant he picked up the man's demeanor and the attitude of the two women to the stranger. It felt *very* Bad.

"Bad," the dog said simply. "Out."

Dave's eyes grew wide and he snorted. "It *is* true. I thought your grandfather had gone crazy." He shook his head and laughed mirthlessly. "Jesus, that *is* something. No *wonder* Seville wants that thing back. Wow."

Elizabeth moved in front of the dog and glanced at Barbara. "Let's carry him back in there." Barbara nodded and the two women picked the dog up and carried him into the middle of the living room. When they had settled him on the plaid dog bed, Barbara stepped back and sat on the edge of the couch. Elizabeth sat beside her dog, stroking his head and neck and holding him in place. "It's OK, it's OK," she soothed the dog. "OK, Dave, go ahead."

"I don't work on dogs unless they are securely restrained and muzzled. That's how I've protected my hands all these years. I want him muzzled."

Elizabeth opened her mouth to protest but Barbara stood up quickly, her face carefully neutral. "I have a muzzle I can get; it won't cause 'im any discomfort and will make it easier for your father to concentrate on what he's got to do," Barbara said. She disappeared for a moment and came back bearing a muzzle.

"Easy, boy, it's OK." She slipped the muzzle on, then resumed her seat on the edge of the couch. With the dog restrained, Dave approached. "Stand him up."

Elizabeth tried, but the dog was simply too weak, and she struggled to hold both ends of the limp dog up. "Never mind," he said impatiently and squatted down next to the dog. He produced a pair of latex exam gloves and put them on. The dog weakly rolled his eye at the snapping sound the gloves made, for long ago he had come to associate the sound with painful experiences. Taking the dog's head in his hands, Dave looked at his eyes. The doctor then examined minutely the dog's whole body, finding the small, scabbed wound on the side where the pen had entered his body. Pulling the scab off, he probed the direction and depth of the wound with his finger. As the man began palpating Damien's abdomen, the dog's mouth cracked open, and his shallow panting became faster. The tip of Damien's tail began to wave in an appeasement gesture.

"I need a thermometer."

Wordlessly Barbara slipped from the room and returned in a moment with a thermometer case marked "DOG" in black ink. She shook it down, handed it to Dave, and resumed her seat on the couch arm.

Barbara was determined to keep her mouth shut. This was no longer her affair. The dog was obviously Elizabeth's, and Elizabeth obviously had the dog's best interest at heart. She had concerns about the young girl's ability to handle these two obviously dominant men. Outside of that, the affairs of these people did not concern her. She couldn't help but note though, the way Dave handled the dog, quickly, and a little roughly, without the slightest word or gesture to reassure. It was apparent the dog was an inanimate object to him. A piece of equipment. Watching him work, she thought about the difference between the man and his daughter.

The researcher noted the area of intense pain at the dog's left carpus and, holding the foreleg fast, he prodded the joint in an effort to determine the nature of the injury. When Damien grunted at the pain and jerked the leg away instinctively, the doctor jerked it back. "Hold still!" he said harshly. Damien thumped his tail twice in apology and flattened his ears in shame. Dave ignored him and continued to palpate the area, while the dog made tiny grunting sounds of pain. At that moment, Barbara knew David Fletcher.

"Is there a chance he might die?" Elizabeth asked in a small voice.

"Of course," her father replied. "He's been hemorrhaging internally for some time, and there's always the chance of peritonitis. He's shocky and should have been getting fluids. There's probable damage to the liver or spleen—probably the liver or he would have been dead by now."

"He's had one bag of fluid this morning," Barbara said through clenched teeth. "And 500 of Keflex twice a day."

"Oh?" Dave turned toward her, looking her up and down as if seeing her for the first time. "And where did you get *your* degree?" he said.

Elizabeth inhaled sharply. She feared the worst but the tall Australian woman ignored the remark. "Would you like to start now?" she said.

Dave continued to stare at her for a moment. "No. He's subnormal on his temp, and we would definitely kill the dog *immediately* if we tried to put it under anesthetic before we stabilize it to some degree. We need the body temperature up to at least 100 degrees. Get hot-water bottles and blankets, heating pads, whatever you have around here. If we're going to save him, we need to start right *now.*" He walked into the kitchen and Barbara looked over at Elizabeth in sympathy. The young woman still remained kneeling by her dog. She had removed the muzzle and was cradling the broad, smooth head in her arms. A single tear worked its way down her face and she simply rocked the dog, whispering "You're not going to die, not now, not after all this . . ." Damien struggled weakly to lick her face in an agony of concern for her sadness. She buried her face in the dog's neck, and Barbara saw her shake as she fought back the tears. Barbara assumed the last thing Elizabeth wanted to do right now was cry in front of her father. Damien curved his neck around, nudging and licking her in his effort to comfort her.

"OK, OK," the dog said weakly.

"I'll get the hot-water bottles," Barbara said to no one in particular, and fled the room.

It was decided that while they were working to elevate the dog's body temperature, they would place him on the kitchen table to facilitate the other work that needed to be done. The animal was obviously terrified by the sight and smell of the men and their surgical equipment, and Elizabeth sympathized, guessing at the memories that must be flooding back to Damien. When the dog was lifted onto the table; she stayed at his head, reassuring him that she was there. She told him to "be good" during Dave's placement of the IV syringe in his front leg, and Damien held perfectly still, his head turned away from the man. While Dave administered fluids, steroids and penicillin through the IV to combat the shock, Bill prepared the Ketamine/Vallium mixture they would use to knock the dog out. This would be followed by 5 ccs Innovar to assist in keeping the dog out for the extended period they were anticipating. Bill hesitated as he prepared to inject the anesthetic agent into the IV.

"We're going to start now, Elizabeth."

"Thank you, Bill. I'm ready." Her hand went out to the dog's neck, and she grasped the fur, holding on tightly.

"I'll be right here . . ." she whispered, then glanced with embarrassment at her father, who was watching her. Dave looked away. But the solution had had its powerful and mysterious effect, and the dog's body slumped limply on the table.

After he had prepped the area, Dave cut along the abdominal midline in the palpable silence of the room. Elizabeth reluctantly removed her hand from the dog's limp head, and her grandfather moved into position to begin the enucleation of the damaged eye. Bill was glancing over a page copied from a canine surgery book, which outlined the procedure he was about to do. The enucleation of a dog's eye was not something a retired thoracic surgeon did on a regular basis.

"Elizabeth, can you help me here?" Bill asked.

"Sure, what do I need to do?" Her voice sounded uncertain. She had been watching Dave's hand boldly slicing through her dog's abdomen, then lifting ropes of intestines looking for injury, and she felt ill.

"Take that bottle, there, and squeeze it all over the eye and surrounding tissue. Good." As she worked, her eyes strayed back to the gaping hole in Damien's abdomen. Dave's hands were thrust deep inside, feeling for the source of the bleeding. The area was awash in blood. "All right," Bill said, indicating he no longer needed her help. She moved down to where Dave was working, watching with concern as he collected a great deal of the blood in a large syringe. Suddenly he called her, "Elizabeth, hand me a 60cc syringe. It's on the counter, there. Here, take this one and put it in that IV bag. We're going to fill it up; here, take this one too, hurry up, hand me that first one back." The abdomen yielded 700 ccs of blood, which they collected and reintroduced back to the dog through his IV. Dave then went back to his exploring. In a few moments, he found the source of the blood.

"Uhm. It's a two-and-a-half-centimeter tear in the caudal lobe, Bill."

The men continued working in silence, each intent on his own task. After repairing the tear in the liver, Dave was able to scout the intestines for further injuries or punctures, while he kept an eye on hemorrhaging at the site of his work.

Queasy but satisfied that the source of Damien's escalating weakness had been discovered and repaired, Elizabeth turned her attention back to Bill's efforts at the dog's head. That was a mistake. Enucleation is a bloody and gruesome procedure, and at that moment Bill was separating the conjuctiva and episcleral tissue from the sclera with a pair of surgical scissors. The damaged eye rotated loosely as the doctor struggled to gain better access to the deeper parts of the eye socket.

Elizabeth's face went white and she swallowed hard. Dave was closing up, mopping up seeping blood around the inner sutures with gauze squares and throwing them on the floor.

"Feeling OK?" he asked.

"Yup," she said tightly. "I don't usually get queasy, I don't know, its just that that eye . . ."

"It happens." He began putting in the last few outer stitches with the quick expertise that twenty years of constant practice had given him. He placed a piece of gauze on the suture line, pressed down a few times and left it there. Out of habit, he stripped off his gloves, put on a new pair and moved across the table from Bill.

"How's it going?"

Bill was struggling to work in the limited area behind the eye, which was still attached by the optic nerve and vessel in the back.

"I've got to deal with this," he indicated with a pair of forceps, "and then this whole thing should just lift out."

In a few moments they had accomplished the ligation and separation, and Bill lifted the eye clear of the socket and looked around for a place to put it. Seeing nothing particularly appropriate, he threw it on the floor at their feet. Elizabeth closed her eyes.

"Now what?" Dave asked, inspecting the wound.

"We remove a portion of the orbicularis oculi muscle, which will prevent blinking motions postoperatively. We want him to look pretty," Bill said with a small laugh. He trimmed away at the deep hole in the dog's head.

In silence the men finished their work, skillfully stitching skin over the eye socket. Barbara watched from across the room, ready to assist should they need her help, and amazed at the dexterity she had witnessed. It was a gift to be able to heal like that—for the two men had truly *given* the dog his life back. Without them, Damien would have been dead in a matter of hours. But there was something incongruous about what she had just witnessed, and Barbara was trying to resolve it. It seemed strange to her that these two men, to whom the dog meant less than nothing, could save him, yet she and Elizabeth, for all their love, concern and good intentions—could not. But like the dog, she was unable to shake a deep and lingering feeling of distrust and aversion toward these men. She wanted to thank the doctors, but the words would not come out. She puzzled at the conflict she felt.

"Would you blokes like some coffee?" she finally said.

Bill smiled at her. "Sure, that would be great. Mine black, Dave, yours too?"

"Fine."

Barbara started the coffee and then opened a large trash bag. While it brewed, she started cleaning up. Gingerly, she lifted the papers off the floor which held the dog's damaged eye. She tried not to look at it. Waking up, but still unconscious, the dog started making whimpering noises and moving its legs. Dave was standing beside the dog, his hand resting on its chest, talking to Bill. Elizabeth was crouched over the dog's head, whispering in his ear.

"Gentlemen, can we move the dog now? Shall we put 'im on the dog bed in the living room?" she suggested. Dave shrugged at Bill then gathered Damien up in his arms and carried the dog into the living room.

"Here." Barbara pointed. While Elizabeth hovered, Dave deposited the dog on the bed.

"He could use another bag of fluids," Dave said as he straightened up.

Elizabeth turned to her father and embraced him. "I can't thank you enough. You just can't know how important this is." She stepped over to Bill and hugged him warmly. "And, you, you've been wonderful. *Can* you understand how thankful I am? You've saved his life. You've saved his life—you can't know what that means to me."

Bill looked at her seriously. "I only hope we won't regret this day, Elizabeth. You do understand, that your father and I saved the dog because it's obviously a valuable animal—we didn't know how valuable till last night—and there could be very serious consequences if it dies while in your possession. You've gotten very attached to an extraordinary animal, but you must realize you can't hide the dog forever. That dog *belongs* to Joseph Seville, it's his *property*, and whether you like that fact or not, you're going to have to make it right with him, soon. We came here and did *our* part, Elizabeth, to make sure that doesn't happen. Now it's time for you to do yours."

"When Damien recovers his strength, and is well again, I want you to meet him, then you'll be able to . . ."

"*No*, Elizabeth," her father said sharply. "We aren't going to meet the dog—we aren't going to get to know him—that won't resolve the issues here. He is not *your* dog to enjoy. He belongs to another man, and that man, no matter how you feel about him, deserves the animal returned. That dog is stolen property. That's the issue. That is what must be resolved. Obviously you can't stay here forever. You have to finish school, get on with your life. This is an unfortunate episode which you have handled poorly. You've made some very poor choices, and at the *very* least, it has gotten our home visited by police, possibly cost you a year of medical school *if* Seville doesn't manage to get you expelled. You need to take steps *now* to resolve this. We came here in good faith and that's what we expect from you."

Elizabeth was staring at her father with a shocked expression, all the color gone from her face. Her mouth opened, and then shut. She looked to Bill, but he remained impassive. Barbara, concerned about the girl's ability to withstand parental disapproval, shook her head ever so slightly when Elizabeth threw an imploring glance her way. No one spoke.

It was several long moments before Barbara finally spoke up. "I think we can take it from here, gentlemen. I've got antibiotics and fluids. Thank you for what you did here today."

Dave had one last suggestion for his daughter. "Make me proud, Elizabeth. Do the right thing."

CHAPTER FOURTEEN

The friendship that can cease has never been real.
—ST. JEROME

Damien's recovery was marked by his utter fatigue. The dog was de-
pleted in spirit as well as body. Seville, having pushed the dog relentlessly in the pursuit of machinelike perfection, had gotten his perfection, but
at a price. The dog's exhaustion was absolute. He slept constantly, waking
only to eat and totter outside to relieve himself, then collapsing back to sleep
again. Violent dreams punctuated his sleep, when his legs would thrash and
piteous whimpers which alternated with low, murderous growls came from
deep within his chest. At these times, Barbara advised Elizabeth to stroke
him gently without waking him, and to whisper "good dog," and "fine lad."
Damien needed Elizabeth beside him, the Aussie explained, even in his
dreamworld, to encourage and support him while he withstood his foes.

On the night that Barbara had called, Elizabeth left the house in a rush,
taking nothing with her. She had no change of clothes, no wallet, no money.
She was certain that by now the scientist had concluded she had the dog,
knowing that for the amount of money he was offering, the dog would otherwise have been found by now. She assumed Seville was watching her home,
and getting there for the things she needed would be risky. Though she
would have died before admitting it, she was afraid.

Three days after the dog's surgery Elizabeth decided she had to risk the
trip home. She would take Barbara's truck to within a few blocks of her

house, sneaking the rest of the way on foot, through the backyards of neighbors. She wasn't sure who she was hiding from, exactly. She knew Seville would have a watch kept on the house, but just how important to the "outside" world was the theft of one dog from a research laboratory? Would the police watch her house, waiting to pick her up for questioning? Maybe private detectives hired by Seville? He had the money. And he needed the dog back.

Perhaps she was being paranoid, but she didn't think so. Seville had offered a twenty-five-thousand-dollar reward. Only a handful of people knew Damien's real worth, but for that kind of money, every sort of bounty hunter in the world would be after the dog. Elizabeth sighed deeply, contemplating the power aligned against her. Seville had money and the media had sided heavily with him as the victim of random radical violence. As a respected member of the research community, he had the status and the influence to eat her alive if it came down to it.

She wished she knew what Seville was up to. News reports simply said that police were following up "several leads." *What kind of leads?* Had Bill and Dave been followed? If Seville could have her home watched, sooner or later someone would slip up, and lead him to the dog. Once that was done, it would be the easiest thing in the world for him to have the police assist him in reclaiming his stolen property.

Barbara walked Elizabeth out to the truck at 11:30 that night.

"Take care of yourself, mate, it looks like you've got a real bastard after you and Damien. There's no tellin' what he'll do or not do to get 'im back." Here Barbara paused awkwardly, then she jerked her head toward the house. "If anything happens to you, he's safe here, you know that. If they get you, just stay cool, Damien will be all right till you get back."

Elizabeth met Barbara's eyes. "I know. I hope you know how much this means to me. God only knows where this is headed—I don't. But I sure want to thank you for everything."

"I wouldn't have missed this for quids. I'm glad I could help him—and you. You're in the biggest mess of your young life but you're stickin' by your mate, and that makes you bloody right in my book. With the kind of people you have after you, you're going to have to be bitter game kid, to see this through. Now, better get going; you look grotty and I know you're tired. You need to get over there and get back and get some sleep."

"Thanks," Elizabeth said with a grin as she got into the truck.

She pulled up to the curb two blocks from her house, wondering if her father would have left the alarm system on or off. The control panel was near the front door, and she intended to go in the back basement door. She would have to haul ass upstairs to punch in the code in time. She was hoping not to wake Bill or Dave. There was nothing right now she felt she could say to them.

She was going to cross lots by parking on the next street over and sneaking into her own backyard via the neighbors' yard directly behind. She was glad for the black T-shirt Barbara had given her to wear. She left the truck, her heart pounding at the mere thought of trespassing onto her neighbors' yard. Could you get arrested for sneaking across your neighbors' yard? Her childhood had been spent studying and being a good kid—she was unfamiliar with this sort of thing. She couldn't help but feel that *everyone* in *every* house was looking at her at that moment.

She picked up her pace and trotted around the side of the neighbors' house, trying to imagine where the master bedroom would be, and trying to be noiseless. The sounds made by her body and feet were thunderous to her. In a moment she had crossed the backyard and come to the twenty-foot swath of stringy alders and spindly looking firs which made up the "greenbelt" between the two properties. A third of the trees had blown over at an angle, too frail to stand on their own. In the dark, without a flashlight, it was a formidable obstacle.

She struggled out on the other side of the trees after some moments and started across the yard, skirting Bill's garden. She looked for the garden shed where the spare house key was kept. When Bill had taken her truck back to the house, he had taken her keys. She squinted, trying to make out the shed. As she started up the path to the back door there was a sudden flash of light, and she stifled an exclamation of fright. The motion detector had caught her movement and turned on the backyard floodlights. She had completely forgotten about it, and she froze in terror. She waited for a shout. Nothing happened. There was nothing to do but grab the spare key and bolt for the door. She'd either been seen or she'd not—there was nothing she could do about it now. She *had* to get her stuff.

Once inside, she turned and locked the door behind her. She raced upstairs, got to the alarm control box and punched in the code. Then she crept to her room, flinched as she turned on the light, quickly changed her clothes and stuffed undies, socks, T-shirts and jeans into a pillowcase. Grabbing another pillowcase, she went into her bathroom, trying to be quiet as she slipped personal items into the bag. She found her wallet, stuffed it in too. She grabbed up a pen and ripped a square off her desk calendar. On the back she wrote:

Dear Dave and Bill, please don't worry, I'm fine. I've got to see this thing through. Love, Elizabeth.

She left it on her bed. She eased down to the back door and paused. There were no sounds from the house. She exhaled deeply. OK. As she reached for the door, she remembered the floodlight. The timer had turned it off, but it would come back on, the moment the stepped out the door. She went down the hall to the fuse box, wishing she had a flashlight.

"Elizabeth."

She about jumped out of her skin. Her father's voice had come from behind her, the way she had just come. She turned to face him, just barely able to make out his tall, solid outline in the light from the window.

"Dave?"

"What are you doing?"

"I just came to get a few things—I didn't want to wake you guys."

"I mean, what are you *doing*? Where is this going to stop?"

"I don't know. I really don't. Just try and understand why I'm doing this, and try not to worry."

"Of course I'm going to worry, Elizabeth. You're running around town like a criminal—you *are* a criminal in the eyes of the law now—hanging around with who knows what kind of people, ruining your life over a stolen dog. A *dog*. Do you think it's fair," he continued, "to ask me to stand by and watch you put yourself further and further into peril, over that lab animal? You're obsessed—I understand he's an interesting and fascinating pet, but you're at a time in your life when you need to be thinking about your career, not an animal." He paused, waiting for a reply, but Elizabeth stood rigid in the dark, unable to speak.

"You've got to see this for what it is. That dog is an *animal*. He's *not* a human. He can't be your friend. He can't reason, he can't think. He lives in a simple world which revolves around eating and sleeping. As long as he gets fed, he's going to be happy—I know, I've worked with dogs a lot longer than you have. Now listen," he said as his voice and shape grew closer, "right or wrong, that dog belongs to Joe Seville. You may not have stolen it from his home, but right now *my* daughter *is* in possession of his stolen property. You sent a gang of hoodlums to his home and the man was *assaulted*, his home damaged. That doesn't make me very proud. I've talked to him, Elizabeth, and you've put him in a terrible predicament. He needs that dog back—he has some kind of presentation scheduled—and he's willing to work with you regarding your concerns. I'd like to see you handle this thing in a responsible way." He was standing right in front of her now, looking down, the faint light gleaming on the bald part of his head. Elizabeth steadied herself, taking a moment before answering to make sure she had control of her voice.

"People used to think," she said softly, "that the world was flat. They believed it was absolute truth. Philosophers, people whose thinking we still respect today, thousands of years later, they *believed* in something, and it was dead wrong. And they believed that the sun went around the Earth. One day," she said, her voice growing stronger and colder, "this *convenient* nonsense about dogs being unable to think or feel emotions will seem as ridiculous as *those* ideas. You're an educated and intelligent man, yet you can't see what is right before . . ." She stopped unable to find the words. She tried again. "We—you and I—we suddenly live in different worlds, I guess. What you do, what you . . . I see things differently now, Dave. I see *you* differently now. I don't like this new vision, I guess I would rather have not had all this happen, so things could go on like they always have, but it *did* happen. And it's hard to come to terms with what you are."

"And what *am* I," her father's voice was ice, "besides a concerned parent?"

Elizabeth chose her words carefully. She didn't want to hurt her father, she loved him, but right was right and wrong was wrong. "What you would do to my friend bothers me. If Damien had gone to your lab, instead of Seville's, *my God*, what you would have done! Without thought, without remorse. It's not killing to eat, it's not killing to put them out of misery, it's using them cruelly because you *can*, because they suffer in silence. A few people stick up for them, but the majority look away because they're scared. They're so damn scared to die, they'll allow any amount of suffering on the off chance it may let *them* live a few more months or years. How can they stand themselves? Don't they have any pride?

"What you are, Dave, is someone who can be a loving, wonderful father on one hand, and turn around and stand over someone like Damien and casually watch them suffer and die. For *grant money*. For a paper. You see my *friend* as a 'basic model'; a research tool, because the law lets you. And then you deny him his intelligence, to *justify* your exploitation."

In the reflected light she saw her father's face was hard, but she was growing more angry and frustrated, and she found it easy to face him and say these things.

"I'm sorry to hear that you feel this way," he said. "It hurts to find that you love a stray dog more than your own father." He turned away, but Elizabeth grabbed his arm, a thing she had never done before.

"It's not like that and you know it! I don't love Damien *more* than you—I love him *differently*. It's not so black and white. Can't you see what Damien and I have been through together? How can you expect me to not help him? *Damn it*, Dave, I hate what you *do*—what you stand for. I'm sorry but I do. I know you really feel that what you do justifies the ends—I know that's the argument. I've grown up around it, heard nothing but your side all my life, now suddenly I see the whole picture. Now I know the other side, the side that was never told to me. And it stinks. What you do—it's *not* necessary. You *know* that, I've heard you speak about it. There *are* alternatives. It's just easier and cheaper this way."

"I save human life. You would have too."

"That's not good enough. Lots of things could save *more* human life. Think of the advances if you experimented on prisoners, or street people, right? You'd get better, more accurate results in your research, *doctor*. If the ultimate goal is saving human life, why not do it right? So what if you kill a few less than desirable people—it will be for the good of all mankind, right?"

"Don't be ridiculous."

"The argument is sound. The end *does not* always justify the means. It seems ridiculous to you to even conceive of using humans, so why can't you understand that for those of us who share friendship with a dog, the idea of using them seems just as inconceivable? Why is a murderer, or a child rapist better than a kind and faithful dog who has harmed no one?"

"People come first. There's no comparison."

"That excuses everything?"

"Yes, it does."

"Your attitude is 'kill 'em all, make 'em suffer, it's all about me—save *me*,' huh?"

There was a long, uncomfortable silence. David Fletcher stood only a few feet away from her, but he seemed remote and unknowable. A brilliant stranger who had shared his home with her for years.

"I guess we have to agree to disagree," she said quietly, uncomfortable with his silence. She loved her father deeply, but the things he had just said made it difficult to find common ground. He knew he was right, and she knew she was right.

She had to make a choice, *right now.* Could she stay, and live in this home built and maintained on the bodies of dogs like Damien? A house sustained by the lives of dogs lying this night in David Fletcher's lab, their surgical suffering unrelieved by even simple pain medication. Dogs which lay blinking in the dark, waiting in silence; long-suffering animals who each morning would greet her father's arrival with a weak wag of their tail, and a kiss for the hand that reached for them. She had been a hypocrite too long. She turned to go.

"If you get arrested," Dave said from behind her, "don't expect me to use any of the money I've earned through my *despicable* research to bail you out. I think that's fair, don't you?"

Elizabeth was shocked but not surprised by what was implied in his statement and his tone. Her eyelids dropped for a moment in silent remembrance of all the good that had gone before. He was a good man, and he had been a good father. He had extended to her the opportunity for a good life. She felt a sudden wrenching anger that this issue had come between them, but it had, and it could not be ignored. She simply could not do what he asked, in good conscience. Her desire to hug him good-bye was an ache, but she knew it was impossible. But her sadness was also tinged with defiant anger.

"No, you're right, I don't think that would be appropriate, Dad. Keep your blood money. Damien and I will be all right."

She walked to the cubbyhole where the fuse box was and, using her sense of touch, turned all the switches over to the off position in order to disable the sensor light in the backyard. Without a word, she walked back down the hall, past her father's form and out the door.

The lights were off and the yard was very dark. She was home free. Then she hesitated. Something, an unspoken Voice, told her look to her right. In the side yard, illuminated by the glare of the street light, stood a man, twenty feet away, just standing, watching her. Her eyes flew open and a shot of adrenaline made her stomach cramp and her hair prickle. He didn't move, she didn't move—she didn't breathe.

Who was it? A police officer? Seville?

She couldn't see clearly enough to make it out.

Oh sweet Jesus, what do I do now? Run for it?

Could it be possible that the man did not see her? He appeared to be looking straight at her. For a long, horrible, frozen moment she waited for her eyes to adjust to the darkness. Then, gradually, she recognized him. It was Tom.

Tom! They are *watching the house after all. And I've walked right into the trap I knew could be here.*

She stayed still, unwilling to make the first move. She had always found Tom's presence nonthreatening, even gentle, and even now she found it difficult to think of him as "the enemy." But she knew she *must.* He *was* the enemy, as dangerous to Damien as the doctor. Obviously, Seville had placed him here to watch for her, and the light coming on must have attracted him to the backyard. Thirty seconds went by. The man was as still and remote as a stone statue in the dark. Elizabeth was stiller.

Could it be possible he had not seen her? Was the yard dark enough that she could see him, illuminated by the street light, but he could not see her? There was no way to tell, and it was maddening. If he could see her, it was unlikely that he would just grab her—it was not *her* they wanted. They would let her go, and follow her to the dog. If he didn't see her, well, that would be one for the books. She had no alternative but to try and leave. She turned and began to creep away, her blood cold, her body tense.

Tom watched her go. She seemed an all right sort, but he wondered what motivated her to put herself in so much peril, so much conflict, for the sake of a *dog.* He considered the idea that perhaps she felt some sort of responsibility for the animal. Tom could understand responsibility, devotion to one's duties and obligations in life; that was his nature. It was a great source of personal pride for him that, over several arduous years, Seville had come to place complete trust in him. His reward had been a position of confidence with an important man, and deeper than that, the feeling that he was really indispensable to Seville. That was important to Tom. As he marked the direction in which the girl disappeared, he decided it *must* be some sense of fidelity, some deep commitment to the animal, that caused this behavior in

Elizabeth. She must feel she was doing the right thing. The usually unperturbable Tom gave a joyless sigh as he moved toward the front of the house. *So am I*, he thought to himself.

Elizabeth was reasonably sure she had gotten away without being followed, but she felt a gnawing anxiety. The only real answer to the whole situation was to get away, out of the state, far from Seville's relentless efforts. She had money; her main problem was transportation. She didn't dare drive her own truck, nor Barbara's, she was too young to rent a car, and the dog was too weak and too readily identifiable to move in public. The Aussie, however, insisted she stay at least another month, giving the dog much-needed time to recover. If they came to *her* door, she said, she would deal with it, she assured Elizabeth with a lop-sided grin.

Where could she go? She must shun friends and family, she had a large and injured dog to hide, and no car. It seemed an impossible situation as she sat beside Damien stroking his head. Impossible, yes, but the alternative was unthinkable.

I have nothing.

She reached out and laid her hand between the dog's pointed ear stubs, and he smiled up at her with his remaining eye. "They ain't got you, Buddy," she said fondly. The dog nuzzled her, his tail slowly thumping out his contentment. Damien also, had nothing. With no stability, a questionable future, and gravely injured in several places, he was content to simply be allowed to lie by her side. He stared into her eyes, his serious expression tinged with concern. Elizabeth shook her head. She was concerned about him, yet with all his problems the dog, in turn, was concerned about *her* tension, her uncertainty. *What was Damien thinking right at this moment?* she wondered. She wished she could ask him. She guessed it didn't really matter, after all. Whatever Damien's perception of the world, it was *enough* like hers that they could communicate, cooperate and commiserate.

Through the weeks of grace, Damien's recovery was steady and rapid. Barbara went back to her part-time job at a nursery, leaving Elizabeth home to watch TV, wander the property with the dogs, and ponder her uncertain future. One evening, she was startled when a strange man walked in the door. With Damien standing beside her in plain view, she panicked, but Barbara came quickly and laughed, reassuring her that he could be trusted. His name was Mark Pagel, he was a teacher, and from then on he came nearly every evening for dinner and to walk with Barbara, hand in hand, across meadows streaked with the long shadows of fir trees and along the forest paths of the fifty-acre farm. He had stayed away at first at Barbara's request, but the Aussie felt it was time to let him in on their secret. Elizabeth was wary, but Mark's soft, low-key manner, and Barbara's obvious devotion to him, persuaded her to accept him as a friend. She was amused that the man seemed only interested in the tall Australian woman, and not Damien. If Barbara had a talking dog with a twenty-five-thousand-dollar reward on its head staying at her house, he didn't seem to be the least bit surprised.

The month passed, and the fall air was now filled with the acrid scent of yellow maple leaves and freshly mowed grass. In Barbara's vegetable garden there really *was* frost on the pumpkins, and the sprawling vines turned black and withered about the fruit. The old apple trees which surrounded the house hung fully loaded and the ground beneath them was littered with the fallen fruit covered with drowsy hornets. Once the sun rose clear of the morning fog the afternoons were brisk and pleasant. The two women stayed outside, preparing the farm for the coming winter or walking slowly to the pond on the hill behind the house. They sat on its bank, watching Damien stiffly accept the playful submission of Barbara's bitches. Elizabeth would talk, and Barbara would simply listen. Then Barbara would talk, and Elizabeth would feel that *this* is how it would have been to sit and talk with her own mother. The feeling hurt; it hurt to acknowledge the voluntary absence of her mother, and her eyes would struggle valiantly to hold back bitter tears. Barbara noticed.

"Liz," she asked one day, "where's your mum? You don't mention her." It was a direct question, bluntly asked. Elizabeth was taken aback.

"Uhm, she left my dad when I was six."

"Uh huh. Unhappy in the marriage, was she?"

"I guess. I don't really know—I mean it isn't something I can talk to my dad about. My grandfather told me some stuff about it, though." She looked down.

"She doesn't call you?"

"No. Never. Don't you think that's kinda strange?" She shrugged, unconsciously. "I have no mother—she just walked away."

Barbara considered.

"You don't know that she *just* walked away, mate. You don't know that it was that simple."

There was a moment of silence. Across the pond, Cobra put up a mallard drake, and confused by the bird's vertical climb, the dogs stood looking about the reeds with wide, excited eyes, trying to figure out where their prey had disappeared to.

"What I think, Liz, is that she was desperate. Something was so wrong she had to break the strongest bond on Earth to get away. She left her baby—in Nature not even a rat would do that, without good reason."

Elizabeth's eyes jerked toward the woman, to hear her mother compared unfavorably to a rodent. "Well, wait, she . . ."

Barbara turned to face her. "What?"

"Well, I mean, yeah, probably something was wrong, but still, why not take me? Isn't that what *most* mothers do?"

"Your father makes good money; he's rich. He's a good enough sort, I mean he doesn't come home drunk and slap you around, right? He could take care of you. Get your teeth fixed, send you to a good school. She couldn't do that for you, and she panicked. Was she young?"

"Yeah, actually, she was pretty young."

"Your age, huh?"

"Yeah, a couple of years older."

"Uhm." The Aussie leaned back, thinking, and Elizabeth had the uncomfortable feeling a point had just been made. She waited.

"I wonder what the problem was?"

"What problem, you mean, why she left me?"

"Yeah, the problem between her and your dad—I wonder what it was. She left *him*, you know, not you."

From across the pond Damien looked over, catching Elizabeth's eye. She nodded, acknowledging him, and with a quick swing of his tail he went back to slowly following the exuberant female dogs through the reeds.

When Elizabeth didn't answer, the Aussie continued. "Have you thought about it?"

"Not really."

"Perhaps you should. I think you owe her that. I'm not saying what she did was right—I'm not—but you need to know. And I would think *she* needs you to know."

"Why doesn't she pick up the phone? She doesn't care—that's obvious enough."

"For you and me, from where we sit, it's strange, inexcusable. We can't understand what drove her, we can't understand why she feels the way she does—does that remind you of anyone else?"

"Anyone . . . I don't. No."

"Your father, Liz, is asking these same questions about you, right now."

Having seen the curiosity with which Elizabeth viewed the pictures of her husband and daughter in the house, Barbara answered her unasked question as they strolled back toward the house. "My family died in a car accident. My husband, and my little daughter."

"Oh, man, I'm really sorry. I can't . . ."

Elizabeth noticed how the tall woman was looking straight ahead, her expression carefully neutral, and she stopped short.

"A drunk driver," Barbara said, trying to sound matter-of-fact. "They were on the way to her horseback riding lesson."

"How can you stand something like that, how can you deal with it?"

"It's just *life*, mate." Her eyes had filled, and she tipped her head back, pretending to look up, and Elizabeth knew it was to keep the tears from spilling. "Their bloody car was simply on the same piece of road as the drunk's. They didn't suffer, and that's about all you can ask for, I guess. Everything's born, everything dies. I just wish . . ."

"What?"

Barbara shrugged, turning her head away, and Elizabeth knew she had lost her battle to hide her tears. "I just wish she had gotten to, you know—I wish it had happened on the way home. She loved those ponies so much. At least my baby was happy. And with her dad—she just worshipped 'im." She brushed at her cheek with an impatient gesture. "I'm sorry."

Elizabeth sat, horrified. She knew Barbara did not want her sympathy, so she said, "My grandfather came to live with my father and me, after my mom left, and they're all the family I've ever had. I've never lost anyone I was really close to. I just can't imagine . . ."

There was silence.

"Well," the Australian said with forced heartiness, "we had good times together. He was my childhood sweetheart, come back from university to marry me after he became a lawyer. We only live once, and we—he and I and the baby—we did some living. I have my memories now, but it's nice to know we never wasted a day. That's a great comfort to me." Barbara indicated the land about them. "Young as he was, he had made sure to provide for me and the baby. He left me this place, and his ashes are here. Hers too. So we're all still together."

As they talked Barbara smiled at Elizabeth's youthful enthusiasm, remembering the fearful uncertainties and overwhelming passions of her own late teens. One Sunday evening, as the sun went down behind the dark, towering Douglas firs at the edge of the yard, they built a bonfire. Without mentioning it, both women felt this evening was special, a last peaceful moment before the realities of the formidable situation facing the two hunted companions asserted themselves. Without Barbara's succor Damien would have died. The country home had been the perfect haven for the fugitives, but Elizabeth knew that Seville would be relentless in his pursuit, and they could stay no longer. He *would* find them here, and she was not willing to bring that kind of trouble down on their benefactor. The best way to repay Barbara for her kindness was to leave, keeping her safe from their powerful pursuer. Elizabeth had no clear picture of what to do or where to go, but tomorrow she would leave.

There was a sharpness in the evening air now, and it was delicious to pull up close to the warmth, toasting her front while feeling the chill on her back. Somehow, the wandering conversation became a discussion of Barbara's faith—what she called the Old Religion—and how the ancient, Celtic nature-based pagan belief survived and quietly thrived to this day. She talked of the powerful symbolism of the sun and moon, trees, stones and deer by which pagans remembered and reflected upon those virtues they considered important. Barbara talked about the Christian holidays which were, in reality, thinly veiled pagan celebrations having been set in place—and already ancient—before Christianity was born. These celebrations marked the all-important turning of the year's seasons.

It felt good to talk with a woman. She barely remembered her mother, but Elizabeth found herself thinking, *this is how it would have been to talk to my mother; an older, wiser, woman.* She found herself speaking shyly of her youth and teen years, spent pleasing her father and grandfather and preparing herself for a future medical career. There had never been anything in her life about which she felt any passion until time shared in the company of the pit bulldog had gently led her to an appreciation of the natural world she had not known existed. Elizabeth told Barbara how she thought it was Damien's friendship which had awakened something long sleeping in her heart. It felt good, she told the older woman, to feel strongly about something at last, and Barbara smiled.

Elizabeth noticed a strange, orange glow behind the dark tree line, and asked Barbara what caused it. The pagan's eyes were already on the glow, and she kept them there when she answered.

"Don't be in a hurry. You need to watch, to wait, to *feel* for the answer. Don't let others do your thinking for you, don't look to others for answers. Nature's not a snob, you need no priest or preacher to guide you to her truths. She reveals herself equally to all." Elizabeth raised her eyebrows at the gentle rebuff. Obviously the Australian was trying to teach her something, so she sat back, stilled herself, and waited, trying to understand. She had her answer in a few moments when the moon rose above the treetops, full and orange; and she thought it perhaps the most beautiful thing she had ever seen. The speed at which it left the treetops amazed her; she had never known the moon moved so fast. When it cleared the trees, Barbara rose from the fire and walked to a small hawthorne tree a few yards away. She reached out and took something from its branches and came back to her chair. Reaching across, she handed a small leather pouch on a leather thong to Elizabeth. "If you'd like," she shrugged, "put this 'round your neck. I made one for Damien, also."

Elizabeth reached out and took the thing, holding it out to the firelight to see it.

"Is it—pagan?"

"Yes."

"What is it?"

"Just something to help you remember. To remind you of your connection with a world that has gone on before, and will continue after. Maybe you'll find it a comfort to know, mate, there really is nothing new under the sun, eh? And—I envy you and Damien your 'walkabout'; perhaps I just want something of me to go along too."

"So, what's in it?"

"To a pagan, very powerful things indeed, mate. To a Christian," she shrugged again, "nothing."

"Well, what is it, can't you tell me? Is it secret?"

"Secret?" Barbara said with a touch of exasperation. "There's nothing secret about it. Secrecy and dogma are the first and most important sign of deceit. There's an oak's acorn, in there. I can try and explain, if you'd like?"

"Please."

"Christians wear a crucifixion symbol, right, to remind them of the death and rebirth of *their* King. As I understand it, and don't quote me, their belief is that their Supreme Being set up the world in such a way that he would have to impregnate a human female, then send his son to Earth to be tortured and die, so that the 'sin'—which he set up they would be born with—can then be forgiven. Seems like a complicated way to do things." She shrugged with her shoulders and mouth. "The implement of the god's son's torture and death, the cross, is a powerful symbol to them, like our little acorn is to us pagans. In reality, the symbolism of the cross is based on the much more ancient symbolism of the acorn, that is, *rebirth.* The cycle of rebirth seems to be what a lot of the world's religions are based on. Probably because it really is so wondrous. The seed, you know.

"Think about an acorn. In the winter the tree 'dies,' the little acorn falls and lies dead, buried. The crucified Christ, laid in his tomb, represented that. Then, in the spring, from inside of that cold, rock-hard, dead lookin' thing, comes forth a tiny, soft, delicate green sprout. And that little oak tree knows just when to come out. Not too early, not too late. The roots know to go down, the leaves know to go up. *Every* spring that happens. Long before Christianity, long before *any* religion or mythology. Now that's somethin' you can take to the bank. There's no hocus-pocus about it, no supernatural beings, 'just' the miracle of life! That's the mystery—The Mother to us all.

"For us pagans, the Mother life force is real, it's tangible. We don't have to sort it out the way some people do, you know, basing faith on how some bloke or some book tells 'em it should be. I wouldn't want a religion, mate, where I couldn't see things for myself, and had to rely on popes and preachers, elders and rabbis, ministers and fathers, to tell me what was truth. Blokes who tell me *what* to believe. No, mate, and I pity the poor 'uns that search for tangible evidence—search all their lives—often agonizingly, for conformation of their beliefs. For a pagan, well, we don't have that struggle." She shrugged a third time. "We just look around."

Barbara paused, looking now at the flames. "You understand, I think, that the world's various religions are man's attempts to understand the world around him, right? You do see that? OK, well, the symbolism is pretty much the same, I think, worldwide. The King always dies for the good of his people. It was an ancient story when the Christ was killed. And it is, for pagans, *symbolized* beautifully by the death and rebirth of the sun each year. Of course the sun doesn't "die," but the symbolism helps us mark our beliefs—keeps 'em before us. The story of the King dying for his people and then risin' again in the spring is one of the most beautiful pagan beliefs there is—and it was incorporated into early Christianity to help win European pagans over. That's why 'Easter' is a blending of both Middle Eastern Christian and European pagan religions.

"As to your bag there, the items are, symbolic—significant only to remind you—having no power, of course, of their own. Besides the acorn, there's a twig from the slopes of Glastonbury, a place of great significance for pagans, but I won't bore you with *that* tonight. And there's a small piece of the horn of a stag, the powerful and ancient symbol of the Greenman, the male, the winter, the dying, the Father. When you find something which you *know* belongs in this bag, then you'll add it, understand?" She held out another bag across the fire. "Here's one for Damien too."

Elizabeth reached slowly, thoughtfully across the orange glow of the fire's embers. "For both of us?"

"Ah, I wouldn't make one for Roland without making one for Oliver, now would I? Damien, being a dog, is already a pagan—he *knows* the Mother and the Father far better than any of us ever will. He walks with them, always." She said it lightly, like a jest, but Elizabeth could tell she was serious. The girl held both bags in her hand for a moment, looking from the moon, to Barbara, to the fire.

"Winter's coming." She wasn't sure why she said it. It seemed significant.

"Yes," Barbara answered, with a ghost of a sad smile, "it is." She looked at her so strangely, Elizabeth wondered for a moment what it was the woman saw in her future.

Elizabeth slipped one of the thongs over her neck and settled the bag under her shirt. Then she knelt beside Damien and slipped the other thong over his short, strong neck. "These will bring us luck," she told the dog.

"Not *luck*," corrected Barbara, sharply. "That's a silly man-made idea, like evil, sin or magic. There is only *life*. Look—the dingo pulls down a baby 'roo. Good for the dingo, bad for the roo. Is that evil? Is the dingo evil? Did some supernatural being order his actions? If the roo gets away, is that good, is it luck? Good for whom? The dingo's cute little pups go hungry, perhaps starve, is that evil, or the work of angels? Or is it *life?*

"Rest assured," she said, growing serious in her manner, "whatever happens to you and Damien, it will not be the result of malevolent evil forces, or divine intervention, or magic, or dumb luck. It will be life, playing out, as it has since the beginning of time. It will be your skill, your intelligence, your grit, against the skill, intelligence and grit of others. Survival of the fittest if you will. Nature will not interfere in yours or anybody else's life. We are all truly equal in that sense. Let Seville do his worst—you do your best. The friendship you have with him," she nodded to the dog across the fire, "the love you share, *that's* magic. That's the only magic there is, or that you'll ever need."

"Remember, Elizabeth *Fletcher*," Barbara said, rousing herself after a moment's reverie, "You've Irish blood in you—not Middle Eastern—and that little bag is there to remind you to stay true to yourself, and to bind you to *your* people's history, *your* people's religion, which are more ancient than you can imagine. It's a way of thinkin' that might help you along the way."

After a while the conversation dwindled, and they sat in the darkness staring at the flames in mellow contemplation. Before coming here Elizabeth had never sat before an open, outside fire, and she was amazed at the thoughts and sensations she experienced sitting there in the dark. It wasn't at all like the artificial gas fireplace in her father's home, where the flames rose and fell in response to a handheld remote control. Damien lay across the fire from her, watching her face. The dark, reddish gold light flickered on his shadowy form, shifting and dancing like the thoughts in her mind.

Monday morning as Barbara and Elizabeth ate breakfast, they were relieved to see that the dog was not mentioned on the news. The twenty-five-thousand-dollar reward still hung over Damien's head, but at least the tempo of the witch-hunt appeared to be slowing down. Elizabeth intended to leave that evening, after dark. Barbara left for her part-time job at the local nursery while Elizabeth headed for the sink to wash up the dishes before packing her few belongings. She intended to spend this last day giving the chicken coop a thorough cleaning. She wanted to do something to repay Barbara for her extraordinary kindness, and had overheard her speaking of plans to clean the coop to Mark. It was a small thing, but it would please her to be able to do it. Crossing the kitchen, she heard a car pull into the driveway. Fear, sharp as an electric shock, shot through her and she ran to the front door to peek out.

It was Bill.

She jerked the door open and ran out. Damien, lying on a rug near the woodstove, was alarmed at her sudden apprehension and rose to followed her out.

"My God, Bill, they'll have followed you!"

"I don't think so, I'm sure by now . . ."

"They *will*!" she said fiercely. She stood in the driveway, her head cocked, listening for the car. "They will," she said again in an inaudible whisper to herself. Her father had spoken with Seville; he knew she had the dog.

"Elizabeth, we've got to talk. You . . ."

"Bill, I gotta get out of here. You don't understand. You've led them here—unintentionally, but they *will* have followed you. He knows I have the dog, and they'll be tailing you and Dad. I gotta go! I'll call you from a pay phone this evening if I'm able."

She started to turn, but Bill caught her arm. "Elizabeth, you've *got* to listen to me, we *have* to talk. Dave is not going to stand much more of this. He's been talking to Seville and Seville's convinced him . . ." Damien pushed between them quickly, his visage stopping Bill in mid-sentence. Bill let go of his granddaughter's arm and stepped back.

"That dog . . ." he began, but stopped at the sound of cars coming up the winding drive at a high rate of speed. A white van pulled in, followed closely by a dark sedan Elizabeth knew well. Gravel popped as the cars slammed to a stop. She bolted for the side of the house, screaming for Damien to follow her. But the dog hesitated, his protective nature attracted to the hectic and potentially threatening action in front of him. Whoever these strangers were, they were frightening Elizabeth.

"Damien!" Elizabeth screamed again, and she hesitated at the back of the house. "Damien, *come on*!" She watched in horror as the black car's front passenger door opened. Seville stepped out, his eyes on the dog, his expression pleasant, his voice candied.

"Well, Damien, how are you? Come here now, that's a good dog. That's a good dog, Damien. Come *here*!"

Elizabeth saw the dog's back droop and the very tip of his tail wave in hesitant submission.

"Oh, Jesus, *no!*" screamed Elizabeth. She ran back toward the dog. "Come on, *come on*! Damien, *run!*"

Seville never even glanced at her. He kept his eyes locked on the dog, his voice soft. "That's my boy, come on now. Let's go, get in the car." Without turning his head or looking away from the dog, Seville called to Tom and Chase. "Don't get out. Stay where you are; don't spook him." He reached out a hand in the direction of the dog, palm up, as if it had a food treat in it. "Fletcher," Seville said, addressing Elizabeth's grandfather without taking his eyes from Damien, "you stay out of this." Bill, shocked at the sudden unexpected activity, stood motionless, watching in confusion.

"Come on, Damien, let's go, get in the car." Seville began to walk slowly forward, his hand still outstretched invitingly.

Elizabeth groaned. Seville was a powerful and determined man. If he got his hands on Damien, he had the strength to physically take the dog away from her. Damien would not fight him. Seville was only ten feet from the dog, talking calmly, and moving steadily nearer. He glanced up at Elizabeth, only for a moment, but when their eyes met, she saw the grim triumph in his expression.

"*Damien!*" Elizabeth screamed. "*No!* Come with *me!*" The dog's concentration broke, and he swung his head to look at Elizabeth. At that moment, Seville saw the change in the dog's body language and straightened up, stepping forward quickly.

"*Lie down! Now!*" he shouted harshly. The dog recoiled, snapping back to face Seville. Without thinking, Damien began to sink down in a response conditioned to sharp commands by the cruel electric collar.

Elizabeth darted forward and grabbed the loose skin on Damien's neck. She pulled him sharply away, screaming, "*Stop it!* Come on!" Seville lunged forward, swearing, reaching for the dog, his hand grabbing up skin and fur on the dog's side. The sharp pain made the dog grunt and pull away, frightening him and shattering his trance. He raced after Elizabeth without a backward glance.

For a split second Seville watched them go, marking their direction. Then he turned to the men in the vehicles. "Get out on the roads, watch for her. She'll have to come out somewhere. Get everyone out here, stat. Get this area contained." Then he disappeared around the house in pursuit.

Damien ran, confused and uncertain, following The One. They were running from their alpha, and it was an unsettling feeling. The man was close behind them, calling out commands in an angry and threatening manner. If Elizabeth had not bid him follow, he would have had no choice but to slink back to Seville.

In all her life, Elizabeth had never ever felt such intense emotions as she did at this moment. *Everything* was more intense. She felt the very air she was moving through, morning-chill and sharp against her body. She could *smell* the air, and the odor of the moss and rotting wood she was running on. The gray branches, the dark green shiny salal leaves, ferns, fir tree trunks, all were crystal clear, and she seemed to be seeing them—even in the midst of her desperate flight—in amazing detail for the first time. She could hear Seville's pursuit behind them, and it was the most intense, and terrifying, sound she had ever heard. He was coming, he meant to get Damien, and only she could save her friend. She must act, and she must be *right*.

After five minutes of blind, desperate running through dense undergrowth and cover, she realized she could not go on in this manner. The dog was not strong, he was still recovering from two major surgical procedures, and she could not expect him to continue to plow through the tough, almost impenetrable cover. She would have to find a road, a path, something to make their going easier. She hesitated, swiveling about, trying to orient herself to where she had come from, and which direction the road might be. She could no longer hear or see Seville, but it gave her no comfort. She may have given him the slip, but then again, the running of nearby water was covering any distant sounds. As Damien came up beside her she glanced down at him. He was panting happily, smiling at her and looking expectant.

He's enjoying this!

She continued to look around her, calming herself by stroking the dog's smooth, sturdy head and taking slow, deep breaths. She had never been in the woods like this before—really in the woods—with nothing around her but silent gray tree trunks and the dense, unrelenting undergrowth. The dog, however, had been. He glanced about easily. Comfortably. He belonged here, this was his turf. It gave her an idea.

"*Go* on, Damien. *Let's go!* I'll follow you, OK? *Let's go.*" The brindle dog trotted off easily, happily. "Go, Damien. White Pain is coming, go, *hurry!*

Go!" Damien glanced behind him and picked up the pace. He moved through the brushy tangle with much more ease than she had, finding natural openings and game trails with practiced ease. In a few more minutes they arrived at the stream she had heard. It was small, two to three feet across, and damned every few yards by fallen logs and debris. The dog hesitated at the water, jumped it, then turned to look at Elizabeth for direction.

"Let's go down," she said, heading that way while the dog trotted downstream on the far bank. She thought about how to get out of the area, the whole area, not just these woods. And then in a heartbeat she knew how. She would find a road, flag down a car, or maybe go to a home. She would look for a woman, an older woman, and she would act hysterical. She would say she had been walking her dog when a man suddenly tried to attack her, and was chasing her. No woman would question a story like that, and she would beg a ride a couple miles away. She would say she had a jealous boyfriend, and didn't want any trouble with the police. She smiled to herself. That would work well. The only glitch would be if anyone recognized Damien as the dog who had been on the news, and who still had a twenty-five-thousand-dollar reward on his head. It was a risk she'd have to take.

After about fifteen minutes of splashing through the creek, she pulled up at a spot where a large hemlock tree had fallen across the stream at chest height. She leaned against it, catching her breath. Damien was on the bank, and when he noticed her stopping he jumped up on the log and walked out to where she was leaning. He nuzzled her face, and stood, tail wagging, happily looking about. He was panting pretty hard and Elizabeth realized he was out of shape. She wondered if Seville was still in pursuit, behind them, or if he had turned back. She wondered if he had called for the police. Would they help if they thought it was just a stolen dog? She had a fleeting thought about the one phone call you were supposed to get from jail. Bill *might* bail her out.

Suddenly, right under her feet, she heard a strange, wet, trilling, splashing sound, unlike anything she had ever heard before. She leaped back, looking down at the water spilling past her. A large salmon, easily two and a half feet in length, her sleek back inches out of the shallow water, was struggling up the current. Elizabeth stared in wonder, having never been this close to a live salmon before. From his perch on the log, Damien stared down as well. The fish made another drive, the sound Elizabeth had heard coming from the rapid strokes of her tail against the shallow water. She drove five feet ahead then stopped, resting again, with her big, powerful mouth gaping as if she were panting from her exertion.

Elizabeth remembered dimly that salmon go upstream in the autumn to breed. This fish had come from somewhere in the whole Pacific ocean to find, and enter, the one correct river, and then turn off at the *exact* stream where she had been born. She was coming home to breed, and then to die. She was struggling forward to complete her work, and something in her effort touched Elizabeth deeply. The big fish was cut and scarred all over and the end of her nose was a mass of damaged white flesh. But she was going, doing what she must, and nothing would stop her.

Elizabeth squatted next to the fish, spellbound. The big salmon lay half over in the shallow water, resting. Far below them now, Elizabeth heard the sound of another fish, coming along behind. With a feeling of profound respect, Elizabeth reached out and gently touched the back of the fish.

"Go on, girl, you'll make it," she said it quietly, just wanting to touch something so wondrous, so magnificent. She hoped something of the fish's strength of character came away with her hand. Looking down, she saw a small scale stuck to the end of her finger. With wonder in her eyes, she looked back at the fish, then her eyes rose and swept the great, gray trunks of the evergreens about her. "Thanks," she whispered. Still crouching beside the stream and the gasping fish, she took the time to open her pouch and carefully place the scale within. It was a magic moment, and she knew she would always remember that salmon.

She stood up and stepped back, and the fish drove on again, up over rocks and gravel, going several feet before stopping to rest again, blocked for the moment by a downed log.

"Watch out for Seville," Elizabeth called to the fish. "He's back there somewhere, and he's not going to be in a good mood."

She leaned back against the fallen tree, trying to determine what would be the best way to go. Then she heard another strange sound. She grabbed Damien's muzzle and held it shut to stop the sound of his panting. There was a sound, a whizzing sound rapidly getting louder. It was maddening trying to discern it over the splash of the stream she stood in. Instinctively she crouched down, pulling the dog down with her. They crouched behind the moss- and fern-covered log in the icy water, listening to the strange sound that did not belong in this peaceful forest. As the sound grew, suddenly a silver station wagon flashed by in front of them, on a road not more than forty feet from where they hid. *Oh, for Pete's sake!* Elizabeth stood up, disgusted with herself for not recognizing the common sound of a car's tires on concrete. She crept forward, her hand on the dog's neck, keeping him near.

There were houses on the other side of the road; she could see one, and a few other driveways. This would be perfect, if only she could get across the road without being seen by Seville's henchmen. She scanned the fifty yards or so of road she could see, and crouched in indecision. She really dreaded stepping out into the road, for if she was making a mistake, and Seville or his men saw her, it was over. Really over.

She concentrated on the road again. Once she committed and stepped out, if she was seen, she knew with terrible certainty that neither she nor the dog could run again from a fresh pursuer. This was crucial.

She gave Damien's neck a squeeze. "We gotta do it."

She straightened up and took her belt off. Looping it around Damien's neck, she stepped out and darted across the road, heading for the first driveway. As she approached the house, she scanned it with her purpose in mind. It was a dirty red-brown, with a white "X" painted on the front and garage doors. It was supposed to look like a ranch house. She stopped. There was a huge pile of moldy carpet up against the garage door, two derelict cars in the driveway and more than one beer can in the front yard.

Nope.

Quickly she retreated back down the driveway and checked the road again for traffic. She trotted toward the next driveway. Now that the adrenaline was gone from her system, she realized how exhausted she was. She glanced at the dog. The exertion had caused him to start limping on his sore front leg, and his rear legs were dragging slightly; she could hear his toenails scraping the pavement as he drew his back paws forward.

The next driveway led to a two-story brown house set back off the road. A red, long-haired Dachshund barked at their approach. It started trotting their way. A woman called to the dog, "Jessie, you come back here." They hurried past, headed for the next driveway which was about a hundred feet further down the road, hidden in tall evergreens.

No cars were on the road, so she hurried the tired dog along, jog-trotting to the safety of the next secluded driveway. She turned into the drive and, looking up, saw the familiar black car waiting for her, backed into the driveway and hidden from her view until now. She wasn't ten feet from it.

Elizabeth recoiled as if a snake had struck at her, and thought actually, for a moment, the rush of adrenaline that shot through her might make her faint. Her head swam and she reeled back, blinking. Her legs went completely numb.

It was over—they had her, and yet she found she could not give up. She stumbled back, turning to run out of instinct, though she knew in her heart it was useless to try. She wondered what she would do—actually do—at the exact moment Seville took the dog from her.

"Wait," Tom said. There was something so unexpected about how he said it—the tone—that she hesitated. She had expected a harsh command, or a warning. It was neither. It was a request. "Elizabeth, wait," he said again.

With a shaky inhale Elizabeth drew herself up. They might have her at bay, but she would not beg for a mercy she knew Seville would never give. Her chest rose and fell rapidly with her fear and exhaustion. She turned a pale but defiant face toward the car. Beside her, Damien's head came up. Being a bulldog he didn't waste time in growling. He simply leaned into the belt Elizabeth was holding and waited for an opportunity.

"What are you going to do?" Tom asked calmly from the driver's seat. He asked as if he was inquiring about her summer vacation plans.

"Well, I guess that depends," she replied with an exasperated gasp, still trying to catch her breath. She noticed her hands shaking as if palsied, and tried to still them. Seville was not in the car with him. He would be nearby though. Tom had probably already called him.

"I think it would be better if you just gave the dog to him, before this goes any further. He won't stop until he has the dog back, and he *will* do whatever it takes."

She was exasperated; did he really expect her to say, "Yeah, you know you're right after all, this is getting to be a hassle, here you go, take the dog off my hands!" Were *all* men like this? Something in his manner, though, kept her from a harsh reply. He was so serious. Perhaps he did feel some concern for her and he just saw things differently. Then she chided herself. *This* was Seville's right-hand man, he was only trying to convince her to give up the dog or, she thought with a quick glance back at the road, he was stalling her until Seville arrived. She tensed; she had no choice but to try to run for it.

Tom saw her stiffen. "Please," he said softly, "don't run."

She sighed heavily, exhausted and uncertain. "Don't play with me, Tom. What are *you* going to do? Call him?"

There was a long, long pause. "No. I didn't last time, either."

She felt light-headed again. So Tom *had* seen her at her father's house. He hadn't told Seville, and he hadn't followed her. The implications of the action staggered her. Tom was *helping* her.

"I don't think you'll make it out," he continued. "He has a lot of people willing to help capture the dog because of the reward money. They have the area pretty well blocked. It would be a lot safer for you, *and* him," he nodded at Damien, "if you just gave him the dog."

Dirty, exhausted and frightened, she hesitated in her flight, wanting, desperately, for this man to understand.

"Tom, is there one thing in your life that you would give *everything* up for? One thing that your heart refuses to be complacent about? If you and I traded places right now, and you were me, and Damien was that thing, what would you do? Whatever happens, I'll have done my best, and it will have been worth it. It will have been *right*."

Watching her eyes, he seemed to consider her words. After a long while, he nodded down the road. "Go on," he said.

Wary, Elizabeth tipped her head, unable to believe.

"I feel bad about my part in this," he said. "I don't like the way he treats you. It's not right." Elizabeth suddenly felt very, very fond of Joseph Seville's aide. She turned to go, then turned back.

"Tom, you and Damien have two things in common—you have good hearts and you both deserve better than Seville."

Tom almost smiled. "Maybe you'll make it," he said. "But you have no food, no money? How . . ."

"I don't know, Tom. I really don't. I don't know what I *can* do, but I do know what I *can't* do." A distant sound made her glance down the road nervously, and she turned to go again.

"Wait."

She turned back quickly, suddenly suspicious. The way he had said that made her uncertain. Maybe he was stalling her! How could she have been so stupid! He *was* Seville's number two. Why did she think he would help her? Tom was looking down uncomfortably; looking awkward.

It is a trap.

She was looking around wildly, expecting to see Seville when Tom held his hand out of the car window. There was money in it. "Here," he said simply.

Her breath came out in a long, hard sigh which blew her disheveled hair off her face. She stepped forward and took the money. She held his eyes for a long moment. They were gray, like Seville's, but they didn't look at all like Seville's eyes. And they didn't make her feel like Seville's eyes did, either. They made her feel suddenly very lonely. She wished she could hug him.

"Thanks."

"It's just not right," he said simply. "If you do get out of here—somehow—come to the empty land behind the treatment plant, down on the point. Evenings. If it's breezy." He looked down. "You know, if you need anything."

Why, he's shy, Elizabeth thought. Then her forehead furrowed. *If it's breezy? Huh?*

A vehicle was coming. Scrambling behind the car, she pushed into the dense undergrowth with the dog behind her. Tom was right, if Seville had mobilized volunteer bounty hunters against her, she would not be able to get past them in the daylight. Her plan wouldn't work now. She would have to hole up somewhere and wait for dark.

She hoped *whoever* was after her would think she hadn't gotten across the road in front of Tom's watchful eyes, and would concentrate their search on the area around Barbara's house. She was thankful the sun was coming out and it was getting warmer. She slowly followed the brindle dog through the woods, replaying over and over in her mind the strange conversation she had just had with Tom, and remembering how his eyes had made her feel.

CHAPTER FIFTEEN

Who looks outside dreams, who looks inside wakes.

—C. G. JUNG

For Damien, life had taken a sudden and unexpected turn for the better. Hour after hour went by and much to his pleasure Elizabeth showed no intention of going back inside. From the moment of his capture he had been the victim of long periods of unintentional yet painful sensory deprivation. Locked up inside a cage, crate, kennel or room, Damien had suffered. Any dog, kept from Nature, suffers a death of spirit few humans can comprehend. But now he and The One were moving through the autumn forest, and all was right with his world.

The morning had been startling. When Seville had arrived and commanded him, he had been reluctantly moving to obey when Elizabeth stepped in. A horrible, confusing scene ensued, in which the brindle bull-dog had experienced a moment of indecision. The question of allegiance was complex for Damien; he felt a compelling need and desire to obey both the humans. Seville however, had won the dog's fealty through merciless application of electric shock and force of will, while Elizabeth had won the dog's heart through something far stronger.

In consequence Damien had run away with The One, openly defying their alpha, a very shocking thing. However, Damien was a dog, and running through the woods was so pleasant he soon forgot his disobedience as powerful, wonderful, heady scents slammed into his senses. The cool, shady, dappled forest morning filled him with emotions lost these past weeks with Seville. How had he borne it when the simple scent of crushed grass on Seville's shoes had caused his soul to writhe with longing? Now, surrounded by an entire forest, he ran, aching with his pleasure.

An Ancient Presence hung palpable among the tall gray trunks of the evergreens, welcoming him. Nature was the Mother and the Father to whom he was a perpetual dependent, and trotting along in the scented shade felt like a sweet homecoming. The dog felt the forest Presence in a way no man could.

But the forest was *not* his home.

He was not a wild animal—he was a dog, unique among all species on earth, for his place was with humans, not Nature. In the beginning of time Damien's kind forged a mysterious allegiance with Man, and that tie was stronger now than any which bound him to his ancestral beginnings. An incredible pain in his psyche had finally eased upon entering this forest, but Damien would not hesitate or look back should Elizabeth bid him leave it. His place was with The One.

So they had run away together through a glorious autumn day, headed he neither knew nor cared where. They had wandered on, at a slower pace, for hours. The sun slanted through the trees, its light brassy and only giving warmth when they huddled together in spots sheltered from the brisk wind which rose in the afternoon. There had been a solid frost the night before, not enough to kill the toughest plants, but enough to prove that summer had slipped away and that winter was coming. Damien felt the strong stirring in his being, the autumnal urge to take advantage of this time of grace, and to put things in order for the winter dying that was coming. Big, bright yellow maple leaves twirled from the trees overhead, dropping with tiny whispers of sound to the forest floor around them.

He found the little creek again and they continued down its course. Two hours later, after fighting their way through nearly impenetrable cover, they came to a deep, long ravine which emptied out into the Sound. The salt smell of the air and the cries of seabirds announced their arrival at land's end, long before they could actually see the water.

Elizabeth picked a secluded spot on a dripping clay bank, where, surrounded by large ferns and the trunks of trees which had fallen down from above, they could sit in perfect privacy while watching back up the way they had come for signs of pursuit. Out of the wind, Elizabeth and Damien huddled together for warmth. Beside her, the patient dog licked his sore feet; they had become the soft paws of a laboratory dog.

As the day progressed only an occasional person passed by on the wild, gravel beach, and the two companions hiding among the trees on the bank above escaped detection. Elizabeth talked to the dog, but it didn't sound like the kind of talk he needed to listen to carefully, so he didn't.

They sat all day until sunset, Elizabeth straining to hear any sounds of pursuit over the dripping, running rivulets of water coming out of the clay, Damien resting beside her, trying to discern what it was that made her uneasy. With the dark came the chill of an autumn evening. Damien had been kept inside a climate-controlled environment so long that his coat was now thin and inadequate for outside living, and he became uncomfortable. It had been twenty-four hours since he had eaten, and he was hungry.

He rose and stood across from the girl, staring at her. "Eat," he finally said.

Elizabeth snorted a laugh. She had left the house with only a T-shirt on, and she was shivering also. "You read my mind; I'm starving too. We'll have to go down the beach till we see a road. We need to find shelter somehow tonight. God, it's cold! My feet are freezing. This really sucks."

She stood up, and they moved down the ravine to the beach. In the dark, their progress through the tangled undergrowth was slow. The dog led the way, tail gently waving, happy to be going again, and hopeful about dinner. When they reached the beach they walked easily on the gravel and sand, with enough moon to show the way nicely. Houses began to appear along the shore. As soon as they could, they cautiously crossed a lawn and went up the driveway to the street. The One seemed to know where she was going, so Damien was content to follow along, thinking about food, and taking stock of the many canine urine marks along the way.

"This really sucks," Elizabeth said again, walking slower. "This really, really sucks."

They moved slowly, partly because they were staying off well-lit main roads, partly because they were completely lost, and partly because Elizabeth didn't feel so hot. She told herself she was keeping the pace slow for the recovering dog, but she couldn't help noticing he had no trouble keeping up. She found a piece of twine and tied Damien to a tree in the shadows outside a convenience store. With Tom's money she bought a small bag of dog food, three hot dogs and a Coke for herself. After they ate they pressed on, hopefully headed back toward town and the empty ground behind the sewer plant Tom had mentioned. She had no real idea what she would ask of Tom when she got there, or even if she could trust him. He could easily change his mind but she realized grimly she had nowhere else to go, no one else to turn to. Seville would have Barbara's house watched, obviously. Bill had said her father was talking with Seville, and if he was doing that, if Seville had had an opportunity to sway him, she had little doubt her father would call the police if she showed up at his home with the dog. Her only hope was to throw herself on the mercy of Seville's aide. Not a comforting thought.

She stopped at a pay phone then stared blankly at it, realizing she did not even know Barbara's last name. She would have to try her at work later. Pushing on through the long, dark, cold hours before dawn, Elizabeth came to understand how desperate her situation was. Damien was still weak from his surgeries, and all afternoon she had felt like she was coming down with the flu. She had always been susceptible to influenza, and now the stress of the last few weeks had caught up to her. She felt surreal, stumbling along the edge of the country road in the pitch dark, wearing wet tennis shoes and a T-shirt, a limping dog on a piece of twine at her side. Shaking her head, she thought again and again, *how did this happen?*

Daylight broke, and they were still miles from their destination. Elizabeth had no choice but to crawl back into a thicket of moss-covered hazelnut trees which lined the edge of the road. It was too risky to move by day. The brush she pushed through as she crawled back into the cover of the squat trees was wet from the morning's heavy dew, and her clothing got soaked. Elizabeth stopped and looked for several moments at the dark brown leaf mold which made up the floor of the little thicket she stood in. In the moist soil, tiny mushrooms sprouted here and there, and large fungi grew against the tree trunks. Moisture falling from the limbs dripped about her, and the very sound of it was dismal. Tentatively, she knelt down on the wet dirt. She looked at Damien and he looked back. "This can't be happening," she said. She put her hand to her head and squeezed her eyes. They burned, and she had a splitting headache. She tied Damien's twine around her ankle and resolutely curled up on her side.

If I had a pillow, I might be able to do this.

The feel of the cold dirt on the side of her face was a strange, sobering sensation. She really *was* on the run. She had no car, no money, no place to sleep. She realized, with chagrin, that she was very thirsty, and would have no opportunity to get water for several hours.

I'm a freakin' refugee.

Then she looked at the dog.

He's more like an escaped prisoner of war.

Damien crawled up beside her and she curled around him. He settled on his side, kicked a hind leg out, and put his head over her arm with a sigh. Elizabeth gently stroked his broad head. "Kinda rough on you too, huh?" The dog reached over and gave a quick lick on the cheek. "You're welcome," she said. She was grateful for the warmth of the dog's body against her torso. "Well, we did what we had to do, didn't we? And *somehow*, I've gotten you away from him. We'll make it, Buddy, I don't know how, but we will."

A line from a favorite song came to her mind and she smiled bitterly at the aptness of it; *where do I go, now that I've gone too far?*

Sitting in the stillness of the predawn, she thought of her father and grandfather, and she grew still as a sudden and complete sense of loss came over her. How could her affection for a loved one harm others she loved? She thought of the pagan, Barbara, who had said there was no good or evil, only Life, and that what was good for one, might by necessity, harm another.

She broke down and cried then, bitterly, for what *was*. Her father did great harm, and yet he did great good. She had done great harm to him, and yet she had done great good for Damien. She had done great harm to her own life, and yet for her soul, she had done great good. Saving Damien had been the right thing to do, and yet the loss of her family hurt her now like a physical pain. Good and bad existed together, and were simply a matter of perspective.

So she sobbed, wanting nothing more than to go home and embrace her father, and tell him that she loved him, but she could not, and it hurt her with an excruciating pain. Damien, stricken by her grief, whimpered, and tried desperately to lick her tears away.

Elizabeth tried to sleep, but it was impossible. She lay shivering and wet, curled around the dog on the damp ground. The dog's sturdy presence assured her. She might be protecting him, but he surely protected her.

As morning came on, sparrows and wrens in the thicket began to hop about the arching branches, brown tails jerking, their birdsong clear and sweet. Elizabeth became aware of the lightening of the sky, and she watched with interest how the coming sun gently brought color to the gray thicket.

Color, she thought, *is a gift every morning from the sun.*

She spent the day resting, too cold and uncomfortable to sleep. She wondered what Barbara was doing, having come home to find her and the dog gone. Had she found the police waiting patiently in her driveway? Or just Seville and his bounty hunters? What would she have said to Seville? Oh, what Elizabeth wouldn't have given to be a fly on the wall at that moment!

That night she used the last of Tom's money to buy another small bag of dog food, and some bottled water for herself. She wasn't hungry, and it occurred to her that it wasn't a particularly good sign, since she hadn't eaten all day. The two friends trudged on in the dark, but Elizabeth had to stop several times, sitting on retaining walls and curbs, to rest. She felt weak and awful. Her head and stomach both ached, her muscles hurt and she felt hot and cold, in waves.

They reached the empty and desolate spit of headland behind the sewer treatment plant shortly after sunrise. Elizabeth had made up her mind to ask Tom to help her get away. There was no other alternative. He'd have to get her some dry clothes, and shoes, and then drive her out of town, getting her just far enough out that she could hitchhike somewhere without the dog being recognized. He was her only chance. She tortured herself, wondering what to do if he refused, or—and the thought chilled her very blood—was waiting there with Seville? Touching the bag at her neck, she thought of the salmon, with its bloody, raw snout. That fish had had a job to do, and it had kept going. Alone in all the world, that fish had gone on, facing each new obstacle uncomplaining, unrelenting, undaunted. Thinking about the fish helped, and Elizabeth kept moving.

The land where she would wait for Tom was fill, man-made land pushed out into the inlet. The ugly mixture of dredged clay and muck that was piled willy-nilly and strewn with broken pieces of sewer pipe and old dock pilings, was not a popular destination for walkers or fishermen. The entire west side was a log yard, stacked with huge stacks of logs awaiting transport to Japan. The east side was bare, with a marginal beach at high tide, and long stretches of mudflats at low tide. Here and there, decrepit docks with weeds growing out of the tops of the remaining pilings rotted away unattended. It was a perfect place to hide, but she wondered how Tom had known about it.

A heavy marine fog rolled in as the sun rose, leaving the air damp, cold, gray, and smelling of salt water. Elizabeth was cold, really cold, and her shivering was now continual and violent. She felt weak, listless, and her head ached so fiercely she could think of little else. She looked about for a likely place to spend the day.

The east side offered little in the way of cover. Aware now that she was suffering from an influenza, she knew she needed to sleep, and for that she needed real privacy. She could not afford to be discovered by a stray jogger. If anyone recognized Damien here, it would be over, for unlike the salmon, she knew in her heart she could go no further.

She walked over to the log yard and eyed the twenty-five-foot-high log piles dubiously. They looked precarious and it made her nervous just to stand beside one of them. However, the spaces between some of the larger bottom logs provided a dry and perfect hiding place. It seemed her best option. She crawled back a few feet into an opening between the bottom logs and sat down, her arms around her knees, her head pressed against her arms.

"This *really* sucks," she said to no one in particular.

Damien lay beside Elizabeth all day, waiting. The cold, moist marine air caused him some discomfort also, and he slept fitfully, starting up at distant sounds and periodically nudging his listless companion. By evening, as the light began fading, he knew without question that something was very wrong with Elizabeth. She was curled up on her side in the rough bark hunks which layered the ground between the logs. She was shivering so hard her teeth made audible sounds as they hit together, and twice she had roused herself, only to lean over and retch up yellow fluid. Then she would lie back with a moan. The dog watched anxiously, incessantly pacing and listening to the vague but insistent urgings of The Voice.

Get help. Find a human.

Animals seek to hide themselves away in times of trouble, for drawing attention to a weakness will ultimately invite death. However, the special symbiotic relationship between man and dog provides a unique exception. Damien understood that while he could not help Elizabeth in this situation, she was still his responsibility, and he must do *something.* The Voice insisted he leave her and go find human help. Damien resisted, pacing in and out of the log piles in distress. He did not want to leave his companion—besides, experience had taught him that humans were Bad, mostly. He resumed his pacing, while unrelenting waves of uneasiness battered him.

Darkness fell, and the dog retreated into the hole beneath the logs. His human no longer spoke to him when he nudged or licked her. For several moments he paced around the prostrate body of his companion, and then he lay down, huddling as close to her as he could. Elizabeth instinctively lifted one arm and pulled him closer, holding him to her. Her body felt cold against his.

Damien awoke to find Elizabeth unresponsive. She was barely conscious, her fever extinguished by hypothermia, and the dog was alone with his anxiety. He hung around the front of the log pile, still unsettled about how to deal with this Bad Thing. His thoughts quite naturally turned to Seville. If the man came he would give commands; he would restore order. Damien sat beside Elizabeth's still, cold body, his tail wrapped around his legs, and wished the man would come.

By late afternoon the dog was completely unnerved. A chill wind had come up again, and Damien sat outside the opening in the logs where Elizabeth lay, shivering and squinting into the moist wind.

Go! The Voice kept saying. *Help her. Find a human. A human must come here.*

Finally, he had no choice. It just felt too Bad to stay there any longer; he must do *something*. He trotted out of the log yard toward the open ground on the east side of the headland. Humans had controlled his every action for so long it was now an uneasy feeling, this strange and unwelcome freedom he had regained.

Unless he was engaged in an important or time-sensitive project, a couple of times a week Tom tried to leave work early, meaning, somewhat less than an hour after the time he was supposed to leave. To actually leave at the agreed-upon five o'clock was inconceivable for the resolute employee, and had rarely occurred. But some days, particularly the Fridays when Christina came, he would quietly finish up and then drive to the beach. Seville had no idea where he went, nor did he care; Tom's private life was just that.

Tom possessed three great passions in life. The first, to remain invaluable to the man who was, above all else, the powerful father figure the young Thomas Owen had desired so greatly while growing up. Seville had, in his careless way, fostered this devotion as it suited him. There were certainly benefits in having a loyal, discreet and incorruptible aide and the two men suited each other. The second of Tom's passions was his Pentecostal belief, simple yet profound in its depth. Quiet and reserved in public, Tom surprised many with his passionate and exuberant tenor voice when he stood solo before his congregation and praised God through song. He was considered a local treasure, and passed about from church to church to share his gift.

Third was Tom's passion for flying performance kites. It was something he could do alone, and something he had become very good at. A holdover from childhood days in which a bike was a luxury no one in the family enjoyed, it was the precision and control of kite flying that attracted him as he pursued his hobby now with adult toys. His kites were professional models, expensive and precise, and he could make them do anything.

He liked the empty point of land behind the sewer plant because there was always a stiff breeze, and in its isolation few people went there. He could fly in relative privacy, yet he noted, with perhaps a tiny touch of vanity, that when he worked up near the point, people in houses and boats on either side of the headland could watch his craft.

He went on Thursday out of curiosity more than anything else. He had daylight left, and the breeze was good, but his mind wasn't on the kites, it was on the girl. It had been a couple days since he had seen her, and he couldn't help wondering what had become of her. Would she meet him here as he had suggested? The possibility alarmed him. What *had* he been thinking? What could—or should—he do for her? He hoped fervently that she had left the area.

He tried to remember that she was the "enemy." His boss, consumed with her capture and the return of the stolen dog, had dropped everything to work on finding them. But Tom could not remove from his inner vision how Elizabeth had looked when she had seen him sitting in ambush, waiting for her, in Seville's car. Her head had jerked up like a graceful doe catching sight of the hunter who is there to kill her, and how instead of running, she had stood her ground, frightened, but proud and unashamed of what she was doing. He was haunted by the fear his mere presence had produced in the girl's eyes. This was not a role he relished. Yet, before she left, that fear *had* subsided a little, replaced, when he had not betrayed her, by a warmth that thrilled him to recall. It was a dangerous situation. He knew he must reveal her eventually, for his duty lay with his employer. The best thing was to avoid her, and then the choice would not have to be made.

So why are you here, where you told her you would be?

He had no really good answer to his own question.

He got out his best kite, letting it rise a hundred feet in the air, then turn and plummet straight toward the ground. Ten feet from the earth it abruptly stopped, reversed its direction, and nestled slowly to the ground where it balanced on its tail, quivering with its desire to fly up again. Tom made it hop, each jump a foot higher than the last, while it stood in place. The proud kite danced like a Lippizzan, the restraint of its movement all the more impressive because it so obviously wanted to tear away into the wind.

Luckily for Tom, the kite's tail was on the ground when he first spotted the pit bull, because he dropped the handles. The kite dropped over backward with an undignified rattle, skidded a few yards in the breeze and came to rest against a piece of driftwood. Tom stood perfectly still, staring in horror at the dog which was fifty feet away, motionless, and watching him. He hadn't seen where it had come from. Without moving his head, Tom scanned the horizon for Elizabeth. At every opportunity the bulldog had plainly shown that it did not consider the matter between them closed. Tom swallowed hard and scanned the horizon again. This would be a *good* time for the girl to appear.

The dog didn't move for over a minute and neither did Tom. He was only about forty feet from his car, and he thought perhaps he could make it in time if he ran for it. But he wasn't sure. Then, slowly, the animal began to walk forward. As the grim-looking dog approached, Tom remained motionless, spellbound by the apparition. Twenty feet from him it stopped, its unwavering gaze harsh, the fur on its back rising and falling sporadically. Tom glanced back at his car again. He had stupidly let the dog get too close. He could never make it to the car now. Where *was* Elizabeth? Then the dog spoke to him, for the first time.

"Lux," it said. "Sgo."

Tom tipped his head. An absolute feeling of unreality swept over him. He had seen the dog speak many times, but this, this was different. With Seville the dog simply responded to cues, naming objects it was shown. He had seen it occasionally initiate speech with Elizabeth, but *this* was unbelievable. It was speaking to him, like a man. Or, perhaps, like a demon.

"Sgo. Bad."

Why would the dog be doing this? Why wasn't it attacking him, as it so obviously wanted to do ever since the day he had grappled with Elizabeth in its presence?

The dog barked several short, sharp barks, and then said again, "Lux."

In a moment's flash, Tom thought he understood. Did the dog want to take him to Elizabeth? Could that be it? It seemed far-fetched, and he felt no inclination to step toward the animal.

The dog trotted a little closer. It was now only twelve feet away. It stared at him intently, and then, its head jerking back with its effort to form the words, it said, "Sgo. Lux. Bad."

Tom hesitated, trying to understand. "Bad? What's the matter? Is Elizabeth hurt?" he asked, feeling foolish for speaking to the dog.

The dog's front paws danced in place, his tail thrashing in his relief at being acknowledged. "Lux! Sgo!"

Tom swallowed hard. "OK," he said dubiously. "I'll come." As he turned to gather his equipment the dog was suddenly at his side, anxious, its front paws dancing in the sand, seeming to hurry him along.

"OK, OK, I need to put this stuff away." Keeping a wary watch on the dog out of the corner of his eye, he dismantled the kite and placed it in the trunk. He turned to the dog. "OK," he said. "Let's go."

Damien's relief was exquisite, and he barked his pleasure, turning in quick circles and dashing off in the direction of the log yard, only to run back to bark again, leaving Tom to wonder if the animal had gone mad. Once under way however, the dog settled down to a businesslike trot, leading the way, and Tom trailed behind, trying to imagine what could have happened to the girl. He prayed it was nothing serious, but he hurried, for the dog's insistence concerned him.

The pit bull led him into a log yard, between stacks of logs. Without warning the dog disappeared, then reappeared, showing him an opening between two logs at the base of a twenty-foot-high stack. Tom, dubious, tried to see into the opening.

"She's in—there?"

"Lux!" the dog barked, and disappeared into the hole.

Tom knelt down, still doubtful Elizabeth would be in such a wet, dangerous and small space. He had to get on his hands and knees to look inside.

"Oh, God!"

The girl lay in a fetal position, unresponsive to the whimpering attentions of the dog that nudged and licked her. There was vomit on the ground around her. Her features were sunken and her skin was blue-gray.

"Get *out*, Damien," Tom said, hard. There wasn't room in the crawl space for all of them. The dog removed himself quickly, responding with relief to the stern tone of authority. Tom crawled to Elizabeth and checked her pulse. Her eyes were dilated, but in the faint light under the logs, that told him nothing. Her limbs were rigid. He checked for injuries, but there were none. She was ice-cold to his touch.

Damien crowded into the entrance again, his expression anxious. "Bad," he said, very low.

"What happened to her?"

Tom did not expect an answer, and he got none. The dog suddenly squeezed past him, stepped over Elizabeth, turned and lay down with a sigh, his head on her legs.

Tom considered the dog, which, like an anxious relative, was watching his every move, its fierce gaze softened by concern. "You've done your best for her, haven't you?" It was a stunning revelation to him that the animal could actually feel anxiety for the well-being of its human companion. He was used to thinking of dogs in terms of mindless, disposable *things*. But the dog was looking at him expectantly. The dog *expected* him to help Elizabeth. It trusted him.

He had to get Elizabeth to the hospital, quickly. Gingerly, with one eye on the watchful dog, he pulled Elizabeth into the daylight. He examined her again, hastily, and made the decision that she was suffering primarily from severe hypothermia. He tried to imagine what she had endured over the past few days, waiting for him under the logs while cold, hungry and obviously sick, growing weaker and weaker as her temperature dropped. She shouldn't have waited just for him.

It made him angry.

Why had she done this to herself? Why hadn't she gone home when she became so ill? Was she actually willing to *die* out here, alone and sick and cold, just to save this dog? And the dog—he, too, was obviously cold and hungry—and he hadn't left her. They had both made the decision to stay together.

Tom sighed. Together, they had waited here for him. Looking at the young woman, he thought how harmed she looked. Elizabeth had always been polite to him, and her manner pleased him; she was quiet and serious—not silly like so many girls. Even though she was from a wealthy family and soon to be a medical student, she had always treated him with a gentle deference despite her fierce opposition to what he represented. It was with growing shame that he realized his part in bringing her to this sorry state. He, and the man he worked for, had done this—hunted her relentlessly until she had holed up and dropped, sick and exhausted.

He picked her up and, when he reached the car, carefully placed her on the backseat. He covered her with his jacket. Shutting the car door, he looked at Damien. Once he dropped Elizabeth off at the hospital, he would have to deliver the dog to Seville. There was no other way.

He opened the driver's side door and motioned for the dog to enter. Damien jumped in, but quickly hopped over the seat into the back with Elizabeth.

"No! Damien, come back up here."

But the bulldog had already curled into a ball, pressed tightly against Elizabeth's cold body. Tom stood for a moment, in awe of the dog's single-minded devotion.

After all she has done for him, it's his turn to watch over her, now.

He didn't feel like trying to physically remove the dog, and it ignored his commands to come into the front seat.

Let them be.

After today's parting, Tom knew that Seville would see to it that Elizabeth never saw Damien again.

Considering the actions of the girl and dog, he was suddenly, sharply aware of his role in this situation. What virtue did *his* actions represent? Tom, who had always prided himself on his discipline, his loyalty, his faith and his commitment, saw the acts of his life pale before him. Six years he had devoted to Seville, and yet he had betrayed him in order to let this young woman escape. Why could he not, despite his best effort, sustain the commitment shown by this obstinate young woman and a mere animal?

Friendship.

That was the difference. He had seen it in Elizabeth's refusal to surrender, and he saw it now in the dog, curled around the body of his fallen companion. Tom could not call Seville a friend, and now, looking upon the power of this friendship before him, it was an empty, desolate feeling.

Profound shame swept him. How could he be the one to destroy these two? To bring this girl and her dog to utter desolation? He got in the car, started it, and pulled out into the road. He tried to keep his eyes from the rearview mirror, but they went there, repeatedly. His eyes went to the dog, its head draped protectively over the girl's cold, limp body, watching him. Even the dog *trusted* him. Elizabeth, at great risk, had come to the headland to seek him out, she had trusted him also. These two looked to *him* for protection. His soul writhed. *Why are they trying me like this?*

As he turned onto the road which would take him to the hospital, he tried to find comfort by imagining how pleased and surprised Seville would be, at the moment he handed the dog over to him. Having submitted a paper stating he would produce a talking dog, the animal's theft had put Seville in the most unimaginable position. There would be no words to describe the doctor's relief and gratitude. Tom would be a hero.

A hero because he broke this blameless girl's heart and condemned this remarkable dog to an onerous existence.

He drove hard and fast, angry with himself. It should not be this difficult. He *had* to turn Elizabeth over to the hospital, and when he did, that would be that—the dog had nowhere else to go but back to Seville.

He began to pray, fervently, for the strength to do what had to be done.

Under the protection of the log pile, Elizabeth had lain curled up like a shrimp for twenty-four hours, too nauseated and weak to even lift her head. Then hypothermia had sapped her remaining strength until, wet and ill, she had slipped into unconsciousness. Waking now, Elizabeth had no idea where she was, and an unclear memory of the hours leading up to the present. She did remember running from Seville and her feet being wet. She remembered being on a beach, being very cold and being afraid. She remembered clearly the look and feel of the bark pieces she had curled up on, the smell of seaweed and the sound the seagulls had made as they bedded down for the night on top of her log pile. Slowly she became aware that she was in a strange place, with a ceiling over her.

I'm inside a building.

Damien.

My God! Where's Damien?

The unbearable headache which accompanied the influenza raged on, making her squint against the pain as she tried to bring the room into focus. Her first thought being for her companion, she jerked her head up, unable to remember the last time she had seen him.

Damien lay next to her, stretched out alongside the couch she was lying on. With a gasp of relief, she dropped one weak hand to his shoulders, reassuring herself he was really there. Her other hand clutched at her head as the sudden movement sent a shock wave of pain through her forehead. She groaned and shut her eyes, squeezing them hard, trying to deal with the pain. At that moment, she truly didn't care where she was. She just wanted the pain to stop, or to die—whichever was quicker.

When she opened her eyes again a man was standing beside her. He had something dark in his hand and he was reaching out toward her eyes with it. She recognized the man.

Wherever Tom was, Seville was bound to be near. She had rarely seen one without the other. They had found her and now they would take the dog.

With a groan she struggled to rise against the overpowering nausea. She *would not* give up without some kind of a fight. Beside her, Damien rose to his feet and stood looking at her anxiously.

"Damien, *go!*" she cried in a weak voice, trying to wave him away. Tom moved quickly, placing the cool washcloth on her forehead and reaching gently for her flailing arms.

"It's OK, Elizabeth," he soothed, "everything's all right. Please don't be frightened."

In her confusion she had no memory of Tom as anything but Seville's henchman. She saw only Seville's aide, reaching to catch hold of her and trying to put something over her eyes. She tried vainly to roll away from his grasp. Nausea overwhelmed her.

Damien, confused and agitated, stood back, barking at the two humans. "Damien, be *quiet!*" Tom hissed at the dog. "Elizabeth, ssshhhh, *please* be quiet, I can't have the dog bark in here. It's important that you understand, please *be quiet!*" He reached to touch her gently, to calm her, but she pulled away violently.

"Seville . . ." she gasped, her movement causing another wave of nausea to break over her.

"He's not here. You're safe, please believe me. It's OK, it's OK." He moved the washcloth back up to her forehead from where it had slipped over her eyes. Elizabeth stopped fighting but her eyes remained suspicious, and afraid.

"Please don't let Seville . . ."

"He's not here. You're *safe*. Please believe me—look." Tom swept the room with his hand.

Elizabeth squinted, looking. "Where is he? Where am I?"

"In my apartment. You've been here over twenty-four hours. Elizabeth, you were nearly dead. What happened to you?"

"Seville's not coming here? Is he coming here?" she asked, still suspicious, trying to make her painful eyes focus on the room. She felt another wave of illness coming over her, and her eyes closed against her will. Nausea washed over her like an overpowering wave, pulling her under and dragging her, rip-tide fashion, away from the room and Tom.

"Seville's not coming here. You're safe," Tom said gently, "and so is the dog. Sleep now."

When she awoke Saturday morning her headache was much better and she was able to sit up and look about. Damien still lay beside her, his head laid out upon his outstretched paws. She tried to think, to put her situation into perspective. Nothing made sense. She ran her eyes about the little apartment, which was extremely neat and furnished sparsely. It was masculine in decoration, but here and there were items which Elizabeth wondered at. Small, feminine items of the type found in an old woman's home. She remembered now, she was in Tom's apartment, from which she must surely escape. He could, even now, be fetching the man here to take the dog.

She nearly jumped out of her skin when she noticed Tom was sitting perfectly still in a chair drawn up behind her left shoulder. He was sitting very erect, his head tilted back slightly and his eyes shut, his hands raised, palms upward, a few inches off his lap in a strange gesture of supplication. Elizabeth blinked and squinted her eyes against the remnant of her headache as she stared at the strange sight. She rubbed her face and stared again. Tom had taken her in. He hadn't told Seville. He hadn't taken her to a hospital.

"Hey, Tom," she said tentatively, "you OK?"

Tom opened his eyes and looked over at her, then slowly lowered his arms. "You're feeling better?"

"Yeah. Are *you* OK? What were you doing?"

"What do you mean?"

"Just now, you know, you were doing *something*."

"I was praying," he said with a small shrug, as if it was the most obvious thing in the world.

"Praying." She breathed out and lay back down, rubbing the palm of her hand on her throbbing forehead.

"Haven't you ever seen someone pray before?"

"No, I guess not."

"You've never been to church?"

"Uh-uh."

"You're not a Christian?"

"Uhm, I guess not."

"When you're feeling better, I'd like to talk with you about Jesus Christ."

Oh, oh. Danger, Will Robinson!

Tom actually grinned at her expression. Not his rare but pleasant smile, which was reserved for the witticisms of his employer or polite greetings, but a real grin. "I don't want to do anything that will make you uncomfortable. It's just that my faith requires that I try and help you find your way to salvation, and the only way there is through Jesus."

"I never knew you were religious."

"I'm not religious, I just love the Lord. You would too, if you got to know him."

Elizabeth started to say that the last thing on her mind at the moment was trying to "get to know" someone who lived two thousand years ago but thought better of it. She pushed her sweaty hair back off her face and looked around. "Right now, you know, I'm kinda busy trying to keep Damien out of *hell*—if you know what I mean. When *he's* safe, we'll see about me." She found his concern touching, and then chided herself for feeling so comfortable with this man. He was the *enemy*, and here she was chatting with him. Yet she *did* feel comfortable. Tom's calm, steady presence was simply not threatening.

"I feel like my brain stem has been destroyed. How long have I been out of it? What happened, exactly?"

"You've been very sick. When I found you at the beach you were unconscious. I just didn't know what to do—I thought if I didn't take you to the hospital, you'd die, and it would be my fault. But if I *did* take you to the hospital, well, I knew what *that* would mean. You really scared me," he said, but in a way Elizabeth knew wasn't intended to make her feel guilty. He had been concerned about her and, more importantly she realized, he had worried about what to do with her.

What she didn't know was just how much Tom *had* agonized over what to do. Returning to the apartment with her, he had worked into the early morning hours, first warming her, then struggling to break the persistent and dangerously high fever that had replaced her hypothermia. In the morning, he had had no choice but to leave her alone. All that day at work Tom had worried about her, as well as the thought that though her death was now unlikely, *should* she die, he would be left to explain the girl's dead body in his apartment.

He smiled again, and Elizabeth realized she had never, in all the time she had known this man, seen him smile this much. It was an amazing revelation to her that Tom had not taken her to a hospital, even for "her own good." It appeared he could be trusted.

Tom leaned forward and pulled the blanket up further on her shoulders. It was a protective, comforting gesture, and one that was not lost on Elizabeth.

Cripes, she thought. *Cripes.*

"You should drink something. Let me get you some juice or soup or something. You're awfully dehydrated."

"God, Tom," she said, and immediately mentally cringed at her choice of expressions. "I . . ." Then she stopped, unsure how to go on. She wanted to express her gratitude, but how did one thank someone for something like this? She saw the entire implications of what Tom had done, what he had sacrificed, and she was stunned. She just didn't know how to say what she felt, so she gave up for the time being, and instead considered her physical state. "I'm not sure I'm ready for anything just yet, but thank you. I can't believe what I've put you through."

"I'm going to get a glass of juice; let me know if there is anything I can get you." Tom stood up and moved toward the kitchen. As he rose, Elizabeth suddenly remembered the dog was in the room and instinctively clutched at Damien. In the past, Tom's mere presence was enough to trigger fierce and protective aggression from the dog. Damien, however, calmly watched him walk away, and after a few moments, rose and padded into the kitchen behind Tom.

"Damien—come here! *Tom*, Damien is coming in there, be careful!" The pit bull hesitated at the kitchen doorway, looking back at Elizabeth questioningly.

"Oh, it's OK. I feed him out here, and it's his breakfast time," came the voice from the kitchen.

I really have *been out of it! What's going on here?*

Damien returned her stare, but his ears were swiveled back, listening to the sounds of food preparation in the kitchen, and she could tell his mind was in there. Damien trotted into the kitchen and she heard the refrigerator door open. She could hear Tom speak to him, and in a moment the sounds of the dog eating. Tom came out carrying his glass, and another small glass of juice which he set on the coffee table within her reach. "Here—it's there if you want it."

"Thanks, Tom, you've been really great. I mean, I guess I would have died out there, wouldn't I, if you hadn't picked me up? I got really scared, but by that time I couldn't do anything about it. I really want to thank you," she said, looking down.

He smiled by way of answer.

"How in the world did you and him work things out?" Tom leaned back in his chair, his straight, spare frame looking unfamiliar in the relaxed position. He smoothed first his mustache and then his sort-cropped hair thoughtfully. "I *was* rather uncomfortable when I saw him standing there. I was afraid at first. But he stood way off. He kept looking at me in a strange way, and then, well, he started talking. He'd never said anything *to me* before, ever, and it felt really strange—talking to a *dog*. I should tell you, Elizabeth, I have always thought there was something, well, unholy, about that animal, you know, speaking. Then I realized he was trying to get me to follow him, to where you were. I'd heard of dogs going for help for their masters before, but of course, I never really believed it."

The man glanced down at Damien as he passed by, on his way from the kitchen to Elizabeth's couch. "I realized that the Lord must be using the animal to this purpose, and I thought if the Lord was willing to use the animal," he said with a shrug, "who was I to question it."

"You were my only chance. Damien must have known that. I didn't have the strength to go get help even if I'd wanted to. I gotta tell you, I really thought I was going to die out there, and I was plenty scared. I just didn't know what to do—I couldn't just give up. I wasn't going to hand my dog over because I got the flu or something." She thought of the salmon, and smiled to herself. She hoped the fish had finished her quest. Elizabeth reached for the juice.

"You were very ill," Tom said. "You're too stubborn—you could have died. I think you came closer than you know."

There was a pause that Elizabeth found awkward. "Well, thanks again for taking care of me, Tom. I really mean that. I can well imagine it's been pretty gross. I don't remember much, but I know I was really sick . . ." There was another pause. She felt the need to say something. "If Seville found out . . ."

Tom shook his head. "He won't. This is the last place he would look." His tone was dry.

"Doesn't he ever stop by? Isn't there a danger of that happening?"

Tom shook his head again. "He's never been here in the six years I've worked for him. I don't believe he even knows *where* I live. You're safe here, for as long as you need."

There was another long pause while she considered the implications of his statement. She was suddenly acutely aware of how she must look. Then, her eyes flew open as she realized she was wearing a robe. A guy's robe. Tom's robe—and nothing but her bra and undies under it.

Cheese and crackers! Tom had to undress me!

She felt herself blush to the very roots of her hair. Of course, he would have had to submerge her in warm water to raise her body temperature, and what else could he do? Poor guy, he had done what he had to, just to keep from turning her in. She stifled another grin at the thought of Tom leaving her underthings on. He was *so* straight, so serious. Then she sobered suddenly—and in a self-conscious panic she tried to recall just how long *had* it been since she had last shaved her legs? Washed her hair? Brushed her teeth?

Ohmygod.

She chided herself for being foolish. It had been an emergency. These things happened. Weakly, and in stages, she rose to her feet. There was nothing for it but to be matter-of-fact. It would be best for both of them. "I think I'll go take a shower, if that's OK? Are my clothes dry?"

"Sure. Ah, yeah. I, uh, set them on the counter in the bathroom. I . . ."

She flashed him a calm, reassuring smile as she walked by.

When she came back into the room after her shower, Tom was watching a quiz show on TV. He looked up and watched her walk into the room and she had never felt so self-conscious in her life. Damien rose at her entrance and escorted her back to the couch, and Elizabeth hid her shyness by pounding the dog on the side affectionately as she took her seat.

"Tom, you don't, like, go to confession or anything do you?"

"Confession?"

"Yeah, you know, where you tell a preacher everything you've done, or something. You don't do that, do you?"

"You're thinking of Catholics. No, I confess my sins to Jesus, not to another man."

"Oh, good. That's a relief. I couldn't have slept if I . . ." She let the thought die.

"Elizabeth, you need to trust more."

She buried herself deep in the couch and considered his words. The brindle bulldog jumped up and, after circling around, collapsed with a sigh between her feet. Damien laid his head on her leg and stared at her face, his warm, brown eye content.

I trust him, she thought.

"I think it's pretty freakin' trusting to be able to lie here, comfortably, in the home of one of the two men who have been trying their best to bust my ass for some time, don't you? I mean really," she said.

"You know what I mean."

"I don't, Tom. There's too much at stake for me to trust to the goodness of human nature."

She could see Tom was struggling to understand what it was she thought was at stake. "I've come to the conclusion," she told him gently, "that if I have to explain my commitment to Damien, you wouldn't understand. You know what I mean? Some things are just like that. What that dog means to me, our friendship, what we've shared together—I can't explain that. I can't put that feeling into words. Maybe your religion is like that?"

"Some things just can't be explained, they can only be *felt*." Then she smiled over at him. "I mean, why did *you* help me? I bet you'd have a hard time explaining *that* to Seville, huh?"

Tom was staring at her thoughtfully. He nodded then, as if maybe he finally did understand.

By the next day, as she told Tom, she no longer felt as if she'd been pithed. Wanting to do something to repay him for his kindness, she cooked him her specialty for breakfast—"Omelets Elizabeth," she called them. *Pretty dang domestic,* a voice chided, tauntingly, inside her head. But another voice, with which she sided, could find no fault with the situation. She felt comfortable around her old enemy in a way she would not have thought possible. They were just easy together.

It was Sunday, and Tom left for church. When he returned they sat and talked the entire afternoon and into the early hours of the morning. Tom explained the glass flowers and the rather tacky religious wall hangings as remnants of his mother's presence there. She had come to live with him while she battled cancer, a fight which lasted years, but which she had lost some months past. Her medical bills had made Seville's steady employment particularly appealing, and the job had provided a generous health insurance option which had eased some of the strain. Tom had struggled to pay the bills, and struggled still, which was why he had deferred any idea of higher education. Someday maybe, he said. But for now he was content the way things were.

On Monday, when Tom came home from work, they talked of what the researcher had done that day, hunting for her and Damien. She laughed at the whole idea of Seville snarling his frustration to his aide, while the whole time she lay on Tom's couch eating potato chips and dip, and watching classic romance movies. Then she noticed Tom did not join her in the laughter. It suddenly occured to her the position he was in.

"Tom, don't tell me you actually *like* this guy?"

"I've worked for him for six years. I owe him my loyalty, Elizabeth. The man *trusts* me—completely. I have the keys to his home, his cars. I just, I feel really terrible about this."

"Geez, Tom, he's *such* a jerk. I've seen how he treats you—doesn't that make you mad? Look," she said, "I bet he doesn't pay you shi . . . I mean, you know, I bet he pays you minimum wage or something, huh? After six years together?"

"No, actually he pays pretty well. That's one of the reasons I've stayed. He has money—his father was very wealthy. That's how he could afford to go to school all those years." Tom pushed his food around the plate with his fork.

Elizabeth frowned, "Yeah, he has money, so why is he fooling around with R&D? I don't get it."

Tom shrugged with his eyebrows, still looking at his food. "It suits him. He can afford to do what he wants, and this is what he wants to do—research."

"Yeah, I can see that. It's a strange world, one where you can do things you can't do anywhere else. I thought that all the time, when he was shocking Damien in that metal box. I'd think, man, if someone got caught doing that in their home basement, they'd get thrown in jail. But not if you do it in the almighty name of research. He's not so dumb I guess."

"He's not that bad," Tom said quickly, looking up. "He's OK."

Elizabeth was exasperated. "You're kidding, right? Look what he did to Damien—and I only know *part* of it. Only you and him know what that dog really went through, right? What *did* he put Damien through, Tom? How would you describe it?"

Tom's reply was reluctant. "He . . . went through . . . a lot."

Elizabeth winced at the understatement. "Yeah, and look how he treats *everybody.*"

Tom shrugged, keeping his eyes on his plate. "He treats Novak all right," he said by way of an argument.

"Come on, he works her like a part-time job, Tom. That doesn't count—he probably treats his *car* well too."

Tom frowned, and redirected the conversation. "He treats his kid OK."

Elizabeth sat up. This was news. "His *what*?"

"His daughter."

"Seville has a *kid*?"

"Yes, by his first marriage. She's seven years old now."

Elizabeth sat back, chewing her bottom lip. "Seville has a kid," she repeated in amazement. "What's she like?"

Tom shrugged. "She's . . . OK."

"What's that mean?"

"Well," he hesitated, old loyalties still moderating his words. "She's maybe a little spoiled."

"By him, or mommy dearest?"

"Well, it was a very bitter divorce."

That didn't answer Elizabeth's question, but it was juicy. She sat forward, her expression intent. "*Really?* What happened?"

Tom hesitated again. Gossiping about his boss made him uncomfortable, but the fact that he was so obviously pleasing Elizabeth made it seem worthwhile. "It came about because of . . ." He paused once more.

"What? Why?"

"Novak."

"Are you kidding me? He got caught cheating?" She chuckled. "That's outstanding."

Tom shrugged.

"So how come I've never seen the kid around—does she live around here?"

"Yes. He gets her once a month, for a weekend."

Elizabeth was looking at the roof, rocking back in her chair. "Man, oh man. That's a pip." Then she plunked her chair back down and looked at Tom.

"What do you boys have planned for tomorrow? What's The Evil One up to?"

Tom gave her a disapproving glance before answering. "He's going to get this before the media again. He's certain you have the dog, and he knows you're still around. He's counting on the money to get someone to spot you, and turn you in."

"Yeah, they will too, it's all a matter of time. I'll get my money out of the bank and take off. I've thought about it. What I need is to get away from *here*, get somewhere no one has seen a report about Damien. Like Canada, or Alaska, somewhere really remote, away from Seville. I was hoping maybe you could drive me, some evening, just far enough away I could start hitch-hiking or something."

Tom flinched at the word "hitchhiking." "You're doing this for a *dog*?" Tom looked right at her, and again she noticed how gray his eyes were.

"I'm doing this for a *friend*, Tom. Look what you did for me. You helped me, I'm helping him. Friends see it through for you. That's what I'm do-ing—I'm going to see this through."

The silence was broken only by Damien's soft and rhythmic snoring and, outside, the distant sound of a siren.

"Alaska?"

"Somewhere wild like that, yeah. It could be nice. I could get a job in a cafe or something. I'd be safe—Damien will take care of me. And maybe, in a few years, I could come back, if I kept a low profile." There was a silence and then she continued. "Tom, you're the very first person to ever hear this, but here goes: I don't think I want to be a physician. I don't think I ever have. I think I'm running away from that as much as anything." How strange it was to speak those words.

Tom smiled his gentle smile. "That's kinda funny, really. You getting pushed by folks to be a doctor and not wanting to, and me, well, I can't think of anything I'd rather do, and I can't. God had a different path for me."

"Maybe someday you will be a doctor. Maybe someday *I* will. Right now it doesn't feel right. This is so politically incorrect, but I'd love to stay home and cook all day. Isn't that terrible?" She waited for his reaction.

"Where I come from, that's what most women do." He shrugged. "They seem to like it, why is that bad?"

"Oh, I don't know. It's not PC; the old barefoot-and-pregnant thing I guess. I was raised by two guys who are obsessed with their work and it just never occurred to them that maybe I was different. That I have different drives and motivations."

"I think you should do what you want, Elizabeth. There's no shame in a woman wanting a home."

"Maybe not, but in my family, well, they just could never understand. And, to be honest, I couldn't tell them how I felt. They were counting on me so much—both of them. Now I've let them down."

They sat for several minutes in silence, then Elizabeth stood up and gathered up the dishes. "It feels good to talk about this. I haven't thought of anything else in days. Trudging along in the dark, that's what I was thinking about! I'm sorry you got caught in the middle of this, Tom. It wasn't fair of me to ask you for help—you working for Seville and all. I am sorry. I'm feeling much better now, I'd probably better be going."

She came out of the kitchen and picked up another load of dishes. "You better get to bed; you need your rest for another fun-filled day with Dr. Feelgood."

Tom nodded absently but remained seated, staring into the middle distance. He was lost in thought and she let him be.

The next evening at dinner Elizabeth was unable to draw Tom into any kind of conversation about the day's events. Something was bothering him, and when he sat quietly, hunched over his plate seemingly lost in thought, she was reluctant to disturb him. She was making up her mind to suggest she leave the next morning when suddenly he spoke, continuing their conversation of the night before as if twenty-four hours had not passed in the interim.

"How do you feel about company? Would three be a crowd?"

Elizabeth frowned. "What are you talking about?"

"Maybe I should come along? If that's OK?"

"Huh? Where? Oh, you mean . . ." Suddenly she knew what he meant. "You'd leave Seville?" she joked in her nervousness. But Tom was serious.

"I think I *should* leave. What I'm doing isn't right."

They stared at each other, both too shy to say anything more direct. Elizabeth shrugged. "Yeah, you can come along." It sounded nonchalant, almost harsh, and not at all the way she wished it had.

Tom insisted they prepare to leave and not rush off in a haphazard fashion. He brought her boxes and she, marveling at his neatness, packed his belongings during the day. Together they moved them into a storage unit in the evenings. Elizabeth wrote a long letter to her father and grandfather, to be mailed as they left, hoping to explain feelings and motivations she herself was having trouble understanding. She would call Barbara on the way out of town.

Now that she knew, via Tom, where Seville's reconnaissance efforts were concentrated, she was able to slip out and access her money from the bank and lay in a supply of dog food. They decided together that they'd leave at the end of the week, and that Tom, no matter how uncomfortable it made him feel, could not give notice. He must simply disappear. In the meantime he worked assiduously, trying in his own way to make up for the coming betrayal.

Sir," the female officer repeated impatiently, "all I can tell you is, the man called us and reported he has seen your missing dog, and he requests contact with you. I have no idea why he called *us*, but he left his phone number and we're simply passing on the information if you want it. That's all." The police had had just about enough of Dr. Joseph Seville and his missing dog.

When he hung up the phone Seville said, without turning, "We've got them, Tom—they've been seen."

He dialed the number while Tom sat behind him, frozen in place.

"This is Dr. Joseph Seville; you called the police concerning a stolen laboratory animal."

"Yeah, yeah, I know where it is, I can show you."

"What is the address?"

"Hold it a minute, Doc. Let's talk about this reward before I . . ."

"Give me the address, I'll meet you there."

"Well, I guess . . . Meet me at 8530 Du'Lien, the Rosaleen Apartments. But, I want . . ."

Seville hung up on the man and turned to Tom. "Get the car, Tom. This is it." Seville had a strong feeling this *was* it. He picked a nylon slip lead and moved toward the door. He wouldn't bother calling the police back, they were getting annoyed with him—to them it was a simple stolen dog—and they probably wouldn't respond anyway. If the animal *was* in an apartment, he would get it—there would be no mistakes this time. Even if he had to get physical with Fletcher, it was of no consequence. He stopped and stepped back, picking up another nylon leash. It occurred to him he might very well have to restrain her when he took the dog.

As they pulled out of the driveway into the brisk fall day, Tom dialed his cell phone. He spoke softly, but Seville, sitting beside him in the passenger seat, was listening casually.

"Hi. Listen—something's come up at work and we're going to a location where the dog has been seen. How late I am tonight depends on what we *find there* when we arrive, so I want you to go on without me, and I'll meet you later, at the regular spot, when I can, OK? Bye."

Seville smirked. "Tom, you old dog—a girl?"

"Just a friend I'm meeting after work."

"That's rather an evasive answer," Seville said playfully, his mood ecstatic. "Well, well. What else have you been keeping from me?"

Much to Seville's annoyance, Tom made several wrong turns and then missed the driveway to the apartments, circling back before pulling into the parking area. A man materialized at the driver's door, leaning down and trying to peer into the heavily tinted window. He was a worn-out fifty, with receding hair, yellow whites to his eyes, and a trim white beard. His open shirt revealed a gold necklace nestled in gray chest hair. His teeth showed a lifetime of smoking, his breath a morning of drinking. Seville got out of the car.

"Where are they?"

"You the doctor?"

"Yes. Tell me where they are."

"I want to see the reward money before . . ."

"You won't see *shit* if they get away while we stand here talking. Now, where are they?"

"Look, buddy, I don't see what the . . ."

Seville leaned forward speaking into the man's face. "Let me see if I can make this clear enough for you. If they *see us*, they'll bolt, do you understand that? You'll get *nothing*. If you want your money you'll tell me where they are, and you'll stay *right* here, out of my way. Now, which unit?"

"Well, OK, I guess. It's D-24."

"Tom," Seville snapped, "let's go." He scanned the visible apartments. "Where is the D wing?"

As Tom slowly stepped out of the car, the man swore and raised one hand, pointing it at the aide. "*Hey!* What are you guys trying to pull? What kind of bullshit is *this*?" he said in a loud voice.

Seville frowned. "What are you talking about?"

"Well ask *him* where D-24 is, he *lives* there!"

There was absolute silence while Seville stared at his aide, and Tom, unable to meet his eyes, stared at the pavement, his face a sickly white color. Slowly, when he couldn't stand it any longer, Tom raised his eyes to the doctor's. It was the worst moment of Tom's life, and the expression on Seville's calm face was the worst he could have imagined in any nightmare. It was the moment of consummate betrayal. For Tom it was a moment far worse than simple, physical death.

"Let's go, Tom," was all Seville said.

They walked to the apartment together, and Tom opened the door. They stepped inside and he shut the door behind them. Seville glanced around, then stood, fingering the slip leads he had brought with him. "Why?"

Tom's mouth worked, but no words came out.

"I want an answer, Tom."

"She needed help. She would have died out there." Tom knew that was a partial lie. She hadn't been dying when first he had helped her. "She was alone. She was wet, and cold and sick."

"She used you, that's all."

"*No.* It wasn't like that at all. She never once *asked* for my help."

"No?" Seville said sharply, his voice ice. "She didn't even *need* to ask? You just decided she should steal my dog, and you would help her behind my back. I bet the two of you had some good laughs at my expense, hum?"

Miserably Tom collapsed on the edge of his couch, looking down. There was no defense he could give and he knew it. Seville walked over and stood in front of Tom, considering him, his eyes hard and thoughtful. At last he spoke.

"Tom, *I* relied on you, *I* needed your help, your dependability. I've put my trust in you all these years, and find that *this* is how you repay my confidence?" He was not speaking loudly or angrily. Tom thought he sounded sad. "You know what that dog disappearing is doing to my career—was it wrong for me to want it back?"

Tom was stricken. He looked mutely at the doctor and shook his head.

"Tom, you've been keeping my stolen property, *and* the thief who stole it, under *your* roof. I'd call that treachery, wouldn't you?" He paused significantly. "Treachery is not a word I would ever have thought applied to you, son."

"I'm sorry."

"Oh, now, Tom, that hardly settles it. You knew what was at stake. You knew what Kotch and the others will do to me if I don't produce that dog. I imagine you and your friend had some pretty good laughs over it. Did you and she giggle about it every night? I imagine you did." Seville turned away with a gesture of disbelief, and Tom stood up quickly.

"It's not like that at all. What she did—*she* believed it was right, so strongly, and things just started happening. She and that dog—they're *friends*. I saw it, and then I just couldn't be the one to take that dog away from her."

Seville had moved to the apartment window, and was standing, hands behind his back, gazing out.

"Where did they go, Tom? Tell me."

"I can't. I'm sorry."

"Yes, you can." Seville's eyes flickered around the room, taking it in, looking, searching for clues to this young man's private life that would aid him now. "There is still time to correct this, son, to choose what's right over what's wrong. To right this thing you've done to me. I've thought of you as a son, Thomas, and to find that you've done this to me . . ."

Tom shook his head, avoiding Seville's eyes. "I'm sorry."

Seville seated himself not far from where Tom had slumped down again on the arm of the couch. Seville had spent his entire adult life studying the manipulation of behavior. He had patience, he had persistence, and now he had insight, the tools necessary to produce in this subject the behavior he desired.

CHAPTER SIXTEEN

Somehow once upon a time
never comes again.

Elizabeth couldn't believe how good she felt. *Really* good. And it was nuts, because she had no reason to. Things were going to hell in a handbasket draped firmly over the arm of fate. Seville at that very moment was discovering Tom's betrayal, the consequence of which would be unimaginable. Add to that the fact she was crossing town in broad daylight, in full view of hundreds if not thousands of people, with a dog which still sported a twenty-five-thousand-dollar reward on its head. Elizabeth was hard-pressed to understand her own high spirits.

Walking to the rendezvous site was incredibly risky, but there was no other choice. With every car that passed she wondered, is this the one that will report us? She walked tensely, expecting to be challenged at any moment. She could only hope that as long as Seville was busy with Tom at his apartment, perhaps anyone sighting them would be unable to reach the researcher until it was too late. Still, it was nerve-wracking.

Tom's warning call had her running high on adrenaline, and the revelation of his complete loyalty to her gave her a feeling of invincibility. They had cut it pretty damn close, but with Tom's help she had escaped Seville's clutches one last time. It seemed strange to think that so much—everything—depended on him now.

She couldn't stop thinking about Tom, and about how he made her feel.

When he was near, his tall, quiet presence reassured her, and made her feel safe and protected. It just *felt* right. Strange indeed, considering how recently he had been the enemy—the right-hand man of her own personal demon. But he had simply been Seville's employee, trapped in his role as much as she had been trapped in hers.

When they had talked together into the early morning hours, she had been pleased to find that Tom was what he seemed—patient, kind and deeply devoted to those things he thought right. Now, during her eleventh hour, he was proving strong enough to defy Seville for her sake. Though they were both still too shy to speak more directly about their feelings, Elizabeth sensed she had struck some chord in Tom's stoic heart. For her own part, though the thought of him now was like a catch in her breast, she couldn't—or wouldn't—put a name to what she felt. Her relationship with Tom, however, felt like a puzzle piece that had slipped into place with a satisfying click.

Tonight the three friends would start a road trip into an unknown future. It was frightening, but it was exhilarating also, setting off on such an adventure together. With friends like Tom and Damien, she felt she could handle anything life threw at her. Her father had lived his life, and now she must live hers. She did not share his dream. She could not feel anger toward her father, the love was too deep, but knowing he had been talking with Seville about her, working to get the dog back to the vet, made it easier to leave. She had cut the bonds of her past life and she felt reckless and wildly free. She *had* rescued her friend. She had won.

She wanted to get word to Barbara so she stopped at a phone booth and looked up the nursery where she worked. She should be there at this time of the day. She waited anxiously while the woman who answered the phone found Barbara and handed her the phone.

"Barbara, it's Elizabeth."

"Bloody 'ell, kid, it's good to hear from you. What's going on? Where are you? Is Damien OK?"

"Yeah, he's great. Seville showed up at your house—I guess you already know that—he followed Bill. I had to run like hell out the back—I'm really sorry—I hope you didn't get in any trouble. Did you?"

"Huh! Don't worry about *that*. I don't give a brass razzoo about their threats. Seville, he's a charmer, ain't he?"

Elizabeth chuckled. "I see you met him. Well, welcome to my world! Listen, I just wanted to let you know I was OK. I know I should have called you sooner—I'm sorry about that—things have just been crazy. When they showed up I just ran. Of course I came down with the flu—I always do when I'm stressed—and then I got *really* sick. I was hiding under some logs but I got so cold I got hypothermia, and then I was too out of it to go get help. I hope you're sitting down because you're not going to believe this. Damien went looking for help, I guess, and found Tom, Seville's Tom, and he took me to his home and didn't tell Seville. He saved my life, I mean really, he saved my life. With the hypothermia I had I wouldn't have made it much longer."

"Seville's Tom?"

"Seville's Tom."

"I find that interesting." There was a moment of silence. "Are you sure you know what you're doing?"

"Tom knew how I felt about Damien and he respected my commitment. He takes commitment very seriously. Seeing what I was going through for Damien, he just couldn't turn me over to Seville. I know you don't believe in luck, but wasn't that pretty lucky?"

"You're right, I don't believe in luck or divine intervention, but I do believe in the power of love. Evidently whatever Tom saw touched him deeply. Perhaps he isn't all bad."

"He is a good person, Barbara. Truly. I don't want you to worry about me, but we have to leave right now. The shit hit the fan a few minutes ago. Tom called to warn me to get out, because Seville found out where I was. We're going to meet in a few hours, hopefully, and then we're leaving. So, I wanted to call."

On the other end of the phone, she heard Barbara exhale.

"I just wanted to call and tell you not to worry. And to thank you again. With all my heart."

"Wait, wait, wait. Back up. You *really* think you can trust this bloke? He works for *Seville*! I saw him here durin' the fuss, and he looked pretty much like Seville's man then. Are you sure *enough* to risk Damien?"

"I can tell. I know." There was a pause. "I think, well, I think we really like each other."

Barbara smiled at all that remained unspoken. "You *think*, huh?"

"Well, you know . . ."

"Well kid, you're there and I'm not. I mean, I guess that bloke could have just turned you in at any time, couldn't he? Bloody 'ell. Well, I'm glad it's workin' out for you. I *was* pretty worried, actually. When I got there, boy, was he *pissed*. I figured if he caught you, you'd have your hands full, for sure."

"Yeah, I know. If you think he was pissed then, wait till he finds out I split with his aide and his dog. Jesus, think of it! I better get going. I've got to meet Tom, and then we're heading out."

"I'll miss both you guys. Take care, and let me hear from you when you can."

"Thank you, Barbara. Good-bye."

"Onya mate, give 'em heaps!"

Damien and Elizabeth made it to the rendezvous site without incident.

"Things are going to start getting better," she assured the dog. "We're heading out for Alaska. Or Canada. Maybe the Yukon, someplace crazy like that. Someplace wild and primitive. No universities, no veterinarians with too much grant money and not enough ethics. You'll *love* it!" she told Damien, "nothing but forests and mountains and stuff. No more cages! No more kennels!"

Elizabeth had come to appreciate that while Damien had an animal's kinship with Nature, he was no longer, properly, a true animal. She saw that to be a dog meant to be forever torn between the worlds of Nature and of Man. Where they were going would be dog heaven for Damien. Reunited with her, in Nature at its most pristine, he could have his cake and eat it too.

She squeezed his head between her hands and gave him a quick kiss on the forehead. Excited by Elizabeth's good humor, the dog bounced around her, barking happily. They walked to the water's edge together. The sun was out, and the air mild for autumn. For a while she threw pieces of driftwood into the sound, watching Damien happily retrieve them. He brought each piece up to her, dropped it at her feet, then stood dripping in quivering anticipation until she threw it again. The image of Damien in a steel cage or in a bare, white room, head on his paws, waiting in weary boredom week after week, month after month, haunted her. She had saved Damien from a lifetime of unthinkable hell, but he, in turn, had given her a gift of equal value. She knew now that, had she not acted to save him, she would have remained forever a shade, a pale soul, who went safely and carefully through an insipid and meaningless life. She would have been a human being whose existence had less nobility than that of the salmon, who lay dead now, rocking gently in the shallows beside her eggs, her great task successfully completed.

After a while her arm grew tired, and she showed Damien her empty hands in a gesture he knew well.

"No more," she said, and he immediately came to sit on the slope beside her, his head level with hers. He looked out over the water, his warm, brown eye taking in the same view she saw. It gave her great pleasure to see his contentment. They looked together out over the calm water and she watched his gaze, watched what things he looked at.

The dog glanced over and noticed her watching him. He reached over and gave her a quick lick on the cheek, a thing he rarely did. He was not an effusive dog, and she was surprised.

"Good," the dog said quietly.

Her breath caught. Still, after all this time, his speech could stun her.

She tipped her head against his and held it there. She put her arm around his shoulders, feeling the wet from his fur come through her sleeve, cold and warm at the same time. Smiling to herself, she knew now that words, hers or Damien's, were unnecessary to the communication between them.

"It is *good*. Thanks for letting me come along for the ride, Buddy. It's been something, hasn't it? Man oh man," she said slowly. "It *has* been something."

They sat together for quite a while, the dog and the girl, her arm companionably around his shoulders, his stocky, stalwart body just touching hers.

They sat for an hour, waiting for Tom, and Elizabeth spent the time wondering again why she didn't feel more frightened, and why she felt *glad* to be leaving behind everything she had thought important. She did not realize such decisions come easily with youth, and were as natural as the tide rising at her feet.

Elizabeth's attention was caught by some barnacles in the water before her. Their fanlike arms had begun rhythmically sweeping as the water covered them, bringing plankton to their "mouths." She knelt carefully at the water's edge, smiling at their quick, greedy grabbing motion.

"Hey, Damien, check this out. *This* is what I want to come back as in my next life. You get to sit, surrounded by your food, and just shovel it in as fast as you can all day. *What* a life." She turned her head to see why the dog hadn't joined her at the water's edge. He usually came crowding when she stooped to look closely at something. Damien was standing above her, his front feet on the top of the small bank they had been sitting on, his head raised in an attitude of total attention. He was looking keenly at something.

Tom. At the thought of the young man coming to collect her, and of the life they would make together starting unequivocally at the moment she stepped into his car, she was swept by bittersweet emotion. She took a deep breath, held it, then exhaled, certain now.

"What is it, Damien?"

The dog remained in place, turning his head to look back at her quickly. "White Pain."

"*What!*" She scrambled up on her hands and knees, joining the dog at the edge.

"Oh, *shit!*"

There were two options. Go left into open ground, or right into the log yard. They were a long way from the point where the headland connected with the mainland, and she knew she didn't have the strength to run the whole way. If they went left they were sitting ducks. She went right; thinking her only chance was to lose him in the maze of stacked logs. For the split second before she started to run, she wondered, *how?* Had Tom betrayed her? Was it conceivable he would hand her and Damien over to Seville after all he had done for them? Had the trust—and love—developing between them been false? Or, had she been spotted while walking here today, and her location reported to Seville by some passerby?

Don't be a fool—it doesn't matter now. This is about you and Damien. Finish the job.

She sprinted right, heading for the log yard. Seville watched them go, then altered his course to cut them off. He had nylon leashes in his hand. After just a few dozen yards, Elizabeth realized she was too weak from her recent illness to run much farther. And hiding in the log yard simply meant waiting to be found by the man who hunted them.

The girl and the dog reached the log stacks forty yards ahead of Seville. She pulled up, panting and thinking. She looked down at Damien.

"Stay close boy, and *don't listen to him.* You stay with *me.* I'll get you out of this, I promise. We've come this far—we'll make it."

She gambled the doctor would penetrate far into the rows of logs, thinking she would go deep in hopes of losing him in the huge yard. She doubled back to the leading edge of the yard, where she had entered, and began to cautiously trot down past the towering piles. She fought to control her labored breathing and listen for Seville's footsteps, but she could hear nothing over her own panting and the cries of the displaced sea gulls. It was fearful work, expecting to see the man step out from behind each stack of logs.

They reached the place where she had seen Seville enter the log yard, and she slowed up. Damien pressed close to her heels, his body language clearly indicating he was scenting the veterinarian. The man had obviously passed through here and she fervently hoped he had turned right, and gone up toward where she had entered. If he had, they were past him, and they could run for the mainland. If he had turned left (but she couldn't think why he would have done that) then they ran the risk of encountering him still. She began walking carefully forward again.

The logs in this part of the yard were large, two to three feet through, and they towered twenty-five feet overhead in their precarious stacks. The footing was treacherous, consisting of large hunks of broken bark, which snapped when stepped on. She noticed that Damien hung back, close to her, ears flat against his head. Seville's presence spooked him.

She still couldn't see Seville's car anywhere. She couldn't stand not knowing where he could be. She crept between two big piles and, holding Damien by the neck fur, she peeked back in the direction they had come. Nothing. But that didn't prove anything. The man could simply be over another aisle. The yard was immense, and there were several rows of logs.

She continued her careful withdrawal. She picked up her pace, feeling now it would be better to just try for the mainland as quickly as possible. As she passed the end of the next stack an arm shot out, grabbing her shoulder. The sudden interruption of her forward momentum jerked her shoulder backward and she swung about, losing her balance and falling heavily onto the bark-covered ground. Without a word, Seville flipped her over, knelt on her back and pulled her arms behind her. She felt her wrists being wrapped with the nylon leash. She kicked and struggled madly, but he was far stronger than her. It felt like a nightmare—her strongest efforts seemed to have no effect on him at all. It was a moment of pure terror.

Then suddenly, there was the sound of a hard, dull impact, Seville was off her, and she was scrambling up, free. Now she experienced a moment of pure relief; the feeling of prey leaping free from predator. Instinctively she began to run blindly, just putting distance between herself and the danger. Then she stopped.

Damien!

She turned back, unable and unwilling to give up on her dog.

Without a sound, Damien had leapt across her body, biting the man in the chest, and shaking him violently with all the strength in his neck and shoulders. Taken completely by surprise, Seville was unable to fight the furious bulldog; he was a rag, a toy, and he lay on his back with an expression of utter shock as the powerful dog dragged him along the ground.

Elizabeth stared in disbelief. Damien was attacking *Seville*. Shocked, she stood too frightened to move. She had known intellectually that Damien was capable of great violence on her behalf, that he was a powerful animal, but now to see him quietly and with complete purposefulness actually *killing* someone froze her in place. And not just *someone*, but the one person in the world Damien feared above anyone or anything else. The loyal dog had given his allegiance to the man he had been forced to work with, had taken every abuse, every frustration, every cruelty Seville had dealt out, without so much as raising a lip toward him. But here, now, the bulldog had found the reason and the courage to throw this man—his god—to the ground and destroy him. And it seemed all the more shocking to Elizabeth because it was for her. This was about *her*. On his own, Damien would have gone meekly with Seville. But he would kill this man rather than have him hurt her.

It was a horrible sight, and the sound of it made her sick. As the dog shifted his grip, bearing ever inward with his jaws in an effort to eviscerate his enemy, his teeth began cutting into Seville's chest, and the doctor cried out sharply. Seville began pushing and hitting at Damien's head, but it was obvious that the dog would not be stopped by such efforts. The man glanced up over the dog's violently thrashing body and his eyes caught Elizabeth's. She had never seen anyone's face look like that.

"Get him off." It was a horrible choking sound, strangely modulated by the dog's shaking action. "Get him off."

"My God!" she breathed.

The dog was standing on the man's body, boring in. Seville had attacked The One and Damien would protect Elizabeth with his life. He would kill this man that harmed her like an avenging spirit, to repay the debt of her long friendship.

The dog had been dragging the doctor along the ground, shaking his powerful neck over and over, but now he stood on him, pinning the man helplessly beneath him. Seville caught Elizabeth's eye again. His face was as white as a lab coat. At that moment, he knew whether he lived or died was up to her. He was in need of a compassion he had never bestowed upon creatures under his control.

"Please," he gasped.

She came forward and grasped the dog around the neck. She was not like the man, she would not ignore an appeal for mercy. The dog's powerful and relentless shaking threw her to her knees but she hung on grimly.

"Damien! *No!* Stop it. Stop, *you're killing him!*" she screamed. If the dog heard her, he gave no sign. Suddenly Damien switched his hold, grabbing up jacket, shirt and flesh lower on Seville's abdomen. The man's hoarse scream sickened Elizabeth's stomach.

"*Damien, no!* Stop! Stop it now! Please, oh my God, *stop it!*" She could think of only one thing to do, and it depended entirely on Damien's love for her—but that was the strongest tool she had right now. She worked her way around to Seville's head, trying not to see his expression. Facing the dog, she put her hands on either side of his muzzle. If Damien shifted his grip on the doctor's torso, even a little, he would crush her hands. The dog's wild eye rolled up to her face.

"Stop it, Damien. Stop it now," she said as quietly as she could through gritted teeth. She moved her hands against his muzzle, pressing them against his fangs. He stopped shaking his hold, and in another moment she felt his grip start to weaken. Seville began trying to pull himself backward, away from the animal.

"*Hold still!*" she hissed at the doctor. "Hold still, don't move."

When the man had moved, Damien had regripped savagely, straight down, his canine teeth penetrating deep into the man's abdomen. When Seville's movement stopped at Elizabeth's command, the dog again listened to the girl's quiet voice, and slowly, with great reluctance, the dog's mouth parted and the material jumped out, spreading back over the man's stomach. It was soaked with blood.

"Don't *move*," she breathed.

The dog looked at her, his eye bright and unnatural, his breathing hard and rasping.

"It's OK, Damien, it's OK. Good boy. *Thank you.* Good job. Now get back! Leave him alone, I'm OK."

344

The dog hesitated, glancing back and forth between Elizabeth's face and Seville's.

"I'm OK, it's all right," she soothed. "I want you to leave him alone." After a moment, the dog stepped back reluctantly.

"Now lie down. Lie *down*! Damien, listen to me. Lie down." She gestured with her hand and Damien sank down on the rough bark beside the log pile, his one good eye boring into the man, his sides heaving with his emotion and exertion.

"Are you OK?" she asked the doctor in a scared voice. Even though she had spoken quietly in order to calm the dog, she was shaking and badly frightened.

Seville ignored her question and slowly got to his feet. He stood hunched over from the pain, one arm across his stomach, his eyes on the dog.

"Please just leave us *alone*. We just want to go. Damien won't go with you—he won't work for you now. Just let us leave. Let's call it even."

Seville remained silent.

"Did Tom . . . tell you where I was?" She had to know. Tom had told her she needed to trust more.

With a grimace the doctor straightened up, keeping his arm across his torn abdomen. He looked at her, his stark gray eyes as unreadable as ever.

"Yes, he did," he said after a moment's hesitation. "You must understand, he was concerned about you and about how this was going to end up."

"I don't believe you." She was trying very hard not to.

"If it's any consolation, he did try; he held out quite a while, actually. It's nothing to fault him for. He's in love with you, you know, and because he *does* love you, I was able to make him see that your running away with the dog might seem pleasant and clever at this time, however it was ultimately going to lead to some very serious consequences for you both. I assured him that if he helped me to resolve it now, I would do everything I could to make things as easy for you as possible. It's the same offer I gave your father, and he accepted as well."

Elizabeth looked down and shut her eyes.

"I'm afraid, Elizabeth, both their lives have been impacted very negatively by you," Seville continued. "Despite that, Tom's thoughts are for your safety and happiness. That's why he told me you were here. He was doing what was best for *you*, and hoping you would trust him enough to see that."

345

Elizabeth looked up. She could not allow her emotions to be a distraction to her right now.

"Look, I just saved your freakin' life, man. The *least* you could do is let us go."

Seville kept watching her and the dog, his eyes going back and forth. He was getting his breath back. And thinking. "All right," he said carefully. "Go on." He shrugged his head at them, indicating the way out of the yard.

Elizabeth stared at him. "You mean it? Why?"

"Go on. I can't *keep* you here, obviously. I'm not the one in control here, am I?"

Elizabeth was instantly suspicious. This was not a change of heart. What was he up to?

"I need to get medical attention. I can't do that until you take the dog away. Go on," he said again, harshly. Again he indicated the way across the empty land with a nod of his head.

Elizabeth looked over her shoulder.

What's out there? Why does he seem to want me to go in that direction?

It seemed reasonable that he knew he was licked, and that for now there was no way he could get the dog, but she was still suspicious. She still hadn't seen his car. Perhaps it was on the other side of the logs. If she could reach it, and if she could get his car keys . . .

Car keys! That was it!

If she left him here, injured as he was, and took his car, she could get out of town and ditch it, before he could make it to the nearest phone.

Grand theft, auto? Not a problem at this point.

She stepped up to him. "Gimme your car keys."

"What?"

"You heard me, give me your car keys. Now! Hand them over."

Seville shook his head.

"Look you jerk, I could let Damien kill you, you know. I've had just about enough of your crap. You hand me those car keys, or I tell Damien to finish the job, OK? We just want to go away. That's all. So hand them over."

"They're in the car."

"No, they're not. You wouldn't do that. Come on, hand 'em over."

"They're in the car," he repeated.

"Oh, *damn* it," Elizabeth sighed in frustration. "OK, put your hands up in the air." Just using that expression made her feel incredibly ridiculous.

"Excuse me?" Seville said incredulously.

"Well—I've got to frisk you. I know you've got them. Put your hands up and don't try anything. You know what Damien will do, and I *swear* to you I won't stop him this time."

"Let me save you the trouble." He reached down and pulled the keys out of his pocket. With a quick pitch, he had tossed the keys over her head, and over the log pile. She heard the tiny *ting* as they hit the ground on the other side. He grimaced with the pain the sudden movement had caused his bitten torso, and then he smiled at her.

She stared at him.

Well, it's what you *would have done if you'd thought of it,* she told herself. *His car is around here somewhere, and he doesn't want me to find it.*

"OK, where's your car?"

That sounded even more ridiculous. Jesus.

"On the other side of the yard. Over there." He pointed over the log stacks toward the access road along the beach. She wondered if it was true. It could be. Then again, he would probably try to direct her the wrong way. Elizabeth made a quick calculation. If she went directly over the log pile, she had the best chance of finding the keys, and it was the surest way to locate Seville's car. She would be able to see all over the log yard from up there.

Damien had come to stand beside her when the man had thrown the keys, and she reached down now and put her hand on the dog's broad head. Damien looked up at her. She was ready to go, but she hesitated. Her frustration at being unable to make the researcher see the necessity of what she did for her companion burned in her.

Why couldn't she find the words?

Was it his fault he couldn't be made to understand, or her fault she couldn't make him understand? How could she feel *so* strongly about something and then be unable to articulate it? But then again, wasn't that the lesson Damien had taught her—that the important things in life defied definition and description?

But she must try.

"Look, I saved your life, and I'm going to ask you to return the favor. Let us go. I know I can never make you understand what's wrong with what you—and my father—do to dogs. You just can't see it. You made this animal's life a *desolation*. For *your* gain. And what did he do? He came to your defense the moment you needed help. In fact, he almost died defending you.

And in return, you shocked the hell out of him with your stupid collar when you couldn't figure out how to teach him or earn his respect any other way. You made his life hell. If the truth be told—*you*, with all your degrees and titles and money—he's a better person than you are, Dr. Seville.

"Now listen, Damien and I have been through a lot together. We're buddies, and buddies watch out for each other. So, all I can do is ask this of you—leave us alone."

Damien and Seville were staring at each other. Both had unreadable eyes. Elizabeth shook her head; she knew she had not reached Seville. It was a waste of time to try.

"Come on, Damien," she said quietly, "let's go." She thought about tying Seville up, but she was afraid to get that close to him again. If he grabbed her, Damien *would* attack him again, and she wasn't sure she would be able to stop him a second time. Besides, it was extremely unlikely Seville would follow her; he was too badly injured for that.

She glanced up at the stack behind her. It was about twenty feet high, made up of eighteen- to twenty-four-inch-thick fir tree logs. They weren't tidy, ends stuck out here and there, and some of the logs were balanced precariously. She had to find Seville's car, and climbing the stack was the only way.

She turned and started up the pile, the dog hopping along beside her. It was a little harder than she had imagined it would be, because when a log stuck out too far, she had to help the dog up onto it. Seville stood watching passively while she climbed, his expression, she thought, seemed almost concerned.

Huh! she though grimly, *he's only worried about Damien's safety.*

She reached the top log and straddled it, looking down at Seville. Damien, happy to see a way off the slippery logs, was hurrying down the other side. He got to the bottom, jumped to the ground and turned to face her.

Elizabeth dropped over the top of the pile, and then hesitated. She wanted to see what Seville would do, the moment he thought she could no longer see him. She climbed back to the top log, and peeked over. Seville had pulled out his cell phone. It had been in his suit pocket all this time. She hadn't thought of that. He was dialing.

"*Shit!*" If he got ahold of the police, it would all end right here. It would end with her being dragged off to jail and Damien going back to the life Seville offered him. *Shit!* She had to stop him. If she had to wrestle it away from him, and if the fool got himself killed by the dog, well then, so be it. She hadn't come this far to give up now. She'd get the phone, then tie the asshole up after all.

God, what a jerk—he just won't quit.

In a panic, she scrambled to the top, then jumped down quickly from log to log, skipping two and three logs at a time. She had to get to him before he got enough information to whomever he was calling to get them to this location. Damien was on the other side, of no use to her now.

Great! I hope he can get over here before Seville beats the shit out of me!

Even though he was injured, she knew she would have her hands full taking the phone away from him.

She heard Seville begin to speak, and she leaped down three logs to a large one near the bottom, which stuck out quite far. When she landed, her feet went out from under her and she fell backwards hard, onto the end of the log. In one hideous moment she realized her weight had dislodged the log, and it was falling away from her. The logs above her were falling. The sound was dull and frightening in its strength. It happened too quickly for Elizabeth to make any sense of it, there was just bright sky and dark logs, and the horrible, deep *tunk tunk* sound of the logs hitting and grinding together, the sensation of falling, then incredible pressure. No real pain, just a strange, dull ache in her hips.

The movement and sound stopped. She lay still a moment.

Thank God, she thought, *I wasn't hurt in all that.*

She was on her back, and she tried to get up. Only her head and shoulders came up. Confused, she tried again, but nothing happened.

There aren't any logs on me, why can't I get up?

She struggled up on one elbow and looked down at her body.

Oh.

She was crushed, completely crushed, her body grotesquely flattened from her waist down to her knees. She looked up wonderingly at Seville, who appeared beside her, the phone hanging limp in his hand.

"Jesus," he whispered.

She stared at the sight of her ruined body, trying to comprehend. It didn't frighten her; she just stared, unsure what it really meant. Then she remembered something—something more important than this strange thing that had happened to her.

"Where's my dog?" She was shocked to hear herself; she sounded weak and strange. It wasn't *her* voice, yet it had come out of her. She tasted blood in her mouth. That was strange.

I must have bit my tongue.

Seville knelt beside her and she reached out, grasping his jacket, trying to pull herself up. She clung to him.

Funny, I can feel this material so strongly, every fiber, but I can't feel any pain—I can't feel my body at all.

She could even feel his warmth on the material, and the sticky spots where the blood had seeped through. Some instinct told her to hold on to the sensations, the sights, the smells—to concentrate on them. The *awareness* of those senses *was* life. She was acutely aware of the pungent evergreen scent put out by the disturbed and crushed logs. When Seville had walked up, she had heard the sounds his body and clothing made as he knelt beside her. The sound of the bark snapping under his feet was loud and distracting. On her left she was lying up against a log. She could see the pattern of its bark looking like a rustic jigsaw puzzle, with each piece outlined in strong relief. Small pieces of gray-green moss caught in the bark stood out in amazing clarity. She clenched Seville's jacket harder; as long as she could feel things this acutely, she was alive, she was fine, everything must be OK—she couldn't really be injured that badly.

She looked in Seville's face. "I'll be OK," she said firmly. "I just need to get up."

"You need to lie still," he said.

Then, she *knew*. An eerie new sensation swept over her as her initial shock receded. She felt her body slipping away from her, even as her mind cleared, and she looked down at what had been her hips and legs. Though there was now a sound like the sea in her ears, her mind was suddenly perfectly, startlingly, clear.

"Oh man, oh man," she whispered.

She choked, then coughed, blood coming into her mouth. She spit it out. "Where's Damien, is he all right?" she asked with growing concern. She felt no panic for herself—she thought it odd that she felt so calm, almost businesslike—but she was concerned about Damien's absence.

Seville looked around. "I don't see him, I'm sure he's fine." He reached down and started to examine her injuries, then slowly pulled his hand back. He looked her in the eye. "I'm sorry, I think you know there's nothing I can do for you."

Elizabeth was aware of blood running into her mouth. She struggled to keep her head lifted up, coughing, spitting, struggling with the blood that was filling her mouth. "There *is* something you can do for me," she said when she could. "You know I can't leave him like this—with you. You know I *can't*. Oh God, please let Barbara take him." She grasped his arm harder. "Please. *Please.*"

"You know I can't do that."

Her heart caught at his answer. She envisioned Damien, his head on his paws, waiting, waiting. Waiting for her, and she wouldn't come. Long, long agonizing hours of a life trapped in a kennel or crate, only to be let out at the whim of his master. The dog would wait, and would he wonder why she had forsaken him?

No.

Damien would never give up hope that she would come. He would never doubt her. His trust in her was pure.

"For God's sake," she whispered, "Don't put that collar on him."

"We'll see," he said, "don't worry about the dog. You need to stay calm."

Elizabeth felt light-headed, a horrid feeling, like being on the verge of fainting, but staying conscious. She fought it, pushing against the ground with her arms, wriggling, twisting, trying to raise her body, willing it to rise. The man's restraining hand made her struggle all the harder. Her worst fear was coming true. If Damien was still alive, if he hadn't been crushed beneath the logs, she would no longer be able to protect him. All she had done would be for naught. Her body fell limp between the logs, ruined, useless and dying, and her eyes closed in bitter defeat. An image came to her, unbidden. The salmon, dead now, rocking in the shallow waters of the pool which had seen its birth and death. Had the salmon made it? Had it died filled with the contented resignation of one who has lived well and welcomes death as a completion of life? Or, like herself, had it fallen short, trying so hard but mortally injured and unable to push itself to the completion of its task?

Seville pulled a handkerchief from his pocket and wiped at the blood that was coming from her mouth.

"Here, let me help you."

"No." She roused herself, weakly pulling her head away from his efforts. "I don't want your help," she said it quietly, as if she were speaking to herself. "I'm not afraid to die. I can't accept your *kind* of help . . ." She opened her eyes and stared, defiant, at the man. "I don't want your help. I've seen the cost." Closing her eyes she smiled a small, small smile, gratified to find that at the end, she would not crawl.

It pleased her.

Unwilling to see darkness yet, she opened her eyes again and looked at the patch of sky directly above her. The moon, three quarters full, showed faint but clear in the daylight. It was there, at midday, but only noticed by those who looked for it.

Without knowing why, it comforted her to know that the moon would continue on its way, eternally. Not as powerful as the sun, but still there, nonetheless. A beautiful, ancient thing, that the eyes of every human generation had looked upon. She wished she could tell Bill to think of her when he looked upon it, sitting in his garden on a warm, sweet-smelling summer evening. Or, if he paused on a frozen winter's night, perhaps then he would be able to *see*. She nodded to the moon, still smiling her small, private smile, and then she closed her eyes again.

"Please," she said so quietly that Seville had to lean down to hear her. "You *must* know this. My father and grandfather—they helped Damien because to them he was *your* dog. You understand? They saved his life because he was your dog. They didn't want any trouble if he died. It's not their fault . . ."

"I understand."

"Would you, would you tell both I love them. Please. Make sure you tell them, will you? Tell them I didn't suffer. The only pain I feel, is here." She placed her right hand on her heart. She faded, seeming to draw away, then choked suddenly on blood and raised her head, swallowed it down with an effort. "Will you?"

"Yes, I will."

She resisted the strange and frightening lightness coming upon her. "Damien!" she called. She had to know what had become of her dog before she could go.

There was a strange pattering sound and Seville rose and backed away quickly. Damien was suddenly there, nosing at her, anxiously snuffling her, sniffing the blood on her. The sight of his rugged golden face gave her a moment of exquisite relief.

"Damien, you're *all right*. You're here," she whispered.

The dog's tail was clamped between his legs and his ears were flat. Like any predatory animal he had a working relationship with death; this, however, was not the lusty and intoxicating death of a prey victim, but rather a mysterious and troubling presence.

"Stay with me." She reached out toward her dog.

Damien nuzzled her, pushing his head under her arm. "Pet," the dog whimpered.

Elizabeth could feel she hadn't long to do what she must. She wanted nothing more than to hug the dog to her, but she could not. She must not. Her breathing was rapid and shallow, and the blood rapidly filling her lungs kept her from being able to get enough oxygen. She struggled to suck in air.

"Listen, Damien. You *must* listen. White Pain *will* hurt you. Go find *Barbara.*" She was wracked with bloody coughing and the dog stepped closer, nuzzling the hands she put to her face. His body felt warm and solid against her.

"Go!" She struck out, her hand weakly pushing at him. "Don't you understand? *Go!*"

The effort cost her dearly, and she lapsed again into violent coughing. The dog glanced at where Seville stood ten feet away, watching.

"Easy, Damien. Steady," he said quietly. "You stay."

"Damn it!" Elizabeth struggled wildly, waving one arm at the dog. "Don't listen to him, Damien. Go on now! Go on. Don't let White Pain touch you. *Go find Barbara.*"

The dog shivered in his anxiety, frustration and confusion. He sat down, hunched miserably, just outside of Elizabeth's reach, his eyes filled with a love and concern as tangible as anything on this earth.

"No," the dog said.

"Oh, Damie . . ." Her frustration complete, the tears came now, not for herself, but for the dog. Damien would not leave her. He would stay, and when she was dead, Seville would take him away. He would have the dog again, and there would be no one to question what he did.

She twisted her head in an agony of sorrow. "I'm sorry, Damie. I'm so sorry." She had lost.

All was lost.

She remembered Barbara's words at the fire, the evening she had been given the bag around her neck. She heard them clearly above the strange rushing sound in her mind, as if it was terribly important. *Rest assured,* Barbara had said, *whatever happens to you and Damien, it will not be the result of malevolent evil forces, or divine intervention, or magic, or dumb luck. It will be life, playing out, as it has since the beginning of time.*

Seville made a movement as if to come forward, toward her but, observing the dog's agitation, he stopped. Elizabeth glanced from where he stood back to the dog beside her, and at that moment a thought came to her. A thought her failing mind grasped at as she had once grasped at twirling maple leafs falling before her face when she and Damien had played among the arboretum's huge trees while sunlight glinted off the morning frost: Barbara would hear of Damien's fate. She would hear that the dog was again in Seville's hands, and she would do something. Elizabeth nodded to herself. Barbara would hear of her death and then she would come for Damien. Barbara was a match for Seville—the pagan woman would prevail where Elizabeth had failed. She exhaled a long contented sigh, the load of responsibility removed from her failing mind. She turned inward then, attending to her dying.

I'm young to die.

I'm not finished.

What would I have become?

With Damien's help she had found the answer to that. At least in death she knew who she was. She wished only, with immense sadness, that Tom could be there as well. With her dying came a strange, certain knowledge that he had remained true. She loved him still.

She stared at the dog for a moment, and then she reached up and removed the leather thong from around her neck. With a supreme effort she reached out and pulled Damien's over his head. She replaced it with her own, then slowly slipped the dog's bag over her own neck. She held it tightly. "Remember me." It was barely audible. "Remember me." She closed her eyes. "I guess it's my turn to wait for you now, Damie." And then she promised her dog, "I *will* wait."

She made an alarming gurgling sound as she fought the blood which rushed into her throat and mouth. She weakly lifted her hands and spread them out, showing them to the dog. She shook her head, eyes filled with regret.

"No more . . ." she whispered.

Seville came forward cautiously, his eye on the dog, to lift her head and turn it to the side. She threw up blood, choked, then locked eyes with her dog. She reached out to him and Damien buried his brindle head against her chest. She pressed her face in his warm neck, hugging him fiercely to her.

Just hold on to him, The Voice which she could hear clearly now, said. *Just tell him you love him.*

And that's what she did, over and over, while the life left her body.

After he placed a call to the police, Seville attended to his appearance. Buttoned up, his sports jacket hid the rips in his shirt, and most of the blood. The rest he could explain as having come from Elizabeth while he tended her. Collecting himself with the ritual of lighting a cigarette, he inhaled the first drag deeply, exhaled just as strongly, and then moved forward to collect the dog. The pit bull was curled up in a tight ball beside its dead companion, its brindle head still resting on Elizabeth's chest. At the man's approach the dog's head lifted and Seville advanced carefully. Though he was reasonably certain the dog would not attack him without reason, he reminded himself he had mistakenly assumed the dog would never have had the courage to challenge him at all, and he had been very wrong.

When I get that shock collar back on you, he thought grimly, *we'll come to quite an understanding, you and I.* Right now it felt far too much like the dog was in control.

Damien watched as the man came and stood before him, then he laid his head back down on Elizabeth's still chest. Seville took the cigarette from his mouth. "Damien, come here."

The dog did not lift his head. "Bad," he said miserably.

"You're coming with me, now."

The dog sat up and gently touched the woman's still body with his nose. Then he stood and faced Seville, his expression asking the question he could not know how to ask.

"She's dead." Seville said, stepping forward with the nylon lead in his hand. "Come on."

Damien stepped back, avoiding him.

"Damien!" he said "Stay!" He quickly stepped forward to slip the noose over the animal's head and Damien side-stepped him again, keeping out of his reach. Several times the man grabbed for the dog, grimacing at the pain it caused his torn torso, and each time Damien avoided him, keeping just out of reach.

"*Damien*, lie down! *Now!*" Exasperated, the man's tone was ugly. Damien squinted and flattened his ears by way of apology, but he would not go with the man—not yet.

Seville considered for a moment, then, holding his aching abdomen, seated himself on a log and regarded the animal thoughtfully. It seemed likely that once the body was removed, it would be safer to press the issue. He would wait.

Damien returned to Elizabeth's body and sat also, watching the man. In the distance both heard sirens coming. Man and dog watched the police cars approach across the field. A few minutes later, the coroner's vehicle joined the police vehicles and soon a ring of men and women stood about them.

Familiar as they were with his search for the stolen lab animal, the police did not question the doctor's account of the accidental death, backed up as it was by the spilled log pile. An investigation had to be made, however, and police specialists arrived, tape was strung, and the officers moved warily around the grieving dog which lay resolutely beside the body. When the interviews and scene work were finished, the coroner called for the dog to be removed so they could proceed with their duties.

"For now," Seville said smoothly, "would you be able to do your work if I got him to move away from the body?"

"I don't care what you do, I just want to be able to work without that dog breathing down my neck."

Seville moved forward, holding out the leash. "Go on, Damien, get back."

Damien held his ground and Seville stopped. Then the man continued forward, speaking calmly, showing the dog the leash in his hand. Damien reluctantly backed away and the coroner and her assistant moved in warily.

"What's up with the dog, Doc?" the coroner's assistant asked. "Was it hers?"

"No. It belongs to me." He saw the man and woman exchange a look. "OK," the man said.

They got to the body and set down their equipment boxes.

"Mother of God," the man said under his breath. Then with the characteristic callousness necessary to their profession, they bent to their task.

Gravel crunched and Seville looked up. Tom's small car pulled up and his former aide got out, looking at the police cars in bewilderment and coming to stand, out of habit, beside Seville.

"How did you know to come here?" Tom asked Seville. He had to know; he had told Seville nothing.

It was on the tip of the scientist's tongue to tell his former employee that it was none of his business, but he shrewdly concluded he did not need a scene here, or questions raised, in front of the police. He needed the area to be cleared and to secure the dog before anything else happened.

"I had a feeling she'd be seen moving in daylight, so I checked my messages. A crane operator," he pointed with his chin toward a distant crane, "called her in."

"Where's Elizabeth?" Seville could hear the rising apprehension in Tom's voice.

"Over there, behind those logs. She's been killed, Tom, in an accident. She was trying to climb that log pile when it fell on her. She was crushed."

Tom stood motionless, his face frozen in disbelief as the coroner photographed the body and finally lifted the ruined remains of Elizabeth into a body bag. Seville watched his former aide, realizing now he hadn't known him quite as well as he had once thought. He could not imagine what the young man was thinking at this moment.

Damien was watching anxiously. These strangers who moved about The One seemed to be Good, and they were touching her gently. Perhaps they would help? The Voice told him they meant no harm. Miserably he followed at a distance as they put Elizabeth's body in the van. He came to the vehicle doors and stood looking in, anguish clear in his very stance. His abdomen jerked imperceptibly with tiny, inaudible whimpers.

"Sorry boy, you can't come with her. You stay here with your—master." The man hesitated at the term. It didn't seem to him that the dog belonged to Seville. Oh well, it was none of his business.

"Is that her blood or your blood on your pants, Doc? Are you injured?" the man called from the back of the vehicle as they prepared to leave.

"I'm fine, go on."

The van carrying Elizabeth's body pulled out, bumping away over the rough ground. Damien stared after it, making no move to follow. The police finished up and followed soon after, eager to leave the scientist to capture his own dog. None of them wanted to be roped into being dogcatchers. Tom had not moved from the spot where he had learned of Elizabeth's death.

Seville regarded them both for several moments, then went and sat on the log near where Elizabeth had lain. He lit another cigarette and waited.

Slowly the dog walked back to the spot where his companion had died. Ignoring the man on the log, he curled up again, where she had left him. He glanced about eerily, then a long, long sigh came from deep within the dog. Only his eye moved, and he looked up from under his eyebrow straight at Tom who still stood, motionless.

Tom continued to stare at the spot where Elizabeth had lain.

Elizabeth was dead. Passed from his life forever.

She had died in an effort filled with more passion than he had ever experienced. Her trust and friendship with the dog had been more *real*, more powerful, more important, than the things in his life, which he held sacred. All his life Tom had struggled to satisfy someone; first an erratic and brutal father, then a stern and silent God who promised eternal hell for disobedience, then a demanding and ascetic employer. In those one-sided relationships he had gamely struggled on, rarely knowing if he had managed to please. But Elizabeth, he had pleased her simply by being himself. Her quiet approval had warmed him like sunlight and her trust had been a precious thing, worth its heavy price. And when, for a brief time, he had been included in her circle of friendship, it had felt like nothing he had experienced before. Now she was gone.

I'm doing this for a friend, she had said. *Friends see it through for you, and that's what I'm doing. I'm going to see this through.*

He hoped at this moment Elizabeth could see into his heart. He wanted, desperately, for her to know he understood, at last, about her friendship with the dog.

A quiet sigh escaped Tom, and he glanced about the log yard. She was here. Perhaps there was a heaven, but she was not in it. He knew she was still here, still with her dog. She would not leave him, even now.

Seville got up, threw down his cigarette and walked over to stand beside him. Tom, watching him approach, noticed his slight stoop and the blood on his shirt. Something had happened and the dog had attacked him. That would explain why Seville was reluctant to approach Damien. He knew Seville was going to ask him to get the dog. For six years Tom had stood beside this man in unwavering loyalty and now, with Seville standing there, silent and annoyed, he felt the separation between them like a cement-block wall. Tom was alone. Like the dog curled up in its miserable ball where Elizabeth had left him, Tom was alone too.

"I assume he trusts you," Seville's voice broke into his thoughts harshly. "Get this around his neck." He held out the nylon leash. "When you get him we'll go in your car—I've lost my keys out here somewhere."

Tom reached out slowly and took the lead. He went to the dog and knelt beside him. Damien held Tom's gaze. For a long moment the brown eye and gray eyes searched each other. Then Tom spoke, low, so that only the dog could hear him.

"You'll come with me now, it's what *she* wants." He would keep Elizabeth's dog safe for her—he would see it through for her sake. He would not fail in this, and in return would be offered redemption from the awful ache he felt for having been absent when she had needed him most. As a man, protection had been a gift he could give to her. Now, having failed that, he would protect what she had left behind. Tom slipped the lead over the dog's head and straightened up. When Damien rose, Seville breathed out quickly.

"Good," he said. "Now give the bastard to me."

Tom moved away and the dog followed at his heels.

"Hey!" Seville stepped forward, roughly grasping Tom's upper arm and swinging him about. "What the hell do you th . . ." Tom and Damien turned as one to face the scientist, the young man's expression resolute and grim, the dog's eye flashing with protective intensity. Tom's firm grip on the leash held the dog to his side. His eyes on the dog, Seville stepped back.

"Don't," Tom said quietly. "Don't do it."

"You're not just going to walk away with my dog!"

"It's not your dog. You should know that by now."

"Don't be a fool, Tom. She's dead, it's over. I'm willing to drop charges, but the dog goes with me."

Tom shook his head. "I'm sorry."

"Now don't tell me you're willing to go to jail over something as foolish as this? It's a simple thing for me to have you arrested. I can understand you're upset right now, but you know I need that dog back. I'm not going to play around about this, Tom, you know that."

Tom considered his words. Seville's persecution would continue to be relentless, that he knew, but the police weren't that interested in a stolen dog case. Right now he just needed to put distance between himself and this man. Seville had no car keys.

"I'm sorry, but I need you to give me your phone."

Seville recoiled, amazement altering his features. "You don't want to do this—it's insanity!"

"Give it to me, please."

When Seville made no move to comply, Tom reached for the jacket pocket where the phone lay. With a quick, aggressive movement of his left arm, Seville knocked Tom's hand away while his right arm pulled back, fist clenched. Without a sound Damien lunged, and only Tom's lightning response and intuition that the dog would leap to defend him kept the dog from his intended target. Pulled off balance by the leash, Damien's teeth clicked together on empty air, inches from the scientist.

"It's all right, Damien. Easy. Doctor, I think you'd better hand me that phone."

Seville still made no move to comply, but this time he did not resist when Tom reached forward and took it from inside his jacket. "Damn you," Seville said softly, and Tom was unsure who he was addressing.

Neither Tom nor the dog glanced back. They went to the little car and got in.

"Tom," Seville called, "it's *just* a dog."

But Damien and Tom could not hear him, for the car was bumping away over the uneven ground, headed north.

AFTERWORD

Damien's character was based on a particular pit bull in my life, but I have borrowed from remembrances of many dogs. I have tried to make Damien's actions and reactions as realistic as possible, however, temperament varies within the pit bull race to the same degree it does in any dog breed. Even among my current pit bull family there is wide variation. Pride is clever, mischievous and carefree, unwilling to fight anyone or anything. Pagan worries and clings. My shy Mhorgana, not clever at all, is a marvel of physical skill. Dirk is arrogant, serious and thoughtful. Grip is a paragon of responsibility, a peacekeeper as well as fearless warrior. Fletcher is incapable of an original thought, and while fierce with other animals, is crushed by the merest frown from any human. Erin Fay is soft and nervous but her heart is true. Butchie, who wants nothing but to cuddle, is consumed with guilt; Maulie, with getting away with as much sin as possible.* Some themes, however, run throughout all my dogs and bulldogs in general; they are highly driven, strongly motivated dogs that adore people but are ever ready to test their mettle against other dogs. Like any working breed, they are not always the best choice for the first-time or casual dog owner. To treat these dogs without respect for their genetic purpose is to do them a huge disservice. Far

---

* And Tori Rose, who waited, so like Damien, for her One, and who steals your heart with her eyes.

363

too many people, many well-intentioned, jump into pit bull ownership without doing adequate research into the needs of these dogs. Because of this, the breed has been reduced in stature from a once-proud symbol of courage and spirit to having its very name synonymous with treacherous viciousness. Nothing could be further from the truth. Or sadder.

Happy, intelligent, rugged and playful, the pit bull offers its human companion the very best that the canine race has to offer in return for simple understanding and responsible ownership. They are possessed of a willing and sensitive nature, and cruel methods of training, such as the electric shock collar, are particularly unnecessary with these dogs. If you are interested in learning more about this breed, please do so before you consider adding a pit bull to your family. There are a variety of organizations which offer frank, responsible discussions on the pros and cons of bulldog ownership. If, after carefully and realistically evaluating your ability to offer a suitable, stable, long-term home to a member of this breed, please consider adopting your future "Damien" from a rescue group. Each day literally hundreds of dogs like Damien die in the animal shelters of America and Europe. Rescue groups help as many as they can, but there remains a shortage of responsible and suitable homes for these victims of human exploitation.

The following websites may help you in gathering information about the pit bulldog.

http://ourworld.cs.com/Dreadlives609/
www.animalfarmfoundation.org
www.outofthepits.org